Debutante

Debutante

~

ANNE MELVILLE

ORION

First published in Great Britain in 1999 by
Orion
An imprint of Orion Books Ltd
Orion House, 5 Upper St Martin's Lane, London WC2H 9EA

A CIP catalogue record for this book is
available from the British Library

ISBN 0 75282 176 8

Typeset at The Spartan Press Ltd,
Lymington, Hants
Printed in Great Britain by
Clays Ltd, St Ives plc.

Putting words on to paper has, over the years, become almost an obsession. To be deprived of the power to continue, for whatever reason, would be a recipe for unhappiness. Making up stories in my head is a habit which goes even deeper. When I can no longer do it, I shall be dead.

Margaret Potter (Anne Melville)
1926–1998

CONTENTS

Foreword

Everyone who was anyone knew in advance that the London Season of 1939 would be quite different from any that had gone before.

This was because King George VI and Queen Elizabeth would be out of the country, visiting the United States and Canada, at the time when they should have been receiving the first debutantes of the year to be presented at court. One consequence of this was that the first presentations would have to take place in March, instead of May. A second consequence was that any hostess hoping for the presence of the king and queen at her party or dinner was forced to arrange the event later in the Season than she would otherwise have done. It was all very unusual and inconvenient.

In other respects, however, everyone who was anyone was confident that the Season of 1939 would proceed in exactly the same manner as every Season before it. It would open on the day of the Royal Academy's Private View – an occasion on which the debutantes, rather than the pictures, were viewed for the first time. And it would come to an end early in August, when Cowes Week and the approach of the Glorious Twelfth started an exodus from London.

In between those dates, several hundred girls of good family, most of them straight out of the schoolroom, would turn into poised, if not exactly sophisticated, young women. Meticulously observing rules of behaviour and dress which had hardly changed in twenty-five years, they would attend luncheons and tea parties, dinners and dances and balls. They would ride in Hyde Park, write polite thank-you letters to hostesses and perhaps help their mothers to arrange flowers: the only house-wifely talent they were expected to possess. They would make friends with other young women, and suitable young men would be introduced to them.

In everything they did they would be under observation from their own mothers and everyone else's; because, whether they realised it or not – and most of them did – the object of their Season was to gain for them exactly the kind of life that their mothers had enjoyed. Each girl was expected to make a good marriage before her twenty-first birthday, and it was taken for granted that she would be a virgin on her wedding day. More than that, she must be free from any whiff of scandal, for her reputation was her most prized possession. Even a kiss could be dangerous, unless an engagement was about to be announced – although, viewed from an opposite point of view, the same kiss might sometimes be useful in making it clear to a tongue-tied young man where his duty lay.

The mothers, for their part, although often reluctant to discuss the facts of life with their vulnerably innocent daughters, were experts in social planning and the management of courtships. Under their tuition, each debutante daughter could hope for a wedding at St Margaret's, Westminster, which would provide her possibly with a title and certainly with a home which would be grand if not necessarily comfortable. She might be aware that poverty existed, but was never likely to experience it.

It was quite likely that she would be in love with her new husband, and in any case she would be expected to be faithful to him at least until she had provided him with two children, one of them male. If, after that time, she were to discover that her husband was attracted by some other young married woman, she would not seek a divorce, but might feel justified in accepting – with due discretion – the advances of someone else's husband.

There were few other ways in which she would be able to relieve the boredom of a life in which there was really not enough to do. Waited on by servants and incapable herself of performing any household duties except their supervision, she would leave even the upbringing of her children to employees. Her days would be passed in entertaining and being enter-

2

tained, hunting, ordering clothes, and taking part in charitable activities: with the prospect of all this stretching on for perhaps fifty years without change. That was how it had been for her mother and that was how her mother expected it to be for her. An unexciting life in some ways; but safe.

In no circumstances would these debutantes, once safely married, be expected or allowed to work for money. Nor, with very few exceptions, were they the kind of young women who were likely to join hunger marches or agitate for political change. If they were to postpone marriage for too long they would be regarded as oddities; and should they marry out of their own class they would be pitied and shunned. But they had all been taught the rules, and it was unlikely that they would wish to break them.

All that had been true in the past, but the world was about to change. For the debutantes of 1939, the Season which marked the end of their childhood was the forerunner of a life which was to prove very different from anything that they had envisaged; but as they danced and sipped champagne they had no inkling of this. Even the mothers gave little attention to international affairs as they plotted to settle to their own satisfaction the most important question of the year: which of the debutantes who came out in the Season of 1939 would be chosen to be the next Duchess of Wiltshire?

PART ONE

The Season

1

'How old are you, Ronnie?'

Lady Veronica Delacourt, looking up from her breakfast, raised her eyebrows in amusement. It was tempting to comment that most women managed to retain some faint memory of the dates on which they had given birth to their babies, but one does not make cheeky remarks to a duchess, even when the duchess happens to be one's mother.

'Seventeen and a half,' she replied. She would celebrate her eighteenth birthday in March, 1939.

'It's time you came out, then. I'll present you at the first Court next year. It will be earlier than usual, because of the royal visit to Canada. Just before your birthday.'

Ronnie received the news with pleasure and without surprise. She had always known that the years of her childhood, in the nursery and the schoolroom, were no more than a period of waiting and preparation for her Season as a debutante. A summer of hectic social life would mark her entry into the adult world. She could hardly wait to tell her governess that the end of her struggle with parsing and Pythagoras was at last in sight.

'Shall I have a ball here at Cleeve?' she asked, but the duchess shook her head.

'London will be better. This is too far for everyone to come. And it isn't really suitable.'

Cleeve Castle was a fake, but it had been a fake for long enough to acquire an authenticity of its own, if authenticity was to be measured in terms of a lack of modern conveniences. It was in 1668 that Charles II, after fathering yet another bastard,

7

had ennobled the complaisant husband of his mistress. The delighted new Duke of Wiltshire, looking for a country seat worthy of his rank, settled on a large stone pile first built by a follower of William the Conqueror and not greatly improved in the centuries which had passed since then. It enjoyed magnificent views, but few home comforts. It was hardly surprising that for that and other reasons the first duchess preferred to remain at His Majesty's court in London.

By the time the royal bastard inherited, Cleeve was crumbling into ruin, but the views were still magnificent, so he pulled it down and rebuilt on the same site – too early, alas, to enjoy the benefits of Georgian architecture. Even the Queen Anne style had not yet penetrated to the north-west corner of Wiltshire. Instead, the old stone was used to make a faithful copy of the towers and battlements which had collapsed, although the domestic arrangements were modernised by providing more staircases and corridors to remove through traffic from intercommunicating rooms. Bathrooms were still unknown, but the relocation of the kitchen enabled food to be served lukewarm instead of cold. There was, however, nothing new or fake about the dampness and the draughts, which survived all change from the eleventh century to the twentieth.

Were a ball to be held at the castle, there would be no shortage of space. By 1938 the banqueting hall, which rose to the height of two storeys, had come to serve mainly as a forum where members of the family might come across each other while on their way to somewhere else; but it had provided a splendid setting for the celebrations when Ronnie's brother, the current Marquess of Lambourn, came of age two years earlier. Ronnie recognised, though, that her mother was right. The entertaining rooms of Delacourt House, the family's London home, would provide a more convenient setting for her coming-out ball.

'Shall I be able to take Prince with me?' she asked. Delacourt House was in Park Lane. It adjoined Hyde Park, so she would be able to ride as often as she did in the country – although no doubt more sedately.

'Certainly you may. It's expected.'

Ronnie had no more questions. That phrase, 'It's expected', summed everything up. The protocol of presentation and

8

Season had been familiar to the Delacourts for generations, and to the families into which they married. The Duchess of Wiltshire knew exactly what arrangements were *de rigueur*. Appointments would be made with dressmakers and milliners and a corsetière. There would be shopping expeditions. Ronnie's dancing master would be quizzed about her readiness for a non-stop round of balls and dances, and any deficiencies would be quickly made good. Lists would be made of young men and women whom it would be suitable for her to meet; perhaps there would be a blacklist as well. Dates of the most important social events would be fixed well in advance. At exactly the right time she would be taught by Madame Vacani how to perform the presentation curtsy. It would all be organised by her mother as Mistress of Ceremonies. Ronnie herself would simply be told what was expected of her.

So she had no need to worry about anything – no need, even, to think about it in advance. Other girls might feel anxious whether they would receive enough invitations or attract enough dancing partners. The daughter of a duke need have no fears on that score. Her place in society was secure and her mother would make sure that she received her due.

However much she might take her debut for granted, though, Ronnie recognised the importance of the announcement over the breakfast table. She was about to take her place not just in society but in real life; life as an adult. Naturally she would still be protected; still subject to her parents' wishes, as she always had been. Nevertheless, this would be her first step towards independence.

Her first reaction was a wish to spread the news.

'Is Pa coming down to breakfast?' she asked.

'Not this morning. He ought not to have gone out riding yesterday. Dr Sidwell warns him over and over again that he must keep out of the fog, but he won't be told.'

Ronnie nodded understandingly. More than twenty years earlier her father had been both gassed and wounded at Ypres. He had lost one lung, and every winter in recent years had seen him struggle for breath with the other. His doctors repeatedly advised him to travel to a warmer and drier climate for the winter months, but the duke's war experiences had given him an ineradicable dislike of foreigners and foreign countries – or, as he put it, Wogs and Wogland, which started at Calais. He made no bones about preferring to die early in the chill of his own damp castle rather than live to a ripe old age on the French Riviera surrounded by Frogs. For Ronnie he had made a concession in allowing a mademoiselle and a fräulein into Cleeve to teach her their languages, which were apparently an essential ingredient of a young lady's education. But he had drawn the line at sending her abroad to a finishing school.

'May I go up to him?' Ronnie asked. She knew that even on her father's bad days he continued to deal with correspondence in bed and was only too pleased to be disturbed.

'Yes, of course. But leave it until after ten o'clock.'

Ronnie nodded for a second time and concentrated on finishing her breakfast. She was an early riser, and an hour on horseback in the castle grounds had given her a good appetite. But for once she refrained from taking a second helping of kidneys and scrambled eggs from the row of heated silver dishes on the sideboard: the Sluggard's Joys. Nobody could call her exactly plump, but her dancing master had once allowed the depressing adjective 'sturdy' to pass his lips. She preferred to think of herself as healthy and energetic – an open-air girl – but perhaps the time had come now to cultivate a more svelte and sophisticated appearance: to look languid and bored instead of lively and eager to learn about anything that did not come out of books.

That thought prompted a return to her bedroom: a round room in one of the castle's four towers. Sitting down at the dressing table, she stared at herself in the glass. She had heard enough about the Season to know that before it even began each of the hundreds of debutantes would be judged by members of the older generation – and by the newspapers – on their rank and beauty. In her case rank was no problem; but beauty? She considered her features critically, as a stranger might do.

Her forehead was wide and smooth: that was good. Her eyebrows were thick: that was bad, but there were ways of improving them. Her dark brown eyes, an inheritance from an Italian grandmother, were set well apart. Good. Her nose was longer than was fashionable these days. Bad. However, to judge from the portraits which hung in the Long Gallery, the nose was something which she shared with every one of her ancestors over the past three centuries, so she might as well decide to be proud of it.

Her lips were rosy, which was fortunate, since she would certainly not be permitted to use make-up. Her complexion was rather darker than she would have liked – another legacy of that Italian grandmother – and even months of indoor activities were unlikely to make her look paler. But her skin was smooth, and the spots which had bothered her a year earlier had all disappeared.

Her hair, strained off her face, was long and dark but very straight. She tugged at the ribbon which tied it loosely at the neck and ran her fingers through it. As though this were a signal, her maid appeared from the dressing room and picked up a silver-backed hairbrush.

'So we go to London at last, your ladyship,' she said in a strangely lilted French accent. Marie had been born Mary Jones in Glamorgan, but a lady's maid was expected to be French, and she had mixed enough with genuine articles in servants' halls to pick up some of the lingo and pronunciation.

Ronnie wondered how it was that the servants always seemed to know what was going to happen before members of the family did, but to ask for an explanation would be to concede a small victory in the friendly battle of words between mistress and maid.

'*Mais oui* and *ooh la la*,' she agreed, mimicking the phoney accent.

Marie was used to being mocked and refused to be laughed out of her efforts to improve herself.

'Your ladyship must ask *madame la duchesse* which of her tiaras she will lend for the presentation, so that I may create *une coiffure magnifique.*'

Already Marie was brushing her mistress's hair higher and higher from beneath before taking it in her fingers and twisting one layer under another to give height and thickness. Until now there had not been much joy in being lady's maid to someone who spent more time in riding clothes than ballgowns and whose hair was perpetually wind-blown. But with a London Season in prospect Marie would be expecting to come into her own at last.

'*Comme ça?*' she enquired with a final, triumphant touch of the comb.

'*Absolument non,*' said Ronnie. She was a girl who made quick decisions. 'Only schoolgirls and dowagers have long hair nowadays. I shall have it cut and permanently waved as soon as we get to London.'

'Then you must have a hairpiece of your own hair. To give dignity to the diamonds.'

'It's too soon to think about that sort of thing.'

'*Mais non, mais non.*' Marie registered horror. 'Always the hair must come first. Before the couturier can create the gown, he must know your ladyship's style.'

'Well, leave it for now, look you,' Ronnie teased. She was in no mood to be bothered with hairstyles. It was still too early to disturb her father, but there was someone else who must be told her news.

Nanny's quarters were in a distant wing of the castle, and now that she was in her seventies and crippled by arthritis she rarely left them. In the past she had been nanny successively to Ronnie's mother and aunts and one of her cousins before coming to Cleeve when the duchess had her first baby.

It was Nanny who had mothered Ronnie for the first seven years of her life, presenting her – neatly dressed and instructed to be on her best behaviour – to her real mother for an hour each afternoon. It was a good ten years since she had been expected to perform any regular duties, but she was an honoured pensioner who would never be asked to leave. Her room, in which a fire was kept burning all day, was one of the cosiest in the castle, but it was the warmth of their mutual affection which led Ronnie to visit her every day.

'I'm to come out next year, Nanny,' she announced without preamble on this occasion.

'Yes, of course you are, dear. Florrie told me when she brought my breakfast. But I didn't need telling. I haven't forgotten you'll be eighteen on March the twenty-first. You'll remember to invite me to Queen Charlotte's Ball, won't you dear?'

'Do I know about Queen Charlotte's Ball?' Ronnie made herself comfortable on the floor, knowing there was nothing Nanny liked better than answering her questions.

'It's for charity. Every year. In aid of the maternity hospital. There'll be a thousand people there or more, but the ones who really count are the Maids of Honour. You'll be one of them for certain, dear. Oh, it's the prettiest of sights to see them lovely girls, all in their white dresses, gliding down the staircases and then dipping into a curtsy. So elegant. So graceful. You won't let me down, I'm sure of that.'

'Another curtsy? Does the King come?'

'No, dear. There'll be a guest of honour, but you curtsy to the cake. It'll have a candle on it for every year since Queen Charlotte was born, and that was a long time ago.'

'Curtsy to a *cake*! Nanny, you can't be serious.' But Nanny was always serious, and the Season, in particular, was no joking matter.

'The ball will be held in Grosvenor House.' She took no notice of the interruption. 'There's a big balcony round the banqueting hall. The nannies are allowed to stand there, where they can see their girls. I was there for your mother, when she was eighteen. Lovely, she was. And now it's to be your turn. How time flies! I'd love to go again, if my legs will let me. All of us nannies are proud of our girls, but I shall be the proudest of them all.'

'Oh yes, you must come, you certainly must. I'll tell Ma.' But there would be no real need of the reminder. If it was part of the system that nannies could be invited, then Nanny would be there. From her cross-legged position on the floor Ronnie rose smoothly to her feet. 'Now I must go and have a chat with Pa. I'll see you again tomorrow, Nanny.'

She found her father in the Queen Anne bedroom. He was propped up by half a dozen pillows in his canopied four-poster bed, reading the letters which his secretary opened and handed to him.

'Good news, Ronnie,' he announced cheerfully, showing no sign of any difficulty in breathing. 'Just heard from Baverstock.' Baverstock was his racing manager. 'Wildflower's foaled. Bay colt. Thought I might name it after you. Bring us all luck, what? Speedwell. What do you think of that?'

'It's a marvellous name for a racehorse – but what's it got to do with me?'

'Good God, child. Doesn't that governess of yours teach you anything at all?'

13

'Not very much, no. But that may be,' added Ronnie honestly, 'because I don't give her much of a chance.'

'Well, ask her if she knows what the Latin name for speedwell is, Lady Veronica.'

'Ah, I see. Pa, have you heard? I'm going to be presented next year.'

'So it's all been decided, has it? Yes, well, I was given advance warning that I might be about to be bankrupted by exorbitant bills for ball dresses, ostrich feathers, white gloves and all that folderol and fiddle-de-dee. Still, what must be must be. You'll be all right, Ronnie. Your mother will see to it.'

'Yes, I know, and it's very generous of you.'

The duke grunted away her thanks and stared briefly at the embroidered peacocks on the tester above his head.

'Something I want to say about this coming-out business.' He dismissed his secretary with a movement of his hand and his expression became unusually serious. Ronnie's conversations with her father were as a rule confined to his favourite subject, which was horses. This one, it seemed, was to be of a different kind.

'I want Chay to go to London with you,' he told her.

Chay was the Marquess of Lambourn, Ronnie's elder brother. He owed his name to the tradition that every prospective Duke of Wiltshire should be named after the royal ancestor. With a new Charles in every generation, family history became confusing. The third duke was still being referred to as 'Young Charles' when he died at the age of ninety-two. From then onwards, alternate heirs were known by some individual diminutive. Chay's grandfather, the eighth duke, had always been called Chas. The ninth duke, Ronnie's father, was Charles. His only son, who would be the tenth duke one day, was Chay.

Ronnie clapped her hands in delight at the news that her brother would be escorting her. It meant that she would never be without a partner – and one who would be the most eligible young man in town. All the other debutantes would long to be introduced to him, so they would have to be specially nice to Ronnie herself. She had had every intention of pleading with her brother to come to London with her, and was delighted to learn that he was already under starter's orders.

'He larked about at Eton,' said the duke. 'Sowed his wild oats at Oxford. Lucky not to have been sent down, from all I hear. But this last year, when I've been a bit groggy, he's really buckled down to learning about the estate. How to run it when I'm gone. He's coming on well.'

Ronnie who adored her elder brother, nodded vigorously in agreement.

'So now it's time for him to think about getting himself married, what? Your Season will give him just the opportunity he needs. Hundreds of well-groomed young fillies with impeccable pedigrees circling the paddock for his inspection. If he can't find the wife he needs there, he never will.'

'You're making him sound like a stallion at stud,' protested Ronnie. 'Kindly remember that your daughter will be one of the fillies.'

'You know what I mean. What we have to remember is, they'll all be after him. Not just the fillies. Their trainers as well. That's something you'll find out quickly enough. It's the mothers with their form books who run the Season.'

'But Chay knows how to look after himself – and he'll be the one who does the choosing.'

'Yes, yes. Point I'm getting at is this: young men get bowled over by a pretty face, often as not. You're the one, Ronnie, with the best chance of learning what the other girls are really like. Chay will see all these title-hunting harpies—'

'Oh really!'

'All right then, these beautiful debutantes. He'll see them when they're on stage, so to speak. You'll get to know them in the wings, when they don't have to be on their best behaviour. Drop him a hint if you need to; that's all I mean.'

'Yes, Pa.' With every moment that passed on this day of days Ronnie was feeling more and more grown up. Never before had her father spoken to her in this way, confiding in her as one adult to another. And she was to be responsible for Chay!

'One other thing.' For the first time since she had entered the bedroom the duke was breathing with greater effort. 'Special year, your coming-out season. Your eighteenth birthday. Plenty of time, I know. But give me an idea what you'd like for a present. A hunter?'

Ronnie hesitated. She loved to hunt – but there were always plenty of horses to choose from in the stables.

15

Heart in mouth, she took the plunge. 'What I'd *really* like, if you're feeling in a magnificently munificent mood, would be a motor car,' she said.

'Hm.' Not many girls had cars of their own in 1938 and for a moment it seemed as though her father were about to refuse, as she had feared. But although he had had little to do with the upbringing of his children, he had always been generous. 'Well, I suppose that's better than asking for an aeroplane, like your brother.'

Chay, who had joined the University Air Squadron while he was at Oxford, would have liked a plane of his own for his twenty-first birthday. The request had been turned down not on grounds of expense, but because an only son must not be encouraged in such a dangerous hobby.

'All right, then,' agreed the duke. 'I'll have a word with Chay. He knows about that sort of thing better than I do.' Chay had been mad about cars from the age of two.

Ronnie herself, although not as mechanically minded as her brother, was more knowledgeable about cars than about the botanical name for speedwell. 'If it could be an MG,' she suggested, 'I'd be able to give Chay some proper competition for once when we race. An MG would be really, really lovely. Please, oh please!'

The duke became severe, or at least pretended to. 'If I give you a motor car, Ronnie, it will be so that you can drive yourself safely from one place to another. I won't have you tearing up and down the public highways. Is that understood?'

'Yes, Pa. You're very kind and generous.' Leaning over to kiss him on the forehead, she made one last hopeful suggestion. 'There's a car called the Magnette. It *is* an MG, but it's designed to be driven decorously on the road.' She crossed her fingers behind her back. 'It's not intended for racing.' Well, perhaps that was not exactly a fib: it was the driver of a vehicle, not the machine itself, who determined how fast it should go. Tearing up and down the public highways was exactly what she had in mind, but that would not be the fault of the car. 'A Magnette,' she repeated, 'would be just the thing.' She left him to his letters.

Outside his door one of the footmen was hovering. 'Miss

Warner asked me to let your ladyship know that she is in the schoolroom, when you are ready.'

'Tell her that I've been delayed, please, William. I'll be with her in a few moments. Or—' She looked at her watch. 'No, don't bother.'

She had wanted to discuss her news with Chay but already she was twenty minutes late for her lessons. This was not unusual, but a sudden qualm of conscience persuaded her not to delay any longer. Soon she would be free of the schoolroom, hooray. For Miss Warner, though, it would not be hooray at all. The announcement would come as a portent of unemployment. Perhaps it would be only right and proper to accept her discipline and make things easy for her during these last few weeks of slavery to books. With a sigh Ronnie moved off towards the grind of algebra. Algebra, ugh! What use was that ever going to be? She could pass the rest of her life quite happily without ever worrying about the value of x.

A light lunch was served in the schoolroom after lessons, so it was not until two o'clock that she was free to look for Chay. As expected, she found him in a workshop which had been converted from one of the coach-houses. Wearing mechanic's overalls, he was tuning the engine of his Maserati with fingers blackened by oil and grease.

'Why don't you leave that sort of thing to Chivers?' she asked from the doorway.

'Because I do it better. Have you come for a ride?'

'Not just now. I've got a stupid old French translation to prepare. It's all such a waste of time.'

'You won't think that when you find yourself sitting next to the French Ambassador at dinner one evening.' He laughed at the startled expression that Ronnie was unable to control. 'You do realise, don't you, that the point of learning French is to be able to converse intelligently with Frenchmen? Well, later on, then. Half past four? We could have a race.'

They would race on the castle track. Chay had been only twelve years old when he begged his father to build it for him. Since the local police had already been making deferential but insistent complaints about the speeds at which the juvenile marquess was driving through the neighbouring villages, the duke felt it best to agree. The park was large and wooded enough for the track to be constructed out of sight and hearing of the castle, and over the years it had become a local amenity. The duke allowed learners to take their first nervous lessons on it and offered prizes to boys from the village school for bicycle races. But first and foremost it was Chay's playground.

Friends from Eton and, later, Oxford came to pit their skill against him, but Ronnie was the resident competition. From the age of eight she had been allowed some kind of vehicle of her own to drive, but always a slower one than her brother's. If she could cajole her father into giving her the MG, the odds would no longer be loaded against her.

'Pa tells me you'll come to London for my Season.'

'Yes. Three-line whip. Ma needs me to keep you out of mischief. Pa demands that I find myself a wife. Spanner, please.'

Ronnie was well accustomed to being treated like a nurse in an operating theatre, feeding the car surgeon with the necessary instruments. With a quick glance to see where he was working, she handed him the correct size of spanner.

'Don't you want to? Find a wife, I mean?' she asked.

'Well, as a matter of fact, I rather do. And I'm not going to meet anyone while I'm under the Maserati or struggling with accounts in the estate office, am I? So although I expect you to be properly grateful at the prospect of being escorted by the most handsome and charming chap—'

'And the most eligible.'

'And, as you say, the most eligible.' Chay grinned as he handed the spanner back. 'Hang it all, I've lost the drift of my sentence now.'

'You expect me to be grateful. And I am, I really am. But as Pa has so tactfully put it to me, you'll be able at the same time to study all the fillies parading in the paddock and pick a winner. Tell me how you'll choose. What do you want in a wife, Chay?'

'Beauty. Loyalty. Affection. A sense of humour would be a bonus.'

'Money? Pedigree?'

'Money's not too important. For all that Pa complains daily of imminent bankruptcy, we seem to get by. Pedigree? Well, any girl who marries me will be a duchess one day, so you could say that I shall provide all that's required in that direction. All the same, I do need to find someone who will know how to behave

18

as a duchess. But at the same time, I shall want to be absolutely sure that she likes me as a chap and not just as a future duke, if you see what I mean. Screwdriver now, please.' For a moment he worked without speaking. 'The important thing, Ronnie – for you as well as for me – is to step into the marriage market with your eyes extremely wide open.'

'Marriage market! What a vulgar expression!'

'That's what the Season is. Don't pretend you didn't realise. I shan't be the only stallion sniffing around for a brood mare. And all the fillies will be whinnying to attract a blue-blooded mate. That's why they're being presented.'

'That's quite enough of this ridiculous—' Ronnie had to pause while she summoned the Parts of Speech to her memory and worked out whether the word she wanted was metaphor or simile. 'Enough of this ridiculous metaphor. You make it sound quite disgusting.' Her dream of the Season was one of romance. 'Anyway, how can you know?'

'It's not ridiculous. I've done this escort business before. While I was at Oxford. Remember? Many's the time I've driven back at five in the morning after a ball to be ready for a tutorial at nine.'

'And did the girls throw themselves at you then?'

'It's the mothers who do the throwing. They're the ones who run the Season.'

'That's exactly what Pa said.'

'That proves it, then. He probably remembers from his own salad days. I doubt if anything has changed much in the past thirty years. The mothers have instincts, and they know the ropes. Their antennae tell them when a chap is content to be a carefree undergraduate; but the moment that same chap is thinking about settling down, their experience tells them that it's time to pounce. They'll start closing in on me from the moment we arrive in London. If you're tired of horsy meta-phors, you can say I'll be a sitting duck.'

'What a vain, arrogant man you are, Lord Lambourn!' Ronnie giggled.

'What a realist, you mean. When they look at me, they don't see me at all. They just have a vision of coronets and strawberry leaves and ermine. Now, let's see how this sounds.'

He started the engine and listened intently. 'Sweet. Sweet.'

Turning it off he got out of the car, pulled the bonnet across and closed it.

'Seriously, though, Ronnie,' he said. 'You're the one who is really going to be up for grabs in the marriage market, and it's easy to be swept off your feet when you've drunk too much champagne and Ma is whispering how particularly desirable a certain young suitor might be. So many thousand acres, so many blue-blooded generations, such glittering prospects—'

'I'm perfectly capable of making up my own mind,' Ronnie interrupted indignantly. 'You're talking as though I'm an absolute ninny.'

'All I'm doing, whether you appreciate it or not, is giving you a piece of sincere brotherly advice. You may think of the Season as a few months of non-stop frivolity, and so it is in its way. But make one bad decision and you'll have to live with it – him, I mean – for the rest of your life. So I'm warning you to keep your wits about you; and when in doubt, run to your beloved brother for counselling.'

It was tempting to tell him that she had only that morning been asked to perform the very same role for him. Instead, Ronnie was silenced by a flurry of uncertainty. Perhaps it would be best not to entrust herself too completely into her mother's keeping. Now that she was about to become an adult, it was time that she started making her own decisions.

Chay wiped a grimy hand on his overalls. 'Now shoo!' he said. 'Get your French translation out of the way and then we can think about racing. The four-thirty handicap over ten circuits this afternoon. To be followed next year by an unusual race in which the runners turn out also to be the trophies. The nineteen thirty-nine Delacourt Marriage Stakes. Which of the two of us, do you think, will be first past the post then?'

2

Along the corridors of Queen Mary's High School ambition was on the move.

The four o'clock bell had just released from their classroom imprisonment three hundred girls wearing gymslips and walking with the curious but rapid heel-and-toe movement which they had developed to circumvent the 'no running' rule. Within a matter of minutes they had reached the cloakrooms, exchanged their indoor shoes for sturdy black lace-ups, buttoned and belted their navy-blue mackintoshes and plonked their navy-blue felt hats more or less securely on their heads. The weekend had begun, and it was time for tea.

Peggy Armitage, however, marked out as a sixth-former by her more becoming uniform of navy-blue skirt, white blouse and green and blue striped tie, walked briskly against the flow. Friday was her day for special coaching.

What were the usual ambitions of seventeen-year-old girls at schools like Queen Mary's in 1938? To become Captain of Hockey? To be allowed to wear lipstick and high-heeled shoes? To be noticed by the tall, dark-haired boy on the bus? To sing the solo in the Christmas carol concert? To be kissed by Ronald Colman? Or just to finish with lessons and settle down to the same kind of life as their mothers? Peggy's ambition was none of these.

Queen Mary's was reckoned by the parents who competed for the privilege of paying its fees to be the best girls' day school in Nottinghamshire. Every year it sent out into the world forty well-mannered eighteen-year-olds with Matriculation Exemption and Higher Certificates. What it did not very often do was to send any of its girls on to university – for the simple reason that few of them had any wish to go.

But Peggy was different. She longed to go to Oxford. It was not that she had set her sights on any career for which a university degree was essential. Her ambition was simpler than that: just to become an Oxford undergraduate would be enough to satisfy her. At the age of fifteen she had read a book called *The Wandering Scholars* and was enthralled by the picture it painted of young men through many centuries following their teachers all over Europe in the quest for knowledge. Some of them had come to rest in a swampy, unhealthy part of England, and from their early lectures and disputations had grown the great university of Oxford.

Peggy ached to be part of that tradition of scholarship. While her fellow sixth-formers thought of romance in terms of cuddles in the back row of the cinema, Peggy's romantic love was for a university in a city she had never visited. She was a glutton for knowledge and saw a particular beauty in old buildings and ancient traditions. Her mouth watered unbearably at the thought of so many books nestling under all those medieval towers and spires, waiting for her to discover them.

Her father, who had left school at the age of fourteen to make his fortune, found it hard to understand why his elder daughter should wish to keep her nose buried in books instead of preparing to accompany her mother to the tea parties and tennis afternoons and charity dances which provided the framework of social life in Newark. But he was an affectionate family man who liked to give his wife and daughters what they wanted. If Peggy wanted Oxford, she could have it.

Peggy had needed to explain that it was not as simple as that. Oxford might not want her. There were not very many places for girls at Oxford, because all but four of the colleges were for men only. Naturally, then, the competition for those places was strong. Without being immodest, she knew that she was the cleverest girl of her age at Queen Mary's, but she would find herself up against the cleverest girls from every other school in the country. Unlike London University, for which Higher Certificates were sufficient qualification, the Oxford colleges had their own entrance examinations and only a handful of candidates would be accepted by each. Her chances of getting in, she told her father, were pretty slim.

This information had aroused Mr Armitage's fighting spirit and he demanded a council of war with some of Peggy's teachers. She should do well in her history papers, he was told, and it would be a simple matter to give her extra practice in Latin and French translation. But there was a stumbling block, erected to prevent mere swots from monopolising all the places. It was an Oxford speciality known as the General Essay: hard to prepare for because it was designed to test intelligence rather than knowledge.

So what was to be done about it? Mr Armitage asked. Under his insistent pressure Miss Downie, the classics mistress, who was an Oxford graduate herself, agreed to coach Peggy in the particular blend of logical thinking, felicitous phrasing and pertinent, even witty, comment which was likely to find favour. It was to this weekly coaching session that she was now on her way.

Bill Brownlow was already waiting in the sixth-form reading room. Bill was a lanky seventeen-year-old whose hair stood up from his head as though in amazement at the speed in which he had recently grown. His strong hands and wrists protruded from blazer sleeves which were several inches too short, and his trouser legs also ended unfashionably high above his large boots. He was as determined as Peggy to get to Oxford, but the county school he attended was even less experienced than Queen Mary's in preparing candidates. It had appealed for him to be given tuition there, and Mr Armitage, who had readily agreed to pay a fee for Peggy's extra coaching, expressed no objection to letting a bright lad share the hour with her. Miss Downie assured him that the two of them would benefit from bouncing ideas off each other.

In one respect, though, their requirements were different. Peggy would be taking her Higher Certificate examinations in June of the next year and then returning to school for an extra term in order to sit the Oxford entrance exam in November. Bill's mother could not afford to support him for an extra year, so he would sit the examination that very month, a year earlier. And it would not be enough for him merely to win a place. He needed a scholarship to meet the cost of the fees.

In spite of their different situations, Peggy and Bill had much in common. Not just the shared ambition, but the shared realisation that to achieve such an ambition was a matter not of daydreaming but of hard slog.

It was a lesson learned by Bill from his widowed mother, who had achieved her own ambition of giving her son a good start in life by scrubbing floors at the local hospital in order that he could stay on at school. And Peggy had learned it from her father, who, with little education and no capital, had started his working life selling fabric from a stall in Newark's market square. While still in his teens he had discovered a demand for cheap but stylish ready-made clothes, and worked with such determination to exploit it that he now owned two factories and also gave employment to dozens of women doing piecework at home. Peggy had inherited both his clearsightedness and his willingness to work.

Miss Downie bustled in and greeted her two pupils cheerfully.

'Since this is Bill's last session before his exam, we're going to do things differently today,' she told them. 'Instead of discussing how you might tackle different subjects, and then practising in your own time, I want each of you to write an essay on the spot, under examination conditions. So sit down and make yourselves comfortable.'

She supplied them with paper and checked that their fountain pens were filled. 'You have fifty minutes,' she told them. 'But before you start, what is the first rule?'

'Think before you write,' they recited in unison, grinning at each other. Then, at the separate tables which had been set facing each other, they looked down eagerly at the words written in Miss Downie's neat classicist's script.

' "Beauty is in the eye of the beholder." Do you agree?'

Thoughtfully chewing the end of her pen, Peggy looked up to discover that Bill was staring straight at her. She was amused to realise what he was doing. His beholding eye would have to work overtime to see beauty in her freckled face, her snub nose and wide mouth. If she could feel proud of anything at all in her appearance it was only her thick chestnut hair – and that, in accordance with school rules, was strained back into a thick plait.

Bill caught her eye and flushed before looking down again at the paper and beginning to write. Peggy, still at the thinking stage, felt at a loss, but at last inspiration struck. Earlier in the term she had written an essay about the relationship of words to the objects they described, and much of the argument was relevant in this context. She too set to work and when their time was up, they had both covered more pages than had seemed possible at first.

Generously overrunning the hour, Miss Downie quickly read through what they had written and pointed out some infelicities and flaws in their arguments. But her final verdict was encouraging, as she assured Bill that he would make a good job of his essay in a week's time.

'So that's the end of your coaching,' she said. 'I hope you feel that it's helped.'

'It's been marvellous of you, miss,' he replied. 'I can't thank you enough. It would really have thrown me, sitting down to something like this for the first time ever.'

Peggy held out her hand to him. 'Good luck, Bill. I do hope you get your scholarship. You'll let me know, won't you?'

'Yes. I'll write to your father either way. It was good of him to let me share your lessons. With any luck we'll meet again at Oxford in a couple of years.'

They shook hands, smiling. Peggy went off to collect everything she would need for the weekend's homework from her desk in the upper sixth room and then cycled the short journey home. Mr Armitage, when he rose in the world, had been able to afford one of the old merchant houses in the centre of the town. A townie born and bred, he had no wish to set himself up as a country gentleman.

Peggy was greeted in the hall by her fourteen-year-old sister, Jodie.

'You'd better tell Mummy you're back. She's having kittens.'

'Why? She knows I'm always later home on Fridays.'

'Not usually as late as this, though, are you? Anyway, Daddy came home early and wanted to speak to you. I suppose she forgot about your late night, and it doesn't take much for her to work herself into one of her states.'

Mrs Armitage, plump and cuddly and with few interests outside her family, was always imagining disaster, but Peggy knew that all her fussing sprang from love. She smiled affectionately as she reported her return.

'Oh darling, I was so worried. I couldn't think what had happened to you.'

'General Essay day, remember? I've been trying to decide whether beauty is in the eye of the beholder.'

'What does that mean? No, don't tell me; it doesn't matter. I was just bothered because your father wants a word with you before we have tea.'

'Sounds ominous. What have I done wrong?'

'You never do anything wrong, darling. It's something you'll like.' Mrs Armitage's eyes were bright with excitement as she gave her elder daughter a loving hug. 'I do hope . . . Well, off you go.'

Peggy found her father seated in his den, warming himself in front of a glowing fire and grunting in satisfaction as he turned over the pages of his new catalogue of clothes and prices.

'Ah, Peg, here you are. Sit you down. Make yourself comfortable. I want to have a little chat. We have a problem, a family problem, and it seems you're the only one who can solve it.'

'What sort of a problem?'

'Money.'

For one awful moment Peggy's heart juddered to a standstill. Had something terrible happened to the family business? Would it prevent her from going to Oxford even if she managed to pass the entrance examination? Was he about to say that she must leave school and go out to work to earn her own living?

'What's happened?' she asked, hardly daring to listen to the answer.

He laughed at the way she had fallen for his little joke.

'Prosperity has happened, my girl. Best year ever. Money rolling in from all directions. I've been a rich man for years, but this year I'm an extremely rich man. More than I know what to do with. You can think of yourself as an heiress, Miss Armitage.'

'Oh.' Peggy let out the breath she had been holding. 'I thought . . . What's the problem, then, Daddy?'

'Spending it's the problem. We're very comfortable here and I'm not prepared to up sticks and buy a grand mansion with no neighbours except sheep and cows. As for your mother, I've never been able to get her to spend money. She doesn't want expensive clothes, she doesn't want valuable jewellery, she thinks six servants are quite enough and she's never allowed me to send her daughters off to boarding school to be turned into posh young ladies.'

'I'm glad about that.'

'Yes, well, you may be. But you can see my difficulty. Here am I, longing to find something I can give her to show that I think she's the best wife any man can have, and here's she saying no thank you, no thank you, to everything I suggest. What's the use of money that just sits in a bank?'

'So?'

'So, a couple of weeks ago I asked her again, and for once she came up with something she really wanted. Sir Richard Grant is mayor this year, as you know, so Lady Grant is organising the annual Christmas party for poor children. Your mother has been invited to join the committee.'

'So that Mummy will do the work and Lady Grant will get all the credit.'

'Well, that's the way of the world. Anyway, they got chatting, she and Lady Grant, about their daughters. You and Jodie, Rowena and Emma. It put an idea into her head. Do you know what a debutante is, Peg?'

'Sort of.' There were pictures in the papers every summer of girls wearing long dresses and tiaras. One of them would be picked out as 'Debutante of the Year'. All of them had fathers with titles. Some of them even had titles of their own.

'Your mother would like you to be a debutante. What do you think about that?'

Peggy was too astounded to think anything at all. 'That's ridiculous!' she said at last. 'I'm not that kind of girl.'

'What kind of girl? You are a young woman of good character, perfectly worthy to be presented to His Majesty King George VI as a true and faithful subject.'

'Presented by who? I mean, whom? Mummy wouldn't have the foggiest idea . . .'

'That's true, but she wouldn't be presenting you herself. There are rules, but they're not too much of a problem.' He reached to pick up a copy of *The Times* from the floor and passed it over. Ringed in red ink on the front page was a two-line advertisement: 'Peeress would chaperone debutante for 1939 Season'.

'I wrote to the box number,' he said. 'Had a chat with the good lady on the telephone yesterday. Lady Menzies, her name is. Scottish. Widowed. Finding it hard to make ends meet, I'd guess, and not many jobs she's qualified to do.'

'You mean, she does this sort of thing for money?'

'Right. Flat fee and expenses. Good for her and a bargain for you. She'd act as mother. Fix everything up. Not just the court presentation. The whole Season. Parties, dances. Introduce you to people. Make sure you get invitations, make friends. I was impressed. She's done it before. Not every year, because that's not allowed, but often enough to know her way around. She'd want to meet you, of course, before anything was arranged. She'd be putting her own reputation at stake if she took on the wrong sort of girl. What do you think?'

Peggy had passed the stage of being astonished and was by now alarmed. If her father had got as far as approaching this Lady Menzies, he must be taking the matter seriously.

'I think it's a preposterous idea,' she said. 'Daddy, I simply haven't got the right sort of background for that sort of thing. It isn't enough just to be respectable. I mean, these debutantes, they're all aristocrats. I'm different – and glad of it.'

'Hang on a minute,' said her father. 'No one has to stick with the background they're born into. If they did, I'd still be living in Back Lane and sending you out to pawn my Sunday best every Monday to Saturday. I met your mother – well, you've heard this often enough – when I was fifteen and running my father's market stall and she was a girl of twelve helping out on her mother's stall next door. We've come a long way together since then, but she feels that she's reached her limit. For you and Jodie, though, there's no limit. With my money, you can fly as high as you choose, and this is a chance that only comes once. When you're eighteen. Your mother wants to be able to boast about you, Peg, love; just like Lady Grant boasts about Rowena.'

'I'll be the first member of the family ever to get to university, if I can manage it. Wouldn't that be enough for her to boast about?'

'I don't think your mother understands what's so special

about a university. What she's set her heart on is another thing altogether. To get you meeting people that you'll never come across here in Newark. Making new friends. Maybe even marrying one of them.'

'Marrying!' Peggy sprang to her feet. 'Daddy, I'm only seventeen. I'm still at school. I haven't even started living my own life yet. I don't intend to get married for years and years and years.'

Mr Armitage recognised that he had made a mistake. He quickly pulled her towards him in a hug. 'Of course you don't, and I wouldn't want to lose you for years and years and years. But listen now, Peg, and don't be getting so upset about this. This Season thing only lasts from about April to July. You could still take your Oxford exam next November, and go there the next year. All you'd miss would be one school term.'

Peggy was silent. Missing a term's work would be serious. It would also mean missing the Higher Certificate exams, and then, if she didn't win a place at Oxford, she would find herself with no hope of getting into any other university. But her father's suggestion had come as such a shock that she needed a little time to decide how best to argue against it. Think before you speak, as Miss Downie might have said.

'I'm not going to bully you,' her father went on. 'It's for you to choose. All I'm saying is that it would make your mother very happy to see you mixing with the nobs. And I can't deny that I'd be a touch proud as well, to see a daughter of mine up there with the best. But the main thing is that it would make me happy to find something I could give her at last. So don't dash straight off to her and say no. Sleep on it. That's all I ask. After that, it's up to you. Your life. Your decision.'

Peggy nodded her head obediently. It was a stupid thing, but she was near to tears. It was all very well to be told that the choice was hers, but how could she refuse something that meant so much to her mother – and, it seemed, to her father as well? They were acting out of kindness; but it was a moral blackmail, all the same, she thought as she went miserably up the wide staircase of the house which her schoolfriends thought enormous but would probably seem a poky hovel to a proper debutante.

On her way to change out of school uniform before tea, she

passed the door of her sister's study-bedroom. It was wide open and Jodie, who had obviously been listening for her, looked up from her homework and called her back.

'Are you going to do it?'

Peggy went in and sat down on the bed. Jodie was a precocious girl who held strong opinions on almost everything and felt no qualms about standing up to her parents. Her elder sister had often in the past found that a no-holds-barred argument was a good way to clear her own mind.

'Do what?' she asked. 'How do you know?'

'Daddy told me. He wanted to make sure that I wouldn't try to talk you out of it.'

'Would you have done?'

'Of course, and I still shall. I wouldn't make any promises. I think it's a perfectly stupid idea. All because Mummy wants to be able to keep up with the Grants and crow to the neighbours about a daughter who's doing the Season. And because she doesn't want you to go to university.'

'You can't say that!'

'Yes, I can. She doesn't want you to go to university. She doesn't want you to go to university. How many times would you like me to say it?'

'Don't be childish.'

'Well, I'm telling the truth.' Unlike Peggy herself, Jodie did not get on well with her mother. 'She thinks that no man will ever want to marry a blue-stocking, and that's what she wants: for you to get married as soon as possible and have the same kind of boring life as herself. She's afraid you'll sort of grow away from her if you get too well educated. But you know you're clever.'

'For those kind words, much thanks.' Jodie did not often pay compliments to her elder sister.

'Going to university is the right thing for you to do. Then you'll be properly qualified to do a useful job in society. And that will horrify Mummy as well. A daughter of hers working for money, after Daddy's toiled away all his life to make sure that we never need to!'

'Perhaps she'd be right. With millions of people unemployed, ought I to take a job that a poor girl needs more than I do?'

'If you're the right person for the job, yes,' Jodie replied. 'But that isn't the real point. Fancy wasting a whole summer just looking for a husband! I'm sure that's all it would be. Mummy wants to marry you off to some goof with a title. As the next best thing to having one herself. Mrs Armitage and her charming daughter, the Lady Doodah.'

'Well, she wouldn't succeed, would she? If I tell them I'm hoping to go to Oxford, all the goofs will cry "Blue-stocking!" and take to their heels.'

'Not if they find out how much money Daddy's got. And anyway, what will happen is that you'll start pretending that you're as stupid as all the other girls, just because that's expected. Then your brains will go rusty.'

'I'm rusty-brained enough already about most things. I can discuss the French Revolution or the poems of John Keats at length, but I don't know about anything that isn't taught in school.'

'And what are you going to learn if Mummy has her way? Apart from the two-step or the turkey trot or whatever? When I was playing tennis with Emma Grant in the holidays she told me that for the whole summer when Rowena was a debutante she didn't talk about anything except dresses and dances and young men. It's a worthless, frivolous life.'

'You could say that it provides employment for dressmakers and milliners and cooks and all that sort of thing. And Daddy reminded me that it would only be for a few months. I could still try for Oxford in November.' Peggy checked herself uneasily. She was repeating her father's points in the hope that Jodie's opposition would help to strengthen her own resolve, but there was a danger that she might be arguing herself round to an unwanted point of view.

'You'd have missed taking your Higher Certificates in June, though.'

'I don't actually need them. If I pass the Oxford entrance exam, all I need is Matriculation, and I've got that already.'

'But you won't pass it, will you? You'll have forgotten everything you knew and you'll have got out of the habit of studying.'

'Oh Jodie, don't be such a wet blanket.'

'I'm only saying all the things you know for yourself, really. It isn't as if you'd even enjoy the Season. All the other girls will look down on you because you're having to pay some old biddy with nothing to her name but a title to see you through. You'll be the only one without the right kind of mother. And it would all be just in order that some vapid aristocrat can be enticed into marrying you to get his hands on loads of Daddy's lolly.'

'Really, Jodie! Are you suggesting that no one could ever fall in love with me for my own sake? And why should you assume that everyone I might meet would necessarily be a chinless twit? It's very snobbish of you to dismiss a whole class of society because it has a certain label tied round its neck. There must be some intelligent aristocrats. Oxford graduates, even. You don't know anything about it.' Even as she spoke, Peggy became uncomfortably aware that opposing her sister's arguments was bringing her round to the view she had originally rejected as preposterous.

'Oh, ho!' Jodie was amused at the reaction she had produced. 'I *have* made you cross, haven't I? Well, anger's as good as wine for bringing out the truth. *In ira veritas*, as whoeveritwas might have said.'

'I'm not cross. I just think that talking about young men is way off the point. All Mummy wants to prove is that her daughters are as good as anyone else, whatever their class. You ought to approve of that, Jodie, with your democratic views. One of the causes of the French Revolution was the lack of social mobility in France. It's a very good thing that that's not true in England.'

'You think!'

'Yes, I do think. I think I have a right to be accepted into any group of people that I choose to join.'

'You won't make yourself acceptable by discussing the causes of the French Revolution over the turtle soup.'

'Oh, shut up, Jodie. You don't know what you're talking about.'

Jodie, hurt, looked down at her homework again and took up her pen.

'Sorry,' said Peggy. She needed solitude to think and went into her own room – only to find her mother waiting for her there.

'Well?' said Mrs Armitage. 'Isn't it a lovely idea? Just think what fun you'll have. I can't wait to see you wearing lovely clothes. And dancing with handsome young men in ballrooms under chandeliers. It'll be like the pictures, but real.'

'It's not the right thing for me, Mummy,' said Peggy. 'I don't want to disappoint you, but—'

'How can you know until you try? Just look at you now. Inky fingers and no colour in your cheeks. At school all day and then special lessons and then homework all evening. What sort of life is that?'

'The sort of life I like.'

'But it's so dull!'

'Then I'm a dull sort of person.'

'No, you're not. You just haven't had the chance to find out that there's more to life than being clever at your books. What's the use of us having all this money if we can't buy you a bit of pleasure with it?'

'Even if I don't want it?' But of course, Peggy reminded herself, it was her mother's pleasure they were really talking about and not her own. She made an effort to smile. 'Well, I promised Daddy I'd think about it.'

'You think about it, then.' Mrs Armitage stood up, ready to go. 'But I do hope, Peg, darling . . . It would make me so proud and happy. My debutante daughter!'

After she had gone, Peggy stood without moving, looking at herself in the mirror. It was a simple clash of ambitions, wasn't it? Her mother's fighting against her own. The London Season, whatever that might involve, against the equally unknown life of an Oxford undergraduate. Her mother's idea of a daughter's happiness against the daughter's wish to choose her own way of life at whatever cost. Two forms of selfishness in conflict, really, although her parents might think that they were being unselfish. Didn't they realise how humiliating the whole business was likely to be for a girl who hadn't been born into the right circles? Jodie had recognised that at once, and Peggy knew that she was right.

Was it simply cowardice, then, which was prompting her to refuse? She had long ago accepted the challenge of submitting herself to intellectual competition. Was it from fear of failure that she was reluctant to compete instead for acceptance into society?

No, it wasn't. The answer was very simple. There was no

point in competing unless the prize was worth having; and what was the prize in this case? To mix with lords and ladies, and perhaps make friends with some of them. But that brought her back again to her mother's ambition for her, which was exactly that. Mrs Armitage had devoted the whole of her life to her family. It would be ungrateful, wouldn't it, to turn her down the first time she asked for something in return?

Slowly Peggy stretched out both hands towards her own reflection until the two sets of fingers almost touched. Oxford was so nearly within her grasp, but she could feel it slipping away from her. Jodie had been right to argue that missing a term at school would jeopardise her chances, which were probably slight in any case. She sniffed, trying to hold back the tears which were already running down her cheeks.

'You're going to do it, aren't you?' asked Jodie, appearing in the doorway of her room. 'Be a debutante, I mean.'

Peggy did not answer at once. She still knew in her heart that it was the wrong course to take. But if Mummy had set her heart on seeing her elder daughter mix with some of the greatest in the land, it would be cruel to disappoint her.

'I'm not sure,' she said, sighing with uncertainty. 'But yes, I expect I am.'

3

'I hate England!'

Because she was addressing her father, Isabelle spoke in French. It had been agreed between her parents over her cradle that they would bring her up to be bilingual, always conversing with her father in French and her mother in English. Sometimes she wondered whether the marriage would have been more successful if they had chosen one language or the other for the whole family to share. But it was too late to do anything about that now.

Seventeen years after taking that decision, her parents did not even share a home. Isabelle lived in Paris with her mother. For the past three months she had been on holiday with her father in Monte Carlo and the South of France. She was an athletic girl and delighted in the hours of sailing, fencing and tennis which she had shared with him. But now, like a readdressed parcel, she was being despatched back to Paris before being taken to the land of her mother's birth.

Guy le Vaillant, driving his daughter at speed along the high winding corniche towards Nice, was careful not to take his eyes off the road, but his voice expressed sympathy and amusement.

'What's wrong with poor old England?'

'Every time I've been there with Maman the sky has been grey, the food inedible, and the women dressed like either dumplings or Christmas trees.'

'I think you may assume that your mother intends to take Alphonse to London with her, so you're not likely to starve. And she will order your clothes in Paris before you leave, so that the dumplings and the Christmas trees will envy your elegance. It's more difficult to praise the weather, but I understand that dampness is good for the complexion. In any case, it's just for a few months. You can endure that, surely.'

'If only you could come too, Papa!'

'Certainly it would give me great pleasure to see you in all your glory. But if you're to be presented to society as the daughter of respectable parents, it will perhaps be just as well if your papa is not there to be inspected through the lorgnettes of dowager duchesses. They might move on to wonder whether you have inherited your father's character, and that would spoil everything. Anyway, your mother has only been prevailed upon to pay all my debts on condition that she goes unaccompanied and has a free hand to present you at court and guide you through your Season without any paternal embarrassment.'

'While you go on gambling here. You've sold me to Maman for a seat at the *chemin-de-fer* table!' Isabelle put an aggrieved note into her voice, but she was smiling, and her father acknowledged the tease by kissing one finger and touching her cheek with it.

'It's the right thing for you to do at this time in your life, my little one, and your mother is the right person to help you. All I have been able to provide for you is the best tennis coach in Monte Carlo, but she will find you a suitable husband. Once you are married and have your own household, you will be free of her – and if you manage to steal Alphonse from her, I will visit you as often as you wish and shoot little birds with whatever snobby lordling you have managed to ensnare. But in any case, I am still your father. Remember that.'

'Suppose there is a divorce?'

'There will be no divorce.' Guy made the statement with confidence. 'A divorcée would not be allowed to present her daughter at court. Nor would she be admitted to the Royal Enclosure at Ascot. That, we may safely assume, will be decisive, however much your mother would like to be rid of me. You will take your place in English society with all the honour due to the granddaughter of an earl and the beloved daughter of the securely married Lady Patricia le Vaillant, with no skeletons in the family cupboard. It is merely unfortunate that your father's extensive business interests detain him in France.'

'Correction. His extensive patronage of casinos.'

'Yes, but truth is a jewel that must sometimes be hidden from prying eyes. Your mother will doubtless instruct you in the necessity for discretion in the course of your introduction to society.' He applied the brake to the powerful Bugatti as they negotiated the hairpin bends on the descent towards Nice. Neither of them spoke again until Isabelle was standing on the platform of the railway station, surrounded by trunks and watching unhappily as the train to Paris crept in and wheezed to a halt.

'I do wish I could stay with you, Papa.'

Her father enfolded her in his arms and kissed her tenderly. 'It's one of the unjust things in life, that it's often so much easier to love the sinner than the righteous one. I know you find your mother too cold and overbearing.' He threw out his hands in a gesture of regret. 'I wish you could have known her when she was young. Lady Patsy then, not Lady Patricia. So gay. So high spirited.'

As her father summoned a porter and led the way to her reserved compartment, Isabelle shook her head at the impossibility of making such an effort of imagination. Even within the domestic setting of their home in Paris, her forty-year-old mother was always stiffly corseted and correctly dressed for the time of day. In public her coiffure was invariably immaculate and her display of jewellery served to intimidate lesser mortals. As Lady Patricia frequently reminded her acquaintances, her father, before succeeding to his earldom, had been His Majesty's Ambassador in Paris; and her main interest in life – or so it seemed to her daughter – lay in the niceties of protocol and precedence. A dinner would be ruined for her by any *faux pas* in the *placement* and she would talk of nothing else for days. High spirited? Gay? Was it possible?

Sitting with her while the luggage was being loaded, Guy did his best to dissolve her disbelief. 'In England, after the war, there were the Bright Young Things. In Paris, the same refusal to be serious. But Paris had other things which, believe it or not, appealed to your mother when she was your age – when she was rebelling, as you do now, against the excessive formality of

37

her parents' lives. There were writers and artists from America. Dancers and composers from Russia. A kind of intellectual excitement in a world where everything was possible. Difficult to explain, but if you ever come across it, you will know. The mind floating in delight. A sense of unreality. And also, of course, drugs and drink. We were both caught up in the sheer bliss of it all.'

Isabelle listened intently. Neither of her parents had spoken to her before about this period in their lives. She had often wondered how two such incompatible people had come to meet.

'It was too easy for a young girl to be swept off her feet and make mistakes,' Guy continued. 'I had ambitions as a writer, and she was ambitious for me. Saw me as the Balzac *de nos jours*. And was more disappointed by my failures than I was myself.'

'Why did you fail?' asked Isabelle.

'Because I inherited money. Enough to make it unnecessary for me to be successful, although not enough to persuade me that there was no need to increase it. A small fortune can deal a fatal blow to ambition. It's helpful to be very rich; and stimulating, although not pleasant, to be very poor. But to possess a small, plump cushion against failure makes failure inevitable. Or so I tell myself now.'

'So how did that affect the marriage?' asked Isabelle.

Guy sighed with regret. 'I bore your mother off, out of her own milieu towards what seemed another heaven, but we never reached it. And then I betrayed her by proving to be unreliable. No good as a writer. No good as a husband. You must always remember, Isabelle, that between the two of us, your mother and I, I have been the one to blame. It's hardly surprising that she wishes to see you take your place in a society where everyone knows his rank and what is expected of him. So that there will be no disappointments. I shall go on trying to win another fortune at Monte Carlo and no doubt I shall continue to fail, but you must put yourself in your mother's hands, and she will make sure that you have a triumph.'

'By a triumph, you just mean a good marriage, don't you? Suppose I don't want to get married?'

'That will be your choice, and I shall respect it. But you'd do well to consider that marriage will bring you a degree of independence. How else are you to escape from being merely your mother's daughter, financially dependent on her and perpetually under scrutiny to be sure that you are preserving your reputation?'

'By reputation, do you mean virginity?'

Guy laughed as he stood up, preparing to leave the train. 'Virginity is a word that no nice English girl should utter aloud. It might suggest that she knows what it means.'

'I'm not an English girl.'

'You're about to become one. You must get into training. But no, reputation is truly what I meant. Far more fragile. Many's the young man who has found himself trapped by an impulsive kiss into learning that he must regard himself as engaged. Otherwise the young lady concerned will be considererd "fast". But if she is thought to be "fast" already, he has a chance of escape. Your good reputation, Mademoiselle le Vaillant, is your strongest weapon. Blunt it, and it becomes useless. But preserve its bright, shining point and your mother will tell you exactly when to strike.'

Smiling, he moved into the stance of a fencer, aiming for her heart; but almost at once became serious again. 'What I am saying is that on the day you promise to love, honour and obey your husband, you will achieve a measure of freedom.'

Isabelle found this as hard to believe as his previous description of a bubbly Lady Patsy with literary interests. He was thinking of a French marriage, she suspected, while she was being steered towards an English one. But there was no time to continue the discussion, for whistles were blowing and it was time for her father to leave the train.

Isabelle hurried to the window for a last goodbye, and her father looked up at her with a twinkle in his eye.

'One other thing,' he said. 'You're far too good a tennis player for the country house weekends at which you'll be invited to play. You'll be in danger of humiliating not only the other girls, but the young men as well. In the interests of making yourself popular, you may need to learn how to lose.'

'Is that what I have to remember as your last word to me?' Fighting her growing unhappiness, Isabelle did her best to keep her voice light-hearted. 'You ought to be giving me fatherly words of advice to apply to life in general instead of just the tennis court.'

'All right then, I will.' Guy spoke more seriously than usual. 'Because you love me, Isabelle, you may find yourself tempted to marry a man who is like me. If that happens, your mother will forbid it, and she will be right. Before you allow yourself to become angry with her, remember that I have said the same thing.'

Isabelle felt her eyes filling with tears. The engine whistled. It had seemed such a jovial, holiday whistle when it announced its departure for the Riviera three months earlier. On this occasion, though, it sounded long and mournful, and she felt that the engine could hardly muster the strength to pull out of the station as it carried her away on the first part of her journey: to Paris, to England, and to the start of a new life.

4

Soon it would be too cold to paint outside. The autumn of 1938 had been a mild one in the Bavarian countryside, but now the year was drawing towards its close. Already the first flurries of snow had begun to fall, although not yet to lie.

Anne Venables was looking forward to the snow. It would present a new challenge. In the three months since her arrival in Germany Herr Frankel, her art teacher, had opened her eyes, encouraging her to look at the world in a new way. He had taught her to see the colours within shadows and to appreciate the spaces between objects. Sitting beside her, he had demonstrated with a few quick strokes how the clouds that she had painted like balls of cotton wool suspended in the sky could be made to seem moving as fast as ships under sail. He had shown her how to paint light on water and promised that as soon as the snow came she would learn the techniques of capturing its subtle glitter on paper. When rain kept them indoors, he had introduced her to the meticulous art of botanical painting, emphasising the importance of reproducing accurately every hair and fibre of the specimens he dissected for her.

Each day, as her teacher announced his arrival at Frau Herzen's house with an old-fashioned bow, Anne thanked her lucky stars that she had not been sent to a finishing school. The reason her parents had despatched her instead to board in a private household, where she could improve her German and take private lessons in music and art, was a shortage of money. But what a relief it was!

Anne was a shy seventeen-year-old, unused to the company of her contemporaries. Howard, her elder brother, had been sent away from home at the age of seven, first to prep school and then to Eton and Oxford, because that was the way in which all Venables boys were educated. But Venables girls stayed at home with their governesses until it was time for them to be 'finished'.

Anne could by now speak German with reasonable fluency, but saw no particular point in the accomplishment. When was she ever, in her ordinary life, likely to find herself chatting to Germans? And although she did her piano practice conscientiously every day, she knew that she was never going to be a Franz Liszt. Nor, to be honest with herself, was she likely to come within a mile of being a Constable either. Even Herr Frankel at his most encouraging never suggested that she had any special talent. All the same, the peaceful hours she spent under his tuition gave her a satisfaction that no other part of her education had ever brought.

Today she had painted a landscape. The scene was a dull one in real life and even duller on paper.

'It's dead,' she sighed, staring critically at what she had done. She spoke in German. It was part of the arrangement that she should speak and hear no English at all during her year's stay.

'Then we must bring it to life, must we not, Fräulein Venables? Something is necessary to attract the eye. So what do you think? A tree perhaps, just there.' His finger pointed.

'But there isn't a tree there.'

'Alas, no. Nature gives us shapes, with outlines and surfaces. But it is what we add or take away that turns Nature into Art. You have done well in learning to paint what you see. Now it is time for you to paint pictures that are better than what you see. Sometimes you will need to add and sometimes to take away. The imagination must improve on the eye. Be bold.'

Half closing her eyes, Anne stared at the watercolour until all she could see was a design of curves where the foothills of the mountains came down to meet the valley. A little higher than Herr Frankel had indicated, she added a dark columnar tree with all the daring he had demanded.

'Very good. Your sense of design is better than your teacher's. That is exactly the right spot. If I owned this land, I would go straight away to plant your tree there. Well, that is enough for today. Your fingers must be cold. Tomorrow we shall make an expedition to the castle on the hill and I will show you what beauty may be found in an old stone wall.'

Anne nodded happily – but alas, there was to be no such expedition. When she returned to Frau Herzen's comfortable house, there was a letter waiting for her.

The envelope bore no stamp; and yet Anne recognised her father's handwriting. Did that mean that he was in Germany, near at hand? She began to read the letter with a hopefulness that soon turned to puzzlement.

Dearest Anne,

I fear that it has become necessary to cut short the time that we had planned for you to stay in Germany. Will you tell Frau Herzen that for family reasons you are obliged to return home before Christmas? Please do everything you can to assure her that you have been happy and well looked after while living with her family – which I feel sure, from your letters, is the case. Thank her also for arranging for you to have such good teachers for your painting and music. I shall of course be writing to her directly myself, but in the meantime you may reassure her that I shall meet all my obligations.

Your Aunt Marian has kindly agreed to accompany you back to England. Pack your things as soon as you receive this letter. She will be calling within a few hours to tell you about travel arrangements.

I hope that this will not cause you too much disappointment. There is nothing to worry about at home, and we are all, of course, longing to see you again.

With love from your devoted father.

'Have you had bad news, Fräulein?' asked Frau Herzen, watching Anne's face as she read the letter.

Anne was unsure what to say. Was there really nothing to worry about? Illness in the family was the only reason she could think of for her unexpected summons home. And if that were the case, could it be her father himself? Otherwise he would surely have been more open with her. Trying to control her anxiety, she realised that the simplest way to answer her hostess was to read out the first paragraph of the letter, translating as she went.

'Oh, but we shall be desolated to lose you!' exclaimed Frau Herzen. 'Especially Claus!'

Anne felt herself blushing. The son of the house was only a few months older than herself. He had taken her into his room on the very day of her arrival to show her a poster on the wall. It depicted the Hitler Youth's ideal young woman – tall, blonde and glowing with good health – and could have been a portrait of Anne herself.

Since then Claus had taken every opportunity to invite her on hikes and bicycle rides with his group. It was a form of showing off to the others: bringing as his companion someone who so closely resembled the perfect girl. Anne for her part enjoyed the open-air activities; and it was fun to be admired and find herself the mascot of what she presumed was the German equivalent of a Boy Scout troop.

'I shall be very sorry to go,' she told her hostess, 'but . . .'

'Oh yes, you must obey your father. I will send one of the maids at once to help you with your packing.'

It did not take long, and by the time her aunt arrived Anne was ready to leave. But conventional courtesies were mandatory in Frau Herzen's household, so coffee and pastries had to be produced for the English visitor before there could be any discussion of trains and boats. Aunt Marian, however, was not to be detained for long. She appeared worried and distracted, but had a firm grasp of the relevant timetables and had made the necessary reservations. Only a short time after reading her father's letter, Anne was on her way into Munich and to the railway station.

It was a tiring journey: first by train across almost the whole length of Germany and Holland, then an overnight ferry from The Hook to Harwich and finally the boat train to London. There Medhurst, the family chauffeur, was waiting with the Alvis to drive them to Yewley House.

Even before the train moved out of Munich station Anne had tried to find out what family emergency had caused her recall. Her aunt reassured her about illness, but would only add that she must wait until her father could explain. Aunt Marian herself, usually so brisk and cheerful, was uncommunicative and looked older than her years. When Anne – grateful that she need not cope with customs and passport formalities at the frontiers by herself – thanked her for taking the trouble to keep her company, the response was accompanied by a heavy sigh.

'It's no trouble, dear. I'd already written to your father to say that I'd decided to return to England.'

Marian was Mr Venables' sister and had been living in Germany for nearly twenty years. She had never married. Every year she came to Yewley for Christmas, but had always looked forward to returning to her own home. Cultural life in Leipzig, she asserted, was far superior to anything on offer in England. It was also a consideration that her tiny income from investments in Britain stretched much further with every collapse in the value of the mark.

'Return for good, you mean?'

'Yes, for good.' But no explanation was offered for this, either, and her obvious unhappiness prevented Anne from pressing the question.

When the journey at last came to an end and the car turned in through the lodge gates, Anne called to the chauffeur to stop.

'I'd like to get out and walk up to the house,' she said. It was not simply that she wanted a chance to stretch her legs: by arriving a few minutes after her aunt she could have her parents' greeting all to herself instead of sharing it.

The drive was not a long one for a house of Yewley's size. Once upon a time the property had been the centre of a huge estate of farmland, woodland and orchard, but an eighteenth-century Venables had gambled much of it away. Little by little most of what remained had to be sold to pay taxes and death duties, and every capital sale caused the family's income to shrink. Now there was nothing left but a few farms and a fine expanse of parkland which made no contribution towards expenses. The Venables were not poor in the sense that any truly poor person would have recognised, but they were indigent rich.

Yewley House stood in a secluded Berkshire valley. It was almost five hundred years old, and Anne's family had lived there for all those years. The Venables were landed gentry who had never done anything to earn themselves a title or a mention in history books. But as an old family and proud of it, Anne's parents continued to honour the tradition of local public service that their position in society demanded of them, even though it was becoming more and more difficult every year to maintain any semblance of the style of life that their ancestors had taken for granted.

Anne thought herself unbelievably lucky to have been brought up in such an old and beautiful place, but often enough over the years she had heard her mother, whose blood was truly blue, compare it unfavourably with her own childhood home and those now occupied by her sisters, Anne's formidably upper-crust aunts.

Rounding a bend in the drive, Anne came to a halt with a sigh of delight at her first view of the house in the pale winter sunshine. How good it was to be home! How lovely Yewley was! How peaceful! From this vantage point she could see both the south and the west façades, with their long, leaded windows. The building was timber framed, with small dark red bricks arranged in diagonal patterns between irregular old beams. Even before going to Germany Anne had often gazed for minutes on end at those bricks, enjoying the subtle shading of colours on the uneven surfaces. Now, thanks to Herr Frankel, perhaps she would have the skill to paint them. She could paint the clusters of twisting chimneys as well, and the carved leaf patterns decorating the gables.

What she would never be able to paint was the smell of the house. The memory of that scent was so strong that even at this distance she felt as though she were surrounded by it: the musty damp of many centuries overpowered by the fragrance of wood. Old floors and old wall panelling and, most of all, the smokiness of log fires which for nine months of the year were never allowed to go out. Her pace quickened as she hurried towards the entrance porch.

Inside she could hear her aunt answering questions in a high-pitched voice, so she took the opportunity to run upstairs and take off her hat.

Her bedroom was exactly as she had left it: the tidily made bed; the ceiling curved like a ship's hull, with its craquelure from which so many pictures could be formed in the imagination; the sloping floor; the leaded window with its view of yew hedges neatly trimmed into arches and pillars with finials of peacocks and squirrels. But when she opened the door which led into the day nursery, which had become her private sitting room, her eyes widened in astonishment. A strange boy was sitting on the floor, surrounded by a confusion of her old playthings.

'What on earth do you think you're doing?' Surprise sharpened the question into an accusation. It was a good many years since she had last felt any interest in most of the objects on the floor, but they were hers. They were private. No one else had the right to play with them without permission – and this boy was not so much playing as spoiling. As she appeared, he was in the process of tipping out a boxful of jigsaw pieces on top of others, from a different box, that were scattered around already.

At the sound of her voice the boy looked round and scrambled to his feet so quickly that he lost his balance and fell over again. He was frightened. And so he should be, she thought. She could see him swallowing the lump in his throat in an attempt to explain, but no sound emerged. Anne stared for a moment and then ran downstairs. The encounter had spoiled her happiness in the return home and when she encountered her mother on the landing she quite forgot to greet her properly.

'What's that boy doing in my room?'

'Ah, there you are, darling. We wondered where you'd got to.' The Hon. Mrs Venables offered a cheek to be kissed. She was not a demonstrative woman and Anne had realised while still in the nursery that her brother Howard was his mother's one and only favourite. Throughout her childhood Anne had sought for ways of pleasing her mother, but had learned that the best way to avoid a rebuff was not to offer any great show of affection.

On this occasion, though, they seemed to be in sympathy. It was clear from Mrs Venables' expression that she resented the presence of the boy as much as Anne did.

'You'd better ask your father. It's all his idea.'

Anne hurried down the stairs, smiled at Aunt Marian, who was busy sorting out her luggage with one of the servants, and burst into the library, flinging herself into her father's arms.

'Welcome home! How we've missed you! Heavens, how you've grown! You're quite the young lady! And more beautiful than ever.'

'Don't be ridiculous,' said Anne, continuing to kiss him vigorously. 'It's lovely to see you again. And looking so well. I was afraid you must be ill. Now tell me, Father. Who's the boy in the old nursery? He's making an awful mess with my things. What's he doing here and when is he going?' She expected to be told that he was the son of some visitor, and about to depart, but her hopes were disappointed.

'His name is Hans Friedman, and he's not going anywhere. He will be staying here.'

'Why? I don't want—'

'Don't let's talk about that now. I'll explain after luncheon. First of all I want to hear all your news.'

The boy took his place at the luncheon table – appearing, for no reason that Anne could understand, to be on the point of tears. He ate little and said nothing while the family chattered about what had been happening to them all.

When the meal was over, Anne followed her father into his study. He sat himself in the leather armchair in whose depths his own father and grandfather had also made themselves comfortable. Anne took the window seat, from where she could see the big beech tree in the centre of the vista to the east of the house, the bare skeleton of its upper branches wearing at its foot a crinoline of the remaining yellow and brown and orange leaves. It brought back to her memory the last conversation she had enjoyed with Herr Frankel. A hundred years ago an earlier Mr Venables had looked at the view and decided that it needed some dramatic addition. Perhaps he had not lived to see the beech as more than a sapling or young tree, but now Anne could enjoy the benefit of his vision.

'Now then, about Hans,' said her father. 'I know you've never taken much interest in what's going on in the world, but while you were in Germany you must have heard about the Kristallnacht.'

Anne shook her head. Frau Herzen had been generous in lending her books to read, but she had no memory of ever seeing a newspaper in the house, and Kristallnacht was not a word that she had heard mentioned. 'No,' she said. 'The glass night? What is it?'

'Well, if you don't know, I'll start at a different point. A year ago Hans was living with his parents in Vienna. They were very well off. His father was a university professor. His mother comes from a rich family and they lived in a big apartment.

48

Nice furniture. Comfortable life. Unfortunately for them, they were Jews.' He paused, waiting for Anne to comment.

'I know that some of the Germans don't like the Jews,' she said uncertainly. She had been surprised more than once by the fierceness of Frau Herzen's comments about one or two of the musicians whose work she had practised.

'And you know that the Germans took over Austria earlier this year.'

'Yes. The Austrians were pleased about that, Frau Herzen said.'

'Some of them may have been, but not all. Since the Nazis arrived there, they've been making all sorts of new regulations. One of them is that any senior Nazi can move into any Jewish-owned property which takes his fancy and evict the owners. That's what happened to the Friedmans. They have lost their home and all their property; Professor Friedman lost his job as well, just for being a Jew.'

'That's terrible.' Anne was already feeling guilty about being so unfriendly to Hans.

'That's not all. Hans's mother has been forced to scrub pavements in the street – not to earn money, but as a humiliation. And then Professor Friedman was arrested and sent to a labour camp. He isn't used to manual labour, and Mrs Friedman doesn't believe that she'll ever see him again.'

'Poor them! Poor Hans! Why isn't she with him here?'

'Because she can't get out of the country. Every Jew in Austria and Germany wants to find somewhere else to go, and other countries are limiting the numbers they'll accept. She was trying to get a visa to come here, but there's a huge waiting list. And then, six weeks ago, there was the Kristallnacht.'

'I still don't know . . .'

'It's called that because of the broken glass that was left all over Germany when every Jewish-owned shop was looted. Synagogues were burned. Jews on the street were killed. Mrs Friedman became so frightened that she sent her son here alone under a scheme named Kindertransport. She had to put him on a train and just wave him goodbye.'

'How could she bear to do that?'

'She thought it was the only way to save his life. But of course the boy himself doesn't understand that. How could he? It must seem to him that he's been sent away because his mother doesn't love him any more. Probably you don't completely understand either, do you? It's difficult to believe that people can be so bigoted and evil.'

'They didn't seem evil. People like Frau Herzen and Herr Frankel. They were nice, ordinary people. Very kind, in fact.' She was silent for a moment, puzzled by the difficulty of reconciling what her father had just told her with her life during the past three months, so pleasant and peaceful. 'So how did Hans come to be here?'

'Britain agreed to take in Jewish children who were in danger, and there was an appeal for funds and homes. I thought we ought to do our bit to help. When Hans arrived at Harwich he was taken to a school hall and given a meal and told to sit still while people like me prowled around and stared and eventually said, "I'll take that one." So he's here and this is his home until his parents can reclaim him. I haven't had much success in persuading your mother that it was a good idea, but she has accepted it and I'm sure you will too, now you know all about it.'

'I can't believe people are being killed simply for being Jewish,' said Anne. 'But if they are, then of course we must help.'

'That's my girl!' He came over to her and patted her hand, grateful to find her sympathetic.

'Shouldn't you have brought two of the children home?' she asked after a moment's thought. 'So that they could be company for each other.'

'I did consider that. But I don't believe that Hans will be able to return to Vienna for a long, long time. For the sake of his own happiness, he needs to become an English boy as quickly as possible, and that will be easier if he has no contact with anyone else from Austria.'

'I can translate for him,' Anne offered.

'That will be very useful. We're having problems in communication. I've done my best with the help of a dictionary, but your mother seems to think that if he doesen't understand something she should just say it again more emphatically. So yes, we'll be glad of your German, but the important thing is to get him speaking English as quickly as possible, so that he can go to an ordinary school.'

'Is that why you wanted me to come back early, because I can speak German?'

'No.' Mr Venables was silent for what seemed to Anne a long time, as though he were wondering whether or not to voice his thoughts. 'This is becoming a rather gloomy welcome home. Not at all what I had in mind. But since we've started . . . I'm very much afraid that before long England and Germany will be at war. Nobody here wants that, but Herr Hitler seems determined to get the whole of Europe into his power, and sooner or later the moment is sure to come when we have to say "Enough is enough". I think that from now on you ought to look at a newspaper every day, Anne, to keep in touch with what's going on. Because whatever happens, it will be your generation which has to pay the price, just as it was mine twenty-five years ago.'

'Is this why Aunt Marian's come home?'

'Yes. She has a lot of Jewish friends, musical friends, in Leipzig. She's helped some of them to get out, but things were becoming very difficult for her and she thought she might soon find herself trapped on the wrong side of a battle line. She had the same worry about you and wrote to tell me that I ought to waste no time in getting you back.'

Anne was still regretful about having her first venture abroad curtailed, but at least she now understood the reason.

'Let's forget about all that for the moment,' her father went on. 'Howard's coming tonight for the weekend, and we have a feast planned, to welcome the two of you home.'

'Lovely. Well, I'll go and be polite to Hans.'

'Thank you, darling. I knew I could count on you.'

He was not an attractive boy – pale and podgy, miserable and nervous – but now that Anne knew the reason for the apprehension in his eyes, she set herself the task of putting him at ease. Together, chatting in German but teaching and learning English words as they went along, they sorted out the jigsaw pieces into the right boxes.

She was just about to change for dinner when she heard the sounds of Howard's arrival to a welcome – after an absence probably only of a week or two – far warmer than the greeting which their mother had extended to her. She ran downstairs to join them.

Howard and Anne were not particularly close. The six-year gap in age and Howard's absences at boarding school had left them with little in common. Mr Venables was right when he pointed out that Anne had inherited all the family's good looks and Howard the brains. Howard had won scholarships to both Eton and Christ Church and, recognising that it was about time for at least one Venables to start bringing in some money, had found himself a good job in the City.

In spite of seeing so little of each other – or perhaps because of it – brother and sister enjoyed an easy relationship. Now they chatted happily together before being chivvied upstairs to dress for dinner.

Over the meal Mrs Venables announced her change of plan for Anne. 'I've been thinking what we should do with you, now that you're not going to be living in Germany after all next summer. I think you'd better come out.'

'You mean, be a debutante? You've always said we couldn't afford that sort of thing. And anyway, I don't want—'

Her mother held up an imperious hand to check her protest. 'I've had a word with your father. Obviously we mustn't be too extravagant, but we can manage a Season. After all, we don't want everyone to think that we're too poor to launch our daughter in the proper manner.' By 'everyone', Anne knew that her mother was referring to the moneyed and titled aunts. 'Besides, it's time that Howard thought about getting married.'

'What's that got to do with me?'

'Naturally, during your Season, Howard will act as your partner. It will give him the opportunity—'

Mr Venables, his eyes twinkling, interrupted to finish the sentence. 'To rope himself an heiress who'd be able to maintain Yewley in the style to which it was once accustomed.'

'I say, steady on.' It was Howard who was protesting now, but his father was not to be stopped.

'You'd be expected to introduce him to all your wealthiest friends, Anne.'

'But I haven't got any friends in London. I wouldn't know anyone except our cousins.' Anne's face was flushed. Until the visit to Germany she had always lived quietly in the country.

The prospect of being pitchforked into an unaccustomed social life in the company of hundreds of complete strangers appalled her.

'You'd soon make friends,' her mother assured her. 'That's what the Season's all about. It's specially designed to introduce you to other girls of the same age. And, of course, to young men. You yourself might . . .'

Anne guessed where that sentence was leading, and her anxiety increased. Seeing her upset, her father came to the rescue.

'There's no need for any more discussion now. It's just an idea for you to think about. We'll have a chat later.'

The subject was dropped, but continued to prey on Anne's mind. She had envisaged a homecoming to a way of life in which everything would continue as before. Hans's presence had dealt the first blow to this undemanding picture; and now the prospect of spending several months in London shattered it completely.

Early next morning she and her brother went out riding together. At the top of a ridge overlooking a placid, lazy stretch of the Thames, they reined in their horses to admire the view. How different from that hateful bustle of London life!

'You don't really want to do this Season thing, do you, Howard?' she asked.

'Why not?' To her dismay, he seemed to find the prospect of it amusing. 'When I was still at Oxford, a whole bunch of us found ourselves on a Lady's List. Lady and List both with a capital L, I should make clear. We'd obviously passed the two acid tests of being decent dancers and safe in taxis. It was actually great fun. And of course, as chaps, we were under no obligation to provide hospitality ourselves. If I were to do it again and see you through, I'd get three months of free meals and champagne at the cost of a few gushing thank-you letters.'

'But you surely don't want . . .'

'To rope an heiress? That's just Father's little joke. No heiress would take a second look at someone like me, all set to inherit a pile of dry rot instead of a title. Also, I have a curious notion that I might prefer to marry for love.' He laughed. 'You do whatever you choose, Anne. All I'm saying is that I'll be happy to back you up if you decide to make your debut.'

53

'Whatever I choose? Whatever I decide? What choice have I got? It sounds as though it's all settled.'

'I actually think you might enjoy it more than you seem to expect. It's perfectly true that Mother's main incentive is to keep up with the aunts, but she's got a good point when she says that you need the chance to make new friends. Both male and female. Stuck away here, you're never going to meet enough people of your own age.'

'I like being stuck away here. It's so beautiful. I'd be content just to sit and paint it all day.' She stretched an arm out towards the river as though she could capture the view and hug it close. 'And she's thinking about a husband, not about friends. To get me off her hands.'

'Oh, come, it's not as bad as that. She can lead you to the trough of the Season but she can't force you to drink the waters of matrimony. How's that for a *mot*? If you're really worried, you know you can always twist Father round your little finger. Come on. Stop mooning over some frosty fields. I'll race you back to the stables.'

Anne chose the first moment when they were alone together to tackle her father. 'I don't want to be a debutante,' she told him earnestly. 'If it's just for Howard's sake, he really doesn't need me. He can get as many invitations as he wants to debutante balls. I shall hate every minute of it and it will just be a waste of your money. I'm sure you don't really want me to do it, do you? Please say that you'll drop the idea.'

She was confident that her father would do as she wished. He always took her side against her mother. But to her surprise, on this occasion he shook his head and repeated almost word for word what Howard had already said.

'I think your mother is right that you need to meet more people and make more friends than you ever will while you're living here. You're not to worry about the money. We shall manage.'

There was a long pause while she tried to think of some more persuasive argument. But her father interrupted her thoughts, speaking in a more serious tone.

'This is all connected with what I was saying yesterday about the possibility that we may soon be at war. The world is about to become a much grimmer place. Your mother and I have lived through all this once and it breaks my heart to think that the same thing may be coming your way and Howard's. It may be that the Season of 1939 will prove to be the last chance you'll have to be carefree. I want you to take that opportunity, so that whatever may happen afterwards, you'll always have the memory of a summer in which you were young and gay and admired for being so very, very beautiful. Do it for my sake, dearest. Go to London and have fun while you can.'

5

What had she expected, then? Rising politely to her feet as the maid showed Lady Menzies into the sitting room of The Elms in Newark, Peggy tutted at her own surprise. She was as bad as Jodie, making assumptions about people just because they happened to have titles.

She had envisaged the visitor – the peeress who was going to present her at court – as likely to be tall and overbearing, wearing pearls and a fur coat and speaking in a lah-di-dah voice. But even her costume of thick Harris tweed could not make Lady Menzies look anything but tiny. Her legs were thin sticks which seemed hardly capable of supporting her. Her face, too, was thin and beaky. As for her voice, it was soft and Scottish as she first of all brushed aside Mrs Armitage's flurry of thanks to her for making the journey north and then turned to Peggy herself.

'I'm very pleased to make your acquaintance, Miss Armitage.'

No one had ever called Peggy Miss Armitage before and the effect on her was unexpected. Within the space of only a few seconds she felt herself to have grown up. She would be going back to school at the end of the Christmas holiday, which had just begun, but she no longer felt like a schoolgirl. A moment ago she had been nervous, knowing that Lady Menzies had come to inspect her and see whether she would pass muster. She had not even been sure that she wanted to be approved. If she were to be pronounced unsuitable, the whole debutante plan would collapse without the responsibility for her mother's disappointment resting on her own shoulders. But the delight of being an adult prompted her to straighten her shoulders, lift her head high and shake hands with confidence.

In the three weeks since her father first raised the subject of the Season, Peggy had made a promise to herself. She was still convinced that it would be a ridiculous waste of time and that she couldn't possibly enjoy it. She had agreed to be presented only as a favour to her mother. But if a thing was worth doing, it was worth doing properly, so she wasn't going to sulk and she wasn't ever going to let anybody guess that she wasn't having a good time. She intended to sneak two hours to herself every day to keep up, if she could, with the schoolwork she would be missing, but for the rest of the time she would do whatever a debutante was expected to do with a good grace. And the first thing she was expected to do was to smile at her future chaperone.

Lady Menzies was smiling as well. Her eyes, as birdlike as the rest of her face, were bright and observant and seemed to be approving of what she saw. It might be all right, thought Peggy. This whole project was crazy, but it just might turn out all right.

The parlourmaid brought in tea and was despatched to inform Mr Armitage that the visitor had arrived. Peggy had been surprised to learn that her father wished to be present for what promised to be a mainly female discussion, but he had made his views clear.

'She seemed to know what she was doing when I spoke to her before,' he said. 'I'm sure she's familiar with all the right procedures, but I want to be sure that she's a good enough organiser to get everything done. And you know what your mother's like. She'll just be so delighted about what's happening that she won't ask any of the difficult questions. If this session goes off all right, then I'll leave you ladies to it in the future.'

The conversation did indeed go well. Lady Menzies won Mr Armitage's heart from the start by announcing that she believed in writing everything down. From a spacious crocodile handbag she produced one well-worn notebook and a brand new ring file.

'You'll be Miss Margaret Armitage as far as the Lord Chamberlain is concerned,' she pointed out, writing that name in capitals on the first page. 'So all your hostesses will use that form of your name, and it will save complications if I do as well. Will that be all right, my dear? As soon as you start to become friendly with the other girls you can tell them that you prefer to be called Peggy.'

Peggy nodded her head. Using her full name seemed an appropriate way of marking her arrival in the adult world.

Lady Menzies turned over a page. 'Now then,' she said. 'Most arrangements can be left until February, but what needs to be considered urgently is the matter of clothes. As you can imagine, the best couturiers are under great pressure as the start of the Season approaches. I've made a list of what you'll need.'

She freed a page from the ring file and passed it across to Mr and Mrs Armitage. Peggy moved to stand beside her father so that she could read it over his shoulder.

The length of the list made her want to burst into laughter. At the moment her wardrobe was a simple one. She had school clothes, Sunday clothes, Saturday clothes and summer holiday clothes. But now it seemed that she was expected to acquire not only a special dress with a train for her presentation at court, but also tea gowns, luncheon costumes, evening dresses and a multitude of special occasion outfits.

'*Three* Ascot outfits?' she queried, reaching the bottom of the page.

'It's usual to wear something different each day, my dear.'

'I don't know that I'm specially interested in racing at all.'

'You won't be going to Ascot to watch the races, my dear. You go there to be seen. Then there may be a description of your outfit, and perhaps even a photograph, in *The Times* next day.'

It was just as well, thought Peggy, that Jodie was not present. The fourteen-year-old would certainly have shown her contempt for this sort of thing by hooting with laughter.

'You don't say how many evening dresses,' commented Mr Armitage. His willingness to be involved in what might have been regarded as a purely female sphere of interest stemmed not merely from the fact that he would be paying the bills. Women's clothing was his business. Although he had made his fortune from the cheap end of the market, he saw it as a necessity to keep in touch with changing fashions in the world of *haute couture*.

'Most of the debutantes like to have a new dress for their own ball or dance,' said Lady Menzies. 'Or else the presentation gown can be modified for that occasion. Otherwise, your daughter can expect to go to four or five dances every week. Some of the girls find that they can make do with three different dresses.'

'No need for our Peg just to make do,' said her father. 'For the presentation, we need someone who knows all the rules. We'll go to Worth. I'll have a word with Victor Stiebel at Jacqmar about the dress for her own ball. For the rest, I'll put my own designers and machinists to work. It'll be a treat for them, getting their hands on top-class fabrics for once.' He gave a mischievous laugh. 'And after they've kitted you out, Peg, we could use the designs again in a range of party clothes for factory girls. Call it the Debutante range. What would you think about that?'

Peggy's horrified expression was a sufficient answer.

'Never you fret. I'll wait a year,' he promised. 'I'll keep your list, then, Lady Menzies. You won't need to worry about that side of things, although we'll have to come back to you for help with hats. Right, what's next?'

Lady Menzies turned to another page.

'There's only one other question which has to be decided urgently, because so many people will be on the same trail,' she said. 'And that's the matter of a London house. Now then, I have a list here . . .'

At Yewley House in Berkshire Mrs Venables looked up in triumph from the letter she was reading at the breakfast table.

'So that's settled, then: the London house. Hettie has written to say that we can move into Hyde Park Gardens for the summer. So convenient. And it means we can have a small dance for you, Anne, on the premises. I always dislike these hotel affairs. Each one seems the same as all the others and they inevitably attract gatecrashers.'

Anne was in no position to compare venues for dances, but her heart sank at the thought of spending four months in her aunt's grand house. On several occasions during her childhood she had been invited to spend holidays there with her cousins. All three of them were older than she was and had made no secret of how tedious they found it to entertain this country mouse. Anne for her part had been intimidated by the huge high rooms filled with expensive ornaments which she was terrified of breaking.

The house was surrounded by streets so busy with traffic that they were dangerous to cross, and although her bedroom window looked over the park, she had never been allowed to go for a walk there alone. If none of her cousins would accompany her, she had to put up with one of the footmen walking a few paces behind. It didn't feel like going for a walk at all, any more than trotting sedately round Rotten Row felt like riding.

'They'll be on their island when the Season starts.' Mrs Venables was still reading the letter and delivering a précis aloud. Aunt Hettie and her husband owned a small island off the coast of Crete. It was too hot in summer and too cold in winter, but in April and May was a paradise of wild flowers. Or so Anne had been told. She had never been invited to stay there, although that was an invitation she would have welcomed.

'But they'll be returning to England in time for Ascot,' continued Mrs Venables. 'And dear Hettie says that she'll be pleased to give a dance for you herself then, if we can deal with all the arrangements. You must write and thank her, Anne, for being so gracious. "The Countess of Chepstow requests the pleasure . . ."' Mrs Venables was glowing with delight, although as a general rule envy of her two sisters made her critical of their behaviour.

'I'd rather have you,' said Anne. 'Why can't it be the Honourable Mrs John Venables requesting the pleasure?'

'Don't be ridiculous, Anne. Surely you must realise . . .'

But Anne did not stop to realise anything. Ever since the edict went out that she should be a debutante she had been nervous and prickly. Her mother's snobbery about titles had never bothered her before, but now it was touching her directly and she didn't like it. Rather than be reduced to tears by another lecture, she left her breakfast unfinished and stalked out to find a coat and go for a walk.

Her father, following her from the room, took her by the hand. 'Come into the library for a minute,' he said, and led her there. 'Now then. If you're going to develop a phobia about titles, it will spoil your summer, and I'm not having that.'

'But it's so stupid. What's Aunt Hettie ever done – or Uncle Patrick, for that matter – that everyone should start kow-towing before them?'

'We haven't got time to discuss the feudal system, the growth of the aristocracy, the rules of primogeniture and the role of the House of Lords,' said her father. 'Much less to reform them all before lunch. After all, you might just as well ask what I have ever done to deserve the ownership of Yewley.'

'That's different.'

'Not different at all. Property and titles can both be acquired by merit or money, but in my case and your uncle Patrick's they've come down by inheritance. A social hierarchy exists, which you will have to accept. You have a perfect right to determine your own attitude to it. When it comes to other people's attitudes, though, you must just try to understand them and not let them worry you too much.'

'But how can I avoid the consequences of other people's attitudes?' asked Anne unhappily. 'She's going to make me marry a title, isn't she? Well, I won't.'

For once Anne was not reminded that 'she' was the cat's grandmother. The conversation was too serious for that.

'No one can make you marry anyone if you don't want to. You're not to start getting hysterical about this, Anne. You're perfectly capable of making your own decisions. All that your mother can give you is opportunity. What use you make of the opportunity is up to you. My only demand on you is that you should enjoy your Season, and enjoyment is an attitude of mind. I want you, please, to decide that you are going to be happy.'

This, from her father, was unusually severe. Anne tried to defend herself.

'I did decide that. When you said you wanted us both, Howard and me, to have fun, I promised myself that I would try. But all this Countess business . . .'

'Let me take you back a little way,' said Mr Venables, his voice once again soft and affectionate. 'When your mother was eighteen, she became engaged to be married to a young viscount. I have no doubt at all that it was to be a love match.

Four years earlier than that, your Aunt Hettie had married the youngest son of an earl. Also, I feel sure, a love match. Then the war started. Your mother's fiancé was killed in action. Hettie's two brothers-in-law were also killed in action, so that her husband most unexpectedly inherited the title. Your mother wouldn't have been human if she didn't sometimes feel that she'd drawn the short straw.'

'Only if you're thinking in terms of rank all the time.'

'Yes, well, that was the way she was brought up.'

'She's had you instead.'

'It was a terrible war, that war,' said Mr Venables soberly. 'Those of us who fought in it never expected to survive. And the women who waited at home and read the casualty lists had to suffer not only bereavement but the fear that there would be nobody left to love them. When I asked your mother to marry me at the end of 1915 she was lonely and unhappy. I knew even at the time that I was in some sense a second-best.'

'But—'

'Oh yes, we've been very happy. But there are times, no doubt, when she wishes that Howard could look forward to having a handle to his name. Since that's out of her power, it's true that she's ambitious for you in that way instead. You'll have to accept that. When it comes to the crunch, though, the question of who you marry eventually is entirely up to you. If you pick an absolute rotter, I might use my parental delaying rights to say No: not until you're twenty-one. But I shall never tell you that you've got to choose one man rather than another. Have we got that straight between us?'

Anne nodded.

'Good. Now then. Running your Season is going to give your mother enormous pleasure, if you allow her to do it her way.' He smiled mischievously to break the solemn atmosphere of the conversation. 'After all, what's the point of having a daughter except to bring her out? So if you're plotting bloody revolution, save it for some really big principle. The name on an invitation card is simply not important. Right?'

'Right.'

'Off you go, then, and say something nice to show that you're cheerful again.'

Anne found her mother in the morning room, studying a large calendar for 1939 which was already beginning to fill up.

'It's very kind of Aunt Hettie to offer the house and the dance,' she said. 'I'll write and thank her, shall I?'

'I'm sure that would be appreciated. Now then, we must fit in one or two trips to London. For one thing, we need an appointment at Madame Vacani's . . .'

'Back straight! Back straight! Lady Veronica, you are leaning forward again.'

Ronnie took a deep breath and pulled back her shoulders, fixing her gaze on an imaginary point straight ahead on the mirrored wall of Madame Vacani's dance studio. But it was still not good enough for Miss Betty, who produced a large book and placed it on the top of Ronnie's head.

'Walk once right round the room,' the dancing teacher demanded. 'When you return to this spot, give the small bob. Still with the book on your head.'

Ronnie had mastered the small bob, which would be used when royalty was present at a party. It was the presentation curtsy which was giving her trouble, because it was not a fluid movement, but required her to walk, pause, dip, move, dip again and retreat. She could manage the curtsy as long as she was allowed one hand on the barre to steady herself, but it was a different matter out on the open floor.

'Now,' said Miss Betty, sitting down on a plain wooden chair. 'I am the King.'

Weight on right foot. Left foot behind. Down. Down. Incline head. Up again. Weight still on right foot. Smile. Stand erect. Pause.

'Well done,' said Miss Betty. The book had stayed in place until the inclination of the head. 'Now then, the train.'

An assistant produced what looked like an old curtain, with an attachment to hang it over Ronnie's shoulders. The presentation dress would be long enough by itself, but the compulsory train was an extra hazard. After making her curtsy to the King, Ronnie would somehow have to kick the fabric out of the way before moving on to curtsy again to the Queen. The prospect of becoming entangled in her own clothing and toppling to the floor in front of the whole court was a nightmare. Ronnie bit her lip with concentration and did four deep curtsies in a row, moving three steps to the right after each one without disaster. It helped, she discovered, if she sang the instructions to herself in her head, to the tune of 'Tea For Two'. Left foot back and down and down, incline the head and pause a sec, then up we come, keep straight and straight and smile!

'Very good,' Miss Betty nodded her praise. 'Practise each day, and wear your train for the practice as soon as it's ready.'

The lesson was over. Ronnie joined her mother, who was sitting at the side of the room, frowning over an open notebook.

'What an accomplished young lady I'm becoming,' she giggled. 'I can ride, I can drive and I can curtsy. What are you doing?'

'Working on a list for your first dinner. Chay's given me the names of some of his Eton friends who went into the Guards. There'll be a lot of girls at the start of the Season who won't have partners of their own, so we must try to get a good mix.'

Ronnie looked over her mother's shoulder at the neat handwriting. Each of the young men who was invited to dinner at Delacourt House would be under an obligation to dance with her at the ball that followed. Some of them would become her friends, but for the moment they were only unfamiliar names on a list: Rufus Craig, John Rutherford, Andrew Laidlaw, Malcolm Ross . . .

'The Marquess of Lambourn,' said Lady Patricia thoughtfully.

Isabelle looked up from the letter she was writing to her father. 'What about the Marquess of Lambourn?' But she guessed the answer even before she finished asking the question. Lady Patricia had just returned to the house in Mount Street after taking tea with a dozen other women of her own generation. They had been comparing notes about the eligibility of all the young men of the right age and standing who might be encouraged to partner their daughters, and it seemed that from all the different lists a single *parti* had made his way to the top.

'The Marquess of Lambourn', Lady Patricia informed her, 'is the only son of the Duke of Wiltshire. He is twenty-three years old, and unmarried.'

'I see,' said Isabelle. She rose and walked to the window. It had been a damp English day, but the sky had cleared, and there were promises of spring in the pale afternoon sun. It was nearly March: her presentation at Court was only a fortnight away. Beyond that lay the Season for which her mother's ambitions were now patently clear. Lambourn was the prize for which Lady Patricia would play. Isabelle wondered wryly whether this privileged nobleman had any idea of what was in store for him.

'Also,' Lady Patricia's voice interrupted Isabelle's train of thought, 'his father is ill – wounded in the war. I shouldn't think it will be long before Lambourn inherits.'

'Maman!' Isabelle turned from the window, shocked and indignant, but Lady Patricia met her gaze steadily. It was Isabelle's eyes that fell, and she returned to the table, reluctantly putting aside the letter to her father in order to concentrate on her mother's list of last minute preparations.

6

'How much longer!'

Naturally Isabelle did not speak the words aloud. But she could not control a faint sigh of impatience as she perched uncomfortably beside her mother on the back seat of the Daimler. They had been queueing in The Mall for an hour already and were still nowhere near the gates of Buckingham Palace. The corset she was wearing forced her to sit up straight, but the ostrich feathers which rose from her hair made it necessary for her to dip her head slightly if they were not to touch the top of the car, so that she was frozen into an unnatural position. And – this was the last straw – from time to time complete strangers, able to walk ten times as fast as the car was travelling, came to gawp at her through the windows, as though she were part of a freak show.

Well, that was just what she was. It was absurd that the King and Queen could only recognise the existence of a young woman if she was wearing ostrich feathers. Not to mention the kind of long and very tight white gloves that it had taken a maid and a button hook half an hour to fasten. But there was nothing to be done. She was in the grip of a system from which there was no escape. The car moved on for all of ten yards.

At last they arrived in the palace courtyard. Obeying Lady Patricia's instructions, Isabelle left her evening cloak in the car, although the March evening was cold and her presentation gown – conforming to yet another of the iron rules – was low-cut and sleeveless. But the palace itself was warm and welcoming and the system operated smoothly, because everyone except the debutantes themselves had performed their parts many times before.

In spite of their slow approach, Isabelle and her mother were early enough to find seats in the Throne Room itself. Although the King and Queen had not yet taken their places beneath the red canopy at the end of the room, the scene was a colourful one. The centre of the room was occupied by members of the diplomatic corps, resplendent in coloured sashes and glittering stars and wearing almost as many medals as the soldiers in their full dress uniforms. Even the military band, which was playing as softly as could be expected of so much brass, seemed to be wearing fancy dress. On the rows of red plush chairs arranged down one side of the room, the debutantes them-selves, all wearing white dresses, looked particularly demure in contrast to all this ostentation.

Isabelle found it hard to accept the fact that she was one of them. Because she had spent most of her life in France, she was seeing the occasion through the eyes of a foreigner. It was not simply that she felt an outsider, but that an outsider was what she wished to be. Her father was French. Her name was French. She wanted to be a Frenchwoman.

But she had agreed to be presented, and so she must do it properly. During the next few months she would be expected to make friends from amongst the other girls who were sitting here as patiently as herself. It was tempting to lean forward and study their faces; but the temptation must be resisted. Keeping still was part of the ritual.

A fanfare of trumpets and a roll of drums announced the arrival of the royal party. In a twinkling of tiaras the debutantes and their sponsors rose for the national anthem before settling back on their chairs. Nervously Isabelle checked that her train was correctly looped over one arm. In one hand she clutched her bouquet, while the other gripped the pink card without which the Lord Chamberlain would not recognise her exis-tence.

After so many hours of preparation, the ceremony itself proceeded with a surprising briskness. Diplomatic presenta-tions came first, and then the debutantes were called in order of rank. Lady Patricia was the daughter of an earl but was married to a mere commoner, so Isabelle knew that she would not be among the first to be summoned. She looked critically at the dresses of the other girls as they made their way towards the throne. A full-skirted crinoline style was the fashion in England this season, it seemed. It made the girls who wore it look plump: well, perhaps they *were* plump. Her own figure, which was petite, would have looked ridiculous in such a costume. Her gown had been made in Paris and fitted sleekly over her small breasts and slim hips. She didn't care that it would mark her out as being different, nor that it gave her the appearance of a woman who was older than eighteen. She was confident of its elegance; it was the others who were out of line.

'Lady Patricia le Vaillant!'

As her mother approached the throne in the role of presenter, Isabelle herself stood up. Her Card of Command was examined and a court usher, with the swiftness of much practice, arranged her train on the ground behind her. Isabelle straightened her back and held her head high. It was time for her to play her walk-on part in this comedy.

'Miss Isabelle le Vaillant.'

Counting the steps in an effort to control her nervousness, Isabelle moved towards the King and Queen. In the centre of the red carpet was embroidered a small golden crown. This was the spot on which she must pause. Holding her bouquet in front of her, she sank into the ceremonial curtsy in which she had been coached, inclining her head as she reached the lowest point.

It was as she began to rise smoothly to a standing position again that something very peculiar happened. Not something that anyone else could have noticed, because it was all in her own mind. Her body was making a formal gesture towards someone who happened to be the monarch – and only a few moments earlier her mind had regarded this whole business simply as something which had to be gone through in order that the social life of the Season could begin. King George was smiling at her now. Well, no doubt he smiled at each of the debutantes. But Isabelle realised for the first time what she had just done. She was pledging her loyalty to him, in just the same way that all the brightly dressed soldiers must have pledged themselves when they took their Army oaths. She was part of his court, one of his subjects: not French at all, but British. She found herself moved by the occasion almost to the point of tears. It was all very unexpected.

Such emotions must not, naturally, be allowed to check her performance of the continuing ceremony. Automatically her hours of practice guided her through the procedure. Stand straight, kick train out of way, take one and a half steps towards Queen, curtsy again, kick train away again, retreat backwards towards door.

'Well done!' said Lady Patricia, waiting for her in the Blue Drawing Room. 'So that's over. You're out!'

Still dazed by her act of fealty, Isabelle waited without speaking while one by one the other debutantes emerged from the Throne Room. Most of them began to chatter with excitement as soon as their ordeal was over. Once again Isabelle felt herself to be an outsider and this time she commented on the fact to her mother.

'It's because all the dates are wrong this year, to allow for the royal trip to Canada,' Lady Patricia told her. 'It's not at all usual to have a Court as early in the year as March. Normally you'd have had a chance to meet some of the other girls first at tea parties. But you'll soon catch up and find yourself a place in a good set.'

Nodding her head in a pretence of agreement, Isabelle looked round the room, trying to guess which of these strangers might one day become her friends.

'Who's the beautiful girl with the blonde hair and the rather odd dress, over there?' she asked.

It took Lady Patricia a moment to identify the girl's sponsor, which was the only means of identifying her at this early stage of the year.

'That's the Venables girl. Looks to me as though she's dug her mother's presentation dress out of the attic and had it rejigged. Respectable enough family, but haven't got two pennies to rub together. She'll be looking for someone to replenish the family coffers. And so will her brother. Well, he needn't think he can look in your direction.'

Poor Mr Venables, thought Isabelle in amusement, to have his suit rejected before he had even met her. She watched as the last of the debutantes came into the room and a repeat of the national anthem signified that the ceremony was over.

'That looks an interesting girl,' she said, nodding her head towards the doorway. 'The one who's just come in, with auburn hair. Do you know her?'

The latest arrival was one of the best-dressed girls in the room. Isabelle, who was well educated in fashion, recognised the embroidered satin gown as being by Worth. Although the gown was at home in these surroundings, however, its wearer clearly was not. Like Isabelle herself she was looking round the sea of faces with no expectation of seeing anyone she knew. Her face, slightly freckled, was full of character but not at all beautiful. She was a fish out of water and a fish who showed no sign of wishing to swim. Isabelle felt an immediate sympathy with her, and a hope that she might be one of those who became a friend.

Lady Patricia wasted little time on this identification. 'She's being presented by Mairi Menzies, who does it for money. That means that the girl's a nobody. She may even have a father who's in trade.'

For a second time within a few moments Isabelle felt an amused sympathy for someone who was being dismissed in such a manner before the Season had even begun. Perhaps the insignificant Miss Freckles ought to be introduced to the impoverished Mr Venables so that they could hide in a corner together.

There was no time for such matchmaking thoughts to be developed, for now the assembled company was being invited to proceed downstairs, where champagne or iced coffee awaited them. And now Lady Patricia had her evening's quarry in her sights.

'Follow me,' she said.

The Duchess of Wiltshire was a brisk woman in her late forties, obviously so wealthy and socially secure that she had not bothered to have a new gown made for herself. There was a flurry of introductions and an exchange of compliments on the subject of their respective delightful daughters. Then, while their mothers reminisced on the subject of their own presentation days, many years earlier, the two girls were left to chat together.

Isabelle and Ronnie circled each other cautiously in conversation, willing to be friendly but finding some difficulty in reaching common ground. City versus country, France versus England: their backgrounds were so different that they were reduced in the end to discussing only the ceremony from which they had just emerged. But a breakthrough of a kind came when Isabelle, addressing her new acquaintance as Lady Veronica, in accordance with her recent introduction, found the name being casually dismissed.

'Oh, no one ever calls me Veronica. The King and Queen might, I suppose, if we ever find ourselves having a chat, but I'm Ronnie to everyone else.'

Isabelle was pleased by the step towards friendship – but it was an odd situation, all the same. One of the things her mother had promised her was that the Season would be her great opportunity to make friends with girls of her own sort: and no doubt many of the other debutantes, brought up in isolated country houses, had the same attitude. Yet it seemed that she would not be allowed to choose for herself who those friends should be. Miss Freckles and the impoverished Miss Venables were never likely to become part of her circle. And it would be foolish not to recognise that the main reason – the only reason – why she had been hurried across to meet Lady Ronnie Delacourt was that Lady Ronnie was the sister of Lord Lambourn. She wondered whether Ronnie herself – an unsophisticated country girl, by the look of her – realised this.

Their conversation was interrupted by the announcement that the Duchess of Wiltshire's car was waiting.

'I booked an early appointment with the photographer,' said the duchess apologetically, taking her leave. 'Otherwise one can find oneself queueing all night. You must come to tea, Patsy, on the twenty-second. With your lovely daughter. We can compare our lists.'

'Delighted.' Lady Patricia beamed with pleasure at the success of her manoeuvre.

'Did you know her?' Isabelle asked curiously. Her mother had opened the conversation with the admission that 'You won't recognise me after so many years, but . . .'

'Of course I knew her. It may be twenty years since we last met, but once introduced you stay introduced. Men have their networks through clubs and regiments and all that sort of thing, but this is ours. This is why you have to be so careful not to get involved with anyone unsuitable, because you can never get rid of them.'

So now, Isabelle realised, she and Ronnie were officially linked. They had been seen together. They would be invited to the same parties. They would share dancing partners and would be photographed side by side. They would never be able to get rid of each other. Well, why should they wish to?

There were other similar links to be made before the evening was over. The routine of introductions and laboured conversation was repeated several times before Isabelle felt herself beginning to wilt.

'Are we going to the photographer as well?' she asked.

'Naturally, yes. As soon as our car is called. This is an evening to be put on record. After all, you're never going to look quite like this again, are you, darling?'

I sincerely hope not, thought Isabelle. These ludicrous ostrich feathers! But again this was something she was careful not to put into words.

7

'Is it all going to be as dull as this?'

Ronnie, who was having the time of her life, looked at Isabelle in surprise as the two girls, standing side by side in the cloakroom, patted their hair into tidiness after an exceptionally vigorous polka. 'Are you bored already?' she asked.

'Well, this is my fifth dance in five days – and yours, I'm sure – and three of them have been in the same place.'

Ronnie understood what she meant. Not every hostess was as fortunate as the Duchess of Wiltshire in having a ballroom of sufficient size in her own town house. For the less privileged, the fashionable venue to hire this year was Number 6 Stanhope Gate. For the first dance it had been quite delightful and on the second occasion it was interesting to see how it had been transformed by different arrangements of flowers. But it was true that for this third dance it had become less exciting. The same Harry Roy's band was playing the same music for the same group of dancers.

Nevertheless, Ronnie herself was not bored at all. She didn't really care where the dances were held as long as she continued to be surrounded by the group of Chay's friends who flirted with her and flattered her and were generally jolly.

Chay was looking after her marvellously. At the start of every evening he scribbled his initials against half the numbers in her programme, so that if someone who was out of favour asked her for a dance she could claim to be already bespoke; but it was understood between them that she could set him free at short notice whenever she chose. In practice there was always such competition for her company that the system was hardly necessary.

It was easy to guess why Isabelle might feel differently, because she was being so transparently managed by her appalling mother. It had taken Ronnie no time at all to understand why Isabelle always wanted to sit next to her between dances – in the hope that when Chay came to check that his sister didn't need him to partner her, he might choose the nearest girl for the next number. But if her plan – or rather, Lady Patricia's plan – were to be successful, it was necessary for Isabelle to keep dances free and run the risk of being a wallflower.

'She's after you!' Ronnie had murmured to her brother as they were driven home together at the end of the very first ball. The remark was not meant unkindly. A good many of the debutantes were probably hoping to bring themselves to his notice.

'And should I allow her to catch me?'

'There's nothing wrong with Isabelle herself.' It was Ronnie's own fault that they didn't have much in common. Her father's detestation of foreigners meant that she had only the sketchiest acquaintance with French culture; and she had never learned to sail or fence. 'The question is, would you like Lady Patricia for a mother-in-law?'

'There's a deeper question than that,' Chay suggested. 'Eighteen-year-old girls have an unfortunate tendency to turn into their mothers by the time they're forty.'

'Perhaps Isabelle will become like her father instead.'

'But who *is* her father? Nobody seems to know. A shadowy and always absent figure.'

Ronnie had had no answer to that, but Isabelle's apparently fatherless state aroused her sympathy. Now the two girls chatted pleasantly together as they returned to the ballroom. It was time for the supper dance.

'Isabelle is bored,' Ronnie said to her partner.

Malcolm Ross, who had been a friend of Chay's at Eton and was now a cavalry officer, had been quick to press his attentions on her from the very start of the Season. His broken nose – a legacy of his prowess on the rugger field – gave him a sardonic look and prevented him from being handsome in any conventional sense, but his erect bearing and confident manner conferred on him an air of distinction. He was as tall as Chay, but far more sturdily built. The only thing that Ronnie didn't like about him was his habit of standing too close to her. It was all right when they were dancing, of course, but in ordinary conversation she found his physical presence overbearing. Continually backing away, she was continually advanced upon, as though he needed to feel that his breath was touching her lips as he talked. Yet his willingness to do whatever she wanted made it easy to overlook such a small annoyance.

'Isabelle bored? We can't have that,' he said, beckoning for their glasses to be refilled with champagne. 'Why don't we go off to the 400?'

Ronnie considered the suggestion doubtfully. Nightclubs were absolutely out of bounds – but, knowing that Chay was at hand to keep an eye on his sister, the duchess was not strict in performing her duties as chaperone, preferring to indulge her passion for bridge. It would certainly be fun to sneak away, but there was always a possibility that someone at the nightclub might recognise her and tell her mother, and then she would be kept much more closely under observation. Later in the Season it would be worth taking the risk, but not yet.

'No,' she said. 'We'll have a scavenger hunt. Just four couples, so that nobody notices we've gone. Four couples with cars. If we each write down one thing to find, that will be eight scavenges. Who's got some paper?'

They chose the others and she watched as, with some whispering and giggling between partners, each of the eight items was written down four times.

'Two o'clock,' she said. 'That'll give us all time to clear our programmes for half an hour or so. At two o'clock you should be sitting in your cars but you're not allowed to peep until then. Promise? Scouts' honour!'

Everyone promised. Isabelle's partner would be her second string. When she wasn't pursuing Chay, she was allowed by her mother to encourage Lord John Rutherford, although he was a mere second son and still up at Oxford, only two years older than herself.

'Shall I drive?' asked Malcolm as Ronnie fished in her bag for the keys of her MG.

'Certainly not. You're the one who'll have to leap out and collect the things.'

'You are a bit tiddly, though, Ronnie.'

'You've had just as much champagne as I have.'

'I'm more used to it.'

'Don't care. My car. Is it two o'clock yet? Go!'

They unfolded the scraps of paper. A policeman's helmet was predictable. Malcolm could get that. A spider in a matchbox would not be too difficult, since it didn't have to be alive. A ginger cat.

'A cat!' exclaimed Malcolm. 'Where are we going to find a cat?'

'At the Dorchester.' Ronnie was already putting the car into gear. 'There's one that sits in the ladies' cloakroom all the time. I expect Isabelle chose that. We need to get there first.'

She shot off at a speed which rocked Malcolm backwards, emerging from the mews at the back of Delacourt House without pausing to look out for traffic and roaring into Park Lane. The hotel was not far away, but on the other side of the road. As they approached it, she could see the strip of red carpet across the pavement which signified that another dance was being held there tonight. In fact, at that very moment, one of the debutantes was stepping out on to the carpet, with her chaperone beside her, and waiting while the doorman summoned a taxi.

'Get a move on! There's Rutherford!' exclaimed Malcolm, who could see his Phaeton approaching from the other direction.

Ronnie put her foot down on the accelerator. If they missed this ginger cat she had no idea where to find another. And it would not be possible for Malcolm to go into the ladies' cloakroom, so she would have to jump out herself. Lord John's car, on the correct side of the road, was already slowing down. Without pausing to signal, Ronnie swerved across Park Lane, intending to stop in front of the Phaeton and bring it to a halt short of the entrance. At exactly the same moment a taxi answered the doorman's summons and pulled into the kerb.

'Christ!' exclaimed Ronnie. There was a choice of several things she might hit – the Phaeton, the taxi, the debutante or a lamp-post. In the vain hope of missing them all she tried to get back on her own side of the road while at the same time braking sharply. The Magnette, skidding sideways, plunged out of control towards the red carpet. Ronnie closed her eyes. Whatever was going to happen next, she didn't want to know.

8

'Can you wiggle your toes?'

Through a curtain of confusion and pain and darkness Peggy heard the words, but did not understand them. She was lying in bed; that much at least was clear. So what was a man doing in her bedroom? And why was he asking ridiculous questions about toes?

The man's voice spoke again. 'Don't pretend you can't hear me: I know you're awake. Open your eyes, Miss Armitage. Come on, make a big effort.'

Peggy made a big effort. It was not immediately successful. She seemed to have forgotten how her eyelids worked. Perhaps if she were to take hold of her eyelashes and pull them upwards . . . But her hands were not obeying commands either. As for wiggling her toes, she didn't feel as though she possessed any toes to wiggle.

Yes, she did, though, for at that moment she felt a sharp stab in one of them.

'Oh!' Indignation that someone was sticking pins in her had a more positive effect than his polite requests. Her eyes opened. The darkness dissolved.

A young man, wearing an unfastened white coat, was leaning over the end of her bed, which was not her own bed after all. Her view of her feet was obscured by some kind of frame which was holding the sheet off her legs, but she could tell that he was holding one of them. She was in a hospital, obviously – although in a small room, not a public ward.

'Are you a doctor?' she asked doubtfully. He looked too young to be qualified. Perhaps he was just a medical student.

The young man looked up and gave her a friendly grin. After gently lowering her leg he sat down beside her. 'Laurence Elliott, Bachelor of Medicine,' he said, introducing himself. 'More or less a doctor. In two or three months I shall be let loose on the unsuspecting public. Just for this last year of training, my consultant demands that I stay under his eye, in order that he needn't be called out of bed to deal with people who hurl themselves against lamp-posts in the middle of the night. If you needed a delicate neurosurgical operation, it's possible that I might not be your man, but cuts and fractures are well within my powers. You'll never have a neater row of stitches or a smoother plaster cast.'

'What happened?' asked Peggy.

'Don't you remember?'

She began to shake her head, but found the movement painful. 'No. At least, I remember that we were waiting for a taxi.' She had left the dance early, at two o'clock. Although she enjoyed dancing on the rare occasions when she attracted a skilful or interesting partner, after four hours she had had enough.

'Well, according to the wee Scottish lady who came in with you, you were first of all – at about two in the morning – hit by a moving lump of metal. Viz, a motor car. And then thrown against an unmoving lump of metal. Viz, a lamp-post. Not a pleasant experience. But you'll live.'

'I'm glad to hear it.' The wee Scot must be Lady Menzies. 'Where is she now?'

'She was in a bit of a tizzy, for which I don't blame her. There was a certain amount of blood and you were unconscious and we needed time to find out how badly you might be hurt. I sent her home, because there was nothing she could do to help, and she said she'd be getting in touch with your parents. So by now they're probably in a tizzy as well. Do they live in London?'

'No. I expect they'll come, but it will take them a little while.'

'Meanwhile,' said the young doctor, 'there's someone else.'

'What do you mean?'

'Sitting in a corridor just through that door is a young woman wearing a rather dirty ballgown and a diamond necklace who ought not to be allowed out at night unchaperoned. She's in an even bigger tizzy than your Scottish friend, but in spite of that I have to say that she is the most ravishing creature that I have ever seen in all my born days.'

'How very rude of you,' said Peggy – and felt a little better immediately at the return of her ability to tease.

'I could have added, present company excepted, but you have to remember that doctors are not allowed to fall in love with their patients, so I'm afraid you're out of bounds as far as ravishing is concerned. Anyway, she's desperate to talk to you before anyone else does, and I haven't sent her packing as I ought to have done.'

'Because you wanted to feast your eyes on her, I suppose.'

'Correct. But it's my job to see that you remain calm and untroubled, so if you don't want to see her, I shall tell her now that you're not up to visitors.'

'Who is she?'

'No idea. But she says it was all her fault.' He stood up to leave.

'Aren't you going to tell me what's wrong with me?' protested Peggy.

'You have a nasty cut on your forehead, but it can probably be hidden by a cunning curl for the time being, and thanks to my needlework skills it should eventually fade into invisibility. Your shoulder is quite badly bruised, but will recover. The main damage is here.' He put his foot on the bedside chair and indicated an area of his own shin. 'There's quite an unpleasant fracture. But it's been superbly set and efficiently protected and so this too will eventually be as good as new. I'm afraid you'll have to lay off the Highland reels for a bit, though.'

'Thank you. Could you hold the ravishing creature back just for another five minutes while I sort myself out?'

'A pleasure.'

The door closed behind him, leaving Peggy to her own thoughts. She was not concerned about the cause of her accident, but only with its effects. No more Highland reels, he had said – in fact, it was obvious enough that there would be no dancing of any kind for her for some time. The plaster on her leg offered her a way out of the Season.

She had done her best to become the glamorous debutante of her mother's dreams; and in one respect it had actually been enjoyable, moving from school uniform into the stylish wardrobe which her father had provided for her. Although in his business life he was forced to work with cheap materials, he had always had an eye for beautiful fabrics and Peggy had shared his excitement as they pored over samples of silks from Damascus or lace from France and watched as his chief designer made quick sketches to show what was appropriate for a particular weight and pattern of fabric to be worn by a particular girl at a particular time of day. Peggy had no complaints to make about the dressing-up aspect of the Season.

She had tried equally hard to provide the conversation expected of a debutante at the dinners which preceded each dance. Taking care not to seem too intellectual was an intellectual exercise in itself. But the dances themselves were a form of torture. At each one there would be six or seven young men who were under some kind of obligation to dance with her; but there might be over twenty numbers on her programme. She had realised in advance how hard it would be to make her mark in this society, and how humiliating when she failed, but there were evenings when all her courage was needed to keep a smile on her face as she sat and watched everyone else taking the floor. Other girls in her position, she had soon discovered, escaped to the cloakroom on the pretence that their dresses needed some repair, but she had resolved not to stoop to that.

Hardest of all were the efforts needed to pretend to her parents, when they came to London for weekends, that she was having a marvellous time. Even her father, who must have been aware of the problems she would face, regularly beamed with pride and pleasure in the belief that his money was buying happiness for everyone concerned.

She had promised herself that she would keep up the act to the bitter end – but now, surely, there was a way out. A girl who couldn't dance was left with very little of the Season to enjoy. And the most important part of it had happened. She had been presented to the King. She had made her debut and so she was a debutante. Her mother could boast about her – and, indeed, could indulge her fantasies of the triumphs her daughter would have achieved had it not been for this unfortunate accident.

As for Peggy herself, she could go back to school. There were still a few weeks of term left. She could even sit for her Higher

Certificates, although without having had any time for revision. Yes, if the ravishing creature who was waiting in the corridor was truly the cause of the accident, she had performed a good deed.

The five minutes was up, and the door opened.

'I'm Ronnie Delacourt.'

'Do come in.' Peggy had not met Lady Veronica before. They did not attend the same dinners or dances. Peggy was well aware that invitations to the events of the Season were determined by social rank, and Lady Menzies had made it clear from the start that she would not be able to open the most aristocratic doors. But all the debutantes knew Ronnie's name and could recognise her from pictures in newspapers and magazines.

'How are you?'

'No great damage. Won't you sit down?'

'But your leg!' Ronnie, still standing at the end of the bed, was able to look underneath the frame. 'You won't be able to ride!'

'I don't ride.'

'Don't ride?' The admission threw the visitor off her track and she wore a puzzled frown as she sat down. 'What do you do, then?'

'I read.'

'Oh. Well, I've come to say how desperately sorry I am. Obviously I didn't mean this to happen, but it was all my fault. I suppose I'd had too much champagne to drink and we were racing to get to the ginger cat first although my father made me promise that I'd never race on the roads and I might have killed you and I really am so awfully sorry.'

What had ginger cats got to do with anything? But Peggy's head was still aching too much for her to care about sorting out the details. 'Forget it,' she said.

'I can't forget it. I expect the police will ask questions and then my father will want to know what happened to the car and my mother will be furious that I sneaked out of Lady Gurney's ball. But you're the only one who matters.'

'Then you can tell them all – if you feel you have to say anything – that I have no memory of the accident at all. For all I know, I may have stepped out in front of you.'

'No, you didn't. You were on the pavement.'

Ronnie's honesty was attractive and Peggy was happy to repeat that she had no intention of making a fuss.

'That's too awfully good of you. And I've ruined your Season.'

'I'm not bothered about that. I shall go back home.'

'Oh, you mustn't do that!' Ronnie was horrified. 'You'll make me feel even worse if you do that. Though perhaps that's what you want, to punish me.'

'No, of course not. I just don't see any point . . .'

'You could still manage things like Ascot. I mean, they'll give you a crutch or a stick or something, won't they? And luncheons. And the opera. And you must come to my ball. You're with Lady Menzies, aren't you? I shall get my mother to send you invitations today.'

'That's very kind of you.' Peggy knew that invitations to the Duchess of Wiltshire's ball were the most prized of the Season. But it was only ten days ahead. 'I shouldn't be able to dance, though, so it wouldn't really be much fun for me.'

'I shall make it fun. If you'll promise me that you'll come, I'll promise you a really marvellous evening. Really. You must trust me. Will you?'

For a moment longer Peggy hesitated, but ten days more in London was not too much. She could send for some of her school books and start on revision while she was laid up in bed. And the decisive factor was the delight her mother would feel at the news. Mrs Armitage was making a record of her daughter's Season in a photograph album, and a picture of her Peg setting off for Delacourt House would make this whole ludicrous project worth while for her.

'Thank you very much. I'd be delighted.'

And so it happened that when Mr and Mrs Armitage arrived later, flustered and worried, Peggy did not after all give notice of her intention to abandon the Season. Instead, she was able to report that no great harm had been done and that she intended to be on her feet again in time for – wait for it – the Duchess of Wiltshire's ball.

9

'Oh, Peggy!' exclaimed Mrs Armitage. 'Oh, Peggy love!'

The pride in her mother's voice was sufficient reward for what was certainly going to be a ghastly evening. Peggy couldn't imagine what had possessed her to accept the Wiltshire invitation. Well, she could imagine it all right – it was to give pleasure to her parents and prevent Lady Ronnie from feeling too guilty – but that didn't mean that it had been a sensible decision. She had condemned herself to sitting for four or five hours in a ballroom, watching other people enjoy themselves, while the other people stared at her as a sort of freak. The debutante who couldn't dance.

However, it was too late to regret it now; and at least, as her mother's admiration reminded her, she would have no need to feel ashamed of her appearance when the staring began. Her father's team had done her proud.

All the ballgowns which had been made for her in advance were décolleté, with only straps or thin frills of material to hold them up. Although the bruising of her shoulder was no longer black and blue, the ugly yellow to which it had faded was not something she wished to display. So Jeff Marlow, the company's chief designer, had been called urgently to the rescue – and had created a masterpiece.

The dress was made of the finest possible silk; white, but woven through with gold thread which glinted at every movement. The silk came from India and was much narrower than the usual width of fabric. Jeff had turned this problem into a triumph by forming the skirt from a series of petals, which parted and fell back over a golden underskirt as she moved. He had used the almost transparent silk to carry the dress right up to her neck and had then allowed several layers of it, like petals again, to fall over her shoulders as far as the bruising made necessary.

'You'll have all these society reporter johnnies asking you who your couturier is,' said Mr Armitage, surveying her with as much pride as his wife. 'I can see I shall be losing Jeff if I'm not careful. But at least I seem to have gained a mannequin in return.'

'Don't be silly, Daddy.' But she stood with her head high as he took yet another photograph for Mrs Armitage's album. It was Jodie's half term, and the whole family had come to spend a few days in the rented London house. Jodie's own contribution to the evening had been to suggest that her sister's crutch should also be given a silken wrap.

And now a footman appeared to announce that his grace's Rolls-Royce was at the door. In a letter accompanying the formal invitations the Duchess of Wiltshire had promised to send a car to collect Lady Menzies and her protégée and had suggested that they might prefer to delay their arrival until after half past ten. By then most of the other guests would have been received and the approach to the ballroom would be less crowded.

Five minutes later – for the distance to Delacourt House was short – Peggy laughed aloud at the sight that greeted her. Four footmen in livery and wearing powdered wigs were waiting for her with a sedan chair! Her arrival might be late, but it was not exactly going to be unobtrusive.

Entering into the spirit of Ronnie's arrangements, Peggy did her best to look dignified – or, at least, unruffled – as she was carried up the first flight of steps from the pavement and then up a wide curving staircase densely lined with flowers. In the ballroom, the band was already playing, but the dancers parted like the Red Sea before the sedan chair as it made its sedate progress across the floor. A wide chair – no, a throne – upholstered in red velvet was waiting for her, and once she was settled into place, one of the footmen knelt on the floor to place a stool in the most comfortable position for her plastered leg before retreating backwards as though she were indeed royalty.

All the mothers and chaperones stared with undisguised curiosity, but the dancers showed a greater tact in resuming their waltz. Peggy searched the floor with her eyes until she identified Ronnie, who was dancing with more energy than grace. Her partner had a smoother style. He was a tall young man, elegant in his uniform of white tie and tails and moving with an easy confidence. He was the most handsome young man Peggy had ever seen in her life. She leaned over towards Lady Menzies, whose chair beside her was slightly lower.

'Who—?' But at that moment the music speeded up as it approached its end. Ronnie's partner swung her vigorously round and round three or four times before they came to a halt. In a joking manner which aped the formality of an earlier century, he gave an elaborate bow while Ronnie in turn dipped in a curtsy. They were smiling at each other affectionately – and it was the same smile. Peggy guessed the answer to her unfinished question even before Ronnie came hurrying across to greet her.

'Lady Menzies, Miss Armitage, it's so very good of you to come. May I introduce my brother, Chay. Chay is going to make sure that you have an enjoyable evening, Miss Armitage. I'm sorry about all the staring, but I thought it would be best to let everyone have a gawp and then they won't bother about it any more. Nobody knows exactly how you were hurt, except Malcolm Ross, who was in the car with me, and Chay because I told him.' She paused uncertainly.

Peggy, reading her thoughts, responded in the hoped-for manner. 'And Lady Menzies, because she was there at the time as well. I haven't mentioned it to anyone else outside my family.'

'You're more than I deserve, and I can't thank you enough. If my parents were ever to find out what really happened I'd be confined to barracks for the rest of the Season and never allowed to own a car again. Well then, I'll leave you to Chay. If you need to be rescued, wave your crutch and I'll come running.'

Left alone in front of the red throne, Chay addressed himself first of all to Peggy's chaperone. 'Lady Menzies, my mother asked me to mention that there is bridge in the Green Drawing

Room. I can promise you that our charge will not be left alone, and she's hardly likely to run away.'

As soon as she had vacated her chair, he drew it forward so that he could look at Peggy rather than sitting beside her. 'May I?'

'Of course, Lord Lambourn.'

'You must think me very arrogant, promising Ronnie that you are going to enjoy yourself and then inflicting myself on you as though there would be no doubt about your enjoying my company. And I'm not going to give you time to mutter polite insincerities, because I want to ask you what you were thinking about while you watched Ronnie and me dancing. There was such an interesting expression on your face.'

In no circumstances could Peggy give a truthful answer to his question. She had been wondering at that moment whether this was what love at first sight felt like. She didn't actually believe in love at first sight, which was something that only happened in films. She believed that you could only love someone when you really knew him and knew what you were loving. It was not enough that someone should be good-looking and have such an immensely attractive smile. Obviously she couldn't say any of this to a stranger. In some desperation she searched for an alternative.

'I was trying to make up a limerick. It's a bad habit. My sister and I do it all the time.' That last sentence at least was true.

'Will you recite it to me?'

'Um. "There was a young man – not a Mister/Who danced with his beautiful sister./But when he reversed/How the young lady cursed/For he trod very hard on her blister."'

'Ha!' Chay's reaction was unexpected. She expected him, a marquess, to be restrained, polite, a brother undertaking an unwanted duty. But he laughed in delight, so loudly that for a second time Peggy felt all eyes upon her. 'Not a Mister. I like that. Did you think of one for Ronnie as well?'

That was easier, because she and Jodie had already worked one out on this subject.

'I couldn't think how to end it. It starts, "There is a young lady called Ronnie/Who is lively and witty and bonny,/But oh dear! when she drives/You must run for your lives . . ."'

Peggy gave a helpless shrug of her shoulders and was

delighted in her turn when, after a moment's thought, the marquess finished it for her.

'With a hey nonny, hey nonny, nonny!'

Now they were both laughing – and, what was more, the next dance was beginning. The mothers and other chaperones were staring even more fiercely than before as they waited to see whom Lord Lambourn would invite to be his partner and gradually realised that he intended to remain with this crippled nobody.

'That's very good, your lordship.'

'Ah, now,' said Chay. 'Ronnie, as you will have gathered, would prefer not to broadcast the truth about exactly how you and she first met. She has told our mother that you are a good friend of hers – and hopes that you'll accept that description because she wants it to be true. She really is enormously grateful for your discretion. And so I've been asked to find out whether perhaps you'd be prepared to speed up all the formalities of becoming acquainted. In short, to abandon Lady Veronica and Lord Lambourn and move straight to Ronnie and Chay. And allow me, at the same time, to call you Margaret.'

'Peggy.'

He smiled his thanks, as though she were the one doing the favour. It was one of the nicest smiles Peggy had ever seen, because there was a touch of gravity behind the friendliness – just as when he had laughed so uproariously aloud it had been without any loss of dignity. Peggy remembered her conversation with Jodie on the day when the debutante business was first discussed. Not all aristocrats are vapid, she had argued, without believing her own argument. But it was true: beneath his lightheartedness, Lord Lambourn – Chay – was a serious young man. An extremely attractive young man. And they were going to be friends.

'What are you smiling about?'

Another necessary lie. 'I was thinking that you're probably the first partner I've had who hasn't started off by asking me which hunt I ride with.'

'Because you don't ride. You read. Ronnie told me. You ought to get along well with your next sitting-out partner. Howard Venables. We were at Oxford together. He was the only one of my chums there who actually reckoned to do any work.'

'I want to go to Oxford one day.'

'Then Howard's the man to tell you the sort of thing you want to know. My own time there . . .' He leaned forward, chatting about beagling and dining clubs and chaps thrown into fountains. The time sped past. The dance came to an end.

'Let me give you your programme,' said Chay, standing up. The card had a tiny gold pencil attached to it, but Peggy would not need to use it, for there was a name written beside every number. 'I've taken the liberty of putting myself down for the supper dance. If that's all right?'

'You're very very kind.' The supper dance would be longer than any of the others. Already Peggy's doubts about the evening had been banished, and now she felt a positive glow of pleasure warming her whole body. She did her best to control it. Really, Peggy Armitage, she told herself severely, you're beginning to behave just like a debutante.

10

Peggy Armitage was not the only girl to feel anxious as she approached Delacourt House on the evening of the Duchess of Wiltshire's ball. Anne Venables was worried about her dress.

She had quite understood that there could be no question of patronising any of the well-known – and expensive – couturiers: Schiaparelli or Hartnell or Molyneux. She would have been content to buy a readymade ballgown from one of the shops which devoted a special department to such garments, but Mrs Venables had reacted with horror at the very idea. Only the middle classes bought clothes off rails. Mrs Johnson, who had been the family dressmaker for twenty years, must be given the opportunity to create her masterpiece.

It might have been all right even then had Anne been allowed to choose new material for the dress, but instead her mother had announced that she would sacrifice her own presentation gown to the dressmaker's scissors. True, the fabric was very beautiful and had no doubt been immensely expensive in 1912. But the slim skirt was unsuitable for dancing. Mrs Johnson had slit it to the knee to allow sufficient movement and then had covered the slits with an overskirt created from the original train. Probably no one outside the family would realise what had happened, but Anne herself felt embarrassed in advance at the thought of appearing in a handed-down garment. To add to her self-consciousness, the bodice was cut very low, although her breasts were fuller than her mother's had ever been.

'Don't look so gloomy!' exclaimed Howard. He sat facing his mother and sister as the car made its way to Park Lane. 'Anyone would think you were in a tumbril on the way to the guillotine instead of the social event of the season. You'll be the prettiest girl there. You always are. And Lambourn will ask you to dance.'

'Fat chance!' Anne knew that she owed her invitation to the fact that Howard and Lord Lambourn had been at school and university together, but that didn't mean that the marquess would feel any obligation towards his friend's sister.

'No, really. He rang me to fix it. There's some friend of Ronnie's who's due to turn up with a gammy leg. Can't dance. Lambourn's made himself responsible for seeing that there's always someone to sit out with her. And in return for me subjecting myself to a sticky ten minutes trying to make conversation with some unknown and almost certainly boring girl, he'll spend the same ten minutes dancing with you. The things I do for my sister!'

Anne's spirits rose like a rocket – and not simply because to dance with the son of the house would be an honour observed with envy by all the other girls and their mothers. No, there was more to it than that. She was in love with Lord Lambourn.

Well, not properly in love. She had never even spoken to him. It was more of a childhood pash. She had first caught sight of him when her parents took her to Eton for Howard's last Fourth of June. The young marquess was captain of cricket and president of Pop: a school hero. So tall, so confident, so good looking. Anne had lost her heart to him at once, although naturally he could not be expected even to register the existence of somebody's unknown kid sister.

So quiet had her life been since then that there had been no real young man to intrude on her daydreams. And now she was going to meet him at last! He would speak to her, take her hand, take her in his arms to dance. What would they talk about? What could she possibly think of to say that would be of the slightest interest to him? Ten minutes was such a short time. Her elation faded once again into anxiety.

But the dance, when it came, swept her worries away. Anne was tall, for a girl, and Chay – who was over six foot – expressed pleasure at having a partner who did not force him to stoop. She was a graceful dancer and they moved smoothly together round the floor. It would have been pleasant enough to let the time pass in a companionable silence, but when Anne revealed her knowledge that she was being used as a bribe to keep the girl with the plastered leg happy, Chay burst out laughing.

'Her name's Peggy Armitage and I thought it was going to be the most frightful bore and that none of my friends would ever speak to me again after being let in for keeping her amused. But in fact she's good fun. Not the usual sort of girl.'

'What's the usual sort of girl?' asked Anne.

'Well, that's a tricky question, isn't it? Because I might want to say that the usual sort of girl at these affairs tends to rate high on beauty but low on brains. But that immediately gets me into trouble, because in the beauty ratings, if I may be personal for a moment, you are definitely the tops, but I wouldn't want you to think that I consider you as usual in any other sort of way. Oh dear, now I've made you blush.'

To ease her embarrassment, he tightened his grip, drawing her closer so that his head was above her shoulder instead of looking down at her décolletage. It was the happiest moment of Anne's life. Half an hour earlier she had been indulging a daydream. Now she was in love with a real man, and he thought she was beautiful.

'Come and let me introduce you to Peggy Armitage,' he said as the dance, too soon, came to an end. They walked together across the floor to the corner in which Peggy and Howard were in animated conversation.

'There were these four girls,' Howard was saying. 'One from each of the women's colleges. And a message came that there was a man downstairs.'

'Oh no!' exclaimed Chay. 'Not that old chestnut!'

'It may be a chestnut to you.' Howard, interrupted, relinquished his seat to Anne, but without allowing himself to be diverted. 'But Miss Armitage has just asked me to explain the difference between the women's colleges, so that she can choose which one to apply to, and has therefore set herself up as the perfect victim – perhaps the only person in England who hasn't heard this before. So kindly don't interrupt. Where was I?'

'Four women and a man,' prompted Peggy.

'Yes. So the girl from Lady Margaret Hall said, "Who's his father?" The girl from Somerville said, "What's he reading?" and the girl from St Hugh's said, "What does he play?" But the girl from St Hilda's simply said, "Where is he? Lead me to him!"'

Even Chay, half groaning, joined in the laughter. Anne introduced herself to Peggy, since no one else had remembered to do it, but kept half an ear open to the conversation between her brother and Chay.

'We still have a lot to talk about, Peggy and I,' Howard was saying. 'I asked her if I could have the supper dance as well, but you seem to have filled her programme up completely.'

'Changes can be made,' said Chay. 'I'll relinquish my rights on condition that Miss Venables will give me that dance in return.' He raised his eyebrows questioningly.

'I should be delighted.'

'In fact the question of partners is slightly academic,' Chay told them all. 'It seemed to me that Peggy might be more comfortable if we had supper away from the general crush. I've arranged to have a table set up in the Chinese Room. The four of us can meet there when the time comes. Ronnie and her partner will join us as well.'

At that moment Ronnie appeared behind Peggy's chair, anxious to make sure that her arrangements were working smoothly.

'There's too much laughing in this corner!' she exclaimed cheerfully. 'People will start complaining that they can't hear the band.'

'Excuse me, please,' said a polite voice. It was the *Tatler*'s photographer doing his rounds, accompanied by an assistant with a notebook.

'Number 43, left to right. Miss Anne Venables, Lady Veronica Delacourt and . . .'

'And Miss Peggy Armitage,' said Chay.

There was a flash. The scene was on record. Three debutantes, eighteen for evermore. All of them smiling at the Marquess of Lambourn, out of shot.

11

'Who *is* that girl?' Lady Patricia's voice expressed irritation, and Isabelle could guess why. Ever since the girl with the crutch had been carried in, she had been the centre of attention, if only because Lord Lambourn was spending so much time with her.

'We were both presented on the same day,' Isabelle reminded her mother. 'I noticed her, because I thought she looked interesting. But you said she was a nobody.'

'Oh, I remember. One of Mairi Menzies' girls. Well, it seems that Miss Nobody has connections. Follow me.'

Oh dear! Isabelle could tell that she was about to be pitchforked into yet another embarrassing situation. Her mother was ruthless about insinuating herself into other people's conversations or obtaining introductions.

At least, on this occasion, Isabelle could claim to be already a friend of Ronnie's. Since meeting for the first time on the evening of their presentation, the two young women had encountered each other at several luncheons and tea parties, and had been invited to many of the same dances.

It would not, of course, be Ronnie herself towards whom Lady Patricia would be casting her line this evening. However, the longed-for introduction to Lord Lambourn had been achieved some time ago. That particular embarrassment was in the past. They were acquainted. They had danced together. There would be nothing too untoward about Isabelle's arrival to join his laughing group. And as a matter of fact she would welcome the opportunity to meet both the freckled girl with the crutch and the tall blonde with the porcelain complexion and beautiful blue eyes.

Their arrival was the signal for a flurry of introductions, but the general conversation within the little group was interrupted by the arrival of a young man, as *soigné* as every other male in his white tie and tails, but with a shock of thick fair hair that had never tasted Brylcreem. There was a sudden silence as each member of the party waited for someone else to welcome him.

'I do believe,' said the stranger sadly, 'that you don't recognise me. Not even Miss Armitage, in spite of my most intimate acquaintance with her leg.'

'Oh!' Peggy's wide mouth broadened in a smile. 'Dr Elliott. Ronnie, do you remember Dr Elliott? You met him when you so kindly came to visit me in hospital.'

There was something a little too gushing about the speed with which Ronnie welcomed him to the group. Isabelle, who was observant, suspected that for some reason she had hoped not to meet the young doctor again. Dr Elliott, by contrast, was quite clearly bowled over by her, and proved it, as soon as this new round of introductions was complete, by asking her for the next dance, a tango.

'I'm afraid I'm dancing this with Chay,' said Ronnie, consulting her programme. 'We practised the tango all winter in the banqueting hall at Cleeve, until Pa said that if he heard "Jealousy" one more time he'd disinherit us. So this is our chance to show off. But . . .'

'But it's the duty of a brother to step aside whenever his sister changes her mind. I know! Well, at least if you're too energetic and dislocate something you'll have a medical man to put you right. All yours, Dr Elliott.'

Lady Patricia had needed only a split second to realise that Chay was now unexpectedly without a partner.

'Such a graceful dance, the tango!' she gushed. 'Isabelle is particularly good at it.'

It was too flagrant for words! Flushing with embarrassment, Isabelle opened her mouth to say that she was bespoken for the next dance, but already Chay had taken the hint and was bowing his head politely towards her. 'May I have the pleasure?'

As he led her on to the floor he gave her a friendly smile. 'Don't let it worry you. All mothers are the same.'

His understanding helped her to relax, and it was helpful,

too, that the dance did not lend itself to sustained conversation. Besides, Lady Patricia had not exaggerated. It was perhaps the hours she spent practising her skill as a fencer which had helped Isabelle to become so lithe and move with such flowing grace. She was indeed particularly good at Latin dances.

Ronnie had not exaggerated either. It hadn't taken Isabelle very long when the Season started to realise that most of the young men who asked her to dance were clumsy and lacking any sense of rhythm; but Chay had certainly been practising. As they moved smoothly but dramatically across the floor, she felt as though they were giving a demonstration.

'I did enjoy that,' said Chay when the music came to an end. 'We must do it again some time.'

'I'd love to.' She smiled in triumph as he escorted her back to her mother. Lady Patricia, unsnubbable, had managed to appropriate two chairs close to Peggy Armitage in order to make sure that her daughter was near at hand when arrangements for the rest of the evening were made.

Her tactics were immediately successful. Hardly had Isabelle taken her seat before she was approached by young Dr Elliott.

'Miss le Vaillant. Lord Lambourn and Lady Ronnie have arranged for Miss Armitage to have supper with them in a private room and I've just been asked, as Miss Armitage's medical adviser, whether I'd care to join them there, with my partner. I was wondering whether by any chance you were free for the supper dance.'

He made no attempt to disguise the fact that it was Ronnie's company he wanted and that any partner would do to provide him with the entrée to the private room. But Isabelle was not likely to be offended by that when he was offering her the same entrée. To be a member of Chay's private party was a privilege she could not have hoped for in her wildest dreams.

'I'd be delighted.' Somebody else's initials were already in her programme, and to let him down at such short notice was disgraceful behaviour. Her mother would have to deal with that – and would do so cheerfully, since there would have been no forgiveness had Isabelle turned this particular invitation down.

There was more to her pleasure than that, however. Isabelle had no romantic illusions about the purpose of her Season: she was to be engineered into a suitable marriage, and that was not something to which she objected in principle. Her father had been right to suggest that marriage would bring her freedom. She would be able to manage a husband in a way that she couldn't manage her mother, and so her real life as an independent woman could begin. Although naturally she reserved the right to turn down anyone she couldn't stand, she had been quick to recognise that it would save a lot of argument if she fell in with her mother's choice. For that reason alone she would have been prepared to set her cap at the Marquess of Lambourn even if she had no particular liking for him. It was a bonus to discover that the prize at whom Lady Patricia's campaign was directed was not only high born and good looking but a very pleasant, decent sort of chap.

She wasn't conceited enough to take victory for granted, and so she didn't intend to make the mistake of letting herself fall in love with someone who might never feel anything for her. But she did genuinely like Chay very much indeed. It wouldn't be difficult to love him if the time for that ever came. Not difficult at all.

12

Like Cinderella, Peggy had intended to be home before midnight. Just as the mere fact of being presented at Court was sufficient to make her a debutante, so an hour's presence at the Duchess of Wiltshire's ball would have been enough to justify any boasts her mother might wish to make about the high social circles in which her daughter was moving. Even Lady Grant could hardly fail to be impressed.

But midnight came and went, and she found herself with no wish to leave. The supper dance was particularly good fun. It was amusing to observe Ronnie's efforts to keep her official partner, Lieutenant Ross, happy while at the same time not discouraging Dr Elliott's insistent flirtatiousness. Even for Peggy, who knew the background, it was difficult to tell whether she was still simply anxious to prevent him from revealing what he knew about the accident or whether she genuinely liked him.

Whatever the reason, politeness demanded that Chay should be attentive to Dr Elliott's supper partner as well as his own, and it was equally amusing to watch him giving his attention to both the tall blonde Anne and the lithe and dark-haired Isabelle – as well as to Peggy herelf. Although it was Howard who made himself responsible for ensuring that she had everything she wanted from the supper table, everyone else was particularly nice to her as well. Her plate and glass were never allowed to remain empty. She was fuzzily aware that she was drinking too much champagne – but what did it matter? Unlike Ronnie on the night of the accident, she was not about to drive a car.

While the others flirted, Howard was earnest. Peggy must let him take her to Oxford, he insisted, as soon as she was able to walk easily. He would show her some of the colleges and they would punt on the river. And certainly she must come to his sister's dance. It would be a small affair, nothing as grand as Ronnie's, but because it would be later in the Season, he hoped that she would be able to dance by then. He called his sister, with Chay, over to join them, and Anne eagerly confirmed that invitations would be sent next day. Yes, the supper dance was great fun.

Time flew past and Peggy was still at the ball, back in her red velvet throne. As a young Guards officer bowed and withdrew, Dr Elliott came to take his place.

'I asked Lord Lambourn if I could have one of your slots. Is that all right?'

'Yes, of course.' One or two of Chay's friends had been hard work conversationally for someone who did not shoot or hunt or play polo. The young doctor would make a pleasant change. 'Although I would have thought you'd prefer to dance with Ronnie,' she added mischievously.

'I can't expect her to let me have more than the one dance. And I only got that because she thought I might have let some cats out of their bags. In fact, of course, I didn't have the foggiest idea about the details of your accident because you kept so quiet about it.'

'But you let her think you did, so that you could win favour by promising to keep quiet?'

'Something of the sort. Reverse blackmail, you might say. Letting her pay the ransom, in the sense of being terribly sweet, before letting on that I had no hold over her until she told me herself. But it's no good, is it?' He gave a sad sigh.

It didn't need much feminine intuition to guess that he was still talking about Ronnie, but he had been so cheerful when he first presented himself that Peggy could not guess what had happened to throw him into gloom.

'What do you mean?'

'Well, a duke's daughter! A cat may look at a king, but a poor doctor isn't encouraged to look at a Delacourt.'

'Didn't you know who she was when you arrived?'

He shook his head. 'You didn't introduce us when she came to the hospital. And I had an emergency this evening, so I didn't get here tonight until after the family had finished receiving. I didn't know this was her own ball. The daughter of the house! I thought she was just one out of three hundred guests and it was the most marvellous piece of luck that I was going to meet her again.'

'How did you come to be invited, if you don't know the family?' asked Peggy curiously.

'It's a sort of tradition in the hospital. Ronnie's father is a pretty sick man, after what happened to him in the war. He has to come in for checks and at one of them something nasty was picked up just in time to save his life. So whenever the Wiltshires have a ball they send an open invitation for some of the junior doctors to turn up. It helps to boost the ratio of males to females. The duchess encourages us to eat and drink as much as we like, but I doubt whether we're expected to make eyes at her daughter. Oh well! Since you're not my patient any longer, may I tell you that you look absolutely stunning in that dress?'

'You may tell me that every five minutes. Except that –' Was it because he had reminded her of her hospital stay that her leg had suddenly begun to ache? No. She was tired, that was all. 'Perhaps you'd be kind enough to take a message to Ronnie for me when this dance ends. To ask if she could arrange for me to be taken home.'

Ronnie came rushing across to protest as soon as she heard. 'It's only three o'clock. You can't leave yet.'

'The plaster's quite heavy. It's tiring. But I've had a marvellous evening. I'm so grateful to you.'

'I'm the one who has to be grateful. And I've hardly had a chance to talk to you myself. Could I come to tea tomorrow?'

'That would be lovely.'

'I'll get someone to bring round a car, then. Hang on till I come back.'

Chay took her place, repeating his sister's regrets. 'Before you go, I have to tell you that you have inspired me to become a poet like you.' He took up a reciting pose. ' "There was a young lady called Peg/Who hobbled around on one leg. When asked, "Will you dance/Or enjoy a romance?"/She said "Sir, you'll excuse me, I beg." I tried it out on Howard and he promptly tried to rival me. You've started a fashion. 1939 may prove to be the

Season of the limerick. Ah, here's Lady Menzies. And your chair.'

He helped her in and replied to her thanks by protesting that it had been a pleasure to meet her. He made it sound as though he meant it.

Back in the rented house, the whole family was waiting up for her, although as a rule they all went to bed before eleven.

'How did it go?' demanded Jodie.

Peggy gave the happy smile of someone who had drunk too much champagne and didn't care. ' "There was a young man – not a Mister/Who danced with his beautiful sister/Till he caught sight of Peg/With her black and blue leg/So he sat down beside her and kissed her." '

'Did he really?' Jodie was wide eyed. 'Whoever he was.'

'No, of course not. I can't think of another rhyme, that's all. I've started a fashion, Chay says. The Season of the limerick.'

'Who's Chay?'

'Ronnie's brother. Lord Lambourn.'

'You're tiddly,' said Mr Armitage.

Peggy agreed. 'It's rather nice, isn't it? Anyway, I've had a lovely time, and the dress was perfect, Daddy, and Lady Veronica Delacourt is coming to tea tomorrow, Mummy, and I'm very happy and it was nice of you all to stay up but I don't think I can stay awake for a moment longer.'

That was not quite true. Lying on her back in bed she had time to remember how Chay had laughed and how Howard had offered to take her to Oxford and how friendly Ronnie and Isabelle and Anne had been in the supper room and what a pleasant young man Laurence Elliott was. What a ridiculous idea it had been that she might abandon the Season and buckle down to taking her Higher Certificates after all. What a wasted opportunity that would have proved to be! No, even though it might be a little while before she could dance, there were plenty of other activities in which she could take part, in company with her new friends. That was what her mother had promised, wasn't it? That she would make new friends; and it was true. Chay and Ronnie and Anne and Chay and . . . A happy debutante, she sank into sleep.

13

It was the morning after Anne's own dance, a fine June morning. She slipped out of the house in Hyde Park Gardens very early and went for a walk in the park. She was grown up now, with no need for relatives to fuss or footmen to protect her.

Filling her lungs with the sweet air of a midsummer dawn, she walked briskly round the Serpentine, startling slug-a-bed ducks into activity. Near the gate she had passed a park keeper picking up rubbish, but here there was no one else in sight. She had the whole huge park to herself. From time to time she gave a little skip of excitement or swirled in a dance, throwing out her arms to embrace the day.

The park, with its gently whispering trees and its calm, reflecting water, was marvellous. London was marvellous. To think that she had once believed she could never be happy anywhere but Yewley! Now she knew better, recognising that the source of happiness lay in herself and not in her surroundings.

The London Season which she had so much dreaded was going well. Something that had surprised her was that several of the more popular newspapers devoted a lot of space to the debutantes, although Anne could hardly believe that their doings were of much interest to the public at large. The diarists who wrote gossip columns tended to concentrate on just a handful of the girls, and to attach a single and always repeated adjective to each name. Anne had discovered that she was the beautiful Miss Venables.

No one but her father – whose opinion was hardly unbiased – had ever called Anne beautiful before, but she didn't let this unexpected accolade go to her head. What it did do was to give her confidence, because she no longer needed to think of herself as gauche and badly dressed.

Without that confidence she would never have been able to behave naturally with someone like Chay. Chay, oh Chay! Just to repeat his name out loud brought a new bubble of happiness to her smile. It was because of Chay that she was skipping round the Serpentine at this unearthly hour of the morning. She was in the park because she had been unable to sleep after the end of the dance. She had been unable to sleep because of her excitement. Because Chay had danced with her three times.

On the first occasion he was fulfilling an obligation. Anne had known in advance that on this special evening she was in no danger of being a wallflower, for each of her male guests would be expected to ask her to dance. But three times! That was beyond the call of duty. It must mean that he enjoyed her company. Might it also signify that his feelings were becoming as deep as her own? Mrs Venables – who had been counting – certainly thought so, for she had congratulated her daughter as though they were successful conspirators. That had been the only bad moment in an otherwise perfect evening.

A sudden panic in the bird world alerted Anne to the fact that she was no longer alone in the park. Someone was cantering towards her along the soft sand of Rotten Row. It was Ronnie. Most of the debutantes came out to ride at an hour when the rest of the world could observe them in their becoming riding habits, but Ronnie rode because she enjoyed it. Her adjective in the world of gossip columnists was 'rollicking'. The rollicking Lady Ronnie. She gave Anne a friendly wave of the hand as she passed.

By the time she returned to her aunt's house, Anne had worked up a good appetite. She found only her brother at the breakfast table. Both Mrs Venables and her sister, exhausted after all their efforts of organisation, had left instructions that they were not to be disturbed, and Anne's uncle, the earl, had sensibly decided some time ago to absent himself from London while his house there was in turmoil.

Howard, however, in spite of the shortness of the night, had to go to work as usual. At the moment when Anne joined him he was leafing through the *Daily Express* to see whether it contained any mention of the Countess of Chepstow's dance for Miss Venables, but he put it to one side when his sister came in and they chatted amicably for a little while about the previous evening.

'I like your friend Peggy,' he said, after they had discussed the flowers and the food and the music.

'You met her before I did. She's your friend as well as mine.'

'Yes. Well. The trouble is, it's such a rotten system, this Season of yours. I mean to say, how can you get to know a girl properly when you only ever meet her at dances? How can you find out what she's like in ordinary life, when she isn't wearing a ball dress?'

'I'll invite her to Yewley, if you like,' Anne offered. 'We could have a house party in September.' And perhaps Chay would come as well, she thought. 'But aren't you planning to take her to Oxford for a day? That will give you more chance to talk. Not that you've done too badly in the past few weeks.' Although Peggy ('the unfortunate Miss Armitage') was no longer immobilised, she still chose to sit out and rest for alternate dances and Howard had been attentive in keeping her company on such occasions.

'No, I suppose not.'

Anne smiled affectionately. There was only a six-year age difference, but until recently she had always felt as though her brother belonged to a different generation. Perhaps it was because his thick-rimmed spectacles made him look older than his age; perhaps it was because Anne herself had always felt ridiculously young. But now she had grown up. They were two young people together, of equal status. She was unable to restrain her curiosity.

'Are you in love with her, Howard?'

'I don't know. How does one tell? Well, yes, I suppose so. But what's the good of that? She's so young. She's even going back to school in September. She wants to go to university – and that's the right thing for an intelligent girl to do. But she won't start at Oxford until next year and then it would be three years of study after that. I could wait. That wouldn't be a problem. In fact, it'll be two or three years yet before I'm earning enough to support a family as well as putting something towards Yewley's expenses. But why should she want to attach herself to me when she'd be enjoying new experiences and meeting new men all the time?'

'I think you should let her answer your questions for herself instead of providing the answers for her. You could have a kind of understanding, couldn't you?'

'Is that something that you'd like if it were you? To be tied down to one chap without having any of the fun of being married?'

Anne didn't answer at once. Should Chay try to tie her down, she would happily agree to any arrangement he suggested. But Peggy's attitude might be quite different.

'I've never met her mother,' she said at last. 'Lady Menzies is only a chaperone, so she won't be putting on any pressure. But most mothers are pushing quite hard to get us married off, or at least engaged. They seem to think that by next year we'll have missed our chance. Who's ever going to look at an old woman of nineteen or twenty?'

'What's that got to do with Peggy?'

'It rubs off a bit, that attitude. I may say quite sincerely now that I'm in no hurry to get married, but all the same I shall feel a failure if I have to wait too long. To have an understanding with someone, an almost-engagement, might be a kind of protection. Freedom to go on living one's own life for a little while, but with all the security of being loved and seeing a happy future ahead in the end.'

'I wonder if you're right.' Shaking his head doubtfully, Howard returned his attention to the newspaper he had been reading. A photograph caught his attention. 'Ah, look!' But even as he spoke his face darkened and he bit his lip in anger. He read the item for a second time before closing and refolding the paper. 'Time I was off,' he said, and left the room with his toast buttered but uneaten.

Anne lost no time in discovering what her brother had read to upset him so much. The photograph that had caught his eye was not of herself, but of Howard and Peggy in conversation. The gossip paragraph beneath it was brief but cutting.

At the Countess of Chepstow's dance last night for her niece, the beautiful Miss Venables, Miss Margaret Armitage was well looked after by Mr Howard Venables. Miss Armitage, now almost recovered from her unfortunate accident earlier in the Season, is the daughter of Mr Henry Armitage, who has made a fortune from manufacturing cheap party dresses for less privileged girls. Mr Venables is the heir to Yewley House and greatly in need of a fortune to support the burden of an old house in pressing need of repair.

'Oh!' Anne was as indignant as her brother. How dare anyone suggest that he only liked Peggy because she was rich? He didn't even know that she *was* particularly rich. No debutante was likely to be exactly on the breadline; indeed, Anne herself was probably one of those with the least pocket money. But only a short time earlier she and Howard had commented on how little they knew about Peggy's family. To accuse him, almost, of being a fortune-hunter when he had no knowledge that there was any fortune to be hunted was terribly unfair.

Should she mention the paragraph to Peggy? Her immediate decision was to say nothing. Perhaps Peggy would never read it. Perhaps no one would repeat it to her.

Had it concerned anyone else, that hope might have been unrealistic, for the closed circle of debutantes and their mothers had little to talk about except each other. But Peggy, determinedly setting aside every free moment to press on with her studies, was not a gossip herself and did not mix much with those who were. By now, though, she and Anne had become close friends, so it was no particular surprise when Peggy telephoned a few days later to ask if they could meet for tea in Fortnum's.

Peggy came straight to the point. 'Have I done something to offend your brother?'

Anne was startled into silence. Her friend, although embarrassed, pressed on.

'I know this isn't a ladylike way to behave. I ought to pretend not to notice.'

'Notice what?'

'Well, ever since Ronnie's ball, right up to the night of your dance, Howard's been really nice to me. Keeping me company when I couldn't dance. Talking. Pretending that he found me interesting.'

'He wasn't pretending,' said Anne.

'Well, then, what's happened? He was going to take me to Oxford. It wasn't definitely fixed, but we'd mentioned two dates when we'd both be free. Last Saturday and today. But I haven't heard any more about it. And last night, at Isabelle's dance – well, I know I haven't got any right to expect him to ask me for a number, even though he always had before, but it was worse than that. He cut me.'

'I don't believe that. He can't have seen you.'

'That's what he pretended, but I know he had. I'd noticed him looking at me across the room. Come on, Anne, spit it out. Something's changed. What is it? I haven't quite got the nerve to ask him, so I'm asking you.'

It didn't take Anne long to realise that she must give an honest answer, but how far should she betray Howard's confidences? 'There was a beastly little paragraph in the *Express* which upset him. Did you see it? About him and you.'

Peggy shook her head.

'It suggested, without quite saying so, that he wanted to marry you for your money.'

'I haven't got any money.'

'Well, I gather your father has a lot. And when a girl gets married, she's often given a settlement by her father. The suggestion was that such a thing would come in handy to deal with little matters like woodworm and dry rot at Yewley House.'

'You're talking about marriage, but he's never said anything about marriage to me.'

'That was because of you going to university. He thought you wouldn't want . . . He's terribly in love with you, Peggy. He told me.'

'I don't call it very loving to break away just like that, without a word. He ought to have talked to me. I thought we were friends. I enjoyed talking to him, and I thought—' She stopped, upset.

'If he were to talk to you now . . . ?'

'No, thank you. You're not to suggest it, Anne. It would make it seem as though I hoped . . . Well, I certainly wouldn't want someone who lets a silly bit of newspaper gossip influence his behaviour. And he's quite right to think that what I want is to go to Oxford, not to get married yet. So there's no harm done, except that I think he's been extremely impolite and rather cowardly.'

Anne was tempted to defend her brother, but she too thought that Howard had mishandled the situation. What was more difficult to judge was whether or not Peggy was still upset, now that she knew the truth of the situation. Had she been sincere in saying that she didn't want to get married yet, or was she simply putting a brave face on what must have felt like a rejection? But there was no time to reflect on this, because Peggy had another question.

'Who told the newspaper about my father, do you think? I'm always with Lady Menzies. My mother's never been to any of the dances or met anybody. I don't talk about my family. Who would have known?'

'Journalists presumably have their own ways of finding things out.'

'Someone has to tell them. I suppose I must have mentioned it to somebody. After all, it isn't as though I'm ashamed of my family, just that I don't expect society people to be interested in them.' She thought hard for a moment. 'Isabelle!' she exclaimed. 'I do remember that at Ronnie's ball Isabelle was very complimentary about my dress. And her mother, too. They were asking me who the designer was. So I explained that it was someone who worked for my father and I expect I mentioned what sort of business he was in. But there's no reason why Isabelle should pass that information on.'

'Lady Patricia was there as well, you said?'

'No reason for her to talk about it, either.'

Anne could think of a reason. It was perfectly clear to all the debutantes in Ronnie's set that Lady Patricia intended her daughter to marry the Marquess of Lambourn. They watched her manoeuvres with amused interest – and, indeed, some of their escorts were even placing bets on her chances of success. Lady Patricia wanted Chay; but Chay, although sympathetically polite to Isabelle, did not conceal his preference for Anne. It was not altogether far-fetched, then, to wonder whether Lady Patricia might wish to publicise the Venables' lack of wealth, indirectly smearing Anne with the label of fortune-hunter by applying it so firmly to her brother.

She could not put forward this theory to Peggy, however,

without revealing emotions which must not be made public. And Peggy, whatever her true feelings, was obviously determined to show that she didn't care.

'I think it's stupid, all this chatter about who's going to marry whom. Who's in love with whom.'

'It's not stupid at all.' Anne, indignant, was defending herself as well as all her fellow debutantes. 'Maybe it's different for you, Peggy, because you know what you want to do with yourself afterwards. But most of us aren't as clever as you. We haven't got any skills. All we're fit for is to get married. And so I suppose that makes us, well, ready to fall in love.'

'Just like in all those sloppy magazine stories.'

'The fact that people write stories about something doesn't mean that it isn't important.' It was becoming clear to Anne that although her brother might be in love with Peggy, Peggy herself had not yet fallen in love with anyone. She didn't know what it felt like. 'Being in love takes you over. You can't help thinking about it all the time. It matters terribly to know whether the person you love loves you in return. If he doesn't, it's so painful that it hurts. And if you don't know, that hurts as well. And the worst thing of all would be if you both love each other and want to get married and then somebody decides that it isn't suitable, and—'

Anne checked herself. She was giving too much away. But perhaps Peggy, who professed such scorn for the whole process of falling in love, would not be sensitive enough to notice. Hastily she changed the subject.

'Which of us is going to have that last éclair?' she asked.

14

Another hostess, another ball. This one – like the Duchess of Wiltshire's two months earlier – was being held in one of the grand mansions which lined Park Lane. Along the whole front of the house was a conservatory which had obviously been well furnished with greenery even before the florists had moved in to fill it with flowers for this special occasion. It was here that Peggy Armitage retreated at two o'clock in the morning.

There was nothing really wrong with her leg any longer and young Dr Elliott, who was showing considerable skill in continuing to acquire invitations to the social events of the Season, had told her that she must take as much exercise as she could bear. And yes, dancing was exercise, he assured her each time he scribbled his initials in her programme.

She did her best to follow his advice, but after the first two or three hours the leg began to ache, as it was aching now. Quite often, if she chose to sit out, someone would come to talk to her. But nowadays it was never Howard; and although Ronnie often chivvied the members of her set to come over, they were such dull young men, who could talk about nothing but their regiments and their horses and the approach of the grouse-shooting season.

And so, at two o'clock, she slipped unobtrusively through the curtains and into the conservatory. It was lit only by candles, and she was able to pull a chair behind a screen of some ivy-like greenery that was dangling from a hanging basket: not precisely hiding, but making herself unobtrusive in case anyone should casually glance in.

The band started to play again. 'Jeepers Creepers'. That was a good one to be avoiding. Far too energetic for a convalescent leg. She relaxed happily and amused herself by plaiting the dangling foliage.

The curtains parted again. Peggy pulled the plaited screen close to her eyes so that she could see through it. The new arrival was Chay, alone. He walked across the conservatory and opened a window before lighting a cigarette. Peggy was tempted to surprise him with a shout of 'Ambush!' but she had left it too late. Instead, concealed in her bower, she watched with interest as he stared out over Park Lane towards the park, drawing on his cigarette and then sighing as he exhaled.

She had never seen him in quite this humour before: tired and apparently anxious. On the dance floor and at parties he was always suave and amusing and it had never occurred to her that this might be an act; or, at the very least, that his public face might be different from his private one. There was something appealing about this mood of what appeared to be depression. It wasn't always easy to see the man behind the nobleman, so to speak, but she was seeing it now – and it filled her with an overwhelming desire to touch and comfort him.

What a ridiculous idea! All the same, she was on the point of revealing herself in order that they could talk, when the curtains parted again.

It was Isabelle who appeared – and who promptly gave an audible gasp of surprise at discovering she was not alone in the conservatory. A more artificial sound Peggy had rarely heard: not just acting, but ham acting.

It had the desired result. Chay turned to see who it was who had joined him. Peggy, still watching, was fascinated to observe how he – a far better actor, it seemed – threw off whatever had been worrying him and smoothly returned to his public persona: the courteous nobleman.

'Hello. Cigarette?' He offered it from a slim silver cigarette case, waited while she fitted it into a long holder and bent over to light it for her.

'It's too hot in there,' Isabelle said. 'Stuffy. I needed a breath of fresh air.'

'Yes.' He made way for her to approach the open window. She leaned out of it, and for a few minutes their conversation was inaudible to Peggy, who became more and more concerned about her situation. Earlier, she had been a voyeur; now she had become an eavesdropper. But once the first opportunity to declare her presence had been missed, it became more and more difficult to interrupt. And fortunately, the conversation, when she was once again able to hear it, was thoroughly banal and not at all secret.

'What a beautiful scent there is in here!' Isabelle said, apparently oblivious to the fact that the conservatory would soon smell of nothing but cigarette smoke. 'It's this little white flower here, isn't it? Do you know what it is?'

'Stephanotis, I believe, but I'm not an expert.'

Isabelle failed to take the hint and led the marquess down the length of the conservatory, pointing here, lifting a leaf there, admiring flowers everywhere. Any minute now, thought Peggy mischievously, she would pull a rosebud from a vase and ask Chay to pin it to her dress.

Isabelle pulled a rosebud from a vase and turned towards Chay. 'Will you . . .' But the sound of 'Jeepers Creepers' coming to a vigorously noisy end seemed to startle her. She gave another little gasp, as artificial as the first. 'Is that the end of the dance? Oh dear. I didn't realise that we'd been here together for so long. And with no chaperone. How compromising!'

'Compromising?' If Chay understood what she was hinting, he gave no sign of it.

'Well, everyone knows that the only excuse for such a long period of privacy is . . .' For a moment her voice faltered. 'Is – well, it sounds silly, doesn't it, but – is a proposal of marriage.'

Was Chay alarmed or amused? It was difficult to tell. Certainly he was startled. 'I think you're going too far back. The proposal in the conservatory is a Victorian convention. Young ladies these days are not quite such delicate plants, are they? But let me escort you back to your mother if you're worried.'

'It's a little late for that, after such a long absence.' Was it Peggy's imagination, or was Isabelle importing a French accent into her voice, as though to suggest that she might be operating under different rules of conduct and expectation? 'My reputation . . .'

It was time to intervene, while Chay was struggling to control a mixture of incredulity, alarm and indignation. Parting the foliage, Peggy stepped out of her hiding place and prepared to show that she too could put on an act.

'It's all right, Isabelle,' she said in a reassuring voice. 'If your mother becomes concerned, you can assure her that I was here with you all the time. I'll be happy to confirm to any gossips that nothing the slightest bit improper took place.'

Isabelle's face was a study: a mixture of shame and frustration and rage. If looks could have killed, Peggy would have been pinched out as sharply as an aphid on a rose bush.

Chay, for his part, was trying not to laugh. He gave up the struggle as soon as Isabelle, head high, had stalked out of the conservatory and back to the ballroom. 'Well, thank you for that,' he said to Peggy. 'My good fairy, waiting in the wings.'

'I ought to have appeared a lot earlier, but when you came in, I could see you wanted to be by yourself, and so did I, so I just kept quiet, and after that it seemed too late to interrupt.' She hesitated, unsure whether Isabelle deserved to be defended, but they were by way of being friends. 'I expect her mother ordered her to follow you here. She must have hated it.'

Chay, pulling up a chair so that they could both sit down, was less forgiving. 'I've been sorry for her in that respect in the past, but really! She's not a child any longer. If she can't stand up for herself against her mother, she's certainly not fit to get married. Obviously they were in cahoots. A conspiracy.'

Peggy found it hard to disagree.

'What shocks me is the stupidity of it all,' he went on. 'Did she really expect that she could get away with that sort of moral blackmail? And if she did, how could she possibly imagine that to trap a man in such a way could herald the start of a happy marriage?'

'Lady Patricia's view would probably be that future dukes are not expected to have happy marriages: merely suitable ones.'

'Then I shall hope to prove exceptional among dukes, just as you, if I may be personal for a moment, are exceptional among debutantes.'

Blushing at the compliment, Peggy was emboldened to ask a question which earlier might have seemed impertinent. 'You looked very worried when you first came in. Is anything wrong?'

Chay, who had been fiddling with his cigarette case, looked up and stared steadily into her eyes. 'Is your discretion as impeccable as your timing?' he asked.

'If I'm warned that something is secret, then I keep it secret, yes.'

'In fact, time is likely to reveal it soon enough, I fear.' He sighed, offered her a cigarette and, when she refused, lit one for himself. 'But until then . . . There are two things, actually. The first is that I signed up today for the Volunteer Reserve. For the Air Force. I learned to fly with the University Squadron at Oxford, and I love it, the feeling of flying. Though flying in order to kill other people will be a different matter, of course.'

'Do you expect . . . ?'

'I'm absolutely sure that we shall soon be at war. Everyone hopes it can be avoided, and so do I, of course; but I don't think we ought to go on fooling ourselves any longer.'

Peggy considered what he had said in silence. The prospect of war was not something that was ever discussed between the debutantes, but over the past few weeks she had noticed a kind of excitement growing amongst those of Ronnie's set who were Guards officers. Mutterings about the need to teach that Hitler blighter a lesson had served as an excuse for what was perhaps a natural hope of action amongst young men who had chosen a career in which promotion depended on the opportunity to prove their skill and courage in battle.

'Does signing up mean . . . ?'

'It means nothing for the moment. Just that I'll be called up before other people. There'll be a need for qualified pilots. I'll have to have much more training, of course. Flying over a peaceful countryside is rather different from getting into dogfights. But at least I'll have a head start.'

'There were two things, you said.'

'Yes. My father is ill. He's been in poor health for years, with only one lung, but now the other lung's giving him trouble, and it may not be very long . . .' Once again he looked steadily at her. 'Ronnie doesn't know. I don't want to spoil her Season, and there wouldn't be anything she could do.'

'I won't tell her. I'm sorry, Chay.'

'It makes everything more difficult. I've been bothered about it for weeks. I'm his only son and almost everything is entailed.

If he dies and then if I were to get killed in a war, there's some sort of cousin in Kenya who'd suddenly find himself a duke. It wouldn't be much fun for my mother, to be widowed and robbed of her home at the same time. You could say that it's my duty to produce an heir before taking to the dangerous skies. But then there's my duty to my country. It hasn't been easy to decide.'

He smiled: that unusually sweet smile that had so much attracted Peggy at her first glimpse of him. 'Well, the decision's made,' he said. 'I can't worry about it any more, but I don't want to broadcast it, either.'

Accepting the lightening of his tone, Peggy had a suggestion to make. 'I'm sure Isabelle would be happy to produce an heir for you at a moment's notice.'

'Yes, I'm sure too.' He stood up, looking round for something in which to stub out his cigarette. 'I shall be eternally grateful to you for helping to save me from such a fate. Thanks to you, I can walk out of the conservatory without embarrassment. A free man still!'

'Oh, I'm not so sure about that.' Peggy grinned mischievously as she too prepared to return to the ballroom. 'You were in here with Isabelle for less than ten minutes, and chaperoned. You have been in here with me for about half an hour, and for most of that time alone. Think of my reputation, sir! Nothing less than a proposal of marriage can save me from ruin!'

There was a moment – well, perhaps only a split second – in which he wasn't sure whether or not she was joking. His mouth fell open and his eyes widened.

Peggy dissolved into delighted laughter. 'April fool!' she exclaimed, with no regard to the actual date. 'It's all right, Chay. You're safe from me.'

He joined in her laughter. 'You're a good sport, Peggy.' Stepping towards her, he stood so close that for a moment she thought he intended to kiss her. But no doubt all the evening's talk of reputation and chaperonage had had a sobering effect, for instead he merely gripped her by the shoulders and gave a friendly squeeze. The incident was over.

The memory of what had passed was not, however, easily banished. That night Peggy lay for a long time awake in bed, replaying the scene in her mind as though it were a film. And just as though it were a film, she was tempted to edit it, exchanging each actual remark for something wittier or altering her position so that Chay would realise how much she would have liked him to kiss her, reputation or no reputation. She wished, too, that she could cut out the realisation that Howard Venables must have watched Chay appearing alone from the conservatory and then – judging by the look on his face – drawn his own conclusions when Peggy herself stepped through the curtains ten minutes later.

Howard, though, seemed to have dropped her already. She wasn't going to worry about him. The man who filled her thoughts was Chay himself. They had laughed together. He had confided in her. From the first moment when they met he had behaved with kindness to her, when he was only expected to be polite. He liked her. They were friends.

Was that all? Was that enough? Peggy tried to examine her own feelings squarely. Yes, they were friends and she valued the friendship; but it would be easy, dangerously easy, to go further than that and fall in love with a young man whom she admired as much for his seriousness as for his gaiety.

Had she in fact fallen in love with him already? Come on now, Peggy, be honest! She had enjoyed Howard's company and conversation whenever it was offered to her. For Chay's company she felt a kind of longing that was quite different. A desire to be near him; to be touched by him as he had touched her this evening. She would have liked him to kiss her.

Now hold on, Peggy, she told herself. Suppose he *had* kissed me. Suppose – a very big suppose! – he'd even asked me to marry him. Then what? Just look at it straight. Chay was going to be a duke one day – perhaps one day very soon. He needed to marry someone who would be a suitable duchess. Peggy wasn't snobbish enough to believe that duchesses were superior human beings just because of their rank, although neither did she share her sister's inverted snobbery: Jodie, who didn't know any, believed that duchesses were particularly useless and over-pampered women. The truth lay somewhere in between. As long as society existed, anyone who was a duchess had a particular role to play. She needed to look the part and to play it with confidence, without wishing all the time that she were doing something else. Probably all those people were right who assumed that to be successful in such a role, a girl needed to be brought up to it. Certainly she needed to want the rank just as much as she wanted the man.

Anne Venables would make a marvellous duchess. She was tall and lovely and sweet natured and little by little she was growing out of her shyness. Even Isabelle would be a good duchess if she ever succeeded in freeing herself from her mother's management. The incident in the conservatory had made her appear gauche, but that was only because she was speaking someone else's script. Usually she was sophisticated and self-assured.

But Peggy herself? No, she couldn't imagine it. She didn't want to imagine it. It was hard to look into the future and see what kind of a life she would lead, but it must be a life she chose for herself and not something that came inescapably with a label. Chay would already have recognised that. That was why he hadn't kissed her. He had chosen friendship, and friendship was what she wanted, wasn't it?

For the sake of her own self-respect, the answer to that had to be Yes. Although the truth was that she didn't know what she wanted.

Yes, she did. She wanted Oxford. Tossing in the bed, she groaned aloud at her own ridiculous uncertainty. She was saved at last by the memory of something Anne had said while they were taking tea together at Fortnum's. 'Being in love takes you over.'

'That settles it.' Peggy spoke the words aloud, since no one could hear. 'No one has taken me over. I am not in love with anyone. I don't want to be in love with anyone just yet. End of fantasy. Go to sleep.'

She went to sleep.

15

'Well, my dear, you *are* flying high!' Lady Menzies wore a satisfied smile as she studied the thick invitation card which had arrived by the early post. 'Lady Ranelegh!'

Peggy had never heard of Lady Ranelegh, but nevertheless understood the significance of the comment and was pleased to be giving pleasure. Over the past four months she had grown fond of the little Scotswoman, who occasionally reproved her for some mistake of dress or behaviour, but for the most part was understanding as well as conscientious. At the beginning of the Season both debutante and chaperone had been well aware that they could not expect the grandest hostesses to take any notice of them, but Peggy's accident had changed all that. The ostentatious display of friendship shown by both Ronnie and Chay at the Wiltshire ball had moved the unknown Miss Armitage from being merely one of Mairi Menzies' paying clients into a higher tier of social acceptability.

From the awed expression on Lady Menzies' face it now appeared that they must have attained even giddier heights. For a professional chaperone, every social triumph was a business asset which could be mentioned when she next set out her prospectus, and Peggy was glad to be proving a successful protégée.

'Who is Lady Ranelegh?' she asked. 'Do I know her daughter?'

'Oh no, dear. No daughter. Lady Ranelegh is quite an elderly lady. She has a salon all through the year. And then this ball in early July. Most of the Cabinet will be there. And members of the House of Lords. She will have invited the Duke and

Duchess of Wiltshire, certainly, and Lord Lambourn and Lady Veronica with them. No doubt your friend has asked . . .'

Lady Menzies frowned slightly to herself and studied the card with more care.

'Well, perhaps not quite that,' she decided. 'A wee bit unusual, this. It seems that Lady Patricia le Vaillant has been invited to take a party to the ball. Coming at such short notice, we must assume that someone has fallen out at the last minute, but never mind. An invitation is an invitation. I expect her daughter suggested you. She's a friend of yours, isn't she?'

That wasn't as simple a question as Lady Menzies might have thought. Yes, Peggy and Isabelle had become members of the same set, if only because Isabelle was always to be found hanging round Ronnie and Chay. But the confrontation in the conservatory had left Isabelle so visibly angry that it was surprising . . .

No, perhaps not surprising at all. Isabelle would be anxious for reassurance that Peggy would not humiliate her in public by gossiping about what had happened. Probably the invitation was a bribe – and since Peggy had in any case no intention of telling anyone what she had overheard, she felt no compunction about accepting the offer.

The invitation was not, as was usual, for a small dinner before the ball: instead, the party would assemble for light refreshments before moving on.

'So many of Lady Ranelegh's friends are elderly, like herself,' Lady Menzies guessed, 'that she probably arranges for an earlier supper than most hostesses. It gives the politicians a chance to break away into little groups and plot together. You may find that there aren't very many young men to dance with you, but never mind. Just to be there at all is a triumph. Your very best gown. And I think we might hire the tiara again.'

'No.' Peggy put her foot down at that. It was one thing to be properly attired to appear before the King, but she didn't want to look like something she wasn't: an aristocrat with jewels which had been handed down the family for generations.

In every other respect, however, she dressed appropriately for the event, covering her grandest ball dress with the full-length satin cloak that her father had given her for her eighteenth birthday. Lady Menzies gave an approving nod as they prepared to set out for the great occasion.

The taxi dropped them outside Lady Patricia's house, but even while Lady Menzies was paying the driver Peggy realised that there was something wrong. When they had been to dinner there on a previous occasion the whole house had been ablaze with light, and through open windows had come the sounds of animated conversation. Today there was light only in the basement. The rest of the building was dark and dead.

Lady Menzies, joining her as the taxi drove away, was equally disconcerted, pulling the invitation from her handbag to be sure that there was no mistake about the date or time.

'I think perhaps, dear –' she began, but already Peggy was pressing the bell. There was a long pause. When the door was finally opened, it was by a butler who had clearly been struggling into his jacket as he came up the stairs.

'Lady Patricia is expecting us,' said Lady Menzies bravely, but both the callers were already expecting the answer they were given.

'I'm afraid her ladyship is not at home.' It was a standard phrase, and not always to be believed, but on this occasion the darkness and silence proved it to be true.

'May I have the invitation card, Lady Menzies?' Peggy held it out to the butler, who read it with surprise and shook his head. As the chaperone, pursing her lips in anger, began to turn away, she was checked by the flash of a photographer who had appeared without warning from some hiding place in the street.

Now it was Peggy's turn to be angry as she began to suspect what had happened. 'Wait here just a moment, please,' she said to the butler, and turned to confront the photographer, who promptly took another picture. 'Who told you to come here? Who tipped you off?'

'I go where the editor tells me. Don't know anything about tip-offs.'

'So which paper do you work for?'

'Not really any of your business, is it, Miss?'

'If you make it my business by printing any of these pictures, I can promise that your editor will hear from my father's lawyer the moment the first one appears. I recommend you to tell your editor that the situation may not be quite as he imagined it and he would do well to investigate it before he does anything he might regret.'

She turned back to the butler, an interested observer of the scene. 'Can you tell me where Lady Patricia and Miss le Vaillant are this evening?'

'At Lady Ranelegh's ball, Miss. They dined early here, quite privately, before they left. I'm sorry that there seems to have been some misunderstanding.'

'That's one way of putting it. Come on, Lady Menzies.' Peggy strode off down the street, knowing that there would be a better chance of finding a taxi in Park Lane. 'Ranelegh House,' she told the driver as soon as they were successful.

'But my dear, we can't possibly . . .' Her chaperone, appalled, tried to protest, but Peggy, who for the past four months had dutifully been following all the instructions she was given, had been roused to act as her father would have acted in such circumstances. Lady Patricia was going to pay for this, even though Peggy herself might be humiliated in the process.

What a contrast there was between the deserted house they had just left and the miniature palace that was Ranelegh House. None of the curtains had been closed, so that a row of Venetian chandeliers sparkled their light out on to the street. And unlike most of the town houses to which Peggy had been invited in the previous few months, Ranelegh House had a garden, lit now by flaming torches. It backed on to Green Park, offering an opportunity for members of the public to pause in their strolling and stare with interest at the beautifully dressed couples who emerged from the ballroom to take the air for a little while before returning to the dance floor. The sound of the band floated delicately through the open windows: 'Begin the Beguine', they were playing as Peggy tugged at the bell chain.

'My dear—' Lady Menzies ventured one last protest.

'I'm sorry, but I'm not going to let her get away with this. I'll try not to involve you.'

She was still holding Lady Patricia's invitation card, which she allowed the footman who opened the door to glimpse: and she was of course appropriately dressed for the ball. No doubt he had been warned to guard against gatecrashers, so she allowed him no time to challenge her.

'Before we go up, would you please take a message to Lady Ranelegh: that Lady Menzies and Miss Armitage are anxious to have a private word with her if she can spare a moment,' she said, speaking as confidently as she could.

There was a moment's hesitation, and then the door was opened a little wider. They were in.

'We'll wait here.'

Several moments passed before the man returned. 'This way please.'

Peggy had expected to be shown into some small private room, but found Lady Ranelegh waiting at the foot of the stairs. Straight backed and severe in expression she waited to hear what these intruders had to say. Peggy's heart sank and she needed all her courage to confront this stiff old lady who would surely support Lady Patricia le Vaillant rather than an insignificant stranger and who would ensure that their dismissal was a public one.

'I'm sure you're aware, as I am now, Lady Ranelegh, that you didn't invite us to your ball. I'd like to explain why we're here, because you may feel as indignant as I do that someone should have used your name in order to humiliate both me and my chaperone.' She handed over the invitation which had arrived in the post and explained what had happened.

After glancing at it with an apparent lack of interest, Lady Ranelegh put her lorgnette up to her eyes and read the card more carefully, frowning as she did so. 'Some unfortunate mistake, I imagine. An incorrect date.'

'The date of your ball is not mistaken. And it was not by mistake that a newspaper photographer was on the spot, waiting to take a photograph of us being turned away from Lady Patricia's door. My chaperone, Lady Menzies, has looked after me so well and organised my social life so carefully that I can't stand by and see her shamed in this way, so deliberately and unscrupulously. She would have preferred not to involve you in any way. I'm the one who insisted, so if you feel that I'm behaving badly, it's only me, not her.'

Peggy paused, feeling that she was becoming confused when she had intended to maintain a dignified mode of speech. But that moment saw the best thing that could possibly have happened. Ronnie, clutching a broken shoulder strap, came running down the stairs towards the cloakroom in which a maid would be waiting with needle and thread.

'Disaster!' she cried as she passed them. 'Lady Ranelegh, this is a most marvellous occasion. Your beautiful garden! Peggy, Lady Menzies, how topping to see you here. Chay will be pleased. You'll find him upstairs.'

Her hostess, disapproving of such a lack of formality, but prepared to be indulgent to the daughter of a friend, watched her disappear. 'You're acquainted with Lady Veronica?' she enquired.

'Yes, Lady Ranelegh. She and her brother are good friends of mine.'

'Hm.' For a second time the lorgnette went up and the invitation was studied. 'You used strong words a moment ago, Miss Armitage. Deliberately. Unscrupulously. But surely Lady Patricia le Vaillant can have no reason to trap you in what you seem to see as a plot.'

Until that evening Peggy had genuinely intended to be discreet about Isabelle's hopeless attempt to entrap Chay into a proposal of marriage, but she no longer felt any need for restraint.

'I can think of a reason,' she said. 'Lady Patricia has certain ambitions for her daughter. Quite inadvertently, I was responsible for frustating them on one occasion. Not by anything I did. Just because I was present at what Miss le Vaillant had hoped might be a private meeting.'

There was another pause for consideration before the old lady turned to Lady Menzies. 'Miss Armitage has been presented, I take it?' she enquired. 'I am not *au fait* with the youngest generation of debutantes.'

'She has been presented, yes. And she has been received by, for example, the Duchess of Wiltshire, the Countess of Chepstow, Lady Mountavon . . .'

'That's enough. I hope, Lady Menzies, that you and Miss Armitage will do me the honour of joining my other guests tonight. But first of all, leave your cloaks and follow me, please.'

Walking with some effort, she led the way up the stairs towards the ballroom, where by now – according to the band's vocalist – a nightingale was singing in Berkeley Square. She paused until the music came to an end and the dancers returned

123

to their chairs. Then she made her way across the floor to where Lady Patricia was waiting for Isabelle to rejoin her.

'Lady Patricia.' The old lady's voice, accustomed to command, was clear and penetrating. She held out the invitation that Peggy had handed to her. 'It seems that there has been some unfortunate confusion in your social arrangements. I'm very pleased to say that Lady Menzies and Miss Armitage have found their way here without your help, and I hope that they will enjoy the rest of the evening. But I think that perhaps you ought to return immediately to your own address in case any other victims of your secretary's inefficiency should present themselves there.'

By the time Lady Ranelegh came to the end of her short speech everyone in the room was listening to it. Isabelle, understanding the snub but seemingly bewildered by it, flushed a deep red. Her mother's face, by contrast, paled as all blood seemed to drain away. There was a moment in which she seemed on the verge of protesting: a moment in which she stared at Peggy with hatred in her eyes. Then she rose to her feet and walked with as much dignity as she could muster towards the doorway.

Isabelle also stood up, but paused in front of Peggy. 'I was fed up about the other night,' she said, her voice thick with embarrassment. 'And I told Maman and of course I could see she was angry. But whatever it is that this fuss is about, I don't know anything about it.'

'Okay.' Peggy kept her voice neutral, unsure whether to believe it.

'Really I don't. If an apology is needed, then I apologise. On my own behalf, I mean.' She held out a hand, her eyes pleading with Peggy to accept it.

Peggy, her battle won, was feeling so empty inside that she hardly had the strength to remain standing. But with Lady Patricia's departure, her need for revenge had drained away. Before an interested audience, the two young women shook hands.

16

Ronnie returned from her decency-saving session in the cloak-room to find the ballroom buzzing with excited gossip.

'What have I missed?' she demanded of Peggy, pulling up a chair close to her. 'Why am I always in the wrong place when exciting things happen? I passed Isabelle and her mother on the stairs and Isabelle was crying. What's been going on? Do tell.'

Peggy shook her head. 'Nothing important.'

'Oh, come on. It's very unfriendly to keep secrets.'

'Is it?' asked Peggy. Her freckled face broke into a mischie-vous grin. 'Always?'

Ronnie was silenced by her memory of the accident, the real version of which had, thank God, never reached her parents' ears.

'Oh well,' she said. 'Laurie will tell me. He's frightfully good at picking up all the scandal. I suppose it's because he has to be so discreet about his patients. Once he's away from the hospital, he really lets rip.'

'How on earth has he managed to be here tonight?' asked Peggy.

Ronnie could understand her surprise. A good many of the Season's hostesses, anxious to make sure that there would be partners for all the debutantes, sent open invitations to officers' messes, hospitals, universities or barristers' chambers; but Lady Ranelegh, who was more interested in the older generation, would not have taken the risk of having to receive an unsuitable guest.

'My invitation was for me and a partner. Chay had his own card. So I asked Laurie.'

'Ought you to encourage him?' asked Peggy. 'I mean, anyone can see that he's absolutely besotted with you. But—'

'But what?' Ronnie lifted her chin in determination. This was a rehearsal for the conversation that she would have to have with her mother before long. 'Perhaps I'm besotted with him as well.'

'What do your parents think about that?'

'Pa's never met him. He went back to Cleeve straight after my ball. As for my mother – well, she wants me to marry Malcolm Ross. She's got this thing about owning land, and Malcolm will certainly have plenty of that one day.'

'Whilst Laurie presumably has none at all.'

'No, but it doesn't matter. I know that Pa isn't allowed to give anything away – land, I mean – because of the stupid entail business, but there are estates that Ma inherited and that she never visits. She owns an island in the Orkneys, for example. She could give us that.'

'But Laurie's a doctor. What would he do there?' asked Peggy. 'Or you, if it comes to that.'

'There are people living in the Orkneys. They get ill, presumably, from time to time. Anyway, he wouldn't need—' Ronnie checked herself. She was running on too fast. But tonight might very well be the night when Laurie would propose. She felt it in her bones. He had asked her for the supper dance, and she had agreed. That was when it would happen.

Before that, she would have to survive another dance with Malcolm – who was also, to use Peggy's phrase, besotted with her. He had, in fact, proposed to her three times already. The first time didn't count, because he was drunk, and the second time didn't count either, because he had obviously felt the need to prove that he hadn't been drunk the first time. On the third occasion Ronnie had claimed that she wasn't ready to think about that sort of thing just yet: nothing personal. But she knew that he would go on proposing until she said yes – or until she could announce that she was going to marry someone else. So it was about time for the someone else to speak up for himself.

Earlier than at most balls, the time came for the supper dance. Ronnie, who usually had a hearty appetite, was too much on edge to be hungry. Laurie, though, had never made any secret

of the benefit to his budget of the free meals he was offered on
these occasions, and so she had to restrain her impatience until
at last he spoke the word for which she had been waiting.

'Garden?'

She nodded happily as she took his arm. They would not be
alone on the terrace, for a good many of the younger guests
were grasping the opportunity of a little fresh air. But there
were secluded corners and summer houses, and even on the
open lawns dark circles of shadow between the flickering
torches offered an illusion of privacy.

Laurie, however, did not take advantage of these, but instead
led her to the furthest edge of the garden and leaned over the
balustrade. Twelve feet below them stretched the flat expanse
of Green Park. Normally at this time of night the park would
have been almost deserted, but the sound of music had
attracted a small crowd of onlookers. Making no pretence of
being on their way to anywhere else, they stared up at the
perambulating guests, from time to time murmuring an
identification.

For an unbearably long time Laurie remained silent, and
Ronnie herself dared not speak for fear of diverting his attention
from what, surely, was to be a proposal of marriage. In that,
though, she was wrong.

'Them and us,' he said unexpectedly, waving a hand in the
direction of what she assumed to be the admiring onlookers.
'Do you ever think about it, Ronnie? The difference between
someone like you, who can spend your days exactly as you
choose, only needing to express a wish to be given whatever
you want; and those people down there who must work hard
all day, whether they enjoy their work or not, and still very
rarely achieve even a part of what they hope for.'

'What have I done to deserve a political lecture?' asked
Ronnie, trying to keep her voice light.

'It's not really political. Personal, more.' Until this moment
Laurie, with his elbows on the balustrade, had been staring
straight ahead, into the park; now he turned to look into her
eyes.

'I'm one of Them, Ronnie. Them with a capital T. It's been fun
– no, much more than fun. Marvellous, being allowed to
pretend for a few weeks that I was one of you. I oughtn't to

have let myself, but the first moment I saw you . . . And I didn't know who you were then, of course.'

'I'm Ronnie.'

'Yes. Ronnie, daughter of a duke.'

'That doesn't make any difference.' Ronnie's stomach chilled with anxiety. This conversation was not going at all as she had hoped.

Laurie made no direct answer to that. His next remark, indeed, seemed to represent a complete change of subject. 'I've finished my training at last. Done my hospital stint. While I was there I had to be ready to take on anything that was going, from delivering babies to stitching up the victims of recklessly driving debutantes, but now I've got a bit more choice. Not a lot, but a bit. If I want to specialise, this is the time to start. I've developed a special interest in nutrition and its effect on general health.'

What did he expect her to say? Was he waiting for her to volunteer a sudden interest in nutrition herself? Ronnie drew breath, ready to associate herself in some way with his plans, but Laurie was still setting them out.

'So I'm afraid that this is going to be my last grand ball. And when the rest of you come back to London again for next year's Season, I shall be in Liverpool.'

'Liverpool!'

'Yes.' Was it her imagination, or was there a trace of uneasiness, even guilt, in his voice. 'Have you ever heard of something called rickets?'

She shook her head unhappily.

'In Liverpool, apparently, there's a lot of it around. Children whose legs aren't strong enough to support them.'

'Why do you have to go so far? There must be children with rickets in London as well.'

'Yes, I'm sure, but nobody's invited me to look at them. Liverpool, on the other hand, has offered me a job. And there's a special chap up there. An orthopaedic surgeon; a top man in his field. I could learn a lot.'

Ronnie frowned slightly to herself, not understanding what orthopaedic surgeons had to do with nutrition. But what did she care about that? It was time to be positive.

'Are you going to invite me to come to Liverpool with you?'

she said, flushing at her own boldness even as she spoke, and holding out her hand so that he could not, in politeness, refuse to take it.

'I can't do that.'

'Why not? You love me. Don't you?'

'Yes, of course I do, my dearest, darling Ronnie. But—'

'And I love you.' Her flush deepened. It was the first time she had spoken the words aloud.

'Oh, Ronnie!' He was about to take her in his arms and kiss her, she knew he was. But he didn't.

'If . . .' This would be carrying boldness too far, that she should almost be proposing to him, but unless she fought, she was going to lose him. 'If we were to get married, Pa would make a settlement. He can't give land, but he's got money. You'd have more choice then. You wouldn't need to go just where there was a job. You could buy a Harley Street practice and stay in London.'

'I doubt whether very many cases of malnutrition find their way to Harley Street.'

'Well, you wouldn't need to work at all if you didn't want to. We could live at Cleeve. There's plenty of room.'

Laurie shook his head sadly. Ever since their first meeting he had been light-hearted and teasing. This serious young man was someone Ronnie didn't know – and he was frightening her.

'Training to be a doctor takes years,' he reminded her, 'and it's a terrible grind. There's all the strain of passing exams and the strain of not making mistakes, and the strain of surviving days and nights without sleep and the strain of telling someone that he's never going to get better or telling someone else that someone she loves is dead and the strain of doing all this without enough money to live on. No one in his right mind would embark on the training unless he had a passionate need to spend the rest of his life trying to heal people. It's a vocation, I suppose. I can't just give it up; not even for you. Because if I did, I might be angry with you one day.'

'Well then, I can be a doctor's wife.'

There was another long silence before Laurie gave a deep sigh. 'It wouldn't work, Ronnie. I've lain awake at nights, every night, trying to imagine it, but it wouldn't work.'

'When two people love each other, that's all that matters.'

'That's only true in films. In real life, being in love may be enough for a year or two, but you wouldn't enjoy not being able to afford all the clothes you want, or the servants. And sooner or later you'd realise that you'd become cut off from all your friends. Not just by living a long way away, but because you weren't going to the right places at the right times. You're not a snob, and I love you for it, but I'm afraid you might find that a lot of people who enjoy the company of a duke's daughter might become less interested in a provincial doctor's wife.'

'I may not be a snob, but you are, if you think that.'

'All right, then; I am. It would make me unhappy to think that I'd taken you away from the society in which you belong without being able to offer you anything comparable to make up for it.'

'So you're turning me down!'

'Oh Ronnie, darling, I love you so much. But it isn't enough. When a girl gets married, she doesn't simply acquire a husband. She has to take on a new life, and it's terribly important that it should be a congenial new life, because she'll have to live it for years and years. I can't offer you that life. I'm terribly sorry.'

He turned away from her, burying his head in his hands. He was crying, Ronnie realised. She had never seen a man crying before, but the sight made her angry, not sympathetic.

'You shouldn't have let me love you,' she exclaimed. 'You had no right, if you were going to say this in the end.'

'I know.' Pulling himself together, he turned to face her again. 'There was a sort of infectious atmosphere, I suppose, at the start of the Season. So many flirtations going on that didn't really mean anything. Just a way of talking. I thought I could flirt as well as anyone else. I mean, I did fall in love with you that first time I saw you, in the hospital, and it was the most marvellous thing seeing you again so soon after that, and I did hope that you might be interested in me, but all the time I told myself that it couldn't possibly mean anything serious to you because I was only one of dozens of men who were competing for you. I thought I'd be the only one to be hurt. I really am so very sorry.'

Through the open windows of Lady Ranelegh's ballroom came the sound of music as the band, refreshed, began to play again. For the rest of my life, thought Ronnie, 'Smoke Gets In My Eyes' will make me want to cry.

'"To every thing there is a season,"' said the serious and unhappy young man who was no relation of that carefree young man with whom she had fallen in love. '"A time to dance." The Bible forgets to mention that there's a time to refrain from dancing.'

'I hope you'll be very happy in Liverpool,' said Ronnie. Forcing herself to walk slowly, she returned alone to the ballroom. Then, for the second time that evening, she hurried down to the cloakroom so that no one should see her tears. The attendant who waited there had mended her broken strap, but could do nothing to repair a broken heart.

17

Like everyone else, the Duchess of Wiltshire had her regular At Home hours, and ten o'clock in the morning was not one of them. Nevertheless, when a footman brought up the card of Lieutenant Malcolm Ross, she nodded her head. She could guess what he was going to say, and it was something she wanted to hear.

The duchess had known Malcolm since he was a baby. His mother, who had died young, had been one of her closest friends. The pattern of autumn visits between the two families had been broken by Naomi's death, but Chay had become a friend of Malcolm while they were both at Eton, and had encouraged him this year to attend the balls to which he and Ronnie were invited. After the first meeting, no further encouragement had been needed and the duchess had noted the young officer's attentiveness to her daughter with complete approval.

It would be a thoroughly suitable match. Malcolm's grandfather and father were both still alive, so it would be a good many years yet before he inherited the earldom and the Scottish estate, but on his twenty-first birthday he had taken possession of his mother's legacy. He would be able to offer Ronnie a fine house and several thousand acres in Northumbria as well as some unprofitable coal mines in Leicestershire. He was not particularly intelligent – but then, neither was Ronnie. She would soon have found herself out of her depth with an intellectual husband.

The duchess had no reason to think that she might be jumping to an unlikely conclusion. Her husband, now back at

Cleeve, had already reported a formal request by the young lieutenant for permission to pay court to Ronnie. There had even been a tentative exchange of letters between the two fathers. Nothing as binding as a contract; just the start of a negotiation which would eventually ensure that the two young people were well set up for a prosperous life together, while being individually protected in the unhappy event of any problems. Moreover, on the way to Lady Ranelegh's ball the previous evening, Ronnie had found it impossible to disguise her excitement. She had been expecting something to happen. Now Malcolm must have come to confirm that those expectations had been fulfilled.

Such a hope was to be disappointed. The young man who bowed politely over the hand she offered him wore a worried expression and wasted little time in coming to the point.

'It's very good of you to receive me at this hour, duchess. I've come to ask whether perhaps you'd be willing to put in a word for me with Ronnie.'

The duchess looked at him in surprise and some alarm as she motioned him towards a seat. 'I should have thought you were well enough able to speak up for yourself.'

'Well, I've tried, but . . . I've asked her to marry me four times. The first three times she kind of laughed it off. Last night I asked her again, and I really thought . . . I mean, she must know how much I love her, and she's not unkind. I told her that I couldn't bear her to laugh again.'

'And did she?'

He shook his head unhappily. 'She burst into tears. I don't know why. It can't have been anything I said. In fact, just for a minute or two she let me comfort her. And then suddenly she kind of pushed me off and said she didn't want to marry me or anyone else and then she ran away. I couldn't find her again after that. She must have been hiding.'

'And you hadn't had any kind of quarrel?'

'Nothing like that, no. We always seem to get on well together. She's interested in horses and cars, and so am I, and we have a lot of the same friends. I'm sure she likes me. I don't understand why she backs away when—'

'I'll have a word,' said the duchess briskly. 'She's very young, you know. Only eighteen. And it's a big step for a girl. If she feels nervous, it won't be anything to do with you.' For a few moments longer she spoke reassuringly, anxious not to say anything that would paint a picture of Ronnie as anything less than a perfect future wife. Then she stood up to indicate that the interview was over. 'On your way out, ask one of the footmen to see whether Chay is anywhere in the house, will you? I'd like a word with him.'

While she was waiting, she went to the window of her writing room and stared across at the park. Ronnie would be riding somewhere out there. She went riding twice a day. Once in the early morning, for her own pleasure, and a second time in mid-morning because that was the hour at which debutantes were expected to parade and be admired in their becoming habits.

The duchess's conscience was not altogether easy in the matter of her daughter's social life. She had arranged everything that needed to be arranged, and for the first few weeks of the season had been conscientious in performing her duty as a chaperone. But sitting against the wall of a ballroom for hours on end was too boring for words. If a hostess offered bridge, the invitation was irresistible – because after all, Chay would always be there to keep an eye on Ronnie. And what harm could possibly come to her in such respectable venues, surrounded by carefully vetted friends and escorted by young men from approved lists; men who knew that their own reputations would be besmirched if they allowed any scandal to touch their innocent young partners?

Nevertheless, there was cause for self-reproach. For twenty-five years Lady Ranelegh had continued to invite to her ball not only the eminent men and women of her own generation, but also all the women who had been debutantes in her own daughter's first Season: the Season of 1914. Their own daughters, this year's debutantes, were welcomed almost as an afterthought: a politeness which need not interfere with the reunion of the middle-aged mothers.

The evening had been a stimulating one – but that did not excuse the fact that the duchess had not noticed any unhappiness on Ronnie's part. The unusually early supper that was always a feature of Lady Ranelegh's ball meant that the Delacourts had made their way there without hosting one of the dinners which were the usual prelude to a big occasion; so the duchess had not even enquired the name of Ronnie's partner, taking it for granted that it would be Malcolm Ross: an assumption that perhaps had been incorrect. And even though she would not have objected, she ought at least to have been aware of the moment when Malcolm disappeared with her daughter to some secluded place. She had left too much to Chay, who might, for all she knew, have been in search of seclusion on his own account in such a romantic setting.

She waited impatiently, but it was not Chay but Ronnie herself who came in.

'William said you're looking for Chay, but he's still out riding, with Anne. I'd had enough.'

'Come and sit down, darling. You're looking tired. Are you feeling all right?'

'Too many late nights,' said Ronnie. 'I might skip the fancy dress do this evening.'

'Did you enjoy Lady Ranelegh's ball?'

'It was all right. It's getting a bit boring, though, meeting the same people all the time.'

'Did anything special happen last night?'

'Yes, but I missed it. Lady Patricia being publicly expelled.' Ronnie, who had looked pale and lethargic when she first came in, brightened at the memory. 'Everyone's been talking about it this morning. Apparently Isabelle's written to her father, asking if she can go back to France. She won't be allowed to, of course.'

'I meant, did anything special happen to you?'

'Why should it?'

'Well, I've had two telephone calls this morning. Diana and Josephine both became engaged last night.'

'Good for them.'

'So, when shall I be able to announce *your* engagement?'

'No idea.' Ronnie stood up to leave, but was ordered back to her chair.

'Sit down, Ronnie. It's time we talked seriously about this. The Season's nearly over. Do you want to be the only debutante of your year who is still unattached at the end of it?'

'Why not? There'll be another Season next year.'

'And another generation of debutantes, young and fresh.'

'While I shall be on the shelf at nineteen? Well, I don't care.'

'You know what Nanny would say to that. Don't care was made to care. Just look ahead, Ronnie, and tell me how you see your future.' The duchess paused. Was this the moment to warn Ronnie that her father was dying? No; they had agreed that nothing should be said to spoil the carefree happiness of her debut. But it was possible to give a warning without being too explicit.

'You can't expect to live at home for ever as the daughter of the house. When your father and I aren't there any more, and Chay is the duke and his wife, whoever she may be, is the duchess, do you see yourself as staying on as the spinster sister, the maiden aunt?'

'No, of course not.' Ronnie fidgeted uncomfortably.

'Well, things don't just happen. They have to be arranged. You're going to need your own establishment. Something suitable to the way you've been brought up. With a sufficient income to run it.'

'And a husband to provide it?'

'Yes. No need to make a face. How else do you expect to be supported for the rest of your life?'

'It oughtn't to be necessary.'

'But it is, isn't it? Just look at this calmly. What are you qualified to do? Well, don't waste too much time trying to think of something. You're qualified to take the place in society to which your birth entitles you. And very quickly, when you have a home of your own, you will qualify to be its mistress because you know how things ought to be run.'

'But apart from that I'm completely useless.'

There was an accusing note in her voice which the duchess found irritating. Was she suggesting that her mother ought to have fitted her for some different role in life?

'It makes sense that you should find someone suitable and settle down with him. Now Malcolm Ross—'

'Oh, Malcolm's been getting at you, has he?'

'He's upset, very naturally, because he doesn't understand why you should turn him down.'

'It's because I'm not in love with him, that's why.'

The duchess struggled to control her annoyance. 'You don't need to be in love with him. As long as you like him enough to see him as a congenial companion, love will grow after you're

136

married. And what you have to remember is that you're marrying not just a husband but a way of life. That's very important, because in any marriage there may come moments when the husband may prove to be a disappointment in some way, but it doesn't matter as long as the two of you are still happy in the way of life.'

'I've heard that theory before.' There was a note of bitterness in Ronnie's voice which caused her mother to look at her in surprise.

'Then you ought to believe it.'

'But how can I pretend to love someone when I know how it feels to be really truly in love? Wanting to touch someone, wanting to be touched; to be kissed. When Malcolm steps towards me, I always want to step back.'

The duchess paid no attention to this last remark because she was perturbed by what had preceded it. But before she could enquire what – or rather, whom – her daughter was talking about, Ronnie had a question of her own.

'Were you in love with Pa when you married him?'

'I didn't know him very well. The marriage was arranged by our parents. But I liked what I knew. And as I've just been telling you, love grew afterwards. I remember—' Suddenly upset, she was unable to finish the sentence. She remembered the day on which the War Office telegram had arrived to inform her, with regret, that her husband had been wounded. She remembered, too, a telephone call from a kind hospital nurse. 'Your husband asked me to let you know that he's here, in England. He's going to be all right.' The depth of her early despair and the breathless surge of her subsequent joy had been enough to tell her that yes, she was very much in love with her husband.

And now the sadness had returned. There would be no War Office telegram on this occasion, but no reassuring telephone call either. She ought to be with him now. It was for Ronnie's sake that she remained in London and Ronnie ought to be playing her part. An unreasonable anger fuelled her unhappiness and as she searched for a handkerchief she turned her head away. She had always been careful not to display emotion in front of her children.

'What's the matter, Ma?'

'Nothing. An old memory, that's all. Of the time when your father nearly died at Ypres. And that's another thing.' She was pulling herself together now. 'You may not be right in thinking that there'll be another Season next year. Even if there is, there may not be many young men around to take part in it. I'm very much afraid that we're going to have another war, even though nobody wants it.'

It was almost irritating to see the surprise on her daughter's face. Did young women these days not take any interest at all in the affairs of the world? But perhaps it was all her own fault, for talking only about parties and clothes at breakfast. That had all been part of the deliberate decision not to spoil Ronnie's debutante summer with any unpleasant news.

But it was time to return to the point.

'This business of falling in love. The first time it happens, when you're still young, it takes you so much by surprise that you often feel you can't control it, that it's the most important thing that's ever happened to you, that you simply must have the man to whom the feeling has attached itself. But the truth is, and you must believe me, that you're really falling in love with love, not with any individual. And it doesn't last. Who is it?'

'It's not important. I'm not likely to see him again.'

'Good. Then what are you going to do, Ronnie? You can't go on simply being a daughter. There are decisions to be made, and I can't make them all for you. You don't have to choose Malcolm Ross if you don't want to, but . . .'

Ronnie gave a lethargic shrug of the shoulders. 'He's all right.'

'Then you must give him a little encouragement. You can't expect a man to go on proposing if he thinks you're going to turn him down every time. A word of apology would be in order. That you weren't feeling well last night, perhaps, or that you ought to have asked for time to think about it instead of being so definite. Just a hint, that's all he'll need.'

'All right,' said Ronnie. Her voice was tired and unenthusiastic as she stood up to leave. But the important thing for her mother was that she had agreed. The duchess had not really expected it to be quite so easy.

18

Lady Patricia's first action on the morning after Lady Ranelegh's ball was naturally to dismiss her social secretary. The hostess's snub had been devastating and public, but its wording, though sarcastic in intention, had offered a very slight possibility of escaping complete humiliation: a tiny chink of light through the keyhole of a door which was intended to close the path between Lady Patricia le Vaillant and society. Yes, of course the invitation to Miss Armitage had been a simple mistake. A confusion of dates. The stupidity of an incompetent girl.

Miss Frith arrived as usual punctually at ten o'clock. Dressed as always in a navy-blue dress with wide white collar, and with her hair neatly waved round her shining, well-scrubbed face, she carried the morning's letters up to her employer's boudoir, also as usual. Her polite enquiry about the enjoyment of the previous evening's ball was equally to be expected, although unfortunate in the circumstances.

Five minutes later she rushed from the room, in tears and totally confused – for it would have been a mistake to give her any detailed explanation of her inadequacies.

Lady Patricia gave a faint sigh as she surveyed the correspondence with which she would now have to deal herself. But the Season was nearing its end. Already the invitations for all the dances and dinners had been received and accepted, and a house had been taken for Cowes Week. She had made up her mind in the taxi returning home on the previous evening that Isabelle should put on a brave face and keep all her engagements. There might be one or two brief moments of embarrassment, but few hostesses would dare to say or write in so many words that she would not after all be welcome.

Isabelle arrived at that moment, bursting into the boudoir. 'How could you do this to Betty?' she demanded. 'She's crying her eyes out downstairs.'

'Who is Betty?' enquired Lady Patricia frostily.

'Oh really, Maman. How many people do you reduce to tears every morning? It's a terrible thing to do, to blame her for something you did quite deliberately yourself.'

'You forget yourself, Isabelle. I don't admit—'

'You don't admit what everyone in London knows now? Well, I've told her that she's not to leave the house until I come down with a reference from you to help her get another job.'

'You must realise that I can't possibly—'

'If you won't do it, I shall write it myself. And everyone will guess why. And then I shall phone up all my friends.' She paused, and added sombrely, 'If I still have any. I shall ask them all to look out for a job for her.'

'This is none of your business, Isabelle.'

'Just for today it's my business. I agree that it won't be for much longer. I've written to Papa, telling him that I want to go back to France.'

'And he will write back ordering you to stay in England. If there's another war, France won't be a safe place for an English girl.'

For a moment Isabelle looked startled, before presumably deciding that talk of war was irrelevant to their present discussion. 'I'm not an English girl, I'm a French girl.'

'You are my daughter. You are descended from a noble English family and you are doing the Season in England. It would be ridiculous to abandon it and waste all the contacts you've made.'

'Contacts! You promised me that this was a time when I'd make new friends. Well, I shouldn't think now that anyone's ever going to speak to me again. Especially Peggy, considering what—'

'Miss Armitage is of no importance. A nobody.'

'That's not true. She's clever and friendly and I like her. And anyway, even nobodies have feelings. It wasn't her fault she was in the conservatory that time. I wish I'd never told you about it. I never wanted to follow Chay in like that. You made me. I ought to have stood up to you then. Well, I'm not staying here to be bossed around any longer. If I can't go back to France, then I shall find somewhere here to live on my own.'

Lady Patricia was not unduly alarmed by this threat. 'And where will you find the money to pay the rent? To eat?' she enquired.

'I'll get a job.'

'You? Don't be ridiculous, Isabelle. What are you qualified to do?'

'I can speak French. Translate it, or be an interpreter. There must be people who need that sort of thing. I shall go to an agency.'

'Listen to me, Isabelle.' It was time to re-establish authority.

'I've had enough of listening to you. I'm tired of being told where I should go, what I should wear, who I should marry – even if the person you choose doesn't want me. I'm going to look after myself from now on. Other women can do it.'

'You're not a woman, you're a child. A minor. A dependent daughter. And women of the lower classes may work, but no one in society would even consider—'

'I don't wish to be part of society. And after what happened last night, society will be glad to be rid of me.'

'This is all quite—' But Lady Patricia checked herself as the door opened to admit the butler. Infuriating though one's daughter might be, one did not raise one's voice to her in front of servants.

'Miss Armitage and Miss Venables are downstairs.' He was holding their cards on a silver tray.

'Tell them that I'm Not At Home. Naturally.' Really, temporary staff were more trouble than they were worth. How could anyone in his right mind have expected her to be at home at this hour of the morning.

'It's Miss le Vaillant they have called to see, your ladyship.'

Isabelle's face lit up in incredulous delight. No longer a sulky child, she ran from the room. Twenty minutes passed before she reappeared with a look of triumph in her eyes.

'Peggy Armitage is very anxious that I should keep the engagements which have already been accepted for me. She doesn't want to feel that she's responsible for spoiling my

Season. She's a really sweet girl. I like her very much. And Anne's going to back me up. She says people won't cut me if they see I still have friends.'

Because the completion of the Season's social events was so important, Lady Patricia managed to hold back her opinion of the ostentatiously rich Miss Armitage and the genteelly poor Miss Venables. They had no right to interfere in what was none of their business; but since their visit had had the required effect there was no cause to object. But her restraint did not survive Isabelle's next announcement.

'So I told them that I didn't want to go on living here and Peggy said there was plenty of room at the house they've taken and she was sure that Lady Menzies would chaperone me as well as her.'

'You . . . You . . .' Lady Patricia's indignation robbed her of breath. She could have claimed that her daughter had no right to leave the house without her permission, but instead put forward a purely social objection. 'The occasions to which someone like Miss Armitage is invited are not at all on the level of those which you are expected to attend.'

'I'm not sure that you're right about that.' The fighting note had disappeared from Isabelle's voice, perhaps because she knew that she had won. 'Ever since she became a friend of Ronnie and Chay, she's been at all the best places. Anyway, Anne Venables promised that if there are times when my invitations don't fit with Peggy's, I could go with her. So I shall be all right. I've told Estelle to start packing my clothes. So it seems that I shan't be a social leper after all. I'm sure you'll be pleased about that.'

Not many people could leave Lady Patricia le Vaillant at a loss for words, but her daughter had managed it. There was no point in uttering threats or orders which she could not enforce. But it would not take long for Isabelle to discover the difficulties of life without an allowance. She would return.

The sound of footsteps approaching the door made her wonder if the return was to be even sooner than she could have expected, but it was Miss Frith, her face tear-swollen but determined, who came into the room.

'I've come for my reference, Lady Patricia. And a week's wages in lieu of notice.'

The impudence of it! But perhaps she had some kind of right to the money. Lady Patricia had no wish to become involved in a sordid squabble over cash. She indicated that her ex-social secretary should bring her handbag within reach, and extracted the necessary notes.

'Thank you, your ladyship. And the reference?'

'You can't possibly expect me to say—'

'Miss Isabelle promised me—'

'Unfortunately Miss Isabelle has forgotten about you.'

There was a long silence in which the two women stared at each other, each determined not to be the first to give in. It was Miss Frith, as expected, who spoke first, but not, unfortunately, in surrender.

'Well, I suppose that if you don't think me worthy of a recommendation, your ladyship, you won't be surprised if I use my own discretion in dealing with the photographs.'

'Photographs? What photographs?'

'They've just arrived from a newspaper. Pictures of Miss Armitage and Lady Menzies, with the proof of four paragraphs to be printed beside them. The editor feels he ought to have your confirmation that you still want to have the story published. But according to Miss Isabelle, the details need to be amended.'

What a fool Isabelle was! Did she really want the details of her humiliation splashed all over the London evening papers?

'Those photographs were addressed to me. Hand them over at once.'

Miss Frith took a package out of the capacious handbag in which she kept her notebook, but she kept a firm grip on it, waiting. This was nothing short of blackmail. One should never give in to blackmail. On the other hand, the price was not particularly high. A few scribbled words. Without speaking, Lady Patricia turned back to the desk at which she had been sitting and wrote the required recommendation.

Miss Frith read it carefully before handing over the packet of photographs. 'Thank you, your ladyship. I hope that you and your daughter will enjoy the rest of the Season.'

She left the room with her head held high. Such a little mouse she had seemed at her interview as she listened to the duties she would be required to perform, and again later as she made notes and accepted instructions and nodded her head in understanding. What had just happened must be all Isabelle's fault. A stupid, wilful, undutiful daughter. Without warning Lady Patricia found herself overcome by rage. Had Isabelle been in the room, she would have slapped her face. Had the interfering Miss Armitage dared to appear, she would have taken her by the shoulders and shaken her and shaken her until the girl cried out in pain and apologised.

Her fists clenched and her teeth ground together as the rage grew. A red mist blinded her eyes and seemed to be smothering her mind and even blanketing her lungs so that she could hardly breathe. With a sudden furious gesture she swept to the floor everything that lay on the writing surface of the bureau, and then began to pull out each tiny drawer in turn and hurl it across the room.

Estelle, her maid, came running, her tongue clicking with shock as soon as she saw that the white carpet was stained with ink from her employer's fountain pen. She went down on her knees, preparing to dab it clean. As though it mattered what happened to the furnishings of a rented house! All the same, the presence of a servant was enough to restore Lady Patricia's self-control.

'Leave that to a housemaid,' she said abruptly. 'I need you to dress me.' For she was still wearing the peignoir in which she habitually took breakfast in her bedroom. But on returning to her dressing room she paused in an uncharacteristic state of confusion. Her social secretary's disgraceful behaviour had temporarily put out of her mind that far more important matter of Isabelle's escape to the sanctuary of Lady Menzies' chaperonage. How tongues would wag when they learned that Lady Patricia le Vaillant had been deserted by her daughter!

She would have to be ill, of course; there were no other possibilities. Not with anything infectious or contagious, but with something which would confine her to bed, preventing her from performing the necessary duties of chaperonage. As she waved Estelle aside with a murmured reference to a feeling of faintness and the need to return to her bed, her mind was already running through a list of appropriate illnesses.

Beneath her social calculations, though, a fierce hatred was simmering of the two impudent girls who were so deliberately distancing Isabelle from her mother. One of these days she would teach them a lesson.

19

Anyone who was anyone was at St Margaret's, Westminster – except for the bride, who was late. Mrs Venables, sitting with Howard and Anne, looked at her watch to check the time. Well, brides were often late. But she might have expected this one to be different and to spring from the car on the dot of three o'clock rather than to keep waiting not only the congregation but also the crowd of onlookers and photographers who had gathered to see the Duke of Wiltshire's daughter in all her finery. Lady Veronica was such an impulsive girl as a rule, in a hurry to pursue an idea as soon as she had taken it into her head. Her decision to marry Malcolm Ross was itself an example of that. The suddenness of the engagement had surprised all her friends, and it was also characteristic that once the marriage had been arranged, she had wanted the wedding to take place as soon as possible. On this occasion, no-one had wanted to check her impatience. War seemed increasingly inevitable and, as an army officer, Ross would of course be among the first to be called into action. Everyone had been in a hurry. Now, though, Lady Veronica was undeniably late.

For her own part, Mrs Venables did not mind the delay at all. It provided an extended opportunity for her to smile at acquaintances and to emphasise by her presence that her daughter had become one of Lady Veronica's closest friends. But she could tell that the bridegroom was becoming anxious, unable to resist the temptation to turn in his seat from time to time and look down the empty aisle. It was impossible for the Venables contingent, sitting on the bride's side of the church with several rows of large hats in the way, to catch any glimpse of the duchess, or even to see whether she had yet taken her seat. But Lord Lambourn, who as a rule was notable for his calmness, was certainly showing signs of unease, almost as though he wouldn't put it past his sister to make a dash for freedom at the last moment. He was acting as one of the ushers, but by now all the guests had arrived. For the past few moments he had been standing at the end of the front pew with a worried expression on his face, looking back towards the door of the church as though wondering whether he should investigate what was wrong.

For Mrs Venables this was merely a pleasant social occasion and she was in the happy position of not minding that one of the Season's good catches must be cut off her list. Anne would be no good as a soldier's wife. She was too shy to be at home amongst the hard-riding, hard-drinking set of Guards officers. Her love of art and music and plants and solitude would never have endeared her to Malcolm Ross, or to most of the other young men who had thronged the ballrooms of Mayfair this Season.

This made it all the more extraordinary that it was Anne and not her brother who might perhaps emerge successfully from the social opportunities with which she had been presented at such cost.

It was difficult to be sure whether it was a relief or a disappointment that Howard had for some reason brought to an end his promising friendship with Peggy Armitage. There could never have been any question of the Armitages and Venables mixing socially, of course, and this might have led to difficulties, but the self-effacing manner in which Mr and Mrs Armitage had entrusted their daughter to the care of Lady Menzies suggested that they knew their place. And at the time when the relationship looked most promising, Mrs Venables had done her homework, as any responsible mother should. She had been able to report to her husband that Mr Armitage's fortune was quite sufficient to put Yewley back into a good state of repair. Mr Venables had pretended not to be interested, brushing the information aside with the comment that Howard must be left to make his own decisions; but he must certainly have been pleased at the thought that his heir might be spared the financial worries which had

147

dogged him for years. If only Howard himself had behaved more sensibly!

Looking at the possible alliance from the Armitages' point of view, such a family could not realistically expect their daughter to marry into the titled aristocracy. They would have been pleased enough to see her accepted by an old family, respected in its neighbourhood for generations.

It was also true that Peggy was a more acceptable young woman than might have been expected of someone with her upbringing. Her cleverness was sometimes too sharply expressed – but Howard was clever as well, and enjoyed that kind of conversation. On the whole, if he had asked his parents to accept the daughter of a self-made man as a daughter-in-law, they would not have made a fuss. But instead he had backed away and would finish the Season as unattached as when it began.

Anne, though! With a little careful management, Anne might have a triumph – which would be all the sweeter because it would enable her to outrank her aunts and cousins.

Giving credit where credit was due, Mrs Venables recognised that her daughter's first encounter with Lord Lambourn was not the result of her own efforts, but because Howard had been to the right school and made friends with the right people. Indeed, in making out her original list of acceptable matches, her ambition had stopped short of including a future duke. Anne, beautiful though she had become in the past few months, did not in her mother's opinion possess the confident personality needed by a duchess. It was unfortunate, in the new circumstances, that Anne herself seemed to share that view, since no one who saw them together could fail to recognise the young marquess's admiration for her. If only the child could somehow be persuaded to become more positive – and to recognise that although it might be up to the man to speak the words of a proposal of marriage, it was often necessary for the woman to give him an indication that the time was ripe.

Since most members of the congregation were chattering amongst themselves, there seemed no harm in doing the same. She leaned across Howard to speak to her daughter.

'I hope you'll manage to have a few minutes on your own with Chay at the reception,' she said. 'It's a well-known fact about weddings that they're infectious. Other people start thinking about marriage as well. A little striking while the iron is hot would be a good idea.'

'Really, Mother!' Anne's pale face flushed and she looked anxiously around to see whether anyone had overheard.

Between them, Howard was laughing. 'Really, Mother!' he repeated. 'Haven't you learned yet that the harder you push Anne one way the more likely she is to run in the other? Even if,' he added mischievously, 'your direction is really the one in which she'd like to go.'

Anne's flush deepened. She changed the subject. 'Do you think that's Isabelle's father she's sitting with? Two rows behind us, at the end of the pew.'

Observing and being observed was what most of the congregation had come to do, so Mrs Venables felt no compunction about turning in her seat to take a good look. So Lady Patricia had risen from her bed of unspecified illness, had she? Well, of course, she would not have wanted to miss the opportunity presented by another grand Delacourt occasion. No doubt she had summoned Isabelle's father in an attempt to bring their defiant daughter under control. What a handsome man he was, with an easy, smiling expression – so different from that of his wife, who always looked as though her face was as stiffly corseted as her body.

But something was happening. One of the ushers was hurrying up the aisle to speak to the bridegroom and his best man.

'Don't tell me Ronnie's going to leave Malcolm standing at the altar!' exclaimed Howard.

'Don't be ridiculous!' Mrs Venables dismissed the possibility. 'A duke's daughter! Unthinkable!'

'I'm not so sure,' said Anne. 'I was talking to her at her tea party yesterday and I think she's quite frightened. Not certain whether she's doing the right thing.'

'Every bride gets that feeling at some point,' Mrs Venables told her. 'It's quite natural. A kind of stage fright. It never lasts. All the same . . .' She glanced at her watch. Twenty minutes late. She had come to attend a society occasion, but how much more interesting it would be if she were to find herself a participant in some kind of scandal. And she was not the only one to feel like this: a general whispering was buzzing through the congregation. There was no doubt at all about it. Something was up. What had happened to Lady Veronica?

It was true that Ronnie was impulsive. Once she had decided upon some action, she was impatient to get on with it immediately. That did not mean, however, that she was always punctual. Many a young man had been left to drum his heels while she chatted on the telephone or argued with Marie about what dress she should wear.

On her wedding day, however, there was no excuse for hanging around. Naturally there was no choice of dress. The House of Worth had made her a wedding gown of the finest silk, embroidered in silver, which sparkled and glinted at every movement. The waist was pinched in, revealing how much weight she had lost in the past few weeks, but the skirt was full, making it easy to walk. There had been a dress rehearsal on the previous day, so that the six little bridesmaids and the two maids of honour could practise carrying the long train, and everything had gone smoothly.

Marie, too, had demanded and – with some impatience – had been allowed to practise various elaborate hairstyles; although the veil, she lamented, would prevent the final choice from being seen at its best. So once the process of decking out the bride began, it was completed so efficiently that Ronnie was standing in the hall of Delacourt House three minutes before the appointed time. It was her father who was late.

He came at last, walking with more care than usual down the winding staircase, and even before he reached her she could tell that this was one of his bad days.

'You're not well, Pa!' she exclaimed. 'You ought to rest.'

'And miss my only daughter's big day? Certainly not. I shall never get another chance to be father of the bride. And what a beautiful bride! The stable lads have certainly made a good job of grooming you.'

'Oh really, Pa!' Sometimes her father carried his equine analogies too far. 'But you look pretty distinguished yourself.'

'It's the uniform.' He was, of course, wearing morning dress, meticulously pressed, which gave a svelte line to his thin body.

'All men look their best in uniform of one kind or another. You'll notice that with Malcolm. Most of the time you've only seen him in mess dress or his penguin suit. It won't be like that all the time.'

He was giving her a warning – and it was something she had realised for herself already. For the past few days, in fact, she had been in a state of panic as she considered how little she knew about Malcolm, except as a partner in escapades or at dances. What would he be like at breakfast? If they had children, what kind of father would he be? And, most disquieting of all, what would he be like at night?

On this last subject she had tried to elicit some information from her mother, but the duchess had merely given her a reassuring pat – which was not reassuring at all – and said, 'As long as you love each other, darling, it will be all right. Just do what comes naturally.'

Ronnie's anxiety, as she prepared to go out to the waiting car, must have shown on her face, for the duke looked at her more searchingly.

'Too pale, really,' he said. 'Marie could have given you a little colour now that you're just about to become a married woman. But never mind. A beautiful bride. Off we go, then.'

Marie, who had been awaiting her opportunity, sprang forward to gather up the train, and with many exclamations of *'Attention un moment, s'il vous plait, milady. Comme ça. Parfait!'* helped to settle her mistress – and the dress – smoothly into the Rolls.

Sitting straight backed, Ronnie waited for her father to join her, but saw with alarm that he was needing to lean against the open door while he summoned the strength to climb in. The chauffeur, Chivers, hurried to help him, but once inside he collapsed forward, allowing his grey top hat to slide to the floor as he gasped for breath.

'Where are your pills?' Ronnie began to feel in his pockets, but they were all empty. The line of a gentleman's suit should never be spoiled.

'Just taken two.' He managed to lean forward and tell Chivers to move off.

'Pa, dearest, you mustn't . . .'

'Can't stop now. Late already.'

It was Ronnie's turn to slide open the glass panel. 'Back to Delacourt House,' she ordered. 'As fast as you can go.'

'To St Margaret's,' commanded her father. In the mirror Chivers' eyes could be seen wavering indecisively between his two passengers. But the duke was his employer. Instead of turning back at the southern end of Park Lane, they continued on towards Westminster.

By the time the car drew to a halt the duke's breathing was so shallow and fast that it was clear this was more serious than any other of the attacks which had regularly affected his lungs ever since the war. Ronnie took command.

'Tell one of the ushers to ask Lord Lambourn and her grace to come here at once,' she ordered the chauffeur, still angry with him for disobeying her earlier instructions. While she waited, she made no attempt to move, although the crowds who regularly flocked to society weddings had their cameras at the ready and the fidgeting bridesmaids were anxious to take up their duties. Chay and his mother came hurrying out of the church and stepped into the back of the car to face her. The duchess gave a gasp of alarm as she took in the situation.

'We must go home and send for the doctor,' said Ronnie.

'But the wedding . . .' began her mother, although the expression of anxiety as she took her husband's hand showed that she too understood how serious the situation was.

'The wedding will have to be cancelled. Postponed, anyway. You must see . . .' Ronnie's eyes filled with tears. It was clear to her – and it must surely be equally clear to the others – that her father was dying.

'Just a moment,' said Chay. He had a word with one of the policemen who was keeping the spectators off the street. When he returned, he made an attempt at a reassuring smile, although his face was as pale as Ronnie's own. 'There's an ambulance waiting very close, in case anyone in the crowd should collapse. It will be here in a couple of minutes, to take him to hospital. That's the best thing, Ronnie. Truly.'

'But I can't possibly . . .'

'Yes, you must.' The duchess, guessing that her daughter was still thinking about the wedding, spoke firmly, while continuing to squeeze her husband's hand and stroke his cheek in a display of affection which Ronnie had never observed before. 'I shall go to the hospital with Charles, naturally. That can be explained. But there can be no question of cancelling the ceremony at this notice. All those people waiting for you. The bishop. And Malcolm. Think how he must be worrying at this moment. You have a duty of kindness. And a position in society to maintain. I do understand how you feel, Ronnie darling, but you can be driven to the hospital within an hour.'

Unusually – for she was not a demonstrative woman – she kissed her daughter on her tear-damp cheek. Then the ambulance arrived, causing a frisson of speculation amongst the sightseers.

After her parents had been driven away, Ronnie burst noisily into tears. But although Chay put a comforting arm round her shoulders, his message was as unwelcome as her mother's.

'You can't let Malcolm down now,' he said. 'We're already twenty minutes late. He must be imagining all sorts of explanations. Humiliations.'

'In a week or two . . .'

'In a week or two Pa may be dead. No need to be mealy-mouthed about it. We both know, don't we? Then the family will be in mourning and it would be unthinkable . . . And by the time a decent interval has passed, Malcolm will be in France and goodness knows how long it will be before he sees you again. You can't ask so much of the man you love, Ronnie. Now dry your face and straighten your shoulders and off we go.'

Ronnie did as she was told. Moving like an automaton she stepped out of the car and stood still while the bridesmaids and maids of honour fussed around her train. Chay kissed her lightly and then offered his arm. The wedding service was, at last, about to begin.

Inside the church the organist, whose fingers had been meandering over the keyboard in an increasingly desultory fashion, broke with relief into the Wedding March. Every head turned to see the bride appear – and there was a collective gasp as it was observed that she was on the arm not of her father but of her brother. What was more, she had been crying and was still not far from tears.

The same question rippled along every pew. 'What's happened to the duke?' So strong was the atmosphere of curiosity and anxiety that the bishop who was to conduct the service – himself a distant relative of the Wiltshires – took the unusual step of making an announcement before the wedding began.

'I am sorry to have to tell you that His Grace the Duke of Wiltshire was taken ill while on his way to St Margaret's and has been taken to hospital. The reception will still be held at Delacourt House as arranged, after this service, but the family hopes that you will understand if they themselves withdraw from it to be at his bedside. And now, dear friends, we are gathered here today . . .'

The service continued. The bride, of course, had her back to the congregation, so that any distress she was feeling could not be seen. Her shimmering dress was both beautiful and stylish and her head-dress exactly appropriate for a young aristocrat. Her long train had been carefully arranged behind her by the six sweet little bridesmaids who were now twirling their posies under the watchful eyes of the two maids of honour. Everything – save for the fact that it was Chay who gave the bride away – proceeded just as expected.

Mrs Venables gave little attention to the marriage vows, which a man like Malcolm Ross would probably not keep for very long, and instead considered how the day's events would affect her own plans.

It was easy to guess that the family had been divided about how to deal with the duke's collapse – and from that it could be deduced that he was not merely ill but dying. Ronnie, to judge from her tearful expression, must have wanted to postpone the wedding. The duchess, one of the old school, would have argued that personal distress should never be allowed to interfere with social obligations. And Chay? Thinking calmly, Chay must have realised that the groom, a serving officer, was likely to find himself posted into battle before very long, while the bride would be expected to enter a period of mourning as soon as her father died. He might have seen the marriage in terms of now or possibly never.

A family like the Wiltshires would take mourning seriously. So now it was not merely unlikely that Anne would have any opportunity to speak to Chay during the reception: he would also certainly withdraw from the house party which had been arranged at Yewley House for the first weekend in September.

Ronnie had already sent her regrets, because she would be away on her honeymoon. But Chay had accepted. The arrival of his acceptance had been a moment of triumph.

Mrs Venables had had great hopes of that house party. It would show Anne in her very best light, confident in her home surroundings. Her love for the old house and its gardens could not fail to endear her to a man who was also devoted to the home of his ancestors through many generations. She could have shown him her paintings and played the piano to him as well as joining in the tennis and croquet and games of charades which were the expected amusements in every weekend of this kind. And now the duke's collapse had spoiled all these plans. Really, thought Mrs Venables as the service ended and the organ swelled triumphantly into the Trumpet Voluntary, it was too, too trying.

Each of the thirty-two clocks in Delacourt House had struck midnight before Ronnie came back home, exhausted and crumpled, to find Malcolm anxiously waiting for her. He had been asked to act as host at the reception, in order that the guests should not feel completely abandoned. It had been followed by a dance which in normal circumstances would have continued into the small hours. But the sombre atmosphere had caused the guests two by two to leave early and it was to a silent building that she now returned.

'Darling!' Malcolm hurried out of the library to take her into his arms and smother her with wet kisses. 'I was afraid . . . How is he?'

'Still alive,' said Ronnie, resisting the temptation to wipe her lips dry. 'They're giving him oxygen. With a sort of machine to pump it in. But there's nothing, really, that they can do. The lung that's kept him going seems to have packed in completely. Ma and Chay are going to stay all night, but they sent me home.'

'Quite right. You're worn out. Come to bed.'

For a second Ronnie hesitated. She had eaten nothing since breakfast and by now was aware of her hunger, but there seemed something inappropriate about asking for sandwiches when her father was dying. She nodded her head and began wearily to climb the second flight of steps.

When they reached the upper gallery she turned automatically towards her own bedroom, but Malcolm took her by the hand and turned her in the other direction.

'The honeymoon suite awaits you,' he said. 'This way, your ladyship.'

It had always been intended that the first night should be spent at Delacourt House. As he flung open the door the scent of flowers, beautifully arranged in pale pyramids of colour, almost overwhelmed her. The tester bed had been given new hangings and the satin sheets were already turned down, awaiting the happy couple.

Sitting beside the door, Marie woke with a start and produced her button hook, ready to unfasten the many tiny silk-covered buttons down the front of her mistress's dress so that it could be taken away to join generations of tissue-wrapped Wiltshire wedding gowns; but Malcolm waved her away. Hurt, she closed the door quietly behind her, leaving the bride and groom to face each other.

How handsome Malcolm was, even with his broken nose! He was still wearing the mess uniform which suited him so well; now he pulled off the sash and began to unfasten the jacket.

Ronnie smiled at him. She was tired and she was unhappy and she wanted nothing better than to tumble into her own familiar bed and sleep for hours. But this was Malcolm's wedding night and she must play her part with at least a pretence of cheerfulness. They were chums, after all.

The effect of the smile on her husband was as though she had puffed a bellows towards a smouldering log to send flames suddenly roaring up the chimney. Tossing his jacket on to a chair he stood close to her and began to fumble with the tiny buttons. But his fingers were too thick and clumsy. To Ronnie's dismay he tore her dress open and tugged it off her shoulders so that it fell to the ground, leaving her only in her silk French camiknickers.

'Ronnie!' he exclaimed. 'Oh Ronnie, Ronnie.' Now it was his trousers and underpants which tumbled to the floor. To take off his socks and shoes he needed to sit down, but his eyes remained fixed on his wife's body.

Ronnie too was staring. She had seen Malcolm stripped to the waist before, but never completely naked: that would have been unthinkable. Trying to control her panicky breathing, she asked herself why she should feel so dismayed, even disgusted, by the man who was advancing towards her. She was in love with Malcolm, wasn't she? Wasn't she? And she had visited the stud when her father's racehorses were being mated, after all. But this was going to happen to her. Suddenly all her father's horsy analogies had ceased to be jokes and were coming true.

Malcolm slipped the thin straps off her shoulders, picked her up and carried her to the bed. And then he was on top of her, heaving up and down, muttering incomprehensible words, thrusting into her.

'Just do what comes naturally,' her mother had said, and Ronnie did her best. She tried to relax her body and allow whatever was happening to flow over her, but it hurt. She made her body rigid, pushing it hard against her husband's, but that hurt even more. Then came one thrust which hurt more than all the rest put together.

Malcolm's heaving and moaning came to a halt. He lay on top of her, his head on her shoulder and his hand stroking her body. For a long time he was still. Then he raised his head to look lovingly down at her.

'Sorry,' he said. 'I'm very sorry. I should have tried . . . It was having to wait so long. And worry. It'll be all right next time. It's only the first time.'

Ronnie nodded in what she hoped was an understanding manner.

'You'd probably like a bath,' he said.

Yes, she would, for her body was sticky and bleeding. Though how odd it was that she should apparently need his permission for such a little thing – and in her own home.

'But don't be long,' he added. 'I'll be waiting.'

Lying back in the bath, Ronnie thought over the events of the day: her father's illness, the wedding that was far from being the carefree affair which she had expected, and what she could only think of as Malcolm's attack on her. But there was one other matter which she must not allow to enter her thoughts again.

The hospital to which the duke had been taken was the one which had treated his earlier illnesses. It was the hospital to which the Wiltshires, in gratitude, had sent an invitation to their ball for the use of any of its young doctors who was not on duty. If it hadn't been for that invitation, she would never have met Laurie. There had been moments even while she was sitting at her father's side, holding his hand, when she had found herself wondering whether Laurie was still working there or whether he had already left for Liverpool. If she were to stretch her legs by wandering out into a corridor, might she . . . ? She had been ashamed of her hope, but could not quite thrust it away.

Laurie would have been gentle and kind. Laurie would have given her pleasure and made her laugh. Her longing for him now, as she lay in the cooling bath, was almost unbearable. It was the memory of Laurie, she realised now, that had made Malcolm's body so unexpectedly distasteful.

Malcolm was a decent chap. They were friends. But someone – her mother – ought to have realised that she needed time to free herself completely from one man before tying herself down to another.

No, that wasn't fair. She was the one who ought to have realised. She had been a fool – but as Chay had warned her once, she would have to live with it. The bath water was cold by now, because she hoped that by staying away as long as possible she would find Malcolm asleep when she returned. But what difference would one small delay make? From now on he would be sleeping – and not just sleeping – in her bed every night. Every night.

20

The tenth Duke of Wiltshire, a stranger to himself in his new uniform and new title, stood to attention as the coffin containing his father's body was carried into Cleeve village church.

The church was already well populated with marble effigies of his ancestors, reminders of the fact that the dead man had been the head of one of the greatest families in the land. That fact made the present simple ceremony seem curiously muted and parochial. In the normal course of events there would have been a later memorial service in London, almost a society occasion, at which his fellow members of the House of Lords could pay their respects. But this was not a time when any events could be expected to take their normal course. Everyone believed that war could only be a day or two away. Chay himself had already received his calling-up papers. Allowed three days' grace on compassionate grounds, he would have to leave almost as soon as the funeral was over.

There was a sense in which the simple village service and the lack of pomp were suitable enough. The ninth duke had never chosen to take any part in national affairs. He had done his bit for king and country as a young man, and had suffered for it for the rest of his life. So he had been content to live quietly, the custodian of his castle and his people and his land. Caring for them was his way of fulfilling his duty.

As a proof of his caring he had taken pains to ensure that his only son should be well prepared to take over his responsibilities. Chay did indeed feel responsible; but just at the very time when he most needed to take the reins, he was being forced to leave. John Fenton, the agent, was competent enough in day-to-day management. He would be able, no doubt, to see to the general maintenance of the land and its timber. He would deal efficiently with the tenant farmers, although probably they would suffer from an insistence on keeping to exact dates for the payment of their rents. The old duke – though not so old: he was only in his fifties when he died – was always prepared to be sympathetic in cases of hardship for which there was a genuine excuse, but an employee would feel obliged to stick to the rules.

Day-to-day management, however, was not likely to be enough. Fenton would be faced with unprecedented situations and decisions which could have huge consequences.

One decision was crucially important. What was going to happen to Cleeve Castle once the country was at war? A note of warning had been sounded only a few days before Ronnie's wedding, when the county billeting officer had called. No one could deny that Cleeve had room to accommodate dozens of evacuees from the cities, but in spite of that the billeting officer had decided to wait and see what happened.

'If I send you evacuees and then the Army decides to requisition the castle it will be unsettling for the children and I may have difficulty finding other billets,' she had told the old duke as he prepared to leave for his daughter's wedding in London. 'You may feel, your grace, that it would be wise to make some suitable arrangement for the duration yourself rather than have one thrust on you.'

But the duke had already been too tired and ill to contemplate such a disastrous necessity, and now Chay could not think where to start. Everyone knew that occupation by the military would be destructive, and he strongly suspected that school-children might prove almost as bad, if he were to invite even a reputable school to evacuate itself to Cleeve.

Besides, although the castle would certainly be safe from bombing, its lack of adequate heating and hot water would not provide a healthy atmosphere for large numbers of children. The comfort of his family home depended on an army of servants, but already the younger ones had begun to leave, either to join the Forces or to look for work in factories.

Chay castigated himself for allowing his mind to stray to such matters as buckets of coal and jugs of hot water as the funeral service began. But if he were to be honest with himself, his worries about the future were so great that he was finding it difficult to grieve as he ought. He forced himself to fix his eyes and concentration on the coffin, which had been carried in and set down in its place before the altar. The bearers stepped aside, stood for a moment with heads bowed, and then retired.

This was a time when he ought to think only about his father, but his worries about the future would not go away. His own immediate prospects in the RAF were straightforward enough. Alone in the sky he would be expected to display skill and courage and initiative, and because he loved flying it would be a glorious adventure; but from the moment when he reported to a commanding officer he would not be expected to take important decisions but simply to do what he was told.

His mother's life would also be ruled by a sense of duty. If, as everyone expected, the outbreak of war was marked by the bombing of London, it would not be safe for her to live in Delacourt House. There were other possibilities, however. From her grandmother she had inherited the island of Dounsay, in Orkney, and also a house in Devon which was currently let but could be reclaimed. She would want to stay at Cleeve, though; she was president of numerous county organisations, from the Red Cross to the Girl Guides. Cleeve, as it happened, had no dower house on the estate, so any plans for the castle's wartime use, whether under requisition or by voluntary negotiation, must include the promise of self-contained accommodation for the new duke's mother. And her presence would be invaluable in keeping an eye on strangers in the castle.

And what about Ronnie? Chay ought by now to be able to feel that his sister, who was staring down at the printed order of service without making any attempt to join in the singing of the first hymn, was, so to speak, off his hands – a married woman. But she seemed to be finding it difficult to make the transition from daughter to wife.

Ronnie had always been devoted to her father, so it was natural that the shock of his collapse while he was actually in the car with her on the way to her wedding should have affected her deeply. Half guilty and half angry that the ceremony had not been postponed, she had refused to leave Delacourt House during the ten days in which he struggled for breath before finally giving up the ghost. It had been impossible in the circumstances for Malcolm to force her to go away with him on their honeymoon, or to prevent her from travelling to Cleeve with the rest of the family and remaining there for the funeral.

Now Malcolm, like Chay himself, was under orders. He had originally arranged for a honeymoon in France, but the worsening international situation had persuaded him to abandon that plan and instead accept the duchess's suggestion that they should spend it on her Orkney island. Now there would be no time for the young couple to make even that journey. Malcolm must rejoin his regiment, leaving behind a young wife who had had no opportunity to learn how to live either with a husband or without one. Would she be able to cope?

All over England at this moment, no doubt, other girls were facing exactly this situation, and he would have expected someone like Ronnie to be more courageous than most. It was hard to believe that the listless young woman beside him in her black silk suit bore any relation to the high-spirited debutante who had danced the Season away so energetically.

A picture flashed into his mind: a picture that had been caught by a magazine photographer at his sister's own ball. Three girls in white ball dresses, unconsciously forming themselves into a triangle with Ronnie at its apex. Yes, that was the answer to the problem of Ronnie: her friends. In the absence of a husband she must rely on her friends for company. No doubt she would volunteer for some kind of war work, but perhaps one of the other girls would join up at the same time with her, to keep her company. That would be a reassurance to Malcolm as well as to Chay himself. Anne Venables, for example . . . But no; he had promised himself that he would not think about Anne today.

The organ swelled into the last verse of the hymn, fitting for a soldier who had at last succumbed to the wounds he had suffered in action.

> Splendid they passed, the great surrender made,
> Into the light that never more shall fade.
> All that they hoped for, all they had, they gave
> To save mankind; themselves they could not save.

Unlike Ronnie, who remained silent, Malcolm was singing lustily, and even the duchess's voice quavered only on the last few words. She had chosen the hymn, 'O valiant hearts', herself, never having concealed her feeling that the athletic, polo-playing young man she had married in 1914 had died on the Ypres battlefield. Because she was a woman who always accepted her obligations, she had cared for the semi-invalid who was eventually returned to her and had accepted the quiet existence that his state of health made necessary. But it could not have been the kind of married life she envisaged when she had walked down the aisle of St Margaret's, Westminster, twenty-five years before her daughter.

That dream broken by war was one of the reasons why Chay did not intend to propose to Anne, although she was the one he had chosen from among the various contenders for his hand. For a second time he reminded himself that he was not going to think about Anne today. As the congregation settled back into the pews, he forced himself to give his full attention to the service.

It was Ronnie who, much later that day, shattered his resolution. The tenants, after paying their respects to the new duke, had returned to their homes. The Delacourts had few kinsmen in England, but the duchess's brother and sister and some of her nieces and cousins would be staying the night at Cleeve. When Ronnie signalled after tea that she would like a walk, Chay was glad to escape into the gardens.

'Have you thought what you're going to do with yourself, Ronnie, if Malcolm goes off to France?'

'When, not if. Yes, I have. I sat down and tried to decide if there was anything I was good at. A rather shaming experience. The only thing I came up with was driving cars, so I'm going to try and join something called the Motor Transport Corps. It would mean acting as a kind of chauffeur, really.'

For the first time that day Ronnie smiled. 'It was quite funny. I told Malcolm what I had in mind at breakfast this morning, when Ma was in the room with us. He got quite worried because he said I'd be driving dashing young officers around all the time – and I suppose he knows what dashing young officers get up to! So Ma said no, of course not, you had to be very senior to have a driver, and she knew an elderly general who'd be delighted to have me and could be guaranteed to treat me like a granddaughter. So there we are! Even in wartime, all the right strings get pulled.'

'You'll miss Malcolm. It's hard on you, being separated after such a very short time.'

Ronnie didn't answer directly, but answered his concern with one of her own. 'And you'll miss Anne. You would have been going off to spend the weekend at Yewley tomorrow, wouldn't you, if—'

'Yes, and I'd hoped to invite her back to Cleeve. With Howard, but without her mother if possible.'

'Are you in love with her, Chay?'

'Her mother?' Chay put on such a show of astonishment that Ronnie laughed aloud and some of the old animation returned to her eyes.

'Anne, you idiot. Are you in love with Anne? But of course you are. Anyone can see that. Well, surely her mother's on your side.'

'That could be counter-productive. It was an interesting Season in that way. There were lots of mothers pushing their daughters in my direction, but first prize for pushiness goes jointly to Lady Patricia and Mrs Venables. Isabelle, on the whole, went along with what her mother wanted.'

'Until the great rebellion.'

'As you say. Full marks to Isabelle at last. With Anne it's a bit different, though. She's so embarrassed by the way her mother tries to steer her in my direction that she tends to stand back and make it clear that the campaign has nothing to do with her.'

'But she wouldn't go as far as turning you down just to spite her mother. She's crazy for you.'

'That's the sort of thing I like to be told. But she's never said it herself. If I could get her without her mother, she wouldn't have to prove anything. But then—' He paused unhappily.

'Then what?'

'I was thinking while we were in church. About how our parents got married in 1914 and then Pa went off to the war and when he came back he wasn't the same man. I mean, for all I know he may have been a better chap, but not the same. And he might have been killed, and left Ma a widow with a baby. I don't suppose either of them realised, on their wedding day, how terrible war is, but I can't pretend that *I* don't realise. How can I decently ask anyone to take on all that anxiety and loneliness?' He checked himself, dismayed to realise that he was being tactless. Ronnie, after all, had just done exactly that. 'Well, of course, *you* have. You've been very brave.'

'Brave!' Ronnie's voice expressed contempt for herself. 'When someone calculates a risk and then takes it, that's brave. But me! Malcolm caught me on the rebound and lots of my friends were getting engaged and Ma rushed me into a wedding and I never stopped to think. That's not brave. It's stupid.'

'But it's all right, isn't it, Ronnie? I mean, Malcolm's a decent chap.'

'Yes, of course.' But the pause that followed was a painful one, and Ronnie's next question was alarming. 'Do most girls enjoy it, Chay? You know what I mean.'

He knew what she meant and put an arm sympathetically round her shoulders. 'Yes, they do. Perhaps not always the first time or two, but it will soon be all right. Believe me.'

'How soon is soon? We may not have so long. Never mind.' Ronnie sighed away her doubts. 'We've got off the subject, which is you. It's all very well being high minded and not asking Anne to commit herself to you, but if you don't say anything at all how will she ever know you care about her? Instead of being lonely and anxious she'll be lonely and unhappy. You ought to let her make up her own mind which she wants. She's more sensible than I am. She'll think it through.'

'You're certainly telling me what I want to hear.'

'Well, there you are, then. Even if the only thing you say is that you feel you ought not to say anything more, she'll be happy to know.' Ronnie gave a sad laugh. 'Listen to who's talking! The fount of all worldly wisdom.'

'We'd better be getting back.' Still with his arm round his sister's shoulders, Chay turned her to face the castle.

What a dinosaur of a building it was, with its mock-medieval battlements and massive stone walls! Chay loved Cleeve with all his heart, but that didn't prevent him from recognising its absurdity as the mock relic of a long-past age. It was not so much a caricature as the very essence of a castle: a huge version of every young boy's favourite toy, from which tiny cannons could fire matchsticks at painted tin besiegers.

A stranger, looking at it from outside as Ronnie and Chay were looking now, would find it hard to believe that such a building could be a family home. Yet only a few months ago it had been exactly that. Ronnie in the schoolroom, Chay himself tinkering with his cars and racing them, the duchess busying herself with household management and good works and the duke defying ill-health to ensure that what he had inherited from his ancestors should be handed down to the next generation in good heart. They had all been happy, in a quiet way. And although the estate had suffered as much as any other from the years of depression, the local community had been held together by the stability of its centre. Chay had the right to feel proud of his inheritance.

But now? His father was dead. His sister was married, and when she bore her first son, the boy would be heir to a different title, a different home, a different estate. His mother might stay on at Cleeve, but the heart of the castle would shrink to the confines of a widow's quarters. His farming tenants, who in the past had looked inwards, to the family who owned their land, would be forced to take a wider outlook, behaving as the national interest demanded in wartime.

And Chay himself was off to the war, just like his father twenty-five years earlier. He was not frightened of fighting, but he was frightened about what would happen to Cleeve while it was out of his control.

What would he find when he returned? He could give no answer to that question. The only thing he could know for certain, as the years of peace ticked towards their end, was that nothing would ever be the same again.

PART TWO

War

21

The Season had ended, the war had begun, and Peggy Armitage
was a schoolgirl again. It was no fun going back to Queen
Mary's. No fun at all.

'Don't pretend I didn't warn you,' said Jodie.

'You warned me.' Peggy wasn't going to admit it, but it was
her sister's earlier certainty that by doing the Season she would
be abandoning her hopes of Oxford which now provided the
greatest incentive to grit her teeth and settle down to her books
again. But she wasn't enjoying it much.

Take uniform, for example. There were a good many aspects
of life as a debutante that Peggy hadn't much enjoyed, or even
had scorned, but to her own surprise she had liked the dressing-
up side of it. Her father had been generous in more than money.
He had encouraged her to talk to his designers. Young Jeff
Marlow in particular, who came to her rescue when her leg was
in plaster, had explained how different styles demanded
different types of fabric; and, while assuring her that no
expense need be spared for her own wardrobe, had enjoyed
showing her how the designs of her dresses could be modified
to make them suitable for mass production. That had been
education of a different kind.

Now, however, she was back in navy-blue skirt, white blouse
and striped tie. She put them on at seven in the morning and
wore them until six in the evening; there was no longer any
need to change for lunch, for tea and for some evening ball.
Throughout the summer she had moaned about all those
changes, but insidiously they had become an accepted element
in her daily timetable. Each morning nowadays, as she pre-

pared to set off for school, she sighed at her own reflection in the mirror.

But the return to school uniform was only a symptom of a far greater problem. Although carefully protected, there was no doubt that in the course of the Season she had changed from a child to an adult – and now, from her own choice, she was having to pretend to be a child again. Only for two months, admittedly, but it was not only ridiculous but unnecessary. She could have asked her father – who allowed her everything she wanted – to employ a personal tutor for her. It really was all her sister's fault that it seemed necessary to stick to the plan that she had set out for herself.

One thing had not changed. Before Howard Venables had so hurtfully begun to avoid her at parties, talking to him had given her a scholar's view of life at Oxford, and Peggy was still determined to win a place at the university. It was that determination which prevented her from becoming discontented as she set to work again. It was a solitary experience: as the only Oxford candidate at Queen Mary's there was no one with whom she could share the anxieties of the approaching examination, and she missed the intellectual companionship of Bill Brownlow during Miss Downie's tutorials. But Oxford would bring new friendships and with that thought in mind Peggy applied herself once again to the old routines of school work: she studied textbooks and made notes and constructed outlines and wrote the essays that her teachers set her.

Besides, there was another kind of change to be considered. Although the Season had ended in a flurry of chatter about engagements and marriages and house parties and shooting parties, the coming of war had altered almost every plan. Peggy's own new lifestyle might demonstrate a greater contrast than most, but it was unlikely that many of this year's debutantes would be content to continue as social butterflies.

She kept in touch with several of them by correspondence. Ronnie dashed off scribbled notes from time to time, while Anne wrote long letters illustrated by tiny paintings. Mrs Armitage quickly learned to identify the handwriting of these and other correspondents.

'Do you ever hear from Isabelle?' she asked over breakfast one morning. The whole family had been enthralled by the saga of Lady Patricia's behaviour and Peggy's triumph over her.

Peggy shook her head. She had been uncertain from the start whether or not the two of them would keep in touch. They had not been particularly close in the early weeks of the Season and the incident with Chay in the conservatory had really upset Isabelle. It was only her anger at her mother's crude attempt at revenge that had made Isabelle seek not merely forgiveness but friendship – and this had been strengthened when she went on to take refuge with Lady Menzies.

This should have been a firm enough foundation for a lasting relationship, but Isabelle's personality was a complicated one. At one moment she seemed to feel hurt that she was not accepted by the other debutantes as one of themselves; while at another she would deliberately distance herself from them, accentuating the differences that had begun with her upbringing in France. She had been embarrassed by her mother's campaign to marry her off to Chay – yet it seemed that she had hoped it might be successful.

'Not a word since she wrote to thank you for letting her share Lady Menzies with me. It looks as though she's managed to escape.'

'Escape from what, dear?'

'From her mother.' Peggy couldn't help laughing. 'It's an odd thing. It's the mothers who push their daughters into doing the Season and then the Season sort of steals their daughters away from them. Well, with Ronnie it was marriage; but then, marriage was the main point of the Season for her.'

'I hope you don't feel . . .' Mrs Armitage's anxious face showed her alarm.

'Oh, you're different, Mummy.' Realising that it was time to leave for school, Peggy stood up from the breakfast table and kissed her mother on the top of the head. 'You always hoped that I'd come back the same as before, didn't you, and I have. No need for escape here.'

She put on her hat and mackintosh and slung her mock-leather gas mask carrier over one shoulder. Jodie had already left for school on foot. Peggy, who preferred to cycle, was able to consider in silence whether what she had just told her mother was true.

171

It was and it wasn't. She loved and would continue to love her mother, but she too had her escape route planned. Oxford would change her. Her mother, who had been delighted to hear every detail of debutante dances and dresses, would be quite out of her depth when books and lectures became her daughter's main interests.

It was really just a matter of growing up, Peggy recognised. Probably the Season in itself merely accelerated a process which the passing of time would have achieved in any case. Dutiful daughters – still children, really – were fed into a social mincing machine and emerged at the other end as independently minded young women. The change was too abrupt to be comfortable, but it was bound to happen at some point.

What more than anything else turned the Season into a forcing house was the pressure to marry. Wheeling her bicycle through the school gates, Peggy told herself that she was lucky to have escaped the trap. She could not claim all the credit herself. Young men were the hunters as well as the bait, and no young men had pursued her to the point of surrender. She had enjoyed the company of the young doctor, Laurie Elliott, but he had never had eyes for anyone but Ronnie. Howard Venables would have posed more of a temptation, but her father's wealth had frightened him off. She admired him for not being a fortune-hunter, though she would have been happier if he had chosen to persevere. As for Chay, she could never have hoped that he would be more than a friend. Or at least, she *had* hoped for a moment or two, but had soon realised that it could be no more than a daydream. So here she was, heart-whole, reporting into school and once more pursuing her ambition unchanged.

Fitting the front wheel of her bicycle neatly into its slot in the shed, Peggy made her way across the asphalted netball courts and into the school building.

Very little had changed in the past few months. Newark was safely in the middle of England and had no docks or important factories to be bombed. All the same, the hockey field had been dug up to provide emergency shelters, looking like a series of potato clamps. The whole school had to file into them once a week in air raid drill. They were damp and dark and uncomfortable and soon became stuffy; they didn't seem to have been designed with any idea that they would actually have to be used.

As far as the school building itself was concerned, windows had been criss-crossed with sticky tape to minimise the risk of flying glass. The blackout problem had been overcome by having classes only in the hours of daylight, with extra work to be done at home. Apart from that, and the presence of a school prefect at the door each morning to ensure that no girl went inside without her gas mask, there was nothing very much about Peggy's timetable to remind her that there was a war on.

22

The war was a phoney war. No one was being killed at all – or, at least, no one that Ronnie knew – and the bombing that had been widely expected had not happened. In any normal year, most of Ronnie's friends would have left for the country as soon as the Season came to an end, to enjoy the usual round of house parties and shooting parties. But the end of peacetime had had the unusual effect of keeping many of them in London while they decided what form of war work to undertake.

Ronnie's own decision to become a Fany had proved to be a good one. The First Aid Nursing Yeomanry did not require her to do any actual nursing. Instead, as a member of the Motor Transport Corps, her first three weeks had been devoted to a course in maintaining the machines she was to drive. Because she had always been willing to help Chay as he tinkered with his engines she had a head start on her fellow volunteers. For the first time in her life she found herself to be a star pupil.

Thanks to her mother, she had been appointed as driver to an elderly general brought out of retirement to take a desk job and free a younger man for active service. He didn't really need her at all, but his rank entitled him to be transported between his home and Whitehall and then out to lunch and back again. Had she been a member of one of the regular women's services, she might have felt that this was a waste of national resources, but since she was an unpaid volunteer, even this very minor contribution to the war effort was better than nothing – and must be regarded as a kind of apprenticeship for the more demanding work which would surely come her way before long.

So she became adept at driving in the blackout, with only a downward-facing slit of blue light allowed from the headlamps of her car. And like an aspirant taxi driver doing 'the knowledge', she studied street maps, worked out routes from one place to another and practised driving them in her memory. It was not a very necessary kind of efficiency, but because she had never pretended to be efficient about anything in the past, there was a considerable satisfaction to be gained from each successful journey.

Not only was she unpaid, it cost her over £50 to kit herself out. Officially she was still a civilian, but her uniform – complete with Sam Browne belt – gave her the appearance of an Army officer. Very smart, she thought, as she inspected herself in the glass for the first time.

Between journeys, she had time to socialise with the other volunteer drivers. They were all girls of her own sort: wealthy and upper crust. During the day they spent their free time chattering and in the evenings they danced, just as though the Season were still in progress. As a married woman Ronnie no longer needed a chaperone – not that she would have bothered with one in any case – and there was no one to look disapproving when she went to nightclubs. Life was one long party, which gained an added frisson from the unexpected way in which young men turned up for a single night on leave or announced casually that they would be leaving for France the next day.

'Does Malcolm mind you going out at night?' asked Julia, a fellow driver who had been presented at court on the same day as herself. Malcolm was in France with his regiment.

''Course not. He wouldn't want to think of me sitting at home alone in the dark every evening.'

Ronnie answered with more confidence than was justified by the truth, because she saw no reason to make her husband uneasy by over-emphasising her social timetable in her letters. She considered her behaviour to be decorous – for example, she certainly did not allow any of her dancing partners to kiss her or even hold her too tightly – but there was no point in worrying Malcolm by going into details. The activities of the friends they had in common provided enough gossip to be going on with.

It was a problem, in a way, that they had had no time in

which to set up a home of their own. Ronnie was living below stairs at Delacourt House. She used the ground floor when she was there by day, but part of the servants' quarters in the basement had been adapted to provide her with a safe bedroom below ground level. It was a single woman's apartment and she was living a single woman's life.

Malcolm himself was having a good time. As a professional soldier, war offered him the prospect of promotion and the hope of glory. He wrote enthusiastically about lines of communication and defence systems and new responsibilities towards his men. His letters were loving, regretting the shortness of the time they had spent together and looking forward to the future.

Ronnie wrote lovingly as well, but her true feelings were not so simple. The wedding and honeymoon had been spoiled by her distress at her father's collapse and death. She could not have expected her bridegroom to postpone their wedding night indefinitely, but it had not proved a happy occasion.

Ronnie recognised that this was all her own fault. Although her mother had given her no information about what was likely to happen, Ronnie herself had often gone with her father to see his racehorses being mated. She ought not to have been alarmed by the sight of her new husband advancing towards the bed like a jouster with his lance pointed for attack. Her friends had warned her that a soldier previously seen only in uniform would look less impressive in ordinary clothes. They had not prepared her for the reaction she felt on seeing him in no clothes at all.

Malcolm was a young man in the peak of condition: fit and healthy. His body was as good as any man's body could be. And she had promised to worship it. Why, then, did she find the sight of his nakedness unpleasant? Why could she not prevent herself from shrinking away from the touch of his flesh? It must mean that there was something wrong with her. Just once – and with a feeling of shame – she had tried to pretend that it was not Malcolm who was beating down on her but Laurie Elliott; because she had loved Laurie, she thought, in a way that she could not quite love Malcolm. But it didn't work. Until that last evening at Lady Ranelegh's ball, her relationship with the young doctor had been a light-hearted one of words and laughter. Yes, she had wanted him to kiss her, but her daydreams had never gone beyond that. Even if they had, imagination was no match for the weight and the smell and the grunting and gasping of the real man who shared her bed.

Naturally, she had pretended. Malcolm had gone off to France a happy man, confident that he was leaving behind an adoring young bride. And perhaps by the time he returned she would no longer need to put on an act. She would not be taken by surprise again. She would know what to expect. After months of exchanging loving letters she would be missing him, longing to have him back. With every day that passed she must be becoming more mature. Yes, it would be all right.

In the meantime, Malcolm – although absent – acted as a protection. The young men – many of them friends of his – who invited her to nightclubs and danced and flirted with her knew very well that flirtation was all they could expect. She was a bride, to be respected; but there could be no harm in enjoying themselves for an hour or two.

It was hard to remember, sometimes, that there was a war on.

23

Newark might be remote and undisturbed by hostilities, the children of the aristocracy might still be pursuing a frenetic social life in London, but at Yewley House nobody could doubt for a second that there was a war on. On one side were the four Johnson boys: Jeff, Andy, Johnny and five-year-old Tom. On the other side was everyone else.

It had been obvious from the start that if the four evacuated brothers were to be kept together, Yewley, as the largest house in the area, was the best fitted to receive them. Even so, Anne had been surprised that her mother had raised no objections in advance. Almost certainly she intended that it would be the servants and not herself who would look after them. Perhaps also she thought that a group of four would amuse each other and so be less trouble than a single boy. She might even have hoped that they would be company for Hans, who tended to hang around the house waiting for someone to tell him what to do.

That was not how things turned out. The four boys had no idea why they had suddenly been removed from their home and family and made to live in a cold and creaky house in a place where there was no Woolies and no chip shop – in fact, no shops at all within walking distance – and no buses or trams to help with wider explorations. But dirty and scruffy though they might be, they were not unintelligent and it hadn't taken them long at all to realise that their best hope of being returned to London was to make their presence in the country intolerable for everyone concerned.

The principal victim of their campaign was Hans, and it

was Hans who was under attack on one misty Saturday morning in November 1939. Anne heard the shouts from her bedroom window and hurried outside to find out what was going on.

'Thump 'im, Jeff!'

'That way, Andy. Don't let 'im get away!'

"Ow d'you like that, then, yer bleeding Jerry?'

'Stop that!' Anne arrived on the croquet lawn at a run. 'What do you think you're doing?'

"E won't fight,' said Jeff sullenly. 'We give 'im a chance but 'e just blubbers.'

It was true that Hans was crying. There was unfortunately something about him that seemed to fit him into the role of victim even before any aggressor appeared. Atlhough he had grown at a fast rate in the past few months, and the extra inches helped him to look a little less podgy than when he first arrived in England, he was a greedy, unathletic boy and still unhealthily pale and fat.

It was also to his discredit, in terms of playground culture, that he was clever. His first weeks at the village school had been passed in a haze of incomprehension, but in the period between Anne's return from Germany and her departure for London she had found him a quick learner, and once he had broken through the language barrier he made rapid progress towards the top of the class. This was not appreciated by the incoming East Enders, who expected to show themselves as superior to the village yokels who were their reluctant hosts.

Even Anne, who was sympathetic to Hans's situation, recognised that he was not an attractive child. But she and her parents were his hosts and the only family he had, and he was entitled to their protection.

'You'd blubber too if it were four to one against you,' she told the evacuees. 'Hans, you'd better go and clean yourself up. Now then, Jeff. What's all this about?'

'Dun't have to be about nothing,' said ten-year-old Jeff, watching Hans making his stumbling escape. "E's a German and we're supposed to be fighting the Germans. 'E oughtn't to be 'ere at all.'

Anne sighed as she prepared to deliver a short political lecture without having much hope that she could attract the boys' sympathy. It would not be the first attempt to explain the situation.

'Hans is not a German. He's Austrian. Austria is one of the countries which has been captured by Germany.' This was not the occasion to be too precise about words. 'And he's Jewish. The Germans are trying to kill all the Jews. German ones, Austrian ones. English ones if they could. Hans is on our side against the Germans. That's one thing. The other thing is that just as you've been sent here because it's safer for you than London, so Hans has been sent here because it's safer for him than Austria. I know you didn't like having to leave your mother, but at least you'll see her again at Christmas. Hans will probably never see his mother or father again because by now I expect the Germans have killed them. So you ought to feel sorry for him and be nice to him.'

The four boys looked unconvinced.

'It's not just us,' said Andy sulkily. 'All the others at school pitch into 'im as well.'

'Well, you ought to stand up for him. The Yewley House gang, sticking together. You could tell the others what I've just told you.'

The suggestion was received with sullenness. Had her mother, Anne wondered, ever suggested to the village school-teacher that Hans's special situation ought to be explained to the rest of his class? That was something to think about later. For the moment, she decided to make a more practical sugges-tion.

'I'm going to ask you to look after him,' she said. 'You can see he's never going to fight for himself. He needs a bodyguard. Someone to stick up for him and make it clear that anyone who picks on him will have another, stronger fellow to contend with. Which of you will do that?'

There was no response.

'Threepence a week,' Anne said. 'That would be a fair wage for a bodyguard, wouldn't it?'

Four hands shot up. Anne found it hard not to smile.

'I don't think Tom's quite big enough yet,' she suggested, 'but the rest of you could take it in turns. A week each. Starting with Jeff.' She would get three for the price of one, since the official bodyguard of the week would certainly be protected by his brothers. Whether the bribe would persuade any of the brothers actually to be friendly to Hans was doubtful, but at least it might reduce the number of his cuts and bruises.

One effect of the arrival of the evacuees was that Hans no longer bore the brunt of Mrs Venables' annoyance at being saddled with an unwanted guest. When Anne returned to the house she found her mother fuming.

'That Tom has wet his bed again. Really, it's too much. Maggie's already beginning to mutter about the number of extra sheets she has to wash. And Mrs Webster doesn't take kindly to seeing the food she's cooked wasted, all because their majesties have never seen a green vegetable before. As for the mess they've made in—'

Anne hurried out of earshot. She was fed up with listening to grumbles. The war ought to be a noble occasion, with everyone sacrificing their own interests to those of the country. Instead, the life of the family seemed to be dominated by petty details. She had never expected a time would come when she would want to get away from Yewley, but now she was longing to escape.

Ronnie had suggested that she should join her in London, but Anne knew that she couldn't afford to work as an unpaid volunteer. The obvious alternative was to join one of the women's services, in which board and lodging and uniform would all be provided for her, but there was a snag about that as well. Once she had enlisted, her time would cease to be her own. If Chay were suddenly to write and announce that he had a few days' leave and would like to meet her, she might have to tell him that it was impossible. Not that it seemed likely that such a letter was ever going to arrive. She had written to express her condolences after his father's death and had received a friendly reply, but however often she reread the by now well-thumbed note she could not find in it any trace of the love which – surely she was not mistaken in this – he had grown to feel for her.

And so she was unsure what to do and her indecision made her feel unpatriotic and edgy and ashamed. There was no question of conscription yet for young women, but she was fit and healthy and she ought to be doing her bit.

One day she returned from an early morning ride to sniff

with alarm at the smell of smoke in the stable yard. It didn't take long to trace its source to the three elder Johnson boys – who else? – who were having a quiet smoke in the hay loft, passing a cigarette from one to the other. She recognised the cigarette as being her mother's favourite brand, but its theft was a minor matter. She snatched it away.

'Don't ever do this again!' she commanded. 'Don't you realise how stupid it is? Just look round you, at all this hay and straw. It only needs a spark, or the head falling off a match, to set the whole place on fire. Horses are terrified of fire. They'd probably trample you to death in panic. Except that you'd have burned to death before that because you couldn't get out in time.' She didn't feel the slightest compunction in exaggerating the gory details. They had to learn.

'We're not staying here in this stupid old place anyway,' said Jeff, watching resentfully as the cigarette was carefully pinched out. 'Our mum says we can come home for Christmas and there aren't any bombs so we needn't come back. So there.'

He seemed to regard it as a personal triumph – and so, from his point of view, it was. But for the Venables family it had an equally cheerful significance. War on the domestic front might soon be over.

On the national front it had hardly begun. Anne was still puzzling over what part she could play when the matter was solved for her, at least temporarily, by a letter from her aunt.

'Marian's gone off to the Isle of Man in a state of high indignation,' said Mr Venables after reading it.

'To do what?' asked Anne.

'To interview refugees. Or rather, as they're now called, aliens. It seems that we're rounding up all foreigners in case any of them take it into their heads to conquer the country from within. One of the victims is a great friend of Marian's, a musician. She went to a lot of trouble to help him get out of Germany, so she doesn't take kindly to seeing him cooped up in a sort of open prison.'

'That's ridiculous, to think that people who've run away from Germany would ever want to help the Germans!'

'Well, you can see the argument. Ninety-nine per cent of the refugees are probably exactly what they claim to be, but if the Nazis wanted to infiltrate any spies into England, that would be the ideal way to set about it. So Marian's got herself a job interviewing people who don't speak English.'

'I could do that too!' exclaimed Anne. 'My German's good enough. How does one get that sort of job?' Realising that her father was about to object, she hurriedly pressed on. 'I ought to do *something*,' she pleaded. 'And suppose someone like Hans's mother suddenly arrived over here and found herself locked up. It would be terrible. I'd like to help.'

For a moment longer Mr Venables hesitated. But perhaps it occurred to him that when his daughter took her first job away from home it would be an advantage if her aunt were near at hand.

'I'll make some enquiries,' he promised.

Within ten days it was all arranged. Aunt Marian was living in a boarding house in Port Erin, and there would be room for Anne to join her there. To start with, she would act only as an interpreter, but might become an interviewer in her own right once she became more experienced.

Mrs Venables came into Anne's room as she was deciding what to pack. 'You should write to Chay,' she said. 'Telling him your new address is a good excuse. Just to remind him of your existence. After all, he has some responsibility towards you. Taking up so much of your time during the Season so that no one else could really get near you. If I were the sort of woman who made a fuss about the rules of etiquette, I should be justified in pointing out that he had compromised your reputation.'

Her mother was exactly that sort of woman, thought Anne to herself. Any such a suggestion would be enough to wreck her relationship with Chay for good.

'He doesn't need to be reminded of my existence,' was all she said. 'And I don't need an excuse.' She spoke decisively enough to make it clear that her mother was not to interfere. All the same, when she was alone once more, it was difficult to avoid a few tears of unhappiness. Why hadn't Chay written again? Had he had some kind of accident? After all, where aeroplanes were concerned, training must be almost as dangerous as fighting.

Surely, if anything had happened, Ronnie would have told her. So why not write to Ronnie again, and try to discover indirectly where he was?

No, she decided. If he didn't want to keep in touch then it would be humiliating to push herself forward.

But oh, she was so much in love with him. It was stupid to be proud and hold back when perhaps Chay himself might also be waiting, wondering whether the end of the Season had meant the end of more than just a programme of dances.

Anne sat down at her bureau and filled her fountain pen. Her mother was quite right. She needed to tell her friends – *all* her friends – what her new address would be. She had no idea where Chay was at the moment, but if she sent a letter to Cleeve Castle his mother would forward it.

The mere fact of coming to a decision made her happy again, and her happiness turned to joy when she went downstairs for lunch and discovered that a letter had arrived for her by the second post. It was a thin, flimsy letter, not enclosed in the thick envelope which would have enabled Mrs Venables to identify its sender immediately, but Anne recognised the handwriting. Snatching it up, she took the stairs back to the privacy of her bedroom two at a time.

It was dated seven weeks earlier, but the first page provided sufficient explanation of why it had taken so long to arrive.

My dear Anne,

You must be wondering what has become of me. Or at least, I *hope* you have been wondering what has become of me. I wouldn't like to feel that I could disappear from your life without you even noticing.

If you write to me – and I hope you will – you're expected to use the jumble of numbers at the top of this letter which is supposed to track me down wherever I happen to be. (And my name, for the purpose of the envelope, is Charles Delacourt: simpler that way.) Where I actually am is in Canada. The official reason for packing a gang of us off here was that England couldn't provide enough instructors or training planes to cope with the rush of volunteers. I suspect the *real* reason was that England couldn't provide enough sky. Someone high up must have had a nightmare about the cream of Britain's youth crashing into each other all over the place. One thing that is definitely on offer in Canada is plenty of air space in which we can make our mistakes.

We were given about two days' notice that we were leaving

England, and the destination was a state secret – presumably so that Herr Hitler could be made to quake in his shoes at the thought that we might all be flying straight towards him. It went on being a state secret for a couple of weeks after we arrived here, as well, but at last it's been decided that we can reveal the truth.

The letter then read like pages out of a diary. Chay did not dwell on the dangerous voyage across the Atlantic, but he described the long train journey across Canada, his training exercises, his billet and his new companions.

It was not a love letter. There were no endearments, no promises, no hopes that she would wait for him, but Anne didn't care. It was enough that he had written; that he was thinking of her. As she slit her own letter open in order to add another page to it, she was wonderfully, marvellously happy.

She could write to Ronnie as well now, sending her new address without needing to make any subtle attempt to elicit information. And she also wanted to keep in touch with Peggy, whom – to her mother's strong disapproval – she had found the most congenial of all her fellow debutantes.

Isabelle was not on the list of those whom she would inform of her move to the Isle of Man, because she had no idea where Isabelle was. At the end of the Season everyone had scattered. Lady Patricia le Vaillant was one of those who had hurried away from London in anticipation of bombing raids. And Isabelle, who had left Lady Patricia even before that, had simply disappeared.

24

At the moment when her name came into Anne's mind Isabelle was playing tennis on a cold, grey, November day in Oxford. She was out of practice, and losing.

A surgeon on his way to the Radcliffe Infirmary, where she worked, paused to watch the game on one of the hospital's hard courts. For a few moments she managed to attain something nearer to her usual standard of play in an effort to show off – or at least, not to appear too feeble – but before long he gave a friendly wave of the hand and moved on. Without an audience, Isabelle put two volleys in succession into the net.

'Game, set and match!' said her father. 'What's happened to you, Isabelle? You haven't given me such an easy ride since you were ten.'

'I'm a bit tired.' But those were not the words she used. How marvellous it was to be speaking French again. 'A bit tired' was a heavy, plodding phrase: a donkey straining to pull a load uphill. '*Un peu fatiguée*' tripped off the tongue like a racehorse lightly cantering. For a few seconds it even succeeded in making her feel not tired at all, but that refreshment could only be temporary. After three weeks on night duty she was truly exhausted. She ought to be asleep at this moment – but how could she have borne to waste these last few hours with her father?

In fact, tiredness alone was not enough to explain her failure to cope with her father's low sliced backhands. It was a failure of concentration that was to blame. From early childhood Guy had taught her that in any competitive activity, victory goes to the player whose concentration never falters. If she had served more double faults than usual, it was because she was trying so hard not to cry.

Back in her father's hotel, she made one last attempt to change his mind. 'Please, please take me back with you.'

'Don't let's start this again, Isabelle. It's too dangerous. In France we don't have a Channel between us and the Germans.'

'But you're going back.'

'France is my home and I have no other.'

'It's my home as well.'

'You know that's not true. You have a choice.'

'No, I haven't,' said Isabelle bitterly. 'Not while Maman holds on to my passport. You're my father. You ought to be able to order her to let me go.'

'But I'm not going to. I don't know what went wrong this summer, Isabelle, but you must make it up with your mother. She loves you very much.'

'She's got an odd way of showing it.'

'That's not fair.' Guy spoke more sharply than usual. 'She would like to see you happily settled into the kind of life in which she was brought up herself – and with people of the same sort. When she broke away from it herself to marry me, the adventure was not a success, and she doesn't want you to repeat her own mistake. But at least she has recognised now that some things are bound to be different in wartime. She's letting you do what you wish and she's giving you a generous allowance. What more could you possibly expect?'

Isabelle didn't answer. Her father was right to suggest that their last moments together must not be spoiled by a rehashing of an argument that she was never going to win. Only after she had said her tearful farewell to him on Oxford station and was walking wearily back to the Infirmary did she allow the true answer to spell itself out in her mind.

What she wanted was freedom; and she wasn't going to get it. After the humiliations of the Season, and especially the terrible evening at Lady Ranelegh's ball, she had vowed that she would never live with her mother again. In spite of all the obstacles presented by not being twenty-one, it was time to make a life for herself.

So as soon as the war started and it was made clear that she would not be allowed to return to Paris, she announced instead that she intended to train as a nurse and earn her own living. She didn't add – although it was the thought uppermost in her mind – that there must be a good prospect of being sent to an Army hospital in France eventually.

Her choice of work was the cause of another flurry of discussion. It was difficult for her parents to object to the profession of nursing, but Lady Patricia was not prepared to see her daughter – the granddaughter of an earl – working for a weekly wage. Even in wartime there were some proprieties to be observed.

Her father, who had arrived back in England to discuss what should be done about the Paris apartment, was summoned to act as mediator, and a compromise was negotiated. Isabelle was given permission to join the Voluntary Aid Detachment. The VADs were all volunteers who could afford to buy their own uniforms and maintain themselves – girls of a socially accep- table class.

So it was all settled, but Isabelle needed hardly any time at all to realise that she had made a stupid decision. She had escaped from her mother's leading rein only to find herself in a straitjacket of new rules and regulations; treated like a child who mustn't be allowed to stay out late or make unsuitable acquaintances – or play tennis when she should have been sleeping in preparation for night duty. There was little to choose between Lady Patricia le Vaillant and Matron.

In addition to that, she discovered belatedly that she didn't enjoy nursing. With the war on the ground at a standstill, there were very few casualties from the Forces. Instead of the handsome young heroes she had romantically anticipated, her patients were unattractive men with skin complaints or vener- eal diseases or ulcers. She was furious with herself for being a complete idiot, and the really awful thing was that she could never confess to her mistake because that would allow her mother to say 'I told you so.'

So, as the autumn months passed – and France remained a safe place in which to live – she had gritted her teeth and kept a smile on her face. Well, most of the time. Her debutante Season had been a failure, providing her neither with a husband nor with the host of new friends who had been promised. She wasn't going to let anyone guess that her contribution to the war effort was a failure as well. She was only nineteen. Sooner or later she would discover something that she really wanted to do with her life; something – or someone – to provide an escape from all these mistakes.

Her father's departure was a turning point of a sort. It was no use wasting any more time in wondering whether she might persuade him to change his mind. She was a VAD living in Oxford and she must make the best of it. First she must obey his instructions and get herself fit again. She was not a member of the university, but with a combination of cheek and confidence and a flirtatious smile she might be able to insinuate herself into its fencing club. Meanwhile, she could go for a run every morning. And when the young surgeon who had paused to watch her playing tennis with her father asked tentatively whether she would ever be willing to have a knock-up with him, even in winter, she accepted immediately.

It was a dilemma to know whether or not to keep in touch with any of her fellow debutantes. Probably not, she decided. To begin with she had been scornful of them because they were so unsophisticated; and by the end they were probably all scornful of her because of her mother's gaffe. The whole debutante experience was something to be forgotten as quickly as possible.

There was just one person, though, with whom she would be sorry to lose contact: Miss Nobody, Miss Freckles, the unfortunate Miss Armitage. Peggy, who would have had reason to be an enemy, had proved to be generously forgiving as well as entertaining and reliable. Yes, she would send a card to Peggy. And tease her a little, perhaps.

'Dear Peggy,' she wrote. 'I seem to have arrived at Oxford before you. Will you be coming here to take your exam? If so, do give me warning and let's meet.'

That would certainly produce a response. Peggy would be anxious to discover whether it meant that Isabelle had somehow managed to get herself into the university; and if so, how. Isabelle smiled to herself as she stuck on a stamp. Just for a moment she didn't feel lonely any more.

25

Oxford at first glimpse was exactly as Peggy had imagined it: a medieval city peopled by scholars. As she emerged from the last of her three interviews, late on a dark December afternoon, she was overwhelmed by the marvellous manner in which her dream had become a reality.

Somewhere on the outskirts of the city, she knew, Lord Nuffield's factories would be making cars – or perhaps, in the wartime situation, tanks. In the centre of the city there were no doubt plenty of modern shops and cinemas. But the narrow cobbled lane down which she was wandering at this moment could hardly have changed at all in the past five hundred years. Because of the blackout, there was not even a chink of electric light to be seen. Because of petrol rationing, there were no vehicles on the move. On either side of the lane rose high stone college walls, blackened by age, and behind those walls young men and women would be working at their books. The descendants of the wandering scholars. And before very long she, Peggy Armitage, would become part of this great tradition. Happiness hugged her as she walked.

She had sat the entrance examination at school and not at Oxford, because unnecessary travelling was discouraged these days. The fact that she had been summoned for interview meant that she had jumped that first hurdle successfully, and now the interviews in turn had gone well. The last term at school, which she had found so tedious while she was enduring it, had proved its worth in settling her back into the habit of study, reminding her how to collect and remember information, how to organise her thoughts and develop them on paper. And to her surprise, the debutante months had also proved of value. A year earlier, if she had listened to a college tutor claiming that an argument in one of her essays was unsustainable, she would probably have nodded her head in apologetic agreement, assuming that an expert must know best. But an hour ago, confronted with that accusation, she had been mature enough to recognise that she was being deliberately provoked and that it was up to her to defend her case.

So she had done exactly that, to be rewarded with a quiet 'Very good, Miss Armitage.' Perhaps she was being over-confident, but she felt sure now that she would be offered a place at St Hugh's College. Emerging unexpectedly from the narrow lane into the wide space of Radcliffe Square she paused for a moment to stare at the domed library which could be her place of work if she came to Oxford. *When* she came to Oxford.

Her mother would never be able to comprehend the depth of excitement that this thought aroused in her. Even her indulgent father probably reckoned secretly that the gaining of a degree was a waste of time. Jodie was more sympathetic – but even Jodie, whose talent was for mathematics, did not entirely understand a wish to study the past. Yet none of this mattered to someone who knew exactly what she wanted.

All the candidates attending for interview had been invited to spend the night in Oxford. Not, however, at St Hugh's College itself, because the building had been requisitioned as a hospital. Peggy had at first been disconcerted to learn this, but after-wards pleased. Because women had been admitted to the university so very many centuries later than men, St Hugh's was a modern college, some way from the centre of the city. For the duration of the war its undergraduates had been offered instead the use of Holywell Manor, a building whose origins were as old as anything Peggy could have wished and one which was much closer to the other colleges.

The college she happened to be passing at that moment, according to the plan with which she had been provided, was Brasenose. The name struck a chord and she made her way round to the lodge.

'Mr Brownlow? I don't think so, miss. Oh, but hang on a minute, though.' The college porter turned away to consult another list. 'Yes, here we are. He's one of the young gentlemen who were expected this term but who've asked for their matriculation to be deferred till after the war's over.'

'You mean he's joined up?'

'I expect that would be it, yes, miss.'

'Thank you very much.' Peggy didn't greatly mind. She hadn't seen Bill Brownlow since their last lesson with Miss Downie a year earlier; though he had written in great excitement to announce that he had won the scholarship he needed. It seemed a pity to miss the opportunity of saying hello, but really she was happy to be on her own.

Solitude would have to wait, however, for she was on her way to a social engagement. After receiving a card from Isabelle she had written to say when she would be coming to Oxford, and had been invited to meet her at the Cardona Café.

Isabelle, it transpired, was learning to be a nurse.

'Do you like it?' asked Peggy, not attempting to conceal her surprise.

'It's absolutely ghastly. I had this picture of the angel of mercy, you know, mopping the fevered brow, but in fact I spend my time making beds and sluicing out bedpans and mopping up vomit. Disgusting! Acting as a slave to the staff nurses, really.'

'Why did you pick nursing, then, if it's so horrid? Why didn't you join one of the women's services?'

'I would have done if I'd thought there was any chance of getting back to France, but when I asked about that I was told no, they were just back-ups to release more men to fight. The beastly thing is that that wasn't true. Some of the ATS *have* gone to France. But I believed what I was told. Stupid me!'

'Presumably as a nurse you *will* get to France in the end,' suggested Peggy.

'I hope so, once I'm trained. That's the incentive. There are casualty clearing stations over there already. And if ever any real fighting begins, they'll have to set up proper hospitals. Meanwhile –' Isabelle's face brightened – 'this has got me a roof over my head away from home. And the social life's pretty good, even though I'm almost always too tired to make the most of it. Oxford's still full of young men. There aren't enough female undergraduates to go round, and anyway they're all swots, so nurses tend to be in demand for dances and parties.'

Peggy was amused by the change in Isabelle, who nine months earlier had been so docile as she acquiesced in her mother's title-hunting campaign. She might not be enjoying her job, but she was obviously revelling in this new independence.

'So do you feel you are more English than French now?' she asked.

'No.' The answer came without hesitation. 'I've messed up in England and been made to feel a foreigner. You've been nicer to me than I deserved, but most of the crowd will always remember me as that pushy French girl who chased after Chay and lost. So humiliating!'

'I'm sure everyone realised that it was your mother who was doing the pushing.'

'All right: the spineless girl, then. A sort of doormat. But I did actually fall for Chay. Nothing to do with his title. I would have liked . . . But it was so difficult, with Maman doing everything wrong. I still . . . Oh well, that's all over now. As I say, I messed up.'

'Never mind. You're one of us now. Part of the British war effort.'

'Well, England's fighting for France, isn't it? And besides . . .' Isabelle looked almost embarrassed. 'There was an odd moment, on the day we were presented. I wonder whether you felt it as well. As though I was sort of vowing allegiance to King George. And now he's calling the promise in. When everyone else is doing his or her bit, I can't stand aside, can I? Even though emptying bedpans wasn't exactly what I had in mind when I pinned in those ridiculous ostrich feathers. Now that's enough about me. What about yourself, Peggy? How did your interviews go?'

They chattered happily until Isabelle stood up to leave.

'Night duty tonight,' she said. 'I've left the craziest bit of news till last, so that you can go off spluttering with jealousy. I enrolled in London, hoping that I'd be able to keep up with a bit of the night life there, but they thought we were all going to be bombed, so they scattered us around. I'm at the Infirmary here at the moment, but as soon as anyone actually starts getting hurt in this so-called war, I'm on a list to be transferred to a head-injuries unit. And where is it? You may well ask. In St Hugh's

College. So I shall be there before you. Scrubbing floors, I expect, to keep the place clean for you.'

They laughed together as they said goodbye, promising to keep in touch. Then Peggy made her way back to Holywell Manor.

She found the other hopefuls excitedly discussing a notice which had just been pinned up in the lodge. 'The Principal requests the pleasure of the company of all candidates for admission to the college at 9 p.m. this evening for coffee.' A rumour was going round that the results of the examinations might be announced on the spot, instead of by letter.

Peggy stood back quietly, studying the animated group. She was remembering – perhaps because Isabelle had reminded her of it – the day of her presentation at Court. Then, too, she had waited patiently, staring at all the girls in their long white dresses and wondering how she would ever be able to make any friends amongst them; already reconciled to a summer of humiliation.

Well, even in that unlikely society she had succeeded in acquiring friends. Here, by contrast, she was in her own milieu. If she came to St Hugh's, there would be no fear of rejection or humiliation. These girls would be prepared to respect her for what she was, and some might become her friends for life. Even though they were still strangers, she could feel her body flooding with the warmth of her feeling for them.

At a quarter past nine that evening, the rumour proved to be true. The Principal retreated from her coffee party in the drawing room to her office and a secretary requested that Miss Abbott should follow her in. Conversation came to a sudden halt.

Miss Abbott, when she reappeared, was struggling to restrain tears. 'Waiting list,' she said in answer to thirty unspoken questions. 'So I have to hope that there's someone here who'll decide to take up a Cambridge offer instead.' She hurried from the room as the secretary called the next name.

'Miss Armitage.'

Peggy's heart sank. Was the list being called from the bottom up? But no; it must simply be alphabetical. Please let it be alphabetical. Holding her head as high as on that day of presentation, she made her way into the study.

No royal throne here; no crowd of courtiers and pages; no brightness of red and gold. The Principal sat behind a small desk on an uncarpeted floor in a barely furnished room. But she smiled as warmly as King George had smiled before glancing down at the sheet of paper in front of her.

'Miss Armitage? Please sit down. I'm very happy to tell you, Miss Armitage, that the College has elected you to an exhibition. My congratulations.'

An exhibition – which had nothing to do with pictures – was not quite a scholarship, but better than a simple place. As Peggy's mouth broadened into a smile, she had to keep her lips pressed together to prevent her delight from tumbling noisily out.

'In the normal way, you would have received the news through the post in a few days' time. However, there are new regulations to be observed, and some urgency about the decisions which will need to be taken. No doubt you expected that if you were successful in the examination you would begin your degree course here next October, and it will still be possible for you to do so. But in such a case you will be allowed to stay for only two years instead of three before taking up some form of national service. It's envisaged that an emergency wartime degree will be available at the end of the two years. Unless, of course, the war comes to an end before that time.'

Peggy nodded her head in a pretence of understanding, although in reality her mind was still spinning with the only news that mattered. The Principal continued to speak.

'Because of this restriction, the College is offering some of this year's successful candidates, starting with the Scholars and Exhibitioners, the opportunity to come up this January, if they choose. If you accept this offer, you would be able to have two years and two terms in residence, and with a little extra hard work you should have no difficulty in taking the ordinary final examinations at the end of that time. We have room available because several of our second- and third-year undergraduates have left to join the women's services.'

'Yes. I see.'

'You're not expected to take a decision of this kind here and now,' said the Principal. 'You will need to consult with your parents. But should you choose to come up in January, we obviously would want to know very soon. Equally, we would want to know if you decide not to take up your exhibition until after the war in the interests of doing war work, because then we could offer a place to someone else.'

Miss Abbott, thought Peggy. Poor Miss Abbott, desperately hoping that someone would reject the offer in which she had been disappointed. But the Principal was rising to her feet.

'If you will call at my secretary's office before you leave Oxford tomorrow, she will give you all the details in writing,' she said. 'We shall hope to hear from you within a week. Whether in January or October, I look forward to welcoming you as a member of the College.'

'Thank you very much.' Peggy shook the outstretched hand and made her way out through the crowded drawing room. Just like Miss Abbott – although for the opposite reason – she didn't want to talk. She was dizzy with the happiness of ambition fulfilled. She had made it!

That night she slept badly – indeed, hardly slept at all. At first it was excitement that kept her awake. Later, though, as she tossed from side to side on the narrow bed whose wire springs creaked with each movement, a sense of unease crept in. It was strong enough to rouse her from her bed long before breakfast was on offer.

Walking briskly, to stretch her body after the stress of the previous day, she made her way down to the river and walked along the towpath for a little while before turning to look across the water and the meadow beyond. This was the swampy area to which the medieval wandering scholars had come. Enduring its chills and miasmas and fevers they had settled around their teachers. The buildings that were just emerging from the darkness of a winter morning behind the gaunt rows of trees on the further bank – Christ Church, Merton and the tower of Magdalen College – still housed young men who shared her own ambitions and probably also her sentimental love for the spirit of a place. She had longed to take her place here and now she had arrived. So why was she so unexpectedly uneasy?

It was Isabelle who had unsettled her. Isabelle, who hated nursing and had no great attachment to England but was not prepared, all the same, to ignore a sense of fealty. And Bill

196

Brownlow, who had been so anxious to win an Oxford scholarship, but had apparently turned his back on it when a different duty called. And all those second- and third-year undergraduates whose disappearance from Oxford had made it possible for the college to offer immediate places. Peggy had been so absorbed in her own ambition, and the work required to achieve it, that she had not stopped to think whether study was a suitable occupation in wartime. She thought about it now.

It wasn't as though anything she learned could be of any importance to the country. Medical students and engineers would be more useful after they had completed their degree courses, but the same was not true of her. Learning about Magna Carta or the rights and wrongs of the Civil War might play a valuable part in training her mind but the knowledge she acquired would be completely useless in itself.

Frightened by her own thoughts, she tried to keep at bay a sense of desperation. If she were to join up now, she would be equally useless, wouldn't she? She had no skills which would contribute to the winning of a war. None at all.

Isabelle had provided the answer to that argument as well. The value of unskilled women was to free men to fight and to provide them with whatever back-up was needed. That was why, all over the British Isles, housemaids were flooding to work in munition factories and rich, pampered girls like Ronnie were already in uniform. Only she, Peggy Armitage, seemed to think she had a right to pursue her ambitions as though nothing out of the ordinary were happening.

The day was lightening. A thin white mist rose from the surface of the river and clung wispily to the rough grass of the water meadow beyond. The fighting – if there was any fighting – was a million miles away. There was no sound to disturb the peacefulness of the scene. Her heart swelled with desire; but for a place, not a person. This must be how it felt to be in love, and she had never experienced it before. There had been a moment during her Season when she had hoped that Howard Venables might want her to fall in love with him. And there had been another moment when she had wondered whether to allow her friendship with Chay to deepen into something more intense. But now, captured by first love, she recognised that neither of

197

these two emotions had been of the least importance. This was the real thing.

Ronnie, who was presumably in love with her husband, had had to say goodbye to him. Anne, who was certainly in love with Chay, had had to stand aside and watch him go without saying what she longed to hear. War and duty were more powerful than love.

Nothing was decided yet. It would be perfectly possible to be stubborn and selfish and unpatriotic. But as Peggy watched the mist rise and disperse, she could feel tears running down her cheeks. She was in love with Oxford, but not every love affair could demand a happy ending.

26

'I feel like a spy!'

Aunt Marian raised her eyebrows in amusement. 'But you know that you're not, any more than I am.' They were together in Port Erin on the Isle of Man.

'It's different for you,' said Anne. 'You're trying to help people as well as just asking questions.' She knew that after every day spent interrogating alien internees, her aunt spent the evening writing to all her friends and acquaintances, trying to find employment for women who had abandoned homes and incomes to flee to what they had hoped would be a welcoming sanctuary.

Instead of that they had been greeted with suspicion and herded on to this island. In normal times Port Erin was a seaside resort. It was well stocked with boarding houses, where the interned females lived – but not as holiday guests. They were expected to do their own cooking and cleaning, and were seldom allowed to meet their husbands, who had been herded into similar accommodation in Douglas.

Anne herself had been directed to talk to children. The refugees, many of them highly educated, organised their own schools for their children. They accepted Anne as an additional resource for English conversation, even though they realised that she was employed to ask questions and pass on the answers. 'We have nothing to hide,' they assured her. If she needed to discover dates, places, names, examples of persecution so that what the children told her could be checked with the answers given by their parents, there was no objection.

So there was nothing clandestine about the work she had

been doing for the past four months, but all the same she hated it.

'Then give it up,' said her aunt. 'There are plenty of other jobs to be done. More worthwhile, perhaps. For someone of my age, there's not much choice, but for you . . .'

'I'll think about it,' Anne promised, and she began to think that same day. It was a Sunday in March of 1940, and what she liked best to do with her Sundays was to paint the turbulent sea and the banks of clouds which swept in from the west. Every time she painted clouds she remembered Herr Frankel, who had taught her how to make them move across the paper and who now must be considered an enemy.

Once outside, though, she could see that there was no possibility of painting today, for the wind had risen to a gale. Even the huge seagulls who held dominion over this part of the coastline were struggling to make any way against it, and Anne herself had to keep away from the edge of her favourite cliff for fear of being blown over. But the effort of battling against the rough weather somehow raised her spirits while she thought about what her aunt had said.

In the summer, no doubt, the sun would shine and the beaches below would be pleasant playgrounds for the refugee children; perhaps the sea would even be smooth and warm enough for swimming. But when that time came, did she want to be here? No, she decided; she didn't.

It was partly her home that called her. In that calmer, more southerly countryside the gardens would already be coming to life. The first fresh green leaves would be breaking out and peach and plum and cherry trees would be on the point of blossoming. She longed to be back there, to enjoy the familiar changes which each new season brought.

And Chay was back in England: a pilot officer now and posted to an airfield a little to the north of London. Anne felt ashamed of herself for allowing her longing for him to influence her. To give up a job after only a few months was feeble, and in wartime, duty should come before love. But his letter had expressed disappointment at discovering that she was out of range of a two-day leave. As Aunt Marian had pointed out, she could find other duties nearer to home. Turning, Anne gave up the struggle against the gale and allowed herself to be blown back to the town. One decision was made, but others remained to be settled. If she were to return to Yewley House, what should she volunteer to do?

'The Land Army!' shrieked Mrs Venables. 'My dear child, you can't go into the Land Army.'

'Why not?' Anne was startled by the vehemence of her mother's reaction.

'Well, really, Anne. Think about it seriously for a moment. If you were to enlist in one of the women's services, you would have a smart uniform and mix with girls of your own sort. But the Land Army! Those terrible clothes, and just consider what your hands will look like after you've been picking potatoes all day. And the other women! Not at all the right class of people.'

'I really don't think that that ought to be a consideration.'

'Well, try to imagine what it would be like sharing a bedroom with someone who swears and sweats and thinks that having a bath is something to be endured once a year. Someone like the mother of those terrible Johnson boys.'

'I think you're being very snobbish, Mother.'

'To prefer the company of people who share your own kind of upbringing and interests is sensible, not snobbish.'

Realising that she was never going to win her mother's agreement, Anne tackled her father instead. But just as he had supported the plan for her to do the London Season, so once again he surprised and disappointed her by agreeing with his wife.

'The Land Army? I don't think that's at all a good idea, Anne,' he told her. 'You'd have none of the company and community spirit that the women's services can provide. You would find yourself sent to live on a farm which might well be very isolated. If there were any farm labourers still there, they'd resent you as someone who was threatening their own jobs. And you might find yourself with no protection if the farmer chose to overwork you or misbehave himself. No, I'm sorry. If conscription for women is brought in and you find yourself directed to some particular work, then that would be different. But as long as it's all a matter of choice, and you're still under twenty-one, I'm not prepared to give my permission for that. What makes you so keen on the idea, anyway?'

'I like being out in the open,' she said. 'I like to watch things growing. And with the U-boats sinking so many of our ships, it must be important, mustn't it, for us to grow as much food as we can?'

'Then do it here,' said Mr Venables.

'What do you mean?'

'I agree with you that providing food is a worthwhile job, but if you're going to get your hands dirty it might as well be with our earth rather than anyone else's. We've got plenty of land which could be used for new crops, but not enough labour any longer even to keep the gardens in good shape. Wyndham has already warned me that once young Billy is called up one of the walled gardens will have to go. Why shouldn't I be allowed to have my own personal Land Army girl?'

'Why not indeed?' Anne burst out laughing. 'I shall expect to be paid the full going rate. Twenty-eight shillings a week and my board.' She was delighted by the suggestion. Why hadn't she thought of it herself? To continue living at home while feeling that she was contributing usefully to the war effort would be ideal. And with her father as her employer, she would be able to beg the occasional free weekend to visit Chay – should he ever invite her. Pausing only to pull on a pair of Wellington boots, she hurried outside to survey her new domain.

From the back of the stable yard extended three walled gardens, covering three acres in all. The walls were built of the same old brick as the house, although without its distinguishing patterning. One wall supported a range of greenhouses, and another, in the next garden, sheltered raised and cloched beds for propagating and forcing. Against all the other walls were tied a variety of fan-trained fruit trees. Anne had often drawn them, enjoying the shapes of their upraised arms without being greatly concerned about what crops they would yield.

The smallest of the three walled gardens was entirely devoted to fruit, which later in the season would be netted against the birds. Already the ground between the rows of raspberries and strawberries, gooseberries and currants had been neatly hoed. There was nothing more to be done there for the moment.

In the largest garden all the vegetables for the house were grown. Standing quietly in one of the arched entrances, Anne watched young Billy as he dug his way steadily from one side to the other. In another part of the large square Wyndham, the head gardener, was raking and stamping and raking again to create a tilth fine enough for sowing. She watched as he straightened himself and set about marking the first row with string and stakes. He would not want to be interrupted. Not wishing to draw attention to herself, she moved quietly into the third of the walled gardens.

This was the one for her! From this acre of land were supposed to come all the flowers which were needed for decorating the house, but it was easy to tell that, with his two journeymen gone, Wyndham had decided that this must be the area to neglect. A single winter was not long enough to return it to jungle, but already there was an impression of untidiness and no sign of the winter digging which had been evident in the vegetable garden. Anne walked to the centre and looked around her with interest.

She would not be popular with her mother if there were to be no flowers at all, but some sacrifices must be made. The herbaceous border might as well stay, and there was no need to disturb the bulbs in the north border, at present graceful with one of the ten varieties of narcissus which would succeed each other over a period of weeks. But the centre of the area: yes, she could do something with that.

It was tempting to hurry straight off to find a spade and fork and start digging. But the first thing to do was to make a plan. There was no reason why a vegetable garden should not look neat and even decorative. In her mind's eye she divided the area into shapes.

She turned at the sound of footsteps behind her.

'Come to pick some daffs, have you?' asked Wyndham, holding out a trug.

Anne shook her head. 'I want you to take me on as an apprentice,' she said. 'So that I can help you after Billy goes. We need to grow more vegetables. I know you've got too much to do already, but I could look after this plot if you'll tell me what I need to know. About the soil and what's best to grow and which way it should face and – well, everything, really.'

The old gardener looked at her doubtfully, no doubt considering her soft hands, her unsuitable dress and the long blonde hair that was blowing in the wind. 'If that's what you want, miss,' he grunted. 'I suppose we have to get used to everything being different now.'

Anne gave a vigorous nod of her head. Yes; everything was different now. It was only twelve months – almost to the day – since she had made her presentation curtsy to the King and Queen, but last year's Season seemed light-years in the past.

27

'Go home,' ordered General Anderson. 'And take the rest of the day off.'

'Yes, sir,' said Ronnie. 'Thank you very much, sir.' She had just come within a few inches of running down a pedestrian. The pedestrian had stepped out in front of the car without looking where he was going, but Ronnie hadn't been concentrating on where she was going either.

'I know what was distracting you,' said the general. 'I've got a boy out there myself. I hope you'll have some good news soon.'

'Thank you,' said Ronnie. 'And you too, sir.' Neither of them made any pretence of cheerfulness.

She walked slowly back towards Delacourt House. Across St James's Park, where no one was feeding the ducks. Across Green Park, where no one was basking in the unusually hot June sunshine. Everyone was indoors, listening to the news bulletins on the wireless.

Now she was in Hyde Park, which was pock-marked with trenches and air-raid shelters. Was it really only a year ago that she had ridden here twice a day? She sat down on the grass and stared across Park Lane at her home. Would there be a message waiting for her there? Would it say anything that she wanted to hear?

It was not so long ago that people had still been joking about this war which didn't seem to be a proper war at all, but just an accumulation of inconveniences. Now not only had it suddenly become real, but the unthinkable was happening: England was on the point of losing. Belgium had already surrendered. France was just about to surrender. It seemed certain that within a few days the Germans would be occupying Paris. If they were not at the same time marching towards London, it would only be because they couldn't walk on water.

The only light to brighten this gloom was the fact that the sea was calm. The retreating soldiers who managed to reach the coast had a sporting chance of being picked up by boat and ferried back to England. Like everyone else, Ronnie had listened to the wireless whenever she could during the past two days. She had built up a vivid picture in her mind of men in steel hats forming up on the beaches of Dunkirk, wading out into the sea in long lines and being pulled aboard small boats. If the wireless commentators were to be believed, every yacht and pleasure boat in the south of England had made for the English Channel to join in the rescue. And the sea, she reminded herself again, was calm.

The picture in her mind was not a silent one, though: she could hear the scream of planes overhead, machine-gunning the waiting men in their orderly lines. She could hear the explosions of bombs. She could imagine the increasing panic of those who were still trapped too far from the sea, desperately trying to hold off the German advance. Somewhere in that mess of frightened and wounded and dying men was her husband.

Perhaps Malcolm would not be frightened, but he would certainly be angry. He was so proud of his regiment and of his country that probably he had never envisaged a situation in which he would be forced to run away. She remembered him as she had seen him on their last night together: his powerful shoulders, his muscular arms, his smooth skin. She had still been in the process of trying to make herself love his body, and with his skin at least she had succeeded. She would have been happy to lie for hours stroking his shoulders and moving her fingers gently up his neck to his chin, if only she had not known that the movement would be taken as the invitation to more lovemaking.

Today that skin might be dirty and sweating, or torn and bleeding. Perhaps, even, it would be grey and cold in death. Without warning, Ronnie was sick.

Staggering slightly, she made her way out of the park and across the street.

Delacourt House was silent. All the best furniture had been

moved to the country and was stored in the coach-houses at Cleeve. Whatever remained was shrouded by white dustsheets. There were too many windows in the upper floors to be blacked out, so no light was ever turned on there after dark, allowing moonlight to illuminate the ghosts of sofas and chairs. All the servants had left, except for one married couple who had no other home. They acted as caretakers and looked after Ronnie's set of rooms, but even they were not on the premises when she let herself in.

She rinsed out her mouth and splashed her face with cold water before switching on the wireless for company. The evacuation was continuing. It was almost complete. Within a few hours all those who had managed to reach the beaches would be rescued. It was a success. It was a triumph. It was a victory over defeat. She switched the voice off again.

There was nothing forced or artificial about her anxiety that Malcolm should be safe and unhurt and on his way back to her. It must mean, mustn't it, that she was at last loving him as a wife should love her husband? She had been deeply ashamed, in the short time they had together, that she had needed to pretend. But whatever was wrong with her must have cured itself by now; now that she had grown used to the idea of being a married woman, with all that implied. If he were to walk through the door at this moment . . .

But that wasn't likely to happen, and its unlikelihood left her feeling lonely. She needed someone to talk to. Her mother was too far away and too busy: living at Cleeve and organising the WVS throughout the county. In any case, Ronnie had never found it easy to discuss anything too personal with her mother; and where Malcolm was concerned it was hard to conceal a slight resentment that she had been rushed into a marriage that she ought to have been strong-minded enough to resist.

As a rule there was company to be found amongst other Fany drivers. A group of them had appropriated a flat in Ebury Street as a kind of social headquarters where they could chat without bothering about the differences of rank which loomed so large in the other services. But for the past few days this had been almost deserted. All the drivers had someone – brother or husband or fiancé – in France and no one was in a cheerful mood.

She felt a longing instead to chat to her debutante friends, but that was impossible as well. Peggy, who should have been in Oxford, was in Liverpool, doing something too secret to talk about. Isabelle was the one who was in Oxford and almost certainly being rushed off her feet with casualties from the evacuation. Anne was in Berkshire, living at home but working through almost all the hours of daylight. Only a year earlier Ronnie could have phoned up any one of dozens of debutantes to chat just for the pleasure of chatting, but now everyone she knew was busily involved in trying to win the war.

As she ought to be as well. What a wimp she was, to be sitting here feeling sorry for herself! There was no point in going back on duty immediately, since she would not be expected, but tomorrow morning she must report as usual and give the job her full attention. What was the point of worrying about possibilities until they were confirmed? Sooner or later she would find out what had happened to her husband.

As the days passed, she had to cross off possibilities one after the other. If Malcolm was back in England and unhurt, he would contact her immediately. If he was back in England but wounded, it would not be too long before a message came through from some hospital. If he had been killed in France, someone would know. Once three weeks had passed, there was surely no danger of the most dreaded telegram arriving. There was only one possibility left.

So she was mentally prepared for the news that reached her six weeks after Dunkirk: Captain Malcolm Ross was a prisoner of war. As she stared at the words, she had to ask herself how to react. He was still alive. That was good. That was the best possible news. But oh, how furious and frustrated he must be! War had offered him the opportunity to put into practice everything he had lived and been trained for as a professional soldier: to win medals for bravery and gain quick promotion.

And now that had been snatched away. Other men would win the glory and the promotion while he was condemned to be a non-combatant: caged. How he would hate it!

Meanwhile, the war was about to come to England. Everyone at home took it for granted that invasion was only a few weeks away. First the bombs, and then the Wehrmacht. It was Ronnie and not Malcolm who at any moment would find herself in the front line.

28

It was a very small accident to have, in the end, such very large consequences. The patient in the end bed of Ward Three knocked over the jug of water on his bedside locker.

By the summer of 1940 Isabelle had been working at St Hugh's for six months. Her hopes of being sent to France once her training was finished had died with the retreat from Dunkirk, so that now she was trapped in a job she disliked without the reward that would have made it worth while. However, she was not going to allow her mother the pleasure of hearing her admit that she had made a mistake. She was determined to make the best of it – after all, it was a job that had to be done, and as the end of her first year approached she could look forward to escaping from the role of a junior housemaid and being given more responsibilities.

For the time being, however, mopping up spilt water was definitely part of her duty, and she was also encouraged to soothe the men out of their nightmares, if she could.

Before her transfer to St Hugh's she had been warned that men with severe head injuries – in which the temporary hospital specialised – were often noisy and sometimes violent. They shouted. They thrashed about. They swore, sometimes using words that even they didn't know that they knew. If they ever realised afterwards how they had behaved they would be ashamed.

Isabelle understood all that, and so, as she dabbed dry each object on the locker, she murmured reassurance to the bandaged officer in the bed beside it. She told him that he had been having a nightmare but was awake now, and everything was going to be all right. She reminded him that he had escaped from France and now he was in England, in Oxford, in a building which had been built as a college for English girls but which now housed some of the best surgeons in the country so he would be all right, be all right, be all right.

The actual words mattered less than the tone of voice, but in this case the choice of language seemed important as well. The paperback book she was carefully drying was by Sartre. He was a French officer, not British, and the words he had shouted out in panic were in French. She therefore spoke to him in that language.

Next morning, when she brought him his breakfast at the end of her duty, she found him calm and coherent again, but depressed. She lingered to chat for a few moments, rightly guessing that the simple act of conversing in French would cheer him a little. His home was in Paris, he told her, so they talked about that city: their favourite seasons and favourite places. Isabelle confessed how desperately she had longed to return to France when the war began and was told how wise her father had been to forbid it. Paris under German occupation was a desecration; even the thought of it began to upset him and Isabelle felt guiltily that she was doing more harm than good with this conversation. Because she had come to the end of a spell on night duty, she was about to take a three-day break. But she would see him again, she promised, as soon as she returned.

When that day came, she found the bed empty, neatly awaiting some new occupant.

'What happened to Lieutenant Moreaux?' she asked Major Needham, in the next bed.

'He's been moved to the noisy boys' ward. He asked me to tell you.'

Isabelle nodded her understanding. In the interests of allowing most of the patients the chance of a good night's sleep, those who caused the most disturbance were collected together. 'I'll call in for a chat when I can,' she said.

'He certainly seemed to appreciate a bit of a jabber in his own language. Where did you learn to speak French like that? My school never got me very far past the *plume de ma tante* stage.'

'My father's French. Except for holidays to visit my mother's relations in England, I spent the whole of my life in France until about eighteen months ago.'

'That would explain it, then. It sounded, listening to you the other day, as though you wished you were still there.'

'Well, not while the Germans are in occupation. But as soon as we've got rid of them, yes, I shall go back.'

It was the most casual of conversations. It didn't even register with Isabelle at the time that Major Needham must have progressed a little further than the state of his aunt's pen if he had been able to follow the earlier chat. And certainly she did not immediately connect him with the telephone call which came several weeks after he had been discharged.

'Miss le Vaillant. My name's Greenaway. You don't know me. We're trying to collect some information about Paris. Not from tourists or officials, but from people who've actually lived there for some time. I wondered whether you'd be willing to come up to London and have a chat.'

The unexpectedness of the request silenced Isabelle for a moment, and the silence was misinterpreted.

'We'd refund your train fare, of course,' the stranger added.

'Who is "we"?' asked Isabelle. 'Who are you, exactly, and how did you get hold of my name?'

'One of your patients at St Hugh's mentioned it. Chap called Charles Needham. You probably don't remember him particularly. I expect people are coming and going all the time.'

'Yes, I do remember him.' Isabelle was still hesitant, but an excuse to visit London without cost was not to be sneezed at. After she had paid for her board at the hospital, she was left with only nineteen shillings a week out of her pay, and although her mother's allowance was helpful as far as it went, it did not allow for luxuries. The chat that had been mentioned was not likely to last long. She would have time to meet one or two of the friends she rarely saw these days. She gave Mr Greenaway the date of her next free day and the appointment was made.

The conversation took place in a shabby flat in Baker Street. The label next to the door announced that it was the Inter-Services Research Bureau, but there was nothing very military about Mr Greenaway. Grey haired and wearing well-worn civilian country clothes, he revealed as he stood up to shake hands that he needed the support of a stick.

'It's good of you to come, Mademoiselle le Vaillant. May we speak in French?' He was already doing so. 'I like to get all the practice I can.'

Isabelle smiled agreement and waited to discover what this was all about. Domestic life in Paris, it appeared. Mr Greenaway produced a plan and she indicated the area in which she had lived. She was almost ashamed to realise, as the questions began, how little she had moved outside the limited routines of walks with her nursemaid followed later by the regular route to school and expeditions with her mother to shops and art galleries and theatres. The servants had looked after all the day-to-day needs of their life.

Under his coaxing, however, she began to remember the smaller shops of the neighbourhood, the alleys and the concierges. It was during this part of the conversation that she received her first shock. They were talking about the early-morning smell of new bread in the local baker's.

'Ah yes,' said Mr Greenaway putting his finger on the relevant part of the street plan. 'Monsieur Malin. Very sad. He was shot by the Germans, you know, after they occupied Paris.'

Isabelle stared at him in stupefaction. Perhaps deliberately, he misinterpreted her reaction and answered a different unspoken question from the one which sprang to her mind.

'A sniper fired from the window of his apartment. He wasn't even on the premises himself at the time. But it was right at the beginning of the occupation and there was a policy of making an example of anyone who supported resistance. To discourage others.'

'But how do you know about this?' That was the real question.

'Oh, a great deal of information comes out of France. Living under foreign domination is a hard thing to deal with. Most people find it simplest to keep their heads down and accept it. There are always a few who like to be on the winning side and who change loyalties. But there are also a few – or perhaps a great many – who intend to do everything they can to get rid of the conqueror, although they may not see a clear way to do it. We in Britain are their best hope, so they send us as many small facts as they can. By radio and any other means they can find. It's extremely dangerous for them.'

'Yes, it must be.'

'What they hope, of course, is that we can provide some kind of practical help, and we're beginning to think about how that might be done. At the moment we've got our hands full with trying to keep the Germans out of our own country. But one or two of us – old codgers like myself, whose active fighting days are over – have been asked to look ahead. Probably quite a long time ahead, I fear, to a day when our army will be able to get back on the Continent. When that time comes, we shall need to know who our friends are in France. Do you enjoy nursing, Mademoiselle le Vaillant?'

Isabelle blinked at the unexpected change of subject, but answered it honestly. 'No, not very much. I felt it was my duty to do something, but I think perhaps I made the wrong choice.'

'Major Needham spoke highly of you. Said you were very sympathetic and also most meticulous.'

'Being meticulous, I find, is the best way of coping with duties which are often rather unpleasant.'

'Quite. Quite.' Mr Greenaway rose with difficulty to his feet. 'This conversation, mademoiselle, is completely confidential. You won't mention your visit here, or what we have discussed, with anyone at all – not friends, not family, not your superiors at the hospital.'

Isabelle was not at all sure what they had in fact discussed, but she nodded her head in bemused agreement.

'But perhaps at some time in the future we might meet again? For another little chat. To discuss whether it might be possible for you to be of use to both the countries to whom you owe loyalty at the same time.' He held out a hand. 'Thank you so much for coming.'

She was still in a daze as she went slowly down the uncarpeted stairs. What did he mean? What did he want her to do? The only thought that occurred to her was that all those radio operators tapping out their messages about the execution of plump, harmless bakers would need someone at this end to understand and translate what they said. Yes, she could do that.

But if that was all it was, why had Mr Greenaway not said so at once?

Well, she would have to wait and see.

29

Would this be the day: the day when Chay would propose: 'Will you marry me, Anne?' 'Oh yes, yes, yes.'

Because she longed for him to speak, she did not dare to say anything herself. She was happy just to be with him, but her silence was lengthened by the fear that if she were to make some trivial remark it might interrupt the exact moment when he was on the point of putting the question.

So as she lay on her back in the long grass, she stared up into the sky without speaking. Above her she could see the silver flashes of fighter planes diving and dodging, and the patterns of white lines which little by little became fuzzy and dispersed until they were imitations of clouds in the clear blue summer sky. All around her head bees foraged busily amongst the wildflowers, but louder even than their buzzing was the grating drone of bombers, steadily pressing forward with their deadly load, and the sharp rattle of machine-gun fire.

In less than three hours Chay would be inside one of those silver specks. For the moment he lay peacefully beside her, face downwards so that he need not watch the battle in progress, because some of those fighting for their lives would be his own friends. But he could not close his ears as easily as his eyes.

'One down,' he said in a muffled voice, recognising an interruption in the sustained bass note of the bombers. He released Anne's hand to twist round and sit up. They watched together as a Dornier, belching black smoke, staggered for a few seconds in an attempt to remain steady and then plunged screaming towards the earth.

'We have to feel pleased,' he said. 'We have to tell ourselves that half a dozen lives lost there may mean fifty lives saved somewhere in their target area. But it's hard, sometimes, when they're just chaps like me, perhaps with girls like you waiting at home for their safe return.'

He pressed her back on to the grass and kissed her fiercely. It was a hot day at the beginning of August and she was wearing a sleeveless dress with a scooped-out neckline. He covered every inch of her bare skin with kisses before lying back beside her. But still he did not ask the only question she wanted to hear; and she needed to talk.

'Aren't you frightened all the time?' she asked, with her eyes on the column of smoke rising from the crashed bomber.

'When I feel something hit my kite, I shall be frightened,' he admitted, 'but it's simply not possible to live in fear all the time. We have to feel excited instead. Wound up for a battle and determined to win. As though it were a rugger match for the honour of the school. We know all the moves, all the tricks, and we're going to come out on top. So even though every day there'll be some friend whom I'm never going to see again, I can't let that affect me. I have to believe that I personally am immortal.'

'If you're immortal, then why won't you marry me so that we can be immortal together?' asked Anne, throwing patience and modesty to the winds. She was entitled to take it for granted that he loved her. During the past four months he had made no secret of his feelings and they had come very close to a conversation of this kind several times before. It was time to press it to a conclusion. With the Battle of Britain at its height, all ordinary leave had been cancelled for the pilots who were Britain's front line. To take full advantage of one of Chay's rest periods, she had travelled as near to the airfield at North Weald as security allowed.

'Just in case,' he said now, bending a long blade of grass to tickle her neck.

'In case what?'

'In case I'm wrong about the immortal bit. I wouldn't want to think of you . . .'

'Chay, if you're killed —' It was the first time she had ever suggested the possibility in so many words, and she found herself shivering at the thought that it might bring bad luck even to talk about it. 'It would break my heart. Whether we were married or not, it would be the same.'

He shook his head. 'No it wouldn't. Married love is quite different from any other kind of love.'

'And how do you know that, pray?' She did her best to keep her voice light and joking; to pretend that they were not talking about matters of real life and possible death. 'Have you already got a wife tucked away somewhere?'

'I just do know. If I were to die tomorrow, yes, you'd be heartbroken, I'm sure you would, but your heart would heal. Sooner or later you'd meet someone else and be happy with him, and I'd want you to. But if we were married, properly married and living together, and then you found you had to live without me, it would be different. Much, much harder.'

'That's for me to worry about, not you.'

'And then there's the other thing.' He spoke as though he had not heard the interruption, and his voice was serious. 'Being killed is one of the easier options. Bang bang and it's over. There are worse things. I went over to East Grinstead the other day to visit a chap from my squadron who was shot down in flames. They had to amputate one of his hands to get him out of the plane, and he's burnt all over. There's nowhere on his body that he can bear to be touched. And he hasn't got any face that you'd recognise as a face. He'll live, they've promised him. For the moment he's a hero. One of the glorious Few. But in five years' time, he'll just be an unemployable cripple and people will turn away rather than look at him. I can't promise, can I, that that will never happen to me?'

'But you'd still be you,' said Anne desperately. 'It wouldn't make any difference.'

'Yes, it would. You've fallen in love with a chap who was born with a silver spoon in his mouth. I've never had to struggle with anything at all, and certainly not ill health. But anyone will tell you that pain and deformity change the personality. If we get married – and my dearest Anne, I want to marry you more than I've ever wanted anything in my life – you must marry the man you're going to live with for the next fifty years. The man who is as he will be, give or take the odd grouchiness or roll of fat that comes from advancing years.'

'You're thinking of your mother, aren't you?' said Anne

218

sadly. 'But Ronnie said that your father was never bitter about his war wounds. He was kind and good natured. And your mother went on loving him, didn't she?'

'My mother has always been a woman who sees her duty and does it. And although my father's health never recovered, the effect was probably to make him easy to live with. I suspect that Ma might have preferred to play her role in society on a larger stage, but as far as her leading man was concerned she never had anything to complain of but lassitude. For a pilot who crashes, though, there are no gentle illnesses.' Even as he smiled down at her his voice became decisive. 'You're not going to budge me on this. I love you; you know that. Yes, yes, yes, I love you. But. But.'

Once again his lips pressed down on hers. His hands stroked her body, their grip tightening until with a groan of self-restraint he rolled over on to his back again, linked to her only by their little fingers. For a long time neither of them spoke. Then Chay looked at his watch.

'Shall I walk you back to the bus stop or will you walk me back towards the airfield?' On her last visit they had covered the same ground three times, finding it impossible to say goodbye.

'I shall stay here. I love you, Chay.'

'I know.' One last kiss. 'See you again soon.'

She turned her head to follow his tall figure with her eyes as he walked away. Yes, he was one of the heroes on whom his country depended at the moment, fighting to save England from invasion and destruction. And he had been a hero of a different kind when she first set eyes on him at the Eton Fourth of June. 'An arrogant beast,' Howard had told her when she managed to introduce his name casually into some conversation. 'But quite decent underneath.' It was the decent man who had changed schoolgirl hero-worship into love. It was that man, not the young hero, whom she intended to love for the next fifty years.

There was as much pain as pleasure in her love. Sick with desire, she turned her face into the long, cool grass. The bees who had been frightened away by all the movement began to return. Ants and ladybirds and spiders made their busy way through their deep jungle. Wildflowers turned their faces upwards to bask in the sun. The meadow was at peace and she prayed aloud that peace would soon return to the wider world, but her prayer was really for one person only. 'Please, God, keep Chay safe.'

30

The air raid sirens began to wail their alert just as Peggy, finishing a watch at eleven in the evening, stepped out on to the street. For a second or two she hesitated, but she had spent the whole of the past ten hours working inside an underground bunker of reinforced concrete, and the thought of trying to get some sleep in a crowded air raid shelter was unbearable. If she ran, it would only take her ten minutes to get to her cabin. Her digs were in an ordinary boarding house, but if you were a Wren your sleeping quarters were in a cabin: no argument.

Already the wardens were on the street, shouting at stragglers to take cover. August had brought Liverpool its first major air raid and no one knew whether or when others would follow. It was probably not very intelligent to assume that if she couldn't see the warden he wouldn't be able to see her, but Peggy made the assumption and kept her eyes on the ground as she sprinted towards her temporary home. In the black-out she didn't notice the young man who was just letting himself out of a side door of the children's hospital until she hit him.

'Steady!' he exclaimed, clutching her shoulders in an attempt to prevent the two of them from losing balance and falling to the ground together.

'Sorry,' she muttered automatically. Only then did she realise that his voice was familiar. At the same moment he recognised her.

'Well, if it isn't the unfortunate Miss Armitage!' he exclaimed. 'Fancy bumping into you. Or being bumped into, rather. What are you doing in Liverpool?'

'Laurie!' She had last seen Dr Elliott on the evening of Lady

Ranelegh's ball, a lifetime ago. It was a night on which Anne had been radiant and Peggy was angry and both Isabelle and Ronnie were tearful. She herself had been the cause of Isabelle's tears, but she suspected that it was Laurie Elliott who had had something to do with Ronnie's. She had heard no news of him since that time, but remembered talk of his working as a doctor here. As an answer to his own question, it was best only to indicate her Wren uniform. To explain that she spent her working hours listening to wireless signals from enemy ships would be more than careless talk. Radio interception and intelligence was MOST SECRET.

'The ack-ack will be starting up any minute now,' he said. 'You oughtn't to be out on the street. Let's go inside.'

'I can't bear to go into a shelter,' Peggy confessed. 'I'm trying to get home before anything heavy starts to fall.'

'Then I shall escort you. Lead on.'

He took her hand and they ran together along the empty streets. Outside the boarding house Peggy paused uncertainly. It was getting on for midnight. Mrs Kelly's house rules were strict, and gentlemen friends were not allowed over the door-step after six o'clock in the evening. But Mrs Kelly was a nervous lady and would certainly by now be in the air raid shelter at the end of the garden. 'Cup of tea?'

'Lovely. And a chance to catch up with all our news.'

There were four Wrens billeted on Mrs Kelly, and the fixed hours of the meals which she was prepared to serve often found them either working or sleeping, so they had grudgingly been allowed the use of a gas ring and sink in a scullery. Peggy showed Laurie into the sitting room and went to boil a kettle.

She returned to find him fast asleep on a sofa, his head lolling at an awkward angle so that his thick fair hair fell over his forehead. How young he looked! Peggy herself was still under twenty, but at this hour of the night she felt old and tired.

She sat down in an armchair facing him and sipped her tea. It seemed a pity to wake him, though she couldn't resist setting the cup and saucer down a little more noisily than was necessary in the hope that he might stir. But his eyelids did not flutter, not even when she put a cushion beneath his head and took off his shoes.

Returning to her chair, she continued to stare, remembering

him as he had looked in his white tie and tails: flirting, laughing, dancing. Dancing beneath the chandeliers in Lady Ranelegh's ballroom while passers-by, ordinary people, in Green Park looked up at the terraces to envy golden youth at play. Passers-by and golden youth were all ordinary people now. Well, they always had been, but those few months of feeling different had been fun. Dancing, dancing, whirling round and round.

It was Peggy's own head that was whirling round and round as she remembered that unexpected period of her life. She awoke with a start to find the room in darkness and her body stiff and aching. Switching on the light, she found herself alone, but Laurie had left a message on the sofa.

'What disgraceful behaviour, to fall asleep like that! My excuse is that it's forty hours since I last slept, and it comes as a relief to see that you may be in the same boat. When I think how easy it was once to dance until dawn night after night! We must meet again when we can both keep our eyes open. I have a free day next Sunday, emergencies permitting. Have you? If so, do leave a message at the hospital.' Yes, she had. She was due to work the last of her one-to-eleven o'clock watches on Saturday night and then move on to the easiest watch, eight in the morning until one, on the Monday. She could sleep from midnight until seven on Sunday and be fresh for the day. How marvellous it was to have something to look forward to: an ordinary social pleasure.

Meeting Laurie inspired the unexpected pleasure that two expatriates might feel in some remote corner of the world in discovering that they both hailed from the same home town. They had in common four months of 1939; that was enough for them to greet each other as old friends. And friends were what Peggy badly needed. Although she had company both at work and in the boarding house, she was lonely in Liverpool.

Peggy's life had changed on the day – it was Christmas Day, 1939 – when she wrote to tell the Principal of St Hugh's College, Oxford, that she wished to defer the taking up of her exhibition until the end of the war. War was an occasion for sacrifice, and this was hers.

Her parents were surprised by the decision: especially her father, who understood how passionately she had wanted to succeed in the examination. He said nothing to discourage her, though. Too old to enlist himself, his contribution to the war effort was to turn two of his factories over to making workers' overalls and khaki shirts instead of bright summer dresses, but he was proud to have a daughter in uniform.

Mrs Armitage, equally puzzled, was alarmed when she discovered that her elder daughter proposed to join the WRNS, a service that might expose her to all sorts of dangers. But the war had hardly got into its stride when Peggy first paraded for family inspection in her new uniform, so it had been easy to persuade her mother that the life would be no more hazardous than that of a civilian.

Jodie, surprisingly, had not said, 'I told you!' Her comment instead was, 'Good for you!' – although, in true Jodie fashion, it was followed immediately by the declaration that she wouldn't be seen dead in the company of someone wearing that ridiculous pudding-basin hat.

Not that it would have mattered what any of them said. Once Peggy had made up her mind, there was no going back. Within six weeks she found herself undergoing a course that offered far more than training in naval discipline and wireless telegraphy. Many of the other girls were her own age, or even a year younger, but they all shared one common interest from which Peggy felt excluded: men.

Many of the men they discussed were fantasies: film stars. Peggy's burden of school homework had left her with little time to go to the cinema. By now – since a film was often the most accessible form of entertainment to offer itself in a strange town – she had begun to make up for this deficiency in her education. She began to realise that when other girls talked longingly about Ronald or Errol, Nelson or Ty, it was only an exercise in wishful thinking.

Other girls had long-standing relationships of the boy-next-door variety, and these too were endlessly discussed. My Bill, my Tom, my Bobbie. For the rest, every opportunity for meeting young men was eagerly pursued, and the physical character-istics of any who simply passed by were discussed in detail. Peggy found it amusing that she, who had been exposed to the best that society could offer in the way of potential husbands, should be almost alone in being heartwhole and unattached.

She told herself that probably there were many others who were in the same position but determined to conceal it. As though there were something shameful about not being in love.

She was posted to Liverpool as soon as her training course ended. She had no friends there – but no one would expect her to have. There was no shame in it, and before long she was working such killing hours that there was little time for any social life. She reminded herself stoutly that she mustn't think about getting married until she had been to Oxford, because if she did she would probably never get there at all. It was just as well that she seemed able to resist the infection of falling in love. And yet, behind the self-congratulation of that assurance, it was hard not to feel sometimes cut off from the kind of pleasures that seemed so important to everyone else.

It was a time of conflicting emotions. She yearned for Oxford and hated Liverpool, but was determined not to indulge in self-pitying regrets. She had no wish – yet – to marry and settle down to the kind of life her mother led; but she wanted to be loved, as every other girl of her age seemed to be loved. It was all very difficult.

But now, suddenly, there was Laurie. Laurie didn't love her. He had never even flirted with her in the way that he flirted with most of the other debutantes, but he would be a friend, and a link with her other friends. And she would be able at last to join in the chatter of the other girls. My Laurie. As she ironed the summer frock which would replace her heavy uniform for Sunday's meeting, Peggy sang aloud. Even in wartime Liverpool it was possible to be happy.

31

As though to confirm that this must be Peggy's lucky week, that
Sunday proved to be a day of blazing sunshine. They had
arranged that Laurie would pick her up for a bicycle ride at nine
o'clock, and he arrived five minutes early.

'I don't think I've ever seen you in ordinary clothes,' he
exclaimed. 'You looked immensely smart in your uniform the
other night. And of course I remember how stunning you were
in London, in those magnificent ball dresses. Now suddenly
you're equally stunning just in a summer dress.'

'You don't need to pay me compliments,' Peggy told him
sincerely. Just to have his company was pleasure enough.
'Where are we going?'

'I thought we'd head north towards Southport, but not go all
the way, because if we do we shall be on the road all day and
never have time to talk. We'll turn off at some point and head
for the coast. Why not bring a bathing costume in case we feel
like braving the briny?'

They set off side by side. Peggy and Jodie had always been
keen cyclists, so she had no difficulty in keeping up with her
companion, and the lack of traffic made it pleasant exercise.
During her working hours she was hardly able to move at
all. The steady movement of her legs and the freshness of
the air she was breathing made her feel like a newly released
prisoner.

They had left the main road and almost reached the sea when
Laurie came to a halt. 'Elevenses,' he announced.

They leaned their bicycles against a hedge and sat down on a
grass verge, turning their faces up to the sun. From a small

haversack he produced a Thermos flask of iced tea and half a packet of biscuits.

'Not quite in the champagne and strawberries class, I'm afraid.' He poured the tea into two mugs. 'But good enough for a toast to our reunion. If I may be allowed to embarrass you for a moment, I would like to put it on record that of all the debutantes of 1939, you are the one I most hoped I might meet again one day.'

'I'm the debutante you never flirted with. Everyone else, as far as I could tell, but never me.'

'Debutantes as a genus can be divided into two classes: girls to flirt with and girls to fall in love with. But you never managed to come into any sort of categorising. Just a girl whose company was a pleasure.'

'An outsider, in other words.'

'And all the better for it! Your good health!'

They raised their mugs solemnly to each other. It was the start of a perfect day. A day in which they slipped effortlessly back into the easy relationship begun in the previous summer. A day that was the first of several other meetings, all equally enjoyable.

At one of these, on another Sunday, everything changed. Once again the sun was shining, but after three weeks of a September heatwave that Peggy had rarely been able to enjoy, the day was sultry and the air heavy. A thunderstorm threatened and she took the precaution of stuffing a tightly rolled waterproof cape into her gas-mask case before they embarked on another bicycle ride. Again they paused in mid-morning for a cold drink, but this time Laurie led the way into a patch of woodland, which offered a rippling canopy of shade to protect them from the sun.

Tired, they flung themselves down on to a soft carpet of decaying leaves. Peggy lay back, glad to rest, while Laurie propped himself on one elbow to chat.

'I've been longing to ask you, but haven't dared. Curiosity wins in the end, though. If it isn't too sore a subject, what happened to Oxford? Since I hardly imagine that the Wrens are going to let you out again when the academic year starts in October.'

'Oxford has been postponed.'

'You got in all right, then?'

'Yes. But it seemed, well, a bit selfish to enjoy myself when so many people were having such a rotten time. It'll still be there when I'm ready for it.'

'Do you ever regret the decision?'

'It wasn't forced on me. My own choice. I decided I'd never let myself regret it and so I don't.' This was only half true. There had been a good many moments – especially during the first lonely months in Liverpool – when she had reproached herself for being a fool; in the same way that Isabelle had been a fool to volunteer for a nursing job before realising how much she would hate it. But the decision had been made, and what could not be altered must be accepted.

'And it's been worth it?' he asked. 'I mean, the work you're doing now is worth while, is it?'

Peggy knew that he would not expect her to describe her work, but his question was a good one. She spent her long watches struggling to record Morse tappings heard through the atmospheric crackle of her headphones. The groups of letters she transcribed meant nothing to her. They were all passed on to 'Station X', wherever that might be, where presumably someone tried to make sense of them.

Just once, though, she had genuinely felt herself to be useful. At three o'clock one morning – a time when concentration was hardest to maintain – she was trawling through the wavelengths when she recognised the B-bar call signal of a U-boat which had been maintaining radio silence for the past eight days. Even as she called out the frequency she was raising her hand to attract the supervising officer, already convinced by some kind of sixth sense that something significant was happening. The message was so short that it might easily have been missed, but it was followed within the next ten minutes by five other brief signals from U-boats which were known to be operating in the same area. Was it fanciful of her to become convinced that a group of submarines, already stalking a convoy, had just been joined by the one whose leadership they had been awaiting? Whether it was or not, she had passed on her sense of urgency.

Too often in the past weeks she had shivered with horror as news came through of another convoy attacked, another merchant ship sunk. The mental picture of men clinging help-lessly to wreckage in the dark and icy sea and one by one slipping into the depths to drown was enough to give her nightmares. Perhaps on this occasion there would have been enough warning for a U-boat to have been sunk instead. Yes, to answer Laurie's question, her work was worth while.

'Do you regret Ronnie?' she asked abruptly. Perhaps the question was tactless, but it needed to be got out of the way.

'That would be a different kind of regret from yours. Oxford was within your reach. Ronnie was never within mine.'

'If you're referring to social rank, that must have stopped being important the day the war started.'

'But this was before the war. And anyway, *you* can dismiss society because you've been brought up to believe that you're as good as anyone else, and so you are – or a great deal better. But it's easier for someone looking up to say that than for someone looking down to believe it. Ronnie didn't have the foggiest idea of what it would have been like, being married to me. Cruelty to children, it would have been. I'm all for letting people make their own mistakes in order to learn from them; but only after they're grown up – and not when there's a danger that I might be regarded as the mistake myself.'

'I'm sure she felt—'

'She didn't know what she felt. That was why I had to do the thinking for her. The social thing wasn't the most important. She was just too young. She ought not to have got married to anybody at all at that age. Certainly not to me, but not to Ross either, in my opinion. I can understand how hard it must be for a girl, when her mother is pushing her and she can't think what else to do anyway, but all the same . . . You had more sense.'

'What *is* the right age for getting married? For a girl.'

'For someone like your friend Anne, any time now would do, because she's got good judgement. She knows exactly what's best for her. If she gets it, she'll settle down to being a wife and mother without any second thoughts. For you, I'd say twenty-four or twenty-five.'

'Are you telling me that I haven't got good judgement?' Peggy, amused, pretended to be indignant.

'I'm suggesting that you may prove to be one of those rare young ladies who is capable of living your own life rather than merely your husband's. Though why you should think that my opinion is of the slightest value I can't imagine.' Laurie was laughing again in the bantering manner that she remembered as typical of him.

'If I wait till twenty-five I shall have to do the living my own life thing as a spinster. I shall be thoroughly on the shelf by then.'

'Nonsense. You'll be at your peak of beauty and good sense, whereas most girls are pretty at seventeen and then start to go downhill all the way.'

Peggy closed her eyes for a moment. It was something she had worked out for herself – and something which caused her anxiety. Nobody could know how long the war might last, but she would have to stick it out in the Wrens and then there would be Oxford after that. Like every other girl she knew, she took it for granted that she would want to get married one day, once she had had a taste of living an independent life for a while; but she might indeed be in her mid-twenties before she was ready.

'You're not going to fall asleep on me again, are you?' Laurie's voice expressed mock anxiety as he recalled the night of the bump in the blackout. She opened her eyes, smiling.

'Not this time, no. Tell me, Laurie. When you get married, will you expect your wife to be a virgin?'

He looked momentarily startled by a question that was not exactly debutante talk. But he was prepared to give a direct answer to a direct question.

'If you'd asked me that a year ago, I'd have said yes. And if I were to marry a young girl this year or next year, I'd still say yes. But attitudes are changing so fast that I'm not sure . . . There's bound to be a bit of *carpe diem* in wartime. When a girl's saying goodbye to a chap she may never see again, I wouldn't blame her for not wanting to wait for a wedding day. It wouldn't mean that she was promiscuous. And if in fact she never did see the chap again, but married me instead, that would be all right. I'd understand. I think. But at the moment I'm not in the marrying mode, so I can't say I've given much thought to the question. What's your interest in it?'

'I just wonder sometimes. I think you're probably right that I shan't want to get married for quite a time yet, but it seems a long time to wait to . . .' Her voice faltered to a halt. What was she saying?

Whatever it was, Laurie had understood it. He looked down at her for a little while without speaking. 'Is that an invitation?'

Peggy licked her lips nervously. It wasn't much of a compliment, was it, to make it clear that all she wanted was to get the first time out of the way so that she needn't wonder or worry about it any more? 'No, of course not,' she said.

'I rather think it was, you know. And I rather think I'd like to accept with pleasure.' He leaned towards her, his hand stroking up one bare arm until he touched her neck and began to unbutton her dress.

'I didn't mean now, here!' she exclaimed, not caring that she was contradicting herself.

'Yes, you did. If we agree to do it some time in the future you'll get nervous, waiting; wondering when I might pounce. And trying to sneak into some bedroom together would make the whole thing sordid. But the sun is shining and I think you're perfectly lovely and this is going to be the best moment of your life.'

'But I mustn't have a baby, Laurie! I don't want to have to get married!'

'Then how sensible of you to choose a chap like me, who knows what's what.' By now he had unbuttoned her dress right down to the hem. 'Freckles here, too!' he exclaimed in delight, and bent over to kiss them. Then, no longer unhurried, he began tearing off his own clothes.

'Laurie, I'm not sure. I shouldn't have said . . .'

He checked himself for just long enough to grip her tightly and press his lips down on hers.

'Lesson number one,' he said, 'is that it's possible for a girl to change her mind half way, but it isn't possible for a man. You're beautiful and this is going to be beautiful and it's time you got your knickers off.'

Still doubtful, Peggy nevertheless did what she was told, glad that she was not wearing the workmanlike garment that was part of her uniform issue. And suddenly, as his kisses covered her body, her doubts evaporated. Yes, this was the right decision and the right place and the right man. He didn't hurt her as she had expected to be hurt. Although his face seemed to belong to a stranger as he pressed down on her over and over again, through it all he somehow continued to be laughing, as though to reassure her that this was fun.

Not everything about the experience was delightful, though. Last autumn's leaves, that had provided such a soft blanket while they were both dressed, now proved to be prickly, and little bits adhered to her skin where she was sticky or bleeding or merely sweating in the heat. Breathless and excited as Laurie collapsed on to the ground beside her, she tried without success to brush them off; but help arrived from an unexpected quarter. A clap of thunder, so close at hand that it sounded as though Liverpool had been blown up in an air raid, heralded the storm they had been expecting. Pausing only to fling their clothes under the most densely leaved of the woodland trees, Laurie took her hand and led her, naked, out into the rain.

Just for a second she looked around nervously, but there was no one to see them. Happy, and no longer shy, she enjoyed the well-timed shower, using the deluge to clean his back with her hand before he performed the same service for her.

She had never seen a naked man before, but of course she had looked at pictures and copies of classical statues. Laurie had the firm buttocks and muscular arms and legs that she had admired in marble, but his skin surprised her by being as pale and soft as a woman's. What surprised her even more, though, was her own lack of embarrassment as his hands moved over her body.

'Once more,' he said suddenly. 'You're going to ditch me tomorrow, aren't you? So once more now.' All the cleansing work of the storm went for nothing as he pressed her, still standing, against the trunk of a tree; lifting her, moving her until he sensed that she had recovered enough from her surprise to relax and accept him.

They were both drenched by the time Laurie twisted away from her and, gasping her name over and over again, covered her legs with stickiness for a second time. She understood now why there would be no baby, and was grateful.

That night, back in the boarding house, Peggy lay in the five inches of water which was all that anyone was allowed in the bath and asked herself what she thought she was up to. A nicely brought up girl like her! If she were ever to try to explain her actions to her mother she would be met by incomprehension. 'I

232

wanted to get it out of the way. I wanted to know what it was like. I wanted not to have to think about it again, perhaps for years.'

Would the fact that she had enjoyed it make any difference to that resolution? Or had Laurie been right to believe that she would not want this to happen again? Peggy was still too amazed that it had happened at all to attempt to answer that question.

In the confusion of her thoughts she had a sudden picture of the night when she had inadvertently overheard Isabelle's false protestations to Chay about the ruin of her reputation. Isabelle's attempt to manipulate the situation had been clumsy, but she had been playing by rules that were very real and very simple. A woman's innocence and reputation were priceless. Peggy thought that she would never have needed to ask Chay, or anyone in his circle, her question about whether men wanted brides who were virgins. Of course they did: the purity of the aristocratic line must be preserved. And now she had lost her own innocence, and put herself outside Chay's world.

Peggy lay back in the cool water and asked herself whether she minded. In a way, she had been in love with Chay. She had been delighted by his friendship, and she had loved the ease of his manner, his physical grace, and the seriousness that under-lay his public face. But she was level headed enough to realise that Chay had been out of her reach from the start – and not because of social distinctions, but because he adored Anne. Chay would marry Anne one day: of course he would. And tomorrow Peggy would arrange to see Laurie again.

32

Chay was exhausted. In this he was not alone. Everyone at North Weald was exhausted, from the pilots who daily risked their lives in the sky, to the cooks and clerks and mechanics who were in danger of being bombed on the ground. Every time he closed his eyes to sleep he thought to himself, 'This can't go on'; but every awakening brought the knowledge that it would.

Within the past few days the pattern had changed. Earlier in the summer the Luftwaffe had been concentrating its bombing on airfields, destroying as many British planes as possible to clear the way for the invasion that everyone had been expecting. Now, in September, it was London that had become the main target. The reason for this was not very clear to Chay, but he was not required to read Goering's mind, only to cope with the consequences of the change. The enemy now came mainly at night, and night fighting required different tactics from the sunlit dogfights of summer – as well as different patterns of sleep, to which he was finding it hard to adjust.

Forcing himself to move briskly, he went straight from the meal that counted as breakfast, to the workshop hangar, to see whether his Hurricane was fit to fly. On its last outing a bullet had jammed the port aileron, making the return to base a nerve-racking affair. From underneath the plane, as he approached, he heard the sound of whistling.

'You sound chirpy,' he commented as the mechanic eased himself out and smacked his hands to indicate a job completed.

'Got married on Saturday, sir, that's why.'

'Go on! You always said you never would.' Chay was not the

only man on the airfield to feel that it was unfair to expose the girls they loved to the fear of being widowed.

'Well, you know how it is, sir.' The aircraftsman found a rag to wipe the grease off his hands. 'I was feeling a bit gloomy, like. I mean, I know I'm safer down here than you are up there, but . . .' He was silent for a moment and they both remembered the seven cheerful Waafs who had been killed when their hut was bombed during a raid on the airfield. 'I thought to myself sudden, like, "Well, if I buy it, why shouldn't she at least have the pension?" And besides that, she's a good girl and she's never nagged, but I know she'd like to be a Mrs. All the girls want the handle to their name, don't they? If Sal were to find herself on her own and still a Miss, there'd be nothing to show that anyone had ever been sweet on her, like.'

It was an interesting thought, and one that Chay found himself applying to his situation. But of course that was quite different. If he were to marry Anne, she would become rather more than a Mrs. Some girls would have leapt at the title – the picture of Isabelle le Vaillant flashed into his mind – yet for Anne, he felt sure, the title would be nothing in itself, but rather a burden which could be borne only if he went with it.

'How did you fix it up at such short notice?' he asked casually.

'Special licence, sir. If you happen to be feeling in the mood yourself, I've got a spare form I could let you have.' There was a cackle of gap-toothed laughter. 'I'd decided for myself that was the way to do it, with a bit of leave coming up. Got everything arranged. But it turned out that Sal was thinking the same way. Been to the office herself, she had, and turned up with a form of her own. "Come on," she said. "Fill this up and let's get cracking." Made me feel glad I'd done it already.'

'Well,' said Chay, 'I don't suppose you're reckoning to marry anyone else for a day or two, so yes, I wouldn't mind having a look at it.'

He had a look at it. He considered it. He remembered how disappointed Anne had been by what he had said at their last meeting. If she wanted the commitment so badly, why not? After all, it was what he passionately wanted himself.

He had a three-day leave coming up quite soon. Anne was well aware that it was liable to be cancelled without notice, but they had both booked into a hotel near Waltham Abbey. They could have a brief honeymoon there. But to tell her what he had in mind would be to court disappointment if he was unable to turn up. He wrote to apply for a special licence. That didn't commit him to using it. Or so he told himself.

On 7 September, two days after he posted the application, his Wing was scrambled at five o'clock in the afternoon. More than three hundred German bombers were crossing the coast at Clacton, heading for London. They flew in diamond or arrow-head formation, droning steadily onwards with an escort of fighter planes circling high above them, ready to swoop if they were attacked.

Chay's squadron of Hurricanes was one of those detailed to stop the bombers getting through, while squadrons of Spitfires engaged the escorting Messerschmitts and Heinkels. There was no time to think about anything else as he dashed for his plane, took off with the rest of Red section, climbed rapidly in line astern and positioned himself with the sun behind him above the Dornier bombers pressing purposefully ahead on their mission of destruction.

Now he had to pick his target and attack it, but be aware at the same time that he would be the target of enemy fighters. He had to use all his skill and initiative as an individual pilot, but at the same time know the positions of the rest of his section, and be ready to come to their aid if needed. While the battle was in progress, because every ounce of his concentration was re-quired just to play his part efficiently, he had no time to worry about the danger. It was only when he ran out of ammunition and had landed safely back at base that he found himself trembling, needing to sit quietly in the cockpit for a moment or two before he could manage the jaunty walk that was expected of him when he went to deliver his report. And then, an hour and a half later, it was time to go up again.

By the time he was free to sleep, if he could, it was five in the morning, and sleep did not come easily. He had seen two of his friends killed: one in a mid-air collision with a Messerschmitt and the other when his fuel tank was hit by machine-gun fire and exploded. No doubt other deaths had occurred as well: empty chairs in the mess. But they had given as good as they got. The enemy's casualties must have been heavy. He himself had sent two Dorniers spinning out of control to crash far below. Yet so many had been launched in the raid that at least some of them must have penetrated every line of defence. There would be smoking ruins in London now. Women would be weeping for their children or staring in disbelief at what had once been their homes. Men in uniform would be learning that their wives and mothers and daughters had become military targets.

The bombers would probably come again on the next night and the night after that. Chay took it for granted that his leave would be cancelled, but in this he was wrong: so many planes had been damaged that there were more men available than machines.

And so on the next Wednesday he signed himself into the hotel as arranged, noting from the registration book that Anne had not yet arrived. He wondered what she had told her parents about her absence from home. She had of course booked a separate room for herself, but even so, to stay in the same hotel as the man she loved would certainly not have met with their approval. Still, there was no alternative. She had not been prepared to invite him to Yewley, knowing that her mother would fuss and hint and nudge. And on his own side, Cleeve was too far away for such a short leave.

Chay dumped his things in his room and wandered down to the stream at the bottom of the hotel garden. Its gentle whisper refreshed him as he sat on the bank, his arms locked around his knees. A few moments earlier he had been thinking about Anne's mother. Now his thoughts turned to his own.

The duchess's position was perfectly clear and perfectly understandable. It was her son's duty to produce an heir as soon as possible. In normal times she might have expected to scrutinise all candidates for the post of the heir's mother with care, but in the existing circumstances Anne would certainly be acceptable. If Chay were to take her to Cleeve, it would be made plain what was expected of her. And when they married, if they married, she would come under day-to-day scrutiny. Was she pregnant yet? But if Chay were to be killed and leave a widow who was not expecting a baby after all she would be in an uncomfortable position: a useless adjunct to the family. Would it be fair to expose Anne to that possibility?

Why was it so hard to make up his mind? His mother would say, 'Don't dither. Decide and then do it.' His sister carried that attitude to extremes. Ronnie would act on impulse without taking time to think. Chay himself had never in the past been a ditherer. But here he was, with a special licence in his pocket, mentally prepared only an hour earlier to go down on his knees and propose marriage and yet suddenly once again hitting this mental block: it wouldn't be fair. The fact that from the inheritance point of view it was not only sensible but essential simply made matters worse. It wouldn't be fair.

'I thought I'd find you here.'

Chay scrambled to his feet at the sound of Anne's voice. They grinned at each other like a pair of naughty adolescents.

'I think the receptionist is suspicious,' she said. 'I may have looked too happy when I saw your name in her book.'

'None of her business.' Still smiling, Chay moved forward to kiss her, but not as fiercely and passionately as he would have liked. This leave must be as happy and uncomplicated as any of the single days that they had spent together in the past few months. The fact that it would include two nights must not be allowed to make a difference. He was not, after all, going to propose.

Nevertheless, as he prepared for bed that night, he couldn't help wondering. The two nights *did* make a difference. Would Anne be expecting him to come to her room? Was she lying in bed at this moment, listening for the creaking in the corridor, the quiet turning of the door handle? No, of course she wasn't.

There was a creaking in the corridor. Quietly the door handle turned. Anne, wearing a satin dressing gown, let herself into his room and closed the door behind her. Chay had opened the curtains after he turned off the light, so it was only by moonlight that he could see her. She was nervous – frightened, even – but it seemed that she had rehearsed what she wanted to say.

'You're trying to do my thinking for me,' she said. 'You're trying to make my decisions for me. But I want to make my own, and I have. If you don't want me, well, you'll just have to tell me to go away. But I want you, and that's what I've come to say.'

Her dressing gown was half open and now she shrugged it back off her shoulders. She was wearing nothing underneath.

For a moment Chay could neither move nor speak. Because she was a shy and modest girl who must have needed all her courage to behave in such a way, she was standing unnaturally straight, with her chin up and her head held high. Only the trembling of her lips betrayed her nervousness. Chay's eyes lingered on those lips and then travelled downwards over her slender neck, the delicate pattern of the bones beneath, the full breasts and tiny waist, the smooth flat stomach, the long, slim legs, all silvered by the light of the moon. It was too much to bear. Sitting on the edge of the bed, he buried his head in his hands, sobbing.

He hadn't cried since he was three years old, and he didn't know why he was crying now, but Anne knew. There was no more sign of nervousness as she sat down beside him and cradled him in her arms, pressing his head between her breasts.

'You're pushing me away because you believe you're going to be killed,' she said. 'All the time that you're pretending to be sure that it can't ever happen to you, you really feel sure that it will. And so you're trying to make me behave as though I believe it as well. Well, I don't, and so I won't. You're caught up in a battle, and I know it's a bad one, but every battle comes to an end one way or another and people survive. You're not going to be killed. I won't let you think that for a moment. You're a good pilot and you've come through the worst of it and you're going to come through the rest. And I want to be with you now as well as for years and years and years afterwards. It's not fair of you to think that I can't cope with being scared. I can cope with anything at all as long as we have each other.'

How could he resist, when this was what he had wanted for so many months? How could he resist, when to do so would be not self-control but rejection? Still sobbing, but without tears, he pulled her on to the bed beside him, covering her with his body, covering her with kisses. After waiting for so long, he was frantic not to waste another second – but he told himself that he must be gentle, must be slow.

Anne had other ideas.

'Don't worry about me,' she said. 'I love you so much, Chay. I want you to hurt me so that we can be close, so close that we're one person. Oh please, please.' Her hands were on his buttocks, pressing him down, and she made no sound when he entered

239

her. Instead, she enfolded him more tightly with her legs. Her arms tightened round his neck and her body arched to meet his until he emptied into her his whole life, his whole love, freeing himself of the doubts and hesitations which had caused him to waste so much time when he could have been happy.

'I shall have to marry you now,' he said later, laughing in relief and happiness. 'To make an honest woman of you.'

'It's not compulsory,' Anne told him. 'There are no shotguns around. I wouldn't like you to think . . .'

'This is what I think.' He closed the black-out curtains so that he could turn on the light, and felt in one of his pockets for the special licence that only twelve hours earlier he had decided not to use after all. How ridiculous it would have been to let the girl he adored return home as a single woman! As she read it he watched her eyes and lips widening in delight. It crumpled between them as she flung herself into his arms again.

'Oh Chay, my darling, thank you. Thank you so much.'

'So you will, will you? Marry me, I mean. Tomorrow. No, it's today.'

'Of course I will. Darling!'

'Your mother won't be pleased at missing the wedding.'

Anne giggled in agreement. 'Too bad. I wouldn't have enjoyed the sort of posh affair that Ronnie had. This is how it should be. Just the two of us. I only wish we could have longer, but there'll be other leaves.'

Yes, there would be other leaves. Nevertheless, saying good-bye to Anne when this one ended, far too soon, was the hardest moment of Chay's life. At the register office two obliging passers-by had been hauled in from the street. They had been goggle-eyed when they realised that they were acting as witnesses to the marriage of a duke, but had promised to keep it to themselves for a week. Afterwards the happy couple had returned to the hotel and transferred to a room with a double bed so that they could claim that the next duke, if there was one, had been conceived in wedlock.

Back in the mess, Chay had to pretend to his fellow pilots that nothing had changed, despite the spring in his step and the light in his eyes.

He was longing to make an announcement, but he knew that

he must tell his mother first. She would have the right to be hurt and angry if she were to hear the news from anyone else, so when he went to the office to register that Anne was now his next of kin, he swore the clerk, like the witnesses, to secrecy for a week. Anne had promised to say nothing to her own family for a few days, to give a letter time to arrive at Cleeve. A telephone call would be too brusque. He had to explain to his mother why the wedding had taken place without notice to anyone. Then she would be able to spread the news amongst her friends – and pretend, if she wished, that she had known about it all along.

First of all, though, he needed some sleep, for he had had virtually none in the past three days and two nights. He lay down at midnight and seemed only just to have closed his eyes when an orderly awoke him with the news that it was four-thirty in the morning and time to stir himself. Still only half awake he pulled on his Irvin jacket and trousers, and over them his flying boots and Mae West. Then he staggered wearily across to find the Hurricane that would be his and to check it over: petrol, oil, airscrew pitch, directional gyro, helmet, oxygen, radio. All correct. Nothing to do now but wonder when the enemy would put in an appearance.

While he waited in the hut with all the other sleepy pilots, he settled down to write the letter. 'Dearest Ma.' That was the only easy part. He reminded her that she must have noticed Anne Venables as the most beautiful debutante of her year, and that she had probably already guessed that they were in love. Then picking his words carefully – and most certainly making no reference to Anne's appearance in his hotel bedroom – he began to describe the doubts that had at first made him hesitate and the impulse that had changed his mind and convinced him that there was no time to be lost.

The words were not quite right. He would have to try again, copying out some of what he had written and improving the rest. But he couldn't keep his eyes open sufficiently to concentrate. Pushing the unfinished letter into his locker, he rested his arms on the table and his head on his arms and allowed himself to sleep.

He was awakened by the sound of the telephone orderly's voice over the tannoy. 'Dover 26,000. One hundred bandits approaching from south-east. Scramble Red section. Scramble Yellow section. Scramble Blue section. Scramble.'

From then on, every action was automatic. Grabbing his flying gloves, he ran from the hut with the other pilots, fitted on his parachute and settled himself into the cockpit of the plane, whose engine was already running.

Even as he took off and began circling to gain height, a new message came through his earphones, diverting the whole Wing to intercept a second wave of bombers, approaching from the east. They would be using the Blackwater estuary as a guide. The Hurricanes wheeled north, preparing to sweep back and attack the enemy from behind. The Germans painted their Dorniers black for night raids, so it was difficult to see them in darkness while they remained over land, but over water their silhouettes could easily be distinguished. There was a flurry of instructions over the radio as each section was allotted its target. Chay took the message in, but his eyes were on the water, which from this height looked calm amd beautiful. It was a clear night. The moon was almost as full as it had been when Anne first came to him. It silvered the estuary as three nights earlier it had silvered her skin.

'Red 3. Red 3. Bandit above you.'

Chay was Red 3 and, unforgivably, he had allowed his concentration to slip. Instinctively he turned the Hurricane into a steep sideways dive before roaring up again in an effort to get above his attacker. It was one of a formation of Messerschmitt 109s which were escorting the Dorniers, and even as Chay turned sharply again to avoid it he was aware of another plane behind him, raking his tail with machine-gun fire. By now the two other pilots in his section had realised that he was in trouble and were swooping down to help. But the first Messerschmitt made a tight turn and came straight towards him like a determined hornet. It seemed intent on a suicidal collision, but at the last moment it swerved away. Not, however, before putting two cannon shells into Chay's engine.

The explosion rocked the Hurricane and obscured its wind-screen with black oil. Chay was struggling to control the plane, which, without power, was already pointing its nose into a dive, when the tail was shot away by a burst of fire from the second enemy fighter. With a sudden whoosh the engine exploded into flames. The cockpit filled with smoke and the increasing speed at which the machine was spinning downwards forced the flames towards him.

This was the first time that he had had to bale out, but hours of practice enabled him to follow the necessary procedures automatically. Taking a deep breath of oxygen before pulling off his helmet, he tugged at the rubber ball above his head which released the hood of the cockpit. Now his ears were battered by the screaming noise of his descent and his face was flattened by the force of the air pressing against it. One hand tugged away the harness while the other gripped tightly on the ring of the parachute which would save his life in a second or two.

He began to push himself up and out of the cockpit. The wind battered against his head and shoulders, blinding his eyes and numbing his brain. It was trying to suck him out – and that was what he wanted – but something was refusing to let him go. It was hard to work out what it could be, for by now the Hurricane was spinning, but he realised that one foot was trapped under part of the engine which had broken through into the cockpit. He fought to tug it away, but nothing would budge. If this were a car crash, he thought, someone could cut the foot off and get him out. But there were no passing surgeons in the sky.

Was it only days ago that he had been the happiest man in the world, with everything to live for and every possible advantage in life to help him enjoy it? These last seconds seemed to be passing as slowly as hours, but even hours must come to an end. He was not so much afraid as angry, swearing aloud as he pulled fruitlessly to free his foot. Then a second explosion sent a sheet of flame cannoning into his body.

The Hurricane plunged into the calm silver water of the estuary. There were a few moments of steam and turbulence, but before very long all was calm again. The Tenth Duke of Wiltshire's war was over.

33

In late September the Blitz on London was in full swing. No longer was Ronnie a leisured chauffeuse, working office hours in the area around Whitehall. Ever since the raid on the Docklands she had been driving an ambulance through darkness to whichever part of London had been that night's target. The East End was a foreign country to her and bomb craters and the obstructions caused by demolished houses made driving a nightmare; but that was nothing compared to the harrowing duty of helping to load broken and bleeding bodies into her vehicle.

The bombs did not cease to fall while wounded people were being rescued. When she had time to think about it, Ronnie found it strange that her husband – a professional soldier – should be safe, while she was coming under enemy fire. One of the girls who had been presented at the same Court had even been killed: the blast from a bomb had sent her ambulance hurtling straight into the deep water of a dock.

On this particular night Ronnie was behind the wheel of a furniture van. So many ambulances had been rendered unroadworthy that a variety of unlikely vehicles had been called into service. Nobody enjoyed driving the pantechnicon and there was supposed to be a rota to give each of the Fannies in turn the job of struggling with it. But because Ronnie was a more skilled driver than any of the others, her turn seemed to come round with suspicious speed.

The van could hold more stretchers than a regular ambulance, and on her final trip she had to call at four different casualty centres and hospitals before at last the nurse travelling in the back announced that beds had been found for all her patients. By the time Ronnie arrived back at Delacourt House her body ached from the struggle to control the huge van over rough ground, and her head ached from lack of sleep. It was eight o'clock in the morning and she had been on duty for sixteen hours.

She was awakened by a polite cough from Walker, the one-time butler whose duties nowadays were those of caretaker and fire-watcher.

'I'm sorry to disturb you, my lady. There was a telephone call for you from her grace this morning. I took the liberty of mentioning that you had only just returned to sleep. She will telephone again at three o'clock.'

'What time is it now?'

'Five minutes to three, my lady. Knowing that you would have to leave again at three-thirty, I thought –'

'Yes. Quite right.' She had slept for seven hours but was still tired out. Hungry, though. Except for a snatched cup of tea and a bun at about midnight, she had eaten nothing for twenty-four hours. 'I'd like some breakfast. Or tea, rather. Whatever there is to eat.'

The telephone began to ring at that moment. Ronnie put on a dressing gown over the underclothes she had been too tired to remove when she returned home and went along the corridor to pick up the receiver. At the other end of the line, no one spoke.

'Ma? Is that you, Ma?'

There was an odd noise; a strangled sigh. Then she heard her name spoken. 'Ronnie.'

'Yes.'

'Oh, Ronnie.'

'What's the matter, Ma? What's happened? Are you all right?' Ronnie had never known her mother to lose control of her actions or her voice. Even during her husband's funeral she had managed not to cry. There was only one thing that could have caused that sigh of anguish. 'Ma, don't say . . . Tell me. It isn't Chay, is it?' Oh God, she thought, don't let it be Chay.

There was another long silence. Another sigh. 'Yes,' said the duchess. 'Chay. Shot down over water.'

'Is he missing?' It was the last desperate hope. Pilots who

ditched in the Channel were very often rescued, either by their own side or by the enemy.

'No. Dead. Confirmed. Sorry, Ronnie. I can't talk.' There was a click as the connection was cut.

For a moment Ronnie was unable to move. Cold and trembling, she stared at the silent telephone. Then, dashing frantically back to her bedroom, she turned on the wireless. She had missed the first few seconds of the news, which obviously had described the air raids in which she had been involved. 'Eighty-five German planes were shot down in the course of the night,' said the announcer, 'for the loss of seven of our own.'

Seven planes. Seven young men probably dead. Seven families plunged into mourning. She waited to hear whether Chay would be given any special mention: that among the casualties was Flight-Lieutenant His Grace the Duke of Wilt-shire, killed at the age of twenty-five. But no: in death there were no differences of rank. Chay was just one of seven. Except that perhaps he had not been killed last night, but some time ago. It was bound to take a day or two to notify the next of kin, and nothing would be publicly announced until they had heard.

What did an announcement matter? Still too shocked to cry, Ronnie switched off the voice but continued to stare at the wireless as earlier she had stared at the telephone, without seeing it. Her meal was ready, but she was no longer hungry. Like her mother, she found it hard to speak, and could only shake her head before returning to her room to put on her uniform. It didn't occur to her for a moment not to report on time as usual, but she moved like an automaton and sat in silence in the duty room as she awaited the wail of the siren which would summon the drivers into action.

That night it was the area around St Paul's Cathedral which was taking the brunt of the raid. The first bombers to arrive had dropped fire bombs to illuminate a target. The high explosives which were falling by the time she arrived on the scene were wrecking offices and public buildings but not producing many casualties. Although heavily populated during working hours, this part of the City had few homes or residents. She had been sitting numbly at the wheel of her ambulance for some time before she saw the first stretcher being rushed towards her.

246

She jumped out to open the rear doors. Even above the noise of explosives and falling masonry and hissing steam as the hoses rammed water through broken windows she could hear the screams of her approaching passenger and looked down as he was lifted inside. He was a young fireman who must have been trapped inside a burning building. The high-pitched sound was emerging from a circle of black, bubbling flesh that was hardly recognisable as a face at all.

Was this how Chay, handsome Chay, had looked in his last moments of life? Had he known what must happen as his plane screamed towards the water? How long had he had to endure such agony before death took pity on him? The questions churned in Ronnie's stomach and choked her throat. Without warning she heard herself emitting a howl, a scream of disbelief and anguish. Gasping for breath, she buried her head in her hands and began to sob noisily and uncontrollably.

She had no memory of how she got back to base or what happened to her ambulance, but it was still dark when the order came for her to report to the commandant.

Dabbing her eyes dry before she went in, she stood to attention in front of the desk.

'What's wrong?'

A lump in her throat prevented Ronnie from answering. In a moment she was going to cry again. She stared down at her toes in an effort to remain unemotional.

'Your husband?'

Ronnie shook her head. 'No, ma'am. My brother.' Once again the tears began to flow. She felt herself being helped into a chair and struggled to control herself, but it was a moment or two before she was able to steady her breathing with a single juddering sigh. 'I'm very sorry, ma'am.'

'I'm sorry too. You'll want to be with your family.' The commandant was writing a chitty. 'Four days' compassionate leave. Don't feel ashamed. These last few weeks have been hard for all of you, and you've done splendidly. Make sure you get some rest.'

'Thank you very much, ma'am.'

Ronnie had not been to Cleeve since the previous Christmas. She knew, of course, that in the meantime most of the building had been requisitioned by the military, but it came as a shock, nevertheless, when at the end of a long and tiring journey she found herself turned away from the entrance of the castle and directed to what in the past had been a garden door.

The duchess, although restricted to one of the turrets and the long drawing room which faced west over a terrace, had transferred sufficient of her furniture and possessions to her new accommodation to give the drawing room an appearance which ought to have been comfortingly familiar. But as she rose to greet Ronnie, her bleakness of spirit infected the sunny room with the chill loneliness of a prison cell.

The two women embraced. Neither spoke. Ronnie had made the journey to comfort her mother and be comforted, but she had no comfort to give; nor could she have accepted any if it were offered. Some things, she thought, are one hundred per cent terrible. No bright side, no silver lining, no honest way of suggesting, 'Well at least . . .' Chay was dead and would be dead for ever and nothing would ever be the same again. Her father's death had been upsetting enough, but he was a sick man, and, however sad it might be, a father must be expected to die before his children. But this . . .

'Oh, Ma!' exclaimed Ronnie. What else could she possibly say?

The tightness of her embrace expressed more emotion than the duchess had ever before allowed herself to reveal. If she had cried, her tears were dry by now, although they seemed to have etched more deeply than before the lines around her eyes and mouth. When at last she stepped back, she shook her head at the sight of her daughter's pale, strained face.

'You look exhausted. When were you last in bed? We can talk tomorrow. Go and get some sleep now.'

'Where?'

The duchess rang a small bell. Her summons was answered not by a footman but by a maid – a child who must only just have left school.

'Show Lady Ronnie to her room and see if there's anything she needs.'

What Ronnie needed was food. Although she still had no appetite, she guessed that this must account for part of the faintness she felt.

'What's your name?' she asked the girl.

'Paula, my lady,' said the maid, perhaps too new to her work to know that she would be addressed by her surname.

'Show me where the kitchen is, will you?' The area in which cooks and kitchen maids had slaved for two and a half centuries was on the far side of the castle and presumably now dishing out sausages and baked beans to soldiers or civil servants.

Here was one change for the better: instead of a long hot black cooking range loaded with huge cauldrons and insatiably demanding to be stoked, an electric stove had been fitted neatly into the old fireplace of a small room. An open window above a deep sink admitted the cool autumn air to freshen the room, without banishing the smell of the carrot cake that Mrs Stockford was just turning out on to a wire tray to cool.

'Oh, my lady!' she exclaimed. 'We're all so upset.'

Ronnie nodded an acknowledgement. Her expression must have made it clear that she had no wish to discuss what had happened.

For a moment the cook hesitated before adding some extra bad news. 'I don't know whether you've heard about Nanny.'

'What about Nanny?'

'When she was told, this morning, she came over queer. A stroke, Dr Sidwell said it was. He had her taken to hospital, but they don't think she'll be coming back again. She didn't open her eyes when her grace went in to see her.'

'Poor Nanny.' But perhaps lucky Nanny to be spared more bad news. She should have died a day earlier. With no more grief to spare for the moment, Ronnie pulled a chair up to the kitchen table and sat down. Mrs Stockford looked momentarily surprised at the informality but within a few moments Ronnie was presented with a ham omelette. With a home farm at hand to produce eggs and pigs on request, rationing was no doubt perceived at Cleeve as something which only applied to other people.

She forced herself to eat and was then shown up to a bedroom. It was still light, but she closed the curtains and was asleep within minutes. As a result she awoke very early; far too early to disturb anyone. To go to the stables would bring back too many memories of morning rides with Chay. Instead she walked briskly across the terrace, down the steep slope of the mound on which Cleeve was built, across the moat which was as much of a joke as the battlements in a castle which had not been besieged for at least five hundred years. Over the flat meadow on the far side she went, and then on up a gentle rise to the edge of a wood.

She and Chay had often paused here as they rode, turning to look back at the castle. In this wood Chay had built her a treehouse. If she looked to the side she could just see the edge of the race track on which she had spent so many afternoons with him. Chay was everywhere because he had been here before her. She had never known Cleeve without him. He had always been her protector, amusing and kind, and she loved him, oh, how much she loved him!

What filled her heart as she sat down on a fallen tree trunk was a mixture of desolation and amazement. The desolation needed no explanation. The place in her heart which her brother had filled was empty now, and nothing could ever replace him. The cause of the amazement was her realisation that she had never loved anyone else with such intensity.

She had thought herself in love with Laurie, and perhaps in a way she was, but it had been the calf love of someone who had no conception of what true love was like. Probably this was what Laurie himself had realised.

As for Malcolm, she had tried to persuade herself – or had allowed her mother to persuade her – that because she enjoyed his company as a social friend she would love him as a husband. It hadn't worked, had it? His physical presence, instead of arousing her, was alarming; almost repellent. When she learned that he was a prisoner of war she had felt genuinely glad of his safety and genuinely sympathetic about his situation, and had thought that such sympathy must at last be love. But it didn't compare for a moment with the emotion which had overwhelmed her since she learned of Chay's death.

There was nothing incestuous about it. Except on rare occasions such as her wedding day and her arrival for their father's funeral, they had never kissed each other or touched in any but the most matter-of-fact manner, but she had known him more intimately than anyone else, and had loved everything she knew about him. It was impossible to believe that there would ever be anyone else of whom that could be true.

So the bereavement was total; but just because there was

nothing to be done about it she must somehow learn to accept it. Telling herself that as she walked slowly back to the castle did nothing, though, to lessen the shock of hearing her mother's angry outburst over breakfast.

'You realise what's going to happen now? That old rake Giles will inherit. Has inherited.'

Ronnie had had no time to consider the practical consequences of Chay's death. She was aware that the title would pass to someone she had never met: the grandson of the younger brother of the seventh duke. He lived in Kenya and had the reputation of being a gambler and womaniser, but reputation was of no significance where the inheritance of a title was concerned. Already, although he would not be aware of it yet, he was the Eleventh Duke of Wiltshire. The duke is dead: long live the duke!

What she had not fully realised until her mother poured out all the details was that the castle and its lands were entailed with the title. Winner takes all. Well, perhaps she had known in a vague sort of way, but in the past it would never have seemed important. Ronnie herself was always expected to marry and move to her husband's house and Chay would inherit the title and the castle and have sons to inherit it in turn.

Now the duchess was expressing her anger not just against the new duke but against her own son. Chay knew the form. Why had he not married? He had no right to volunteer for such dangerous duty until he had provided the family with an heir. It was thoughtless, cruel.

Ronnie couldn't stand it for long. Abandoning her breakfast, she moved to stand behind her mother's chair and gripped her shoulders. They were not normally a family who touched each other very much, but this was not a normal situation.

'Please don't, Ma,' she said softly. 'I know you're only sounding angry because you're upset, because you loved him so much; but please don't talk that way.'

The duchess gave a sigh of apology. 'I'm sorry, Ronnie. You're quite right. Go and finish your breakfast. You don't look as though you're eating properly. Anyway, nothing will change until the war ends. I don't see a man like Giles coming to England to be starved and bombed. But Chay; why didn't he get married, Ronnie? All those girls who were after him. There

251

must have been one he liked. The Venables girl. He used to dance a lot with her. Poor as a church mouse, but that needn't have mattered. We would have accepted her, your father and I, if Chay had wanted her. Good looking, after all. Too shy, but she would have grown out of that. What was her name? Remind me.'

'Anne,' said Ronnie. Anne, like Giles Delacourt, might not have heard the news yet, but she would be devastated by it. Everyone, all the debutantes, had known that Anne was in love with Chay. And although he hadn't said so in so many words, Ronnie had been almost sure that he had intended to propose to her when he went to the Venables' September house party at Yewley. Their father's death had forced him to cancel the visit, and then had come the war. But the war in most cases had rushed people into marriage rather than holding them out of it. What had gone wrong? she wondered.

'May I see the letter?' she asked her mother. 'Or telegram, or whatever they send.' She knew that there would be nothing personal about it, but the words would provide the necessary final chapter in the record of Chay's life.

'It hasn't arrived yet. Buffie telephoned me. Richard Buffington, Chay's squadron leader. Now then. Arrangements. You'll come to church this morning, won't you?'

'Is it Sunday?' Ronnie had lost track of the days. 'Yes, certainly.'

'Where no doubt we shall be expected to thank God for all his blessings,' the duchess added grimly. 'Then tomorrow I shall have to be at the office as usual. You must stay here and get some fresh air. Have a good rest. Proper food.'

Ronnie was disconcerted by the announcement. She knew that her mother was working full time for the WVS as county president, but she would have expected . . . Well, no, perhaps to continue with a working routine was the best means of preventing emotional collapse. And it was already clear that the two women had no consolation to offer each other. She considered the matter for a moment and then made up her mind.

'If you're not going to be here,' she said, 'I think I might go to Yewley.' A telephone call would be too brutal. But somebody must tell Anne.

34

Anne rose to her feet, unsmiling, in the old schoolroom that was now her personal sitting room at Yewley. She had said nothing yet to her parents, and any other visitor she would have turned away, but Ronnie was a special case and deserved as much of a welcome as she could manage. The telegram, opened and then screwed up and then smoothed flat again, lay on a table beside her.

Ronnie stood still in the doorway as the maid who had shown her up disappeared. 'You know already?'

Anne nodded. 'This came this morning.'

'Ma hasn't heard anything official yet. Why—?'

'I suppose Chay made an alteration on wherever he had to list his next of kin.'

Puzzled, Ronnie reached for the telegram. Anne made no move to stop her and waited while it was read.

'Husband! Oh, Anne!'

Anne opened her arms. She had no more tears left to shed, but she hugged her sister-in-law fiercely for several minutes before drawing away and indicating a chair.

Ronnie read the telegram again. 'Does being married make it better, or worse?' she asked.

'Better, although only the better of bad. It would have been such a waste of so much love if I'd never been able to show it.'

'When did it happen? When were you married?'

'A week ago. Last Monday. Only a week! He had a kind of premonition. He knew that he couldn't go on for ever being lucky.' Anne sat down beside Ronnie and took her hand, squeezing it for comfort. 'I had a phone call this morning, after the telegram arrived. From his Wing Commander. He said that if he had his way every single pilot in his wing would be given the Victoria Cross. Because most of the men who did win it had to be brave just for a few hours, but these men had to go up and fight, and then when they came down to refuel and were safe, they had to go up again. Day after day. Let's go for a walk, shall we? If you see my parents, don't say anything just yet. I haven't even told them we were married. My mother would have – well, not exactly gloated, but she would have been pleased in the wrong sort of way.'

'I'm pleased in every sort of way,' said Ronnie. 'Did I say that? I ought to have said it straight away. I'm just tremendously glad that you're my sister-in-law and that Chay was happy with you before he died, even if it was only for a few days.'

'Three days,' said Anne sadly.

They let themselves out of the house by a side door and walked past the range of walled gardens. Acting on an impulse, Anne pushed open one of the wooden doors and led the way into the vegetable garden.

'This is where I work,' she told her friend. 'Where I ought to be at work now. Digging and sowing and hoeing and harvesting. There's something very satisfying about seeing new life break through and grow so fast.' She looked across at the high rows of runner beans. It seemed no time at all since she had dug trenches and filled them with compost and manure and tied the tips of stakes together and sown the handsome speckled seeds. Now the plants were over six feet high and still heavy with clusters of slender beans.

There had been no frost yet this year, nothing to blacken leaves and signal the dying of the year, but it would not be long before she would have to clear the ground again and dig it, ready for the whole cycle of the season to restart. The onions which had been lying in neat rows to dry in the sun must be brought inside very soon now.

Why was she thinking about onions at such a time? The answer was easy; to prevent herself thinking about Chay and her own widowhood. She allowed the train of thought, however inappropriate, to continue.

'Whenever Howard comes down for a weekend he fills a

254

huge shopping basket with vegetables. Then he takes them into the kitchen and asks to be shown how to cook them. Apparently the food's almost uneatable where he is.'

'Where is he? Did he join up?'

'When he first tried, he was told his eyesight wasn't good enough, but then there was a change of mind somewhere and he was posted off to a country house in the middle of nowhere. It sounded rather grand at first, but it seems that they spend most of their time in a lot of bleak huts. It's all terribly hush-hush. He doesn't talk about what he does at all, except to say how tiring it is. But almost all the other men working there seem to have been picked for their brains, all graduates, so there's an interesting sort of social life. And not dangerous, I suppose. Thank God for that.'

Chay had taken over her mind again, and Ronnie must have sensed it immediately. 'Did you have a premonition as well, Anne?' she asked softly.

'Well, it was more an understanding of the odds. How could they go on, day after day like that, and always come home safely? So many of his friends were killed. And he was so tired. It's fine, what they're saying now, that winning the Battle of Britain has probably saved England from invasion, but at what a cost! Ronnie, you'll stay the night, won't you?'

'If you'd like me to, of course I will. I don't have to get back to London until tomorrow afternoon.'

'I can't put off telling my parents any longer, and it will be easier, somehow, if you're with me.'

'You'll be glad of their comfort.'

'I suppose so. My father's certainly. But mother . . . She'll be sympathetic, of course, but behind it all I know what she'll be thinking. Her daughter is a duchess. She's won the great race of the 1939 Season, when all the mothers were competing for Lord Lambourn for themselves. You realised that, didn't you, Ronnie?'

'Yes, of course. And so did Chay. You must keep reminding yourself of that – that he had so much choice, and you were the one he chose. Right from the start.'

'Yes, I know. It does help. Except that we wasted a year. Oh, well! Let's walk.' She led the way out of the walled garden.

'My mother will be pleased as well,' said Ronnie, as they

strode at a vigorous pace across the deer park. 'She was saying only yesterday how much she wished you and Chay had tied the knot. She'd wanted to welcome you into the family, and now she can. But there is something. I ought to warn you.'

Anne listened intently as her friend explained the details of the entail which would put Cleeve Castle as well as the title into the hands of a middle-aged roué in Kenya unless . . .

'I suppose it will all go into abeyance now,' Ronnie mused. 'For nine months plus a few days' grace, unless you make an announcement earlier that there's nothing to wait for. So I'm afraid Ma is bound to keep a beady eye on your figure. Hard to blame her, really, but not much fun for you. Do you hope—?'

'Of course I hope!' Anne exclaimed. 'It is the one thing that might make this all bearable: that there should be something of Chay still alive. More than anything else in the world I want to bear his child. I wanted it right from—' She checked herself. There was no need to reveal to Ronnie that the wedding night had come before the wedding. 'But of course it's far too soon to know.'

'Of course.' Ronnie took her hand and squeezed it. 'I'll keep my fingers crossed for you.'

There would be others keeping their eyes open for signs of pregnancy, Anne realised. Her own mother would be watching not just her figure but her appetite, her complexion; anything that might offer a clue. To be the mother of a duchess would be trumped by the honour of being the grandmother of a duke.

That night, after she had announced her news and been kissed and cried over and told to be specially careful of herself, with no more digging or carrying heavy loads, Anne went early upstairs to her bedroom; but not at once to sleep. Twice within eight days her life had changed direction. For a week she had been overwhelmed by the happiness of loving and being loved. Now she was alone again; more alone than ever before, because there was so little to which she could look forward. Except . . .

She stood naked in front of a cheval mirror, looking at her body as Chay had looked at it eight days earlier. Her hands, with their short-cut nails and ingrained dirt, were the hands of a labourer, but she had had no cause for shame in the rest of her tall, slender body. She ran those labourer's hands through her long blonde hair and then stroked downwards with them over her full, firm breasts until they rested on the smooth skin of her stomach – her very flat stomach.

Was there anything there? Any spark of life, waiting to grow as the seeds she planted in the spring had grown? If wishing could make it so, it would happen, because they had both wished. She wished again; but now with a more particular request.

'Please God, give me a daughter. Chay's daughter. A daughter.'

A son would be appropriated by the Delacourts. The eleventh duke, taking his place in a long line from the moment of birth and preparing one day to provide an heir in his turn. He would be the owner of Cleeve and his Wiltshire grandmother would insist that he should be brought up there. She would insist, too, that his mother must take her place in society as a duchess – but what was the point in being a duchess without having a duke at her side? A husband-duke, not a son-duke.

A son would have a way of life imposed on him from the moment he was born. A daughter, if Anne had anything to do with it, could grow up to choose her own way of life. And of course she, Anne, would have everything to do with it. A son would belong to his whole family, but a daughter would be claimed by her mother.

A daughter, please, oh please, a daughter.

PART THREE

New Lives, New Loves

35

The birth of Chay's baby was a very public affair. Almost as though she were royalty, Anne thought to herself in amusement; required to have the Lord Chamberlain standing at the foot of the bed to make sure that there were no surreptitious tricks with warming pans and substitutions.

The birth was to take place at home, in Yewley House, so of course her parents would be at hand. Mr Venables, never a fusser, contented himself with adding extra affection to his regular morning and evening hug, but Anne knew how much he was looking forward to seeing his first grandchild. Even Mrs Venables, who had always made it clear that Howard was her favourite child, showed great concern as she checked each day that Anne was eating the right food and taking the right amounts of rest and exercise. She too looked forward to seeing her first grandchild, but in her case – although with unusual tact she did not put the thought into words – there was little attempt to conceal her hope that the baby would be a boy. There was a difference in kind between being an ordinary grandmother and the grandmother of a duke.

The medical profession was well represented. There was the eminent but elderly Harley Street obstetrician, by ducal appointment to the House of Wiltshire, who had brought both Chay and Ronnie into the world in his younger days. He was accompanied not only by a nurse but by the young doctor who would actually supervise the delivery. There was also a midwife, although Anne was never able to discover the difference between her duties and that of the nurse – and to judge from one or two sour passages that she overheard, the two women were not sure either. A monthly nurse and a nursemaid stood ready to care for the baby; and the Venables' own family doctor – not at all pleased to be shut out from what should have been his moment of glory – had been asked to ensure that a wet nurse would be available should Anne's milk prove insufficient.

And, of course, there was the dowager Duchess of Wiltshire. It was natural enough that Anne's mother-in-law should descend upon Yewley House as the day on which the birth was expected approached. In normal circumstances it would have been unthinkable that her grandson – for she allowed no doubts about the baby's gender – should be born anywhere but in Cleeve Castle, but these were not normal times.

The greater part of the castle had been taken over by the Army for unspecified purposes. It was not being used as a military barracks. For the most part it was run by Fannies, and the other occupants were civilians. On the whole, as she explained to the Venables family on her first evening as their guest, it was as acceptable an occupation as she could have chosen for herself. But inevitably it meant that the duchess herself was squeezed into only a quarter of her usual living space with as much furniture as she could cram into it. There was no room for a nursery, much less for a birthing room or accommodation for nursemaids. So here she was, ensconced at Yewley House, waiting.

To the horror of all these people, Anne insisted on remaining active even after the expected date of her confinement had come and gone. Although the shift in her body's centre of gravity made her balance uncertain, she felt full of energy; quite capable of carrying her hoe outside into the fruit cages. Naturally, this was completely forbidden. Reluctantly abandoning the wish to continue her agricultural activities, she took out her watercolours instead. Painting was an approved occupation for a lady.

In the circumstances, there could be no doubt – to within three days – of the date of conception, so on the fourth day after the one she had ringed in her diary it was decided that labour should be induced. Suddenly Anne found herself no longer an individual in control of her own life, but a body, to whom things were being done. The shock and indignation she felt at this was enough to bring on the first contraction and within a few moments her waters had broken.

The labour was a long one. Anne was exceptionally slim and the baby, it seemed, was healthily large. She didn't mind the pain. Although she gasped and sometimes cried out, because the midwife had told her that it was more helpful to make a lot of noise than to hold it all back, she felt that the contractions, each more painful than the one before, in some way brought her nearer to Chay, who must have endured a far greater agony in the moments before his death. But the delay, it appeared, was more worrying to the doctors.

'Forceps, I think,' said Dr Tomlinson, the elderly specialist. Young Dr Green, who had been brought along to agree with his superior, nodded wisely.

'What do you mean, forceps?' asked Anne between gasps; but at that moment the dinner gong rang and the two doctors disappeared. The matter, it seemed, was not as urgent as all that.

'What are forceps?' Anne asked the midwife who came to sit with her instead.

'Is that what they're talking about? Let's have a look at you, my dear.' Unlike the doctors, who lost no opportunity to address their patient as befitted her rank, Mrs Challis was down to earth. 'I think if we worked at it together we could hurry His Majesty up a little.' Her fingers began to work over Anne's abdomen, half stroking and half massaging.

Anne could feel that something was happening. Her breaths were coming faster and the baby was surely, yes, certainly, moving lower down her body.

The midwife took another look. 'I can see your blonde hair there, my dear. Not that they always stay the same colour.' She was talking now for the sake of talking, to take her patient's mind off what was happening. 'Don't push yet, not until I tell you.' There was more stroking, more massaging. 'Are you ready? Wait a minute. Now.'

Anne pushed, and pushed again. With the third push she felt her child slithering into the world. She lay back, sighing deeply and closing her eyes in exhaustion until a faint cry caused her to open them again. Mrs Challis was holding her baby upside down by the feet and patting its back gently. Anne could only see the blood-smeared buttocks.

'Boy or girl?' she asked faintly.

'A dear little girl. Perfect. What a surprise it will be for those two fine gentlemen with their nasty metal instruments, when they finish their port and cheese and find that you could manage it all on your own.' As she spoke she was gently sponging the baby before wrapping her tightly in a shawl and carrying her across to lie at Anne's breast.

'With your help.'

'That's what I was here for. Didn't think there was going to be much chance of getting near you, though. Anyone would think we were all waiting for a Prince of Wales.'

She was not far off in her guess. Anne looked lovingly down at her daughter. 'Mrs Challis, would you be very kind and go down and tell everyone that the baby's arrived? I'll be all right for a bit on my own.'

'My pleasure, dear. But that nurse can earn her keep for once by coming to sit in the corner. No need for her to interfere with you.'

'Thank you. And Mrs Challis, will you make sure that everyone knows it's a girl?'

'Of course I will.'

For just a few seconds Anne was alone with her daughter, whose eyes were closed and whose mouth bubbled and frothed; not yet ready to be considered beautiful by any but a maternal eye. But she belonged to her mother and no one else. Anne loved her so much that it was tempting to press her close to her body; to hug and squeeze. It was necessary to remember how fragile she must be and be content to stroke her forehead with a finger.

Mr Venables was the first of her visitors to open the bedroom door cautiously.

'A quick nip in before the females arrive to goo and gush. Well done, Anne, my dearest darling. And you, my pretty one.' He touched the baby's hand with a finger and they both laughed with delight as she opened her fist to grasp it. 'Welcome to the Venables family.' Then he looked more seriously at his own daughter. 'It'll be a blow to the Delacourts, of course. You'll need to be kind. But as far as I'm concerned, daughters are the thing. And granddaughters, naturally.'

Anne smiled happily as he kissed her again and crossed with her mother in the doorway.

Mrs Venables was not a woman to enthuse over babies as a rule, but this one was different. Nor had she in the past displayed any particularly warm feeling for her own daughter. But it seemed as though, by becoming a mother herself, Anne had in some way qualified to be accepted into a new relationship, and their conversation was as affectionate as she could have wished.

By the time Mrs Venables left, the monthly nurse was hovering, wanting to carry off her new charge, but Anne shook her head. There was one more visit to come, and she was not looking forward to it. She had not needed her father's reminder that her baby's gender would have disastrous consequences for the Delacourts. She might have felt guilty, remembering how passionately she had prayed for a daughter, but was sensible enough to acknowledge that her personal wishes could not have had any influence on the outcome.

The door opened yet again. What had she expected? A weeping woman? A furious woman? The dowager Duchess of Wiltshire, as always, behaved impeccably. She did all the right things, kissing her daughter-in-law, asking to hold the baby, allowing no hint to show itself of the anxiety – even perhaps panic – which she must be feeling about her own future. So warm was her response to the birth that it was Anne who in the end blurted out, 'I'm sorry.'

The duchess made no pretence of not understanding her. 'Not your fault, dear. These things happen in war. It was Chay who ought . . .' But here she did for a moment come near to breaking down. 'I only wish . . .' She shrugged her shoulders and changed the subject. 'Have you thought what you're going to call her, the dear little girl?'

Naturally Anne was well aware of the odd custom of the Delacourts to call every heir to the dukedom after their ancestor, Charles II. Not that this baby was likely to be heir to very much. Had the duchess demanded that the custom be followed in this unusual case, or had she put even mild pressure on the new mother, Anne might well have refused to co-operate, so important was it to her that her daughter should belong only to herself. But the question had been asked in the

265

normal way of a grandmother, and deserved a co-operative answer.

'Charlotte, I thought,' she said, smiling lovingly down at the tiny bundle in her arms. 'My Charlotte.'

36

'To Third Officer Armitage from the Lady of Dounsay, greetings. And congratulations on getting your pip. Or is it an inch or two of wavy gold braid in your case? Anyway, jolly good show. Proper letter to follow.'

Peggy smiled as she read the postcard. Whatever the reference to the Lady of Dounsay might mean, she recognised Ronnie's handwriting and guessed that there would be no proper letter. Ronnie's communications were always brief and hurried scrawls, but always welcome. Especially now, when Peggy was feeling so lonely.

What a crazy system it was that had moved her from a station in which she was doing useful work to an unfamiliar place where she would have to start again from scratch. But that seemed to be an essential ingredient of service life. You were picked up without warning and dropped somewhere else without consultation. It was unusual, she realised, even to have been given a kind of explanation.

It was because she had been earmarked as officer material. First she was removed from Western Approaches to go on an officer training course, and then, as a newly commissioned Third Officer, told that there was no vacancy for anyone of her rank in Liverpool. Instead, she was posted to Orkney.

She had never thought much of Liverpool, but for Lyness there was nothing at all good to be said. The island of Hoy, on which it stood, seemed to be perpetually drenched by rain and perpetually buffeted by a wind that even in midsummer often felt as though it had arrived directly from the North Pole. The town – which was not really a town at all, but a swiftly thrown-together naval base – was ugly in itself and made uglier by the huge oil tanks that were needed to refuel the battleships taking shelter in the waters of Scapa Flow.

Before she arrived there on a blustery day in March, 1941, Peggy knew only two facts about Scapa Flow – the same two facts that anyone else who was interested would have heard. In 1919 the German fleet was made to anchor there after its surrender, and was scuttled by its crews. And twenty years later – only eighteen months ago – in October 1939, a German U-boat nosed its way between two islands through a channel that was thought to be blocked, and sank the *Royal Oak* as it lay at anchor, killing eight hundred men.

Such a thing could never happen again, Peggy was told as she was introduced to the charts of the area, because hundreds of Italian prisoners of war, captured in Libya, had been brought to the Orkneys and set to work to close the gaps between the small islands which formed the eastern boundary of Scapa Flow. With huge quantities of stone they not only made it impossible for a submarine to get through, but also created causeways above the dams, allowing vehicles now to drive all the way from South Ronaldsay to Kirkwall and Stromness.

The Wren with whom Peggy shared her new cabin had been at Lyness since the first week of the war. She had been in love with one of the *Royal Oak*'s officers.

'How can you bear to stay here?' asked Peggy, appalled, when she learned this. 'They should have posted you somewhere else at once.' She was horrified by her own mental picture of a girl staring out into the darkness, praying that there would be survivors and gradually having to accept the truth.

'They did try,' said Moira, 'but I wanted to stay. Near his grave. It acts as a reminder. A lesson you need to learn as fast as you can, Peg. There are only a few of us here – females, I mean – and thousands of men, officers and ratings, coming and going all the time. You can't blame them if each one hopes he's going to get lucky. And it's easy to feel sort of sorry for them and wanting to be kind, but there's only heartbreak in it for you.'

It was a lesson that was to be reinforced only a few weeks after Peggy's arrival. In the third week of May an intelligence source revealed that the pride of the German navy, the *Bismark*, was about to slip out of her hiding place in a Norwegian fjord and join in the attacks on the Atlantic convoys. Shrouded by cloud and rain, she proved to be invisible to the reconnaissance planes that were sent to look for her. If her route was to be discovered, it would have to be through the interception of signals.

Meanwhile, two of Britain's own battleships, the elderly *Hood* and the brand-new *Prince of Wales*, were steaming out of Scapa Flow at full speed, ready to check the *Bismark*'s progress as soon as her location was discovered. Every Wren in the signals centre longed to be the one who would hear and identify some vital call-sign. Peggy found it frustrating that she was no longer one of those who searched for frequencies and strained to hear through the crackling earphones the signals for which everyone was waiting. Now, instead, she was one of those who waited, ready to pass on information and plot interception courses. A whole community was holding its breath.

The signal came at last. Something was passing north of Iceland. It was not long before a cruiser managed to sight and identify the battleship. That was the beginning of a chase that was to cover almost two thousand miles, but long before news broke of its successful conclusion, the staff of the British Home Fleet were silent with shock. In the first gun-to-gun battle, the *Hood* had been sunk. Of more than fourteen hundred men on board, only three had survived.

Peggy was as shocked and silent as anyone else. Often in her time at Western Approaches, in Liverpool, she had had to note the sinking of yet another ship from one of the convoys and had imagined all too vividly the struggles of the drowning men. Those men had all been strangers to her. The *Hood* was different. Only a week earlier she had watched a film as one of a group of six. Now five of that group were dead.

Her cabin-mate's advice had been good. Peggy was upset by the deaths, and more than upset when she thought of the wives and sweethearts whose lives were about to be shattered when they heard the news. But her own heart was not broken. Yes, she thought: she must keep it that way.

It was this decision not to form any close relationships that contributed to her loneliness in this isolated posting. In Liverpool there had been Laurie. Their affair – which had continued for longer than either of them had expected when it began – had not prevented them from remaining friends, but nor had it tempted them into any more permanent relationship.

Wartime uncertainties, Peggy had noticed, affected her fellow Wrens in one of two ways. Some girls desperately needed to feel emotionally secure. They grabbed at marriage, or at the very least wanted an engagement which would allow them to look forward with hope to that ever-receding period 'after the war'. Other girls, afraid of being disappointed by infidelity or hurt by bereavement, were reluctant to commit themselves to anyone. Peggy belonged to that second group.

So loneliness was built into her choice. As the weeks and months passed, she compensated by writing long letters to her family and friends and awaiting their replies with eagerness. From Isabelle she heard nothing. In June, 1941, Anne wrote to announce the birth of her baby and from then on her letters, although as long as Peggy's own, were devoted almost exclusively to the progress of little Charlotte, and Peggy's interest in babies was limited. It was Ronnie, her most slapdash correspondent, who was still in touch with many of the women whom they had both known as debutantes and who provided the most interesting items of gossip.

On this occasion, when at last Ronnie kept her promise to write a proper letter, it contained a piece of news that explained the wording of her earlier note.

I was fascinated to hear you're in Orkney. Are you anywhere near an island called Dounsay? It's so small that it hardly registers on a map, but if you can find it, do pay a visit. Because who is the Lady of Dounsay? Me! Ma inherited it years ago, but it's not at all her sort of place, so she unloaded it on to me as a wedding present. No one from the family has actually visited Dounsay House for at least ten years, so it's probably gently rotting away. I'd love to have a report on it, and you could use it as a country cottage if it's habitable and you felt inclined. Feel free to do anything you like with it.

I've been in touch with Ma, who tells me that one key is more or less hidden in a dovecote near the house, and there's another one in the boathouse: on the north-west coast of Burray. If this all sounds a bit vague, I'm sure the locals will be helpful. Obviously they must be honest! I shall look forward to hearing your description of my wedding present.

One thing of which there was no shortage in Lyness was maps. Dounsay was quickly discovered, on the far side of the Sound of Hoxa. For a few moments, staring down at the chart, Peggy played with the thought that it would be fun to billet herself there and escape from her present bleak accommodation.

It was a crazy idea, of course. Every visit would involve two journeys over water and, in between them, a bicycle ride along the Churchill Barriers built by the Italian prisoners of war. The first crossing could be made by the regular ferry, but to reach Dounsay from the new road would involve borrowing some kind of small boat. The distance across this second stretch of water was very short, but in the darkness – and at this northern latitude there was a great deal of darkness – it would be difficult, and in bad weather it would be dangerous. For an officer attempting to report punctually for duty it would be an impossible choice of residence. End of daydream.

Nevertheless, Peggy was curious, and determined to do as Ronnie had asked, so a fine Sunday morning saw her cycling along the new road. She had prepared herself for disappointment, because a boathouse unvisited for more than ten years might well have collapsed and blown away, but only twenty minutes after leaving St Margaret's Hope she caught sight of it, tucked into a fold of the coastline.

Don't get excited, she told herself as she scrambled down. If by any lucky chance there proved to be a boat in it, it would undoubtedly be rotten and leaky: a death trap. She scrambled down to find out.

There was indeed a boat, placed neatly on one of two racks which had been recently mended. The boat was upside down, making it easy to check that its hull was sound. The ramp that sloped down into the water was sound as well.

Who was maintaining it? Peggy wondered. Ronnie had said nothing about any land agent or caretaker. She looked around and discovered a pair of oars. The island was so close that she could see its landing stage from where she stood. There could be no possible danger in making the crossing.

What she did not find was the key, but she felt confident that she would be able to break in if necessary. She launched the rowing boat and set off over the unusually calm water.

There was someone already on the island. A second small boat bobbed in the water, hitched to a pole by a new rope. Peggy hesitated for a moment. If there was indeed an agent and he was paying a routine visit, she could easily explain her presence. But suppose the house had been occupied by squatters? There could be an ugly scene, and she had told no one where she was going.

Well, she would have to risk it. On this wind-blown island there were no trees to give cover. She tied up her own boat and made her way toward the house.

It was a substantial L-shaped house, built of grey stone, its windows firmly shuttered against the weather with wood from which all the paint had long ago peeled. From a distance it looked deserted, but someone was indeed on the premises, because she could hear music. If there were squatters, they must have a wireless set and a taste for Schubert. She made her way quietly round a corner and saw a pair of french windows open to admit the sun.

Clenching her fists to give herself courage for a confrontation, she stepped into the ghost of a drawing room, in which the carpet and almost all the furniture were covered with white dust sheets. Only the piano was unprotected; and it was the pianist who first caught sight of her. His three companions, all violinists, had their backs to her and came to an untidy halt only when the piano fell silent.

'What are you doing here?' asked Peggy.

The pianist, a heavily built man in his late thirties, rose to his feet. 'I should ask the same thing of you.' His accent marked him as a foreigner.

'I am here to represent the owner. Who has not given anyone permission to use the property.'

There was a burst of discussion amongst the four men. Peggy recognised that they were speaking Italian, although she could not understand the words. It was the pianist who moved towards her while the others lowered their instruments and watched anxiously.

'My friends do not speak English, so I speak for them,' he said. 'My name is Leonardo Cenzo. In better times I am professor of history in the university of Milan. How do you do?'

He held out his hand. Peggy recognised that by shaking it she would be in a sense withdrawing her protest against his trespass, but she found herself confronted by a special kind of confidence. The stranger was taking it for granted that she would not only accept whatever explanation he was about to give, but would find him a congenial companion. It was the kind of attractive self-confidence that Chay had always shown in public, whatever his private anxieties might have been. The difference was that this man ought really to have been alarmed and apologetic.

'I'm Peggy Armitage,' she said, conceding victory with a handshake. 'The owner of the island is Lady Veronica Ross, who has asked me to make sure that the house is secure. Which clearly it isn't.'

'May we talk?' Leonardo whipped the dustsheet off one of the sofas, for all the world as though he were the host. As he gestured to her to take a seat, he whispered something to his friends, who promptly began to play, very quietly, a Beethoven Romance as background to the conversation. Peggy found herself laughing aloud at the cheek of it.

The conversation confirmed what she had already guessed: that the four men were Italian prisoners of war. In civilian life three of them had been members of the La Scala orchestra, and all four, it was easy to tell, had been delighted when their regiment's surrender in Libya had removed them from the fighting. In their free time after each shift of building the Churchill Barriers they had demonstrated their pleasure at being so far from the war by offering to contribute to the local community anything that the authorities would allow. A proposal to give recitals had resulted in the loan of three violins, although not, alas, the cello that Mario would have preferred.

Leonardo himself was only an amateur, but it was he who had discovered the piano.

'I search for signs of old habitations,' he told her. 'Did you know that two, three thousand years ago this place, Orkney, was a great centre of civilisation. On many islands there are Stone Age houses, villages, places of burial. But of course where the men of your navy stay, we may not go. So I have to look in smaller places. I found the boathouse and mended the boat. When I came to the house, many of the shutters were broken and banging. It was easy to come in. We have done no damage. We have repaired the shutters and the boathouse. All we ask is a quiet place to practise. For these –' he gestured towards the violinists – 'it is important that they should continue to play. All this work with stone is not good for their hands. When the war is over it may be hard, I think, for them to return to their orchestra.'

'Are you allowed to wander wherever you please in your free time?' asked Peggy.

'If we ask for permission, it will be refused. But Lucio gives violin lessons to the son of the camp commandant. And I think it is known that none of us have any wish to escape, even if it is possible. There is a blind eye. We – I mean, our own officers – are allowed to arrange for the making of a chapel. Everyone who has a talent is working hard: to make sculptures, to paint beautiful pictures on the walls, to make lanterns and seats and whatever is needed. Now the chapel is only a Nissen hut, but one day it will be a work of art. I and my friends will give the music when it is finished. We need to practise. So much is known. It would be unfortunate if you were to make any complaint.'

Peggy stood up, not yet ready to give him the reassurance he was seeking. 'You can carry on for the moment,' she said. 'I'm going to look at the rest of the house.'

The air was musty and the rooms were dark. She was not after all displeased to find that he had followed her upstairs. As she tugged to open one of the sash windows, its wooden frames swollen by damp, he stood close beside her while he pushed it up and then unbolted the shutters and threw them open.

'This fastening I have fixed myself,' he boasted as the sunshine flooded into the room. 'In Italy I can work only with books, but now I am a Jack of all trades. Is that what you say?'

'Yes.' Peggy was staring out of the window. Between the house and this side of the tiny island was a walled garden, neglected for many years: a jungle. Anne would enjoy taming this, she thought to herself. The young duchess's overwhelming passion – after her love for her little daughter, of course – was

274

for growing cabbages in crescents and tomatoes in triangles, arguing fiercely that vegetables could be made to look just as decorative as flowers. Her friends teased her on the subject, but Peggy sometimes wished that she had an equal enthusiasm for some kind of hobby.

'You have beautiful hair,' said Leonardo, close behind her. 'In the north of Italy, where is my home, this colour of hair is considered the most lovely.'

Peggy turned to face him. He did not step back but held his ground, standing so close that Peggy could hear his breathing. She was disconcerted for a moment, but then recovered herself. 'This isn't my house,' she reminded him. 'I shall report to the owner on what I find. Flattering me isn't going to make any difference.'

'This is not flattery,' he protested. 'You are a beautiful young woman and you have intelligent eyes, like my best students. I think perhaps you are a student yourself, yes?'

He had touched a nerve, but she was not going to admit that.

'Open all the windows, please,' she asked. 'The house needs a good airing.'

It was an order rather than a request, and for a few seconds the two of them confronted each other without speaking. Third Officer Armitage was issuing instructions to a prisoner of war, while Professor Cenzo, fifteen years her senior, was attempting to establish his authority over someone young enough to be his pupil. It was a confrontation that Peggy was bound to win. She watched as he forced open each window in turn. It was almost possible to see the damp blowing away as the dust danced in the sunshine.

They were downstairs in the dining room when the string trio reached the end of the Beethoven and broke into a sprightly Strauss polka. The professor pushed open the last of the shutters, clapped his hands together to brush away the dirt and turned to face the young officer.

'Yes?' he asked, smiling in invitation. 'Yes.'

Before she had time even to be surprised, she was galloping round the wooden floor in his arms. He was a big man, but light on his feet, and his laughter was contagious. What did it matter if he was flirting and flattering? He was not a man who was going to disappear one night into the dark water. He made no pretence of being a hero, and so he would survive. After the war he would return to his real life, and she to hers. There was no risk of heartbreak here. They could be friends. Perhaps even, one day, more than friends.

37

The first stage of Isabelle's journey into a new life was made on a winter's night in 1942, through the blacked-out streets of London and its suburbs, along dark country roads, up steep and narrow lanes. Isabelle fell asleep at midnight. By the time – two hours later – a hand took hold of her shoulder and shook her awake, she had no idea how far she had come or where she was.

There were no words of welcome; indeed, no words at all. Only the light of a torch covered with blue paper guided her across stone floors and up a stone spiral staircase to a narrow and uncomfortable bed. She had become accustomed to narrow and uncomfortable beds at St Hugh's and fell asleep the moment she had taken off her new uniform.

It seemed only a few moments later that she was awakened from a deep sleep.

'It's time to get up.'

The room was still dark and as she forced her eyes open she could make out only a shadowy figure. Her first indignant reaction was to ask – in English – what time it was, until she remembered what Mr Greenaway had told her at their last meeting: 'From the time you enter your training house you are French and only French. You speak in French. You think in French. Every moment of the day.'

That should have made her response simple, but there was a second cause for hesitation: if she was only French, would she have understood the English words? Was this some kind of extra-subtle test? She compromised by muttering something which might have been '*Quoi?*' and turning over to sleep again.

The shadowy figure left the room. If it was a test, she hoped that she had passed it.

She was awakened for a third time at seven in the morning and this time she dressed herself quickly. It was odd what a difference the uniform made. As a VAD she had been a slave – a willing slave, but a slave none the less. Now she was an officer, with the right to command. She pulled the belt tightly round her slim waist and stood up very straight.

Mr Greenaway had made clear the reason why she was to be given officer status: under the Geneva Convention she would have to be treated well by the Germans if she were to be caught while working under cover in France. Isabelle didn't believe for a moment that this ploy would be successful. It was one thing to be an officer in uniform, but an officer in civilian disguise would be a spy. That wasn't something to argue about, though, and certainly her new status gave her a good feeling of being in control.

It was Mr Greenaway also who had decided, after she had volunteered to work for the Special Operations Executive, that she should become a member of the First Aid Nursing Yeomanry, a choice that had nothing at all to do with her nursing experience. As it happened, Isabelle already knew a little about FANY, because Ronnie had been a volunteer driver in its Women's Transport Service, and later had expressed indignation when it was somehow absorbed into the ATS. It seemed, however, to have retained a certain degree of independence; enough to make it useful in unorthodox schemes like this one.

She made her own way down the spiral staircase and emerged into the courtyard of a castle – a proper castle, with turrets and battlements. One of the hints she had already absorbed even before this practical part of her training began was the importance of always moving with confidence and looking as though she knew where she was going. In this case the height of the windows in one of the buildings surrounding the courtyard gave her a clue and she marched without hesitation towards what did indeed turn out to be a Great Hall, its dignity now diminished by trestle tables and tea urns.

After joining the queue for breakfast, she carried her tin tray over to a table and sat down opposite one of three huge fireplaces. The overmantel was carved from stone, and as she stared at it with interest she began to realise that the coat of arms in its centre was familiar. It took her a moment or two to remember where she had seen it before, but at last she was certain: at the Duchess of Wiltshire's ball for Ronnie – the ball to which Peggy had been carried with her leg in plaster. This was the coat of arms carved above the door of Delacourt House.

Pausing no longer than was minimally polite to exchange introductions with the young woman who had just sat down beside her, Isabelle asked a question whose answer she had already guessed. 'What's the name of this house, this castle? Do you know?'

The response, like the question, came in French. 'Cleeve Castle. It's been requisitioned for the duration.'

Isabelle began to laugh. To start with it was a laugh of amusement, but it moved quickly out of control to become almost hysterical. This was the home that her mother had schemed for. If Lady Patricia had had her way, Isabelle would have become the mistress of Cleeve. And now here she was, eating slabs of grey bread invisibly smeared with butter; in Cleeve at last, but far from being its duchess.

Her new acquaintance looked at her in surprise and almost alarm.

Isabelle realised that she must take a grip on herself. 'I'm sorry,' she said. 'It's not anything funny. In fact, it's sad. I used to know the last duke. But I only knew him in London. I never came here. He was killed in the Battle of Britain. He was only about twenty-five when he died. Such a waste.'

Suddenly she was not laughing but crying, an equally inappropriate way to behave, especially in front of a stranger. She had no right to mourn Chay, who had loved Anne and not her. But he had been a marvellous young man. She could have loved him. Indeed, if she were honest with herself, she *had* loved him. Well, once her training was completed, she would have the opportunity to avenge his death.

'Sorry,' she said again and began to ask questions about the timetable of the day.

After her first meeting with Mr Greenaway a long period had passed before she heard from him again. Even when he did contact her for a second time, she only gradually learned what kind of a job he had in mind to offer to a young woman whose only qualification for it was that she had once lived in France as a Frenchwoman and so could presumably do the same again. But this time her life would not be that of a society woman. Instead, she would be acting as a liaison between British intelligence and the scattered and still largely disorganised forces of the French resistance.

Her possible duties were not at first defined. She might act as a radio operator, sending and receiving messages. She might be called on to help the escape of British pilots who were shot down over France. If a good resistance group was already operating in her area, she might help in the planning and executing of sabotage, and would be useful to the group in arranging for arms and explosives to be dropped by parachute. More often, she had already been warned, there was a lack of co-ordination between different bands of men who might all have the same patriotic aim but disagreed about the best means of achieving it; and in that case she might be useful as an outsider in helping to arrange co-operation.

Most important of all, Mr Greenaway had emphasised, would be the task of providing information and creating disruption when the moment came for British forces to return to France and expel the occupying German army. In the months that followed the retreat from Dunkirk, not many people had been able to think sufficiently far forward to prepare for such a moment, for the immediate necessity had been to save England itself from invasion. But while active soldiers planned and fought battles in other theatres of war, a small group of civilians was looking further ahead, and Isabelle had agreed to play her part in their schemes.

And so here she was, ready to be given a new identity: new name, new clothes, new family history, new employment record, new papers. But first, she must undertake a training that seemed well qualified to fit her for a future career as a criminal. She learned to pick locks, conceal documents, break into properties, and evade pursuit by day and night. She was taught how to kill silently and how to protect herself in unarmed combat. She could already shoot, but was made familiar with a variety of weapons and helped to improve her aim and speed of reaction. Explosives experts lectured her and her fellow volunteers on new materials and how best to use them to derail trains, destroy bridges or damage electricity pylons. In a preliminary training course before coming to Cleeve she had already become a proficient radio operator. Now she learned in addition how to maintain and conceal a transmitter. And every day she and the other trainees were forced by an Army sergeant-major to march and run and swim and climb and move heavy loads over obstacles until every muscle was groaning.

Just one hour every week was so quiet that it was almost restful, and only gradually did Isabelle recognise that it was the most terrifying ingredient in the whole of this unusual education. Dr Schleck, a small civilian psychiatrist with a goatee beard and a Viennese accent, came from London to deliver a series of lectures in which almost every sentence seemed to be a question as he tried to make sure that his listeners understood what he was telling them. He warned them that not all Frenchmen would automatically approve of their activities. Some would be actively prepared to collaborate with the Germans. Some would have chosen a quiet life and would not wish to draw attention to themselves; and of these, some would be more positively hostile to underground activity because of the danger that it would provoke Nazi vengeance on civilians.

Little by little Isabelle was made to realise that many of those whom she might expect to be allies would prefer to remain neutral and passive; and that others, while not revealing themselves as pro-German, might even betray her and their fellow countrymen. The lecturer was sending two messages at once: she must learn how to be a good judge of strangers, and she must protect herself against betrayal by surrounding every act of trust with a network of checks and suspicions.

In the last of his lectures, the psychiatrist brought his select class face to face with their last weapon of defence: the suicide capsule. They would each be given one of these, he told them, before they left England. He didn't know the details of how it would be concealed, because the methods changed from time to time. It might, for example, be implanted under the loose fold of skin between finger and thumb, available to be bitten out at a time of desperation.

Isabelle felt her body chill as he raised his left hand to his mouth, miming the action. Mr Greenaway had warned her all along that what he was inviting her to do was extremely dangerous. The risk of death was high. She had accepted that. What Dr Schleck was telling her was that worse things could happen than death.

'But you will never use it,' he told them confidently. 'You will always hope. And because you hope, you can endure. It is necessary for you to have the means of escape, but as long as you know it is there you will never quite despair, because your life will be in your own hands and not in those of your enemies. This small capsule will make you strong.'

In one of his earlier sessions Dr Schleck had described methods of interrogation and devices for resisting them. When describing how the mind could be made to distance itself from the body, he had talked about torture. Isabelle had taken it all in – she had even made notes – but only now, it seemed, was she beginning to understand the true nature of the dangers to which she would soon be exposing herself.

It was not too late to withdraw. This was something that Mr Greenaway had made clear from the start. She was not to think that there would be any shame in changing her mind.

There might not be shame, but there would certainly be a loss of self-respect. Isabelle was not the only one to sit more quietly than usual in the canteen that had once been a banqueting hall after the lecture came to an end.

By the time she had finished drinking her mug of what was called coffee, she had come to two decisions. She did not intend to withdraw, but before she left England, she must make her peace with her mother.

The original breach had to a very slight extent been repaired. For a month after she stalked out of the house in Mount Street to take refuge with Peggy Armitage, Isabelle and her mother had not been on speaking terms. It was her father who had insisted that the silence must come to an end, and, to his daughter's surprise, Isabelle had been given something that came very near to being an apology: an expression of regret that Isabelle should have been humiliated in front of all her friends by Lady Ranelegh.

Since that day Isabelle had called round whenever she happened to be in London, arriving for tea like a social visitor rather than a daughter, but at least not in any spirit of hostility. It was in fact the memory of Lady Ranelegh's snub that helped her to explain on this more important visit why she had volunteered for a dangerous duty that she could not discuss in any detail. She was giving warning that she might one day quietly disappear to serve overseas and would probably not be able to communicate with her family for some time.

Lady Patricia, for all the stiffness of her behaviour, revealed a genuinely maternal anxiety. 'Why should you be the one to put yourself at risk?' she demanded. 'Look at all the others. Your friends. They've all fixed themselves up with soft jobs.'

'That's not true,' said Isabelle gently. 'Ronnie had a terrible time in the Blitz, and Julia Rutherford was killed. As for Peggy—'

But Lady Patricia was not interested in Peggy Armitage. It was easy to tell that her comment had not been a general one. 'What about Anne Venables, then? The Duchess of Wiltshire! What sort of example is she setting, sitting at home with her parents and her baby?'

'She has a perfect right to do it.' Although most young women became subject to conscription when they reached the age of twenty-one, the mothers of young children were exempted. 'Besides, as well as looking after Charlotte, she's working all hours of the day as a sort of Land Girl. It may not be dangerous work, but it's necessary.'

'It should have been you.' Even after so long, it seemed that Lady Patricia had not come to terms with her failure to secure the prize of the 1939 Season. 'If it hadn't been for that Armitage girl! And all the Venables family scheming away!'

'Maman,' said Isabelle gently, 'it was never going to be me. Chay fell in love with Anne the moment he set eyes on her. Anyway, you wouldn't really want me to be a widow at twenty-two, would you?' But that was a stupid question. In Lady Patricia's eyes of course it would be better to be the widowed Duchess of Wiltshire than the unmarried Miss le Vaillant. She pressed hurriedly on.

'That business at Lady Ranelegh's ball is one of the reasons why I'm glad to have the chance of doing something worth while. So that all the girls who thought they could look down on me will be able to respect me instead.' She wasn't referring to

Ronnie or Peggy or Anne when she said that, because they had remained friendly enough to support her, but if that was how her mother understood it, it wouldn't matter.

It was time to go. At all her most recent visits Isabelle's greetings and farewells had been polite rather than affectionate: kisses that were left in the air rather than touching the cheek. Today was different. Who could tell whether the two of them would ever meet again? Isabelle was a realist. She had every confidence in her ability to survive, but Dr Schleck's lectures were not easily forgotten. If it should happen that Lady Patricia was never to see her daughter again, she must be left with the memory – false memory though it might be – of a warm relationship. Isabelle opened her arms, inviting her mother to hug her. After a few seconds of surprise, Lady Patricia allowed herself an unusual display of affection and accepted the embrace.

Four days later Isabelle climbed into an elderly Lysander aeroplane and tried to make herself comfortable as it hauled itself into the night sky. As part of her training she had practised parachute jumping; but within the past month two agents had injured themselves as they landed in occupied France, in one case so severely that she was caught by the Germans without having time to do anything at all. So on this occasion the Lysander would land briefly, allowing Isabelle just three minutes to scramble clear.

England was dark. The Channel was dark. France was dark. But the navigator's course proved to be so accurate that only a single circuit was needed at their journey's end before a grunt of satisfaction indicated that the pilot could see the triangle of three upturned torches flashing a welcome in a field.

'Get ready!' he called back.

Isabelle swallowed the lump in her throat. Would the Germans have heard the sound of an engine and be racing to intercept her? She knew that the first hour in enemy territory was often the most dangerous.

The plane swooped downwards, bumped over rough ground and braked sharply to a standstill. By the time the hatch was opened, four dark and silent figures were running forward to collect the boxes of supplies that were hastily tipped out.

Isabelle was the last to leave, throwing out in front of her the suitcase – French, of course – containing the well-worn clothes which would naturally be owned by a young woman arriving to take up a new job; and also a new radio transmitter. Almost before her feet touched the ground the Lysander was taking off again.

All the boxes had already disappeared, and so had three members of the reception group. The fourth man picked up Isabelle's suitcase, took her by the hand and dragged rather than led her at a run across the field. Without speaking he pushed her down into a ditch that had obviously been prepared as a hiding place in advance, for he was able to pull across a latticework of branches topped with straw to provide conceal-ment.

For an hour they lay without speaking, their ears straining for the sound of a patrol. At last the man pushed the cover aside. 'This time I think they didn't hear,' he said softly. He helped her out of the ditch and smiled in a friendly manner as she brushed herself down. 'I am Alain.'

Isabelle shook the hand he extended. 'And I am Anne-Marie.'

Isabelle le Vaillant no longer existed. This was the beginning of a new life.

38

In the summer of 1943 Ronnie was given a new assignment. She arrived early in order to make a good first impression: this was the first time she had been rostered to drive an American and, since she knew that Major Donovan had only arrived in England the previous day, she had an illogical feeling that she, as one of his first contacts in London, might colour his subsequent view of the whole British nation. It was a heavy responsibility to bear.

Recognising that she would have some time to wait, she had bought a newspaper on the way, and now settled down in the driving seat of the Packard to read it, from time to time glancing towards the doors of the Connaught Hotel to see whether her passenger might be emerging. Most of the space was devoted to the fighting in Russia and Sicily, and to the fall of Mussolini, but even in the thin paper-rationed newspapers of 1943 there was room for a little scandal. Ronnie's eyebrows rose in astonishment as she realised that today's helping of gossip was very close to home.

Giles Delacourt, Eleventh Duke of Wiltshire, had died in Nairobi on 10 July, 1943, almost certainly murdered by the husband of his current inamorata. Ronnie read the details avidly to see how they might affect her own family – and, in particular, Anne. Although he had been three times married, the duke was not legally attached to any wife at the time of his death. More interestingly, although two daughters and one son had the right to call him father, it was apparently not at all clear whether he had left behind him any legitimate heir. In his youth, it was hinted, an impatience of character had made him not always as meticulous as he should have been about the order in which he divorced and married.

Ronnie laughed aloud as she folded the paper in order to read the item again more carefully. Her mother, if she had seen it, would be burning up the telephone wires in an attempt to find out what the situation was. She had always hated the thought of Giles moving into Cleeve and so would probably regard anyone else as an improvement. But if there was no legal heir . . .

'Waiting for me?' said a voice behind her.

As guiltily as though she had been caught with her hand in the till, Ronnie dropped the newspaper on to the passenger seat, jumped out of the car and saluted. 'If you're Major Donovan, yes, sir.'

'Right.' He did not return the salute. Instead, he looked her up and down in such a slow, inch-by-inch manner that Ronnie felt justified in staring equally intently at him. In his case there were a good many more inches to study, for he was well over six feet tall, with a gangling posture very different from the stiff, straight-backed demeanour of the regular officers who had been her usual passengers over the past four years. He was, she supposed, getting on for forty, with a creased and weather-beaten face. His eyes, their blue made even bluer by the tan of his skin, stared at her with an intensity which was not exactly unfriendly, but certainly not friendly: just neutral. If she wanted a smile from him, he was telling her, she would have to earn it.

Ronnie gave a mental shrug of the shoulders and opened the rear door for him, but he shook his head.

'Reckon I'll make myself comfortable in the front. Like to see where I'm going.'

Walking round, he picked up the newspaper that she had left on the passenger seat in order to avoid sitting on it, and let it rest on his lap. Ronnie, whose acquaintance with American voices was gained only from films, pinpointed him as coming from *Gone With The Wind* country rather from the New York of the sophisticated comedies. She took her own seat and waited for instructions.

'This here's a kind of off-duty day for me,' he drawled. 'Tomorrow will be for meetings, inductions, whatever you call them. Liaising with your people. But today . . . Where's the nearest bit of coast to here? English Channel coast.'

'Brighton, I should think, sir. Of course, a lot of the South Coast is a restricted area. I don't know . . .'

'I'll deal with that. Brighton, then.'

As they set off, he looked with interest and some surprise at the deep craters and ruined half houses that were the legacy of the Blitz.

'You in London when all this was happening?' he enquired.

'Yes, sir. At the time when the bombs were actually falling I was moved on to driving ambulances. There were so many casualties that the regular service couldn't cope.'

'I hadn't realised. Don't suppose any of us realised.' They were passing a large block of flats whose façade had collapsed, revealing a selection of wallpapers and fireplaces and staircases that stopped abruptly halfway up the building.

'We guessed that, sir,' said Ronnie, thus losing herself the good mark she might have gained for her ambulance service.

Major Donovan might be slow speaking, but he was quick to pick up the innuendo. 'I've only been in England twenty hours,' he said, 'but that's been long enough to work out that the population of the country divides into two. Half of you are glad that the United States is giving you a hand. The other half can't let go of its resentment that it took us so long to interfere in what was never really any of our business. It'll make things easier if you turn out to be in the first half.'

'I am indeed, sir.' Ronnie's answer, if not absolutely truthful, was prompt enough to sound sincere.

'Another thing. Not too much of the "sir". They've put me in uniform in case I ever need to pull rank – of a sort – to get something done. But you could say I'm still a civilian at heart, and doing a civilian's job.'

'Yes, sir. I mean, yes.'

He pulled a pack of cigarettes from his pocket. 'Smoke?'

'I do, but not while I'm driving, thank you, s—' She checked herself just in time and saw him give a nod of approval before he fell silent, watching to see how competently she handled the car.

Ronnie had no fears on that score. She knew that she was a good driver. Navigating was a different matter, since all sign-posts had been removed to frustrate possible German para-chutists, and she had been given no warning that Brighton was to be her destination for the day. But as long as she continued to press on with confidence in a southerly direction her passenger was unlikely to be aware of any wrong turnings she might take in the maze of streets to the south of the river.

Fortunately she had a good memory for roads, both as they appeared on the map and on the ground – and this would not be her first visit to the resort. In the course of her debutante Season, she had taken part in a midnight road race: to Brighton and back, with at least ten seconds of total immersion in the sea for the men. The girls were allowed to keep their heads out of water, lest their ruined hair-dos should cause questions to be asked when they returned to London at dawn.

What a long time it was since those frivolous days! But thanks to the race, Ronnie was able to identify the right road with confidence once she had left the suburbs behind. Beside her, Major Donovan had apparently decided that she was to be trusted with the car, and was reading the newspaper he had picked up from the passenger seat.

'Never can understand this obsession you British still have with lords and ladies,' he commented.

Ronnie, glancing across, could see that he was reading the item that had so much interested her earlier that morning.

'It's probably more of an obsession with murders,' she suggested.

'Hard to think that John Doe would rate so much space if someone put a bullet in *his* head. But just because the fellow's got a handle to his name . . . Have you ever heard of the dukes of Wiltshire before today?'

'Yes,' said Ronnie briefly, glad that as far as her passenger was concerned she was simply Driver Ronnie Ross.

'More'n I have. What've they ever done to have y'all kowtowing to them?'

The Eleventh Duke of Wiltshire did not provide a particularly good example on which to base a defence of the aristocracy. 'Winston Churchill is the son of a lord,' she said instead. 'The grandson of a duke, in fact.'

'Could be that not being a lord himself was what got him up and into the saddle. Or could be, more likely, because he had an American mother. Think I'll snatch a nap. Short on sleep last night. Wake me when we get there.'

'Yes, sir.' The 'sir' came automatically in response to an order, but this time he made no comment. Perhaps he was asleep already.

He opened his eyes only as the car came to a halt. Ronnie waited with amusement to see his reaction to the building beside which she had parked.

'Holy cow! What's that?'

'The Brighton Pavilion. Built by John Nash for the Prince Regent.'

'You telling me there's a prince regent now?' he asked, puzzled.

'No.' Ronnie hesitated. In spite of Miss Warner's best efforts, she had never been good at remembering dates. 'More than a hundred years ago.'

'I like it! Now then, Miss Ross.' He paused for a second, raising his eyebrows in enquiry as he realised that Ronnie had drawn in her breath and was on the point of correcting him. 'That's right, isn't it? I was told I wasn't to forget that my driver was a civilian. But if that's wrong, and you have a rank, just tell me now so that I can get it straight from the start.'

Ronnie abandoned her impulse to interrupt, because she had no idea what name she could offer instead. She was not plain Mrs Ross but to confess to having a title so soon after her passenger had dismissed the whole British aristocracy as effete would do nothing to raise her standing in his eyes.

'No, that's right,' she agreed. 'Ronnie Ross.'

'So. As I was about to say. Something I want to have clear. Reckon you must have signed something to promise that you'd keep your mouth shut about military matters, right?'

'Yes, sir. The Official Secrets Act.'

'Anything I do, anywhere you drive me, is covered by that oath. I want that to be understood.'

'Well, of course, sir.'

'Don't get me wrong. I'm sure you're discreet when it comes to anything you reckon to be important, but I can kind of imagine you sitting down to chat with one of your friends tomorrow and telling her that you've just had a trip to Brighton. No harm in that, you might think, but there is. Later on I'll be looking at some other bits of the coast, further west. You can enjoy yourself while I'm working, but you don't talk about where you've been. Okay?'

'Understood.'

For the first time that day he smiled at her. It was a very slow smile, seeming to begin underneath his skin and only gradually break through into the open, turning up the corners of his mouth and deepening the lines beside his eyes. He was trying to make up for his lack of trust; but as far as Ronnie was concerned the effort was unnecessary. When she was on duty, she was on duty, accepting orders and – if necessary, reprimands – without bothering to ask herself whether her feelings were damaged. Had a friend needed to remind her of her responsibilities, she might have felt hurt; but Major Donovan was not a friend – and since he knew nothing about her, he was perfectly entitled to take precautions.

She smiled politely back, however, and was genuinely pleased to learn that she could go off duty for the next four hours.

'Would you like the keys to the car?' she asked.

'I don't drive any longer. I'm the only American citizen over the age of five who doesn't drive. That's why I need you, Miss Ronnie. Three o'clock, then, outside this crazy building.'

For a second time that day Ronnie was early rather than punctual at the rendezvous, and drove off in a good mood after the pleasant summer break beside the sea. At first her passenger scribbled notes on his lap – he was a left-hander, she noticed – but after half an hour he looked up and studied the countryside for a little while before asking her to stop.

'What kind of speed can you get out of this car?' he wanted to know.

'I've never pushed it to the limit. We have a speed limit of sixty miles an hour here.'

'No one's likely to notice for sixty seconds. I like to know what I've got under the hood. Give her full acceleration from a standing start. Then just round this bend, if I recollect rightly, there's a long straight stretch.'

Ronnie nodded. 'The Fairmile. In the old days, the stage-coaches used to race to overtake each other along it.'

'You and your "old days"!'

Ronnie did not hear the comment. She was remembering that

it was along the Fairmile that she, with Malcolm as her passenger, had overtaken Lord John Rutherford, driving Isabelle, to be first to Brighton. And now Malcolm was a prisoner of war and Isabelle seemed to have vanished from the face of the earth, and John and his sister Julia were both dead. She felt suddenly very old and very sad.

'Something wrong?'

'No. What do you want me to do, then?'

'Just see what speed you can hold for a mile.'

Ronnie changed into gear and put her foot on the accelerator. It took the heavy car a few seconds to pick up speed, but as they rounded the bend and entered the straight stretch of road it began to fly. Ronnie's eyes brightened with excitement. When she had first been given a car of her own, for her eighteenth birthday, she had been a reckless driver. Peggy's accident had cured her of that, making her more cautious, but she had continued to love speeding whenever she could.

Once she joined the Motor Transport Corps, however, becoming responsible for the lives of generals or the casualties of air raids, she had deliberately reined herself in, almost inventing a new persona for herself. Ronnie the debutante had been put on ice, ready to emerge again after the war. She had been replaced by someone who was competent and steady and safe. It was only an act, but she had been meticulous about maintaining it. Now someone had ordered the real Ronnie to come out of hiding. Her grin of pleasure widened as the needle of the speedometer rose.

From a farm driveway a little way ahead the nose of a tractor emerged. Its driver would see her approaching and pause, wouldn't he? No, he wouldn't. At what seemed a snail's pace he continued to press on. And he was apparently intending to turn right.

There was no time to brake, and the Packard was already at full acceleration. Ronnie's only choice was whether to squeeze in front of the tractor or behind it. Praying that the driver wouldn't suddenly stop dead, she chose to go behind so that she could make use of the farm entrance.

She swerved to the left, just missing the huge tractor wheels, pulled to the right in order to avoid hitting a gatepost. Careered across the road into the verge. Heard a bang as the front wheel hit a milestone concealed by the long grass, and for perhaps another two hundred yards was forced to struggle with the steering before at last pulling to a halt on the correct side of the road.

For a moment she sat without moving, breathing deeply. Then, trying not to reveal how shaky she felt, she got out of the car to inspect the damage. As she had guessed, the tyre had burst. 'Damn!' she said, but not loudly enough to be heard.

Major Donovan came to stand beside her. 'Guess I shouldn't have asked you to do that,' he said.

'You have the right to give me any orders you please,' Ronnie answered automatically, without looking at him.

'Within limits, I take it.'

She did glance towards him then, and saw that he was smiling; but he was quick to recognise that she was in no mood for jokes.

'Got a spare?'

'Yes.' She was already moving to extract it.

'Need a hand?'

'No, thank you.' But as she jacked up the car and strained to loosen the stiff wheel nuts, she couldn't help feeling resentful. She was perfectly capable of changing a wheel, and had done so many times before. And it was part of her job to keep her vehicle roadworthy. And a superior officer who was merely a passenger had no obligations in that respect. And she had turned down his offer. All the same, if he were a gentleman he would have insisted on helping. Unwarranted it might be, but her bad temper increased as she worked her way grimly through the task while Major Donovan sat on the verge in the sunshine and watched.

'You expected to account for your equipment?' he asked as he took his seat again.

'Yes.' Ronnie started the engine and pulled away from the verge. 'But burst tyres are a regular hazard and there's no damage to the bodywork.'

He nodded, and for a little while was silent.

'You handled that real well,' he said at last. 'Been driving long?'

'Since I was a child,' said Ronnie. 'My brother –' Suddenly she couldn't go on. Almost three years had passed since Chay's death, and she certainly didn't think about him all the time, but there were times – and this was one of them – when a picture of him flashed into her mind and she could hardly bear the thought that she would never see him again.

'Something happen to your brother?'

'Pilot. Battle of Britain. Shot down.' And now the tears were flooding her eyes and pouring down her cheeks. For safety's sake she had to pull the Packard to a halt again. 'Sorry,' she mumbled. Groping for a handkerchief, she dabbed herself dry and let out her breath with a deep sigh.

'Sorry,' she said again; and continued her answer to prove that she had pulled herself together. 'My brother was crazy over cars. He taught me about engines. And we used to race. On a race track, not the public roads.' She put the car into gear again and drove on.

'He taught you well.' Perhaps disconcerted by her emotional response to his casual question, he did not continue the conversation but sat in silence until they were approaching the centre of London.

'Drive me to the American Embassy, will you? And I shan't need you tomorrow. Meetings all day. Take the day off and enjoy yourself.'

'Thank you, s—' Not for the first time she had to check herself as she opened the passenger door for him. And if she was not to call him sir, was she not expected to salute either? Yes, of course she must – and in any case that problem was solved when a three-star American general emerged from the embassy. Ronnie sprang to attention and saluted smartly.

Major Donovan raised his left hand towards his forehead. The general raised his eyebrows, but acknowledged the gesture with a salute of his own.

Ronnie's startled expression produced another of the major's slow smiles.

'My right arm is only for show,' he told her. 'You didn't notice?'

She took the question as giving her permission to stare at it. No, she hadn't noticed. His sleeve was not empty and his hand emerged from it in a normal way. But it was true that the arm was hanging in a straight and unmoving fashion, and she had not seen him using it in the course of the day.

'No, I didn't notice. I'm sorry. Were you wounded?'

'Nothing so praiseworthy, I'm afraid. I fell off a horse and hit my head on a spike. Damaged the bit of the brain that tells that arm what to do. The rest of it works all right, though. Eight o'clock the day after tomorrow, then.'

Ronnie smiled to herself as she returned to the car, all her irritation with the day forgotten. How should she spend the unexpected free day? It didn't take her long to decide. She would pay a visit to Anne.

Anne was still living with her parents at Yewley House, looking after her two-year-old daughter with the help of a seventeen-year-old girl from the village. Had her baby been a boy, she would undoubtedly have been summoned to bring him up in that part of Cleeve Castle which had not been commandeered by the War Office. But since Anne had not done her duty by the family, the hateful Giles had officially inherited the title and the estate on the day that Charlotte was born. It was only because the playboy duke had no wish to expose himself to the austerity and dangers of England in wartime that Ronnie's mother had been allowed to keep possession of her remaining quarter of the castle for the time being.

Anne also had read the report of the murder. 'What happens if there turns out to be no legitimate heir?' she asked.

'As far as the title is concerned, you can go back for generations until you hit a younger brother who has direct male descendants now living. This is the stuff of which novels are made, when some tramp living in a doorway is suddenly told to get washed and put on his coronet. If there isn't anyone, of course, the title becomes extinct and all because your little Charlotte hasn't got the right working parts. What happens to the property in that sort of case, I simply don't know.'

'There must be something in the terms of the entail which provides for a situation like that.'

'I think we can trust Ma to be fishing any documents out of her lawyers' strong rooms at this moment, but . . . If there'd been no male heir of any kind when Chay died, it's possible that Cleeve and everything else might have gone to you under his will. But unfortunately there can't be any doubt that Cousin Giles did inherit the entailed property, even if only briefly; so if the entail is broken, presumably his is the will that would count.' Not, thought Ronnie, that there was likely to be very much left to inherit once death duties had been paid on three deaths within four years. Although perhaps Chay's death, being on active service, would be treated in a different way. It was not something she wanted to discuss with his widow.

Anne made no comment aloud, and Ronnie knew why. Even when Chay was alive and Anne was head over heels in love with him, the thought of becoming mistress of Cleeve Castle one day had worried her. Without him at her side, the responsibility for keeping the property in good shape would have been overwhelming, and she had made no secret of her relief that she would never be expected to shoulder it. It was different for Ronnie herself, who loved her childhood home without ever having been required to give any thought to the money and the staff needed to run it smoothly.

'Ma will keep us up to date. I don't suppose that duke number twelve is any more likely to turn up here while the war's still on than duke number eleven was.'

'How's your own war going?'

'It's taken a jolt. I've got a new boss. Major Jack Donovan, over from the United States to liaise, although about what and with whom I don't know. All terribly hush-hush. He sits in the front with me and chats in a very slow sort of voice with this incredible Southern accent. The trouble is, he doesn't know how to treat me. One minute I'm Miss Ronnie and I'm not to call him sir or salute, and the next minute he's barking out orders in a way that makes it clear he doesn't really trust me.'

'How can you expect him to trust you until he gets to know you? I thought your lot didn't have to salute anyway.'

'That was when a Fany was a Fany, with no caste system. Now the ATS is trying to take us over and none of us knows where we are. Ah, here's my Charlotte! I wondered where you were hiding her away.'

As the little girl came running into the room after her rest, Ronnie scooped her up into her arms, and for a little while they romped together on the floor.

'Tea party,' said Charlotte.

'I'd love a cup of tea.' Ronnie continued to chat to Anne while the preparations were carefully made. 'You've heard about Peggy's love nest, have you?'

'I know that she's having an affair with an Italian professor.'

'It's all my fault. I asked her to inspect a house I own in the Orkneys and she found there was someone more or less squatting there already. It's just as well that they can use it as a hidey-hole. I should think she'd probably be shot for treason if anyone discovered that a serving officer was consorting with an enemy alien.'

'He may not be an enemy alien for much longer. It sounds as though Italy's going to surrender at any moment.' Anne gave a sigh. 'I feel so guilty, you know, Ronnie. People like you and Peggy doing such rotten jobs because of the war while I just go on as though nothing was happening.'

'Nonsense. Think of all that food you're growing. And anyway, bringing up Charlotte is more important than anything else. The advantage of living at a time when everyone acts under orders is that if no one gives you an order you can't be expected to do anything.' Ronnie settled herself on the floor. 'Yes, thank you, darling; one lump of sugar. And may I have one of your pink Plasticine biscuits? Lovely.'

For the next half hour she gave the two-year-old her full attention, savouring the pleasure of civilian life.

'Well,' she said at last, reluctantly preparing to leave. 'Back to the unpredictable Major Donovan.'

'I expect he'll grow on you,' said Anne reassuringly.

'Perhaps. Once he's discovered that any girl's heart can be warmed with an orange or a pair of nylon stockings.' She did not, however, really expect this to happen.

39

The first weeks after Isabelle's arrival in France were traumatic.

Alain, the young saboteur who had been waiting to meet her from the Lysander, took her for the rest of the night to an isolated farmhouse where the family was known to be sympathetic to the Résistance. She did not expect to see him again, although no doubt from time to time his group would ask her to transmit messages asking for arms and explosives, and she would pass on details of when a drop might be expected.

After a day's rest Isabelle travelled to the St Denis quarter of Paris, where she had been given a contact address, and arranged a rendezvous. What she did not know was that in that summer of 1943 the whole of an extensive network of agents, covering an area from Le Mans to Reims around the north of Paris, had been betrayed. It was fortunate for her that she was four minutes late for her meeting: just in time to see a dozen members of the Sicherheitsdienst bursting into the restaurant and emerging with two men and a woman under guard.

It took Isabelle a little while to recover from the shock of realising how nearly her life as an agent had ended before it began, and even then her problems were only just beginning, for she had expected to be told where to go, and had no other contacts in the field. Her father was living in America now, and although from her childhood years in Paris she knew the names of her mother's friends, it was no small thing to ask anyone to run the risk of sheltering a foreigner – and besides, she had no way of telling who might be a collaborator.

In the end she took refuge in a pavilion near to the racecourse, to which she remembered being taken for picnics as a little girl.

It had never been intended to act as a residence, but there was water and electricity. She dared not turn on any lights for fear of attracting attention, but at least she was able to set up her transmitter and inform her controller of her predicament.

There were no immediate solutions. The collapse of the 'Prosper' network had obviously thrown the whole system into confusion. Luckily Isabelle had been carrying a considerable amount of money when she arrived in France, to be distributed to agents. So she was not likely to starve; but this was a time of loneliness and anxiety.

Even when, after three weeks, she received instructions, they had a temporary and nervous feel to them. She made her way to Chartres and made a few contacts with local groups. She managed to get a job in the station ticket office, and this proved a useful way of discovering when train cancellations were caused by troop movements. But it was not until the autumn that a new message made her hope that at last she would be able to make the most of her training: a senior agent, currently being briefed in England, would soon arrive to build up a new network from scratch. His code name was Pierre and he would contact her with a sentence containing the phrase 'accident on the line'.

The telephone call came a week later than she had expected.

'Is that Anne-Marie? This is Pierre. I'm sorry to have been delayed. There was an accident on the line.'

Isabelle gave a sigh of relief as she arranged to meet him three days later. It was not simply a question of wanting someone to give her instructions, just that she had not yet felt that she was being very useful.

It was reassuring, as they sat down together in a café, to discover that Pierre truly was a Frenchman, and not just pretending to be one. Also reassuring was the fact that he was in his mid-forties since younger men who were not in uniform were regarded with suspicion and were liable to be stopped and asked for their papers at any time. He was about the same age as her father, in fact, and resembled him in other ways as well, for his eyes seemed always to be laughing and his lips, when he was not speaking, were pursed up as though he were about to whistle.

When a group of Gestapo officers came into the café, Isabelle automatically caught her breath in alarm; but Pierre, leaning across the table to take her hand and kiss it in a pretence of flirtation, looked more light-hearted than ever.

'It's important,' he whispered, 'to be confident always that you are who you say you are.'

'Yes, of course.'

All the same, he waited until the Germans had been shown into a back room before continuing the conversation.

'It wasn't an accident on the line, of course,' he told her in a voice too casual for the enormity of what he was about to reveal. 'I'd been called back to England for briefing and I wasn't prepared to leave until I'd satisfied myself about what really happened to Prosper.'

'And did you?' It seemed unlikely that anyone there would know who it was who had infiltrated the network.

'I think so, yes. It was all set up in London.'

'How could it be? I don't understand.'

'Prosper was summoned back to England and told on the very very highest authority that an Allied invasion was being planned. He was even given an approximate date. A very serious breach of security if it had been true. The excuse for telling him was that there would be an enormous increase in the number of drops to build up supplies. If any of the agents complained about the extra work, they could be told the reason – in the strictest confidence, of course.'

'But there hasn't been any invasion.'

'No. There never was going to be; not this year. It was all part of a plan to persuade the Germans that they must move troops away from the Eastern Front. And before they would believe that, of course, they must be allowed to discover this very certain date. In a huge network like Prosper's there was bound to be someone who would talk in the end. I can't prove anything, Anne-Marie. I'm telling you what I suspect only to impress on you how tight our security must be. You'll have been taught all the systems for making sure that the smaller networks don't have contact with each other. I'm just adding another warning. Neither of us should trust anyone, except each other, too much. We tell London what it needs to know, naturally, but nothing more than that. I must trust you absolutely, for every time you send a message, my life is in your hands. But I can be sure of no one else, and you must feel the same.

Isabelle smiled her agreement happily. It was not just because she found Pierre congenial that she was pleased to be working with him. Until he came she had felt adrift, uncertain what was expected of her, but now she had someone who would tell her what to do and protect her in time of trouble. At last, she felt, she would be able to do something worth while.

40

Captain Bill Brownlow arrived in Cairo with a shopping list as long as his arm, from thirty-one water bottles to – a little optimistically – seven tanks. Egypt was officially neutral, but it was neutral on the Allied side, so to speak, and a good many blind eyes were turned.

Naturally the Army had its own system of requisition and supply, and Bill was aware that sooner or later he would have to report to GHQ to see what could be extracted from Major Oakley, but there were faster ways of getting most of what he wanted. He had made this journey from the desert before and would hand his list to his good friend Sandy at the British Embassy, discuss specifications, and receive the list back two or three days later with a neat column of ticks in the left-hand margin. While he waited, he would attend to his other list, of personal items requested by his men, who all knew that there was no one like Bill Brownlow for haggling in the souks.

Corporal Dai Jenkins, who had travelled with him to share the driving, had a girl in Cairo – just as he had a girl in Alexandria and Swansea and no doubt a good many other places to which he had not yet confessed. Bill sent him off for a well-deserved rest or other relaxation, fixing a rendezvous for the same time next day, while he himself set off on foot, brushing away importunate taxi drivers and shoeshine boys in search of peace and quiet.

There was something different about Cairo this morning. At any time of day or night it was a bustling, crowded, dirty, noisy city, but as soon as he arrived Bill was conscious that this was a different kind of bustle. Ignoring the clubs and hotels which offered special arrangements for British officers, he made for a houseboat hotel on the Nile, in which he had stayed before.

'What's going on here?' he asked Ali, the reception clerk, as he signed his name. 'Something special?'

'Your prime minister has been here.' Ali's voice revealed pride that his city should have had the honour of hosting an important conference. 'And President Roosevelt. Just going, though.'

Bill left his pack and set out for a stroll along the riverside. He had had time to recover from the arduous and dangerous journey across the desert, but even the rail journey from Alexandria to Cairo had been uncomfortable enough to leave him dirty and sweating. He needed fresh air, and time to be alone.

After he had walked for half an hour he climbed to a higher level so that he could stand on one of the bridges. For a little while he stared down at the swirling waters of the Nile, then he turned, leaning his back against the parapet. A group of Wrens was approaching, chatting amongst themselves. His eyes ran over them appraisingly, one by one; in the desert, women were as scarce as water. But when he looked more closely at the third of the four, his eyes widened and he straightened his back, standing almost to attention as they came closer.

Wasn't that . . . Could it possibly be . . . Plenty of women had chestnut hair and a freckled skin, but surely . . .

The last time he had seen Peggy Armitage – to speak to, at least – had been five years ago, as they faced each other across a school table, trying to decide whether or not beauty was in the eye of the beholder. His own eyes had certainly found her beautiful then, although not in a conventional way, and this woman had exactly the same features: wideset eyes, broad forehead and friendly, smiling mouth. Yes, it was Peggy. He was sure.

Bill wasted no time in considering long odds and coincidences. This was what happened in the Army. People bobbed up and disappeared and then bobbed up again. And her parents had told him, when he called at the house once in the hope of seeing her, that she had joined the Wrens.

By now the four women had passed him, but he could easily have caught them up if he had hurried. Common sense, though, told him to wait. His uniform was crumpled and he himself was dirty and sweaty and had not been able to shave for the past twenty-four hours. That was hardly the state in which to present himself for such a reunion. He walked back to the houseboat as quickly as the increasing heat of the day made sensible.

Two hours later he presented himself at the large European-style house on the unfashionable side of the river from which Peggy had emerged. Although she must have been wearing the insignia of her rank on her short-sleeved blouse, he had failed to notice it, but her name was enough to satisfy the officer in charge.

'She's been one of the official conference staff,' Bill was told with a fine disregard for security. 'Now that that's over, you'll probably find her at the Gezira Sporting Club.'

That indeed was where she was, wearing a two-piece bathing costume which revealed that her freckles were not only on her face. She, like each of her friends, was surrounded by a group of four or five young men who were assiduous in bringing her drinks, adjusting the sun umbrella to keep her in the shade, and from time to time tossing her into the pool. It seemed that in Cairo, almost as much as in the desert, women were in short supply.

It would have been easy for Bill to join the group, for he could tell that she had no special favourite amongst her swains. But he wanted her to himself. He would try again in the evening.

Evening came, and with it disappointment. Peggy had left an hour earlier to take ten days' leave. Bill cursed himself for his procrastination, and it was without much hope that he enquired where she was proposing to go.

'Luxor, was what she said.'

Luxor! thought Bill. He could get himself to Luxor, surely, and he himself had plenty of leave due. Corporal Jenkins could take the first batch of supplies back to the regiment – there was bound to be someone just about to end his own leave and return to Al'Irq or somewhere near by who could accompany him. As for the rest of the list, there were always some items – and often the most vital – that only turned up a week or more after the rest. He would be back in Cairo in good time to pick them up. Yes, it could all be arranged.

But tomorrow he would really have to get cracking. He would go back to Sandy, to whom he had passed his list of requirements that morning. He would beard the bureaucratic Major Oakley first thing in the morning, even if it did mean that he might end up with a double ration of some of his requirements. He would leave a note at GHQ, who ought to know but probably did not, giving details of the number of tanks which had been put out of action in his own company alone. He would reserve whatever transport would be needed for the two return journeys. He would spend two hours whistling through the souks at a pace which would bring prices tumbling as merchants realised that this potential big spender had no time to hang about. And he would reserve a sleeper on the night train to Luxor.

That night he slept like a baby, with no sounds of gunfire or approaching aircraft to disturb his dreams. By five o'clock he was lying awake, delighting in the knowledge that there was no need to leap out of bed. His room on the houseboat was exactly at water level, so his window was a porthole. As he stared out of it a skiff, hardly wide enough to contain its occupant, passed smoothly only a few feet away. It put thoughts of Oxford into Bill's mind. He too might have been a young man who rose at dawn to enjoy the river while it was still almost deserted, stretching his back and pushing on his legs as he propelled his craft through the wispy mist that in England would still be clinging to the surface at such an hour.

Well, Oxford was a dream that lay in the past, whilst he must concentrate on the future. Ten hours of hard work and then he would catch the train to Luxor. He was going to see Peggy Armitage again.

41

Peggy gave a deep sigh of contentment as Egypt floated past her. Without needing to move from the shaded upper deck of the river steamer she could enjoy an unending panorama of life on the banks of the Nile. Near one village a dozen women were washing clothes in the river. Ten minutes later, at the next village, the washing was finished and was being carried up the steep bank by another group of women, straight backed and brightly dressed. A man's head bobbed comically up and down behind the dunes as he trotted on an invisible donkey. The villages themselves were Cubist paintings, the square lines of the low mud houses accentuated by sharp shadows; but between each group of habitations the style became Pointillist, as every possible shade of yellow and orange and pink and brown combined in the sand of the desert.

There were many elements in her current satisfaction. It was the beginning of December and yet the sky was blue. How different from the wet and windy greyness of both Liverpool and Lyness! The air was warm, but not unbearably hot. Unlike the atmosphere in Cairo – a crowded, chaotic city which smelt of dust and dung – it was fresh air, and it was quiet. On the lowest deck of the steamer, the poorer passengers would be shouting and quarrelling and cooking and trying to control their hens, but a first-class ticket bought peace. Only when the boat stopped at each landing pier was there a sudden cacophony of traders shouting their wares; and this came as an interesting diversion.

It was the need for just such peace that had persuaded Peggy to travel to Luxor by the steamer rather than the train, although it took so much longer. When she went to the railway station at Cairo to explore possibilities it had seemed to be the scene of a riot. It would have required one battle to reach the ticket office, another to secure a reservation, another to find a porter – and, she had been warned, a complete campaign to secure the sleeper, once attained, against the invaders who would start the journey on the roof but swing themselves inside at the first opportunity.

Peggy could have fought her corner with the best of them, but she was too tired to try – and her decision proved to be the right one. The rest provided by this leisurely journey was a holiday in itself. Indeed, the mere fact of being in Egypt had felt like a holiday, even while she was still working; for there had been many times during the past four grim years when – no doubt like many other people – she had felt imprisoned within the British Isles, wondering whether she would ever be able to see anything of the wider world.

When had she last had a proper holiday? There had been leaves, of course, but a leave only offered a return to ordinary life for a few days. Her mother fussed and pressed food on her, and her father, tired and strained with overwork as more and more of his factory managers and supervisors left to join up, made an effort to return home in the evenings at a reasonable hour. There was no excitement in these visits for Peggy: she was always glad of the opportunity to relax and catch up on lost sleep, but what she expected of a holiday was some new experience in a new setting. For four years now she had longed for it, without ever expecting that it would happen.

Her chance had come in November, 1943. By then, steadily promoted, she was a cypher officer who had had the opportunity to reveal that she was a good administrator. Not until she reported to the *Renown* did she realise how honoured she was to have been chosen for this new posting; because one of her fellow passengers was the Prime Minister, Winston Churchill, on his way to a series of conferences with other world leaders. It was the task of the Wrens who accompanied him to keep him up to date with what was happening on battle fronts and convoy routes all over the world.

So the voyage itself had been work, as tiring as any she had experienced on land. It was an escape from one kind of austerity, but her hours were long, her living quarters were cramped and uncomfortable, and so strict were the black-out regulations that she could not even escape on deck for a cigarette.

The experience was exciting in the good sense, but at the same time it was hazardous: as the *Renown* pursued its erratic course towards Alexandria, everyone on board was well aware of the danger of being torpedoed. Even the humblest ship was at risk; and should a U-boat commander discover that Mr Churchill was within his sights, he would spare no effort to make a name for himself. Peggy had known that her chances of escape would be low if a torpedo did strike, for as well as sleeping below the waterline she spent most of her working hours there in the cypher room or the map room.

All that was behind her now. The series of conferences was over and Mr Churchill had been taken ill, allowing some of the Wrens to take their accrued leave. So here she was, on her way to visit the temples of Luxor and the Valley of the Dead across the river in Thebes; in a country that was not at war and on a boat that nobody would try to sink. It was marvellous to be alone, after so many years without privacy. It was marvellous to have no responsibilities and no need either to give or obey orders. Once again Peggy sighed with happiness.

Soon the sun would be setting. There was a flurry of activity both on the land and in the air. Women and girls came down to the river to fill with water the buckets that they carried in stately fashion on their heads. Flocks of egrets swooped and circled while pelicans skimmed the surface of the water more purposefully and fish eagles clustered in trees, waiting for their moment to pounce. Behind the narrow strip of cultivated ground the sand took on a pinkish hue. Palm trees were silhouetted against the reddening sky and at the same time reflected in the orange water.

The sun itself was huge, falling out of the sky to disappear behind the horizon. Briefly, its rays pierced through the black curtain of night in a brilliant display of crimson, orange and yellow, and then, with a suddenness that took her by surprise each night, everything was dark. Except, of course, for the steamer itself, whose lights still had the power to disturb someone who had spent more than four years observing strict black-out conditions. The lights were part of being on holiday.

There were more lights at the Luxor hotel, when she reached it at last. Lights and music and the sound of British voices: soldiers on leave. Four times as she sat alone in the dining room on her first evening she was offered company, and four times, smiling, she shook her head. On the fifth occasion, however, there was no tentative approach. A young man, whom she had earlier noticed staring at her from his own single table, pulled out the second chair at hers and sat down.

'If you don't mind, I'd prefer—' she began, but she was not allowed to finish.

'Hello, Freckles,' said Captain Bill Brownlow.

It took her a moment to recognise him. At the age of eighteen he had been stubby haired, gangling and shy. Now he was good looking, fit and confident. It was only when he held out his hand to shake hers that she recognised the wrist, with its fuzz of hair, that used to protrude from his outgrown blazer.

'Bill!' she exclaimed – and then added, in mock severity, 'You never used to call me Freckles.'

'I was too much in awe of you then, so now I'm proving how brave I've grown. That's what four years in the Army does for one.'

'I called at Brasenose to see if you were there, when I went to Oxford for my interview,' Peggy remembered, 'but they told me you'd deferred taking up your scholarship.'

'And I called on your family, the first leave I had, to see whether you'd got in all right. They told me you'd won an exhibition. Congratulations. I would have liked to write and congratulate you, but I didn't have the nerve to ask for your address.'

'Silly!'

'Yes. Yes, I was. Have you finished? Shall we go for a walk?'

'What about your dinner?'

'Oh, I had that before I came to join you.' They made their way into the hotel garden. 'Shall we go back to the temple? I've got a torch.'

'I haven't been even once yet. I only arrived this evening.'

'You took the slow boat, I suppose. I was really expecting you to have arrived before me.' He explained how he had glimpsed her in Cairo and had deliberately followed her, but by the faster train.

He continued to chat as they began to stroll. 'While I was eating, I was watching you pushing all the other chaps away. Most girls . . . But I suppose you get bored with being surrounded by men who haven't as much as glimpsed a female in months.'

Peggy didn't comment on his guess. During the whole of her recent period on conference duty there had been a host of young men buzzing around to offer her drinks, picnics, dances, expeditions and invitations to the Gezira Sporting Club to swim and play tennis. Attachés from the embassy, officers on leave, brash aides from President Roosevelt's entourage. She had spent every free moment socialising in a way that reminded her of her debutante season. The atmosphere was one of flirtation, but neither party was expected to take it seriously. She had certainly enjoyed the social life, but had never had any intention of allowing it to continue into her longed-for holiday. Bill, though, was not a flirt.

And Bill had not finished speaking. 'Or else,' he said, 'I suppose you may have formed some more permanent attachment. Some chap that you'll be going home to. So that you wouldn't be interested in anyone else.'

Peggy turned her head to look at him. They were still near enough to the hotel for its lights to illuminate his face, and what she saw in his expression made her heart give a series of jerks, like a car on the point of stalling. The confidence with which he had first approached her had been replaced with a combination of pleading and determination. There was something that he was intent on telling her. He was moving too fast. Far too fast. She started to say so, but was interrupted.

'The summer of 1939,' he said. 'Well, it started before that, when we were having that coaching together. A bad attack of calf love. But that summer, after we'd taken our Higher Certificate exams, a bunch of us went up to London for a weekend to celebrate. And I was walking across Green Park – well, really I was there because the newspaper said where all the parties were going to be and I hoped you might be at this particular one. So I stood and gawped with everyone else, and suddenly there you were, up on a kind of terrace. You looked so lovely. A princess.'

It must have been the night of Lady Ranelegh's ball. The night when Lady Patricia le Vaillant was given her comeuppance by the girl who had started the season as Miss Nobody. 'I wish I'd known,' she said, walking on again.

Bill took her hand in case she should stumble in the darkness. 'Why should you have taken any notice of the son of a charwoman, without a penny to his name, when you were surrounded by all those rich chaps in white ties? But I said to myself then, in three or four years' time, I'll have a degree and perhaps a good job and then perhaps I can bob up again and see if, if . . .' His voice faded away uncertainly into a sigh.

'But of course, I hadn't reckoned on the war,' he continued. 'It's been too long, when you won't have given me a thought. So, as I was saying, I expect there's someone . . .'

Not counting Chay, who had never promised more than friendship, there had been two 'someones'. First of all Laurie, who had educated her in the pleasures of sex. She had not intended to love him, but love of a kind had grown. Not, though, with sufficient strength to survive her posting to the Orkneys. And then there had been Leonardo, who had provided a different kind of education, in art and music, while consoling her at a time when they were both lonely. With him, too, she had known that the affair would only be a temporary one, for he had a wife, whom he loved, back in Milan.

So she couldn't pretend to be the innocent girl with whom Bill, it appeared, had fallen in love. But that didn't mean that she wanted to frighten him off. All this was very odd. She hadn't seen him for five years, and even before that they had enjoyed an easy friendship, but nothing more. As a schoolgirl swot, she had had no interest in boys. Not, at least, in boys to be flirted with and captured as trophies. Just in Bill as Bill: the hardworking boy with the quick brain and imaginative ideas.

'There have been one or two,' she said carefully, 'but only temporary. Nobody at the moment. But that doesn't mean . . . You're going too fast, Bill. We don't know each other, not as adults. Five years ago we were still children.'

'The child is father to the man,' he said cheerfully. 'Or mother

311

to the woman, as the case may be. Some things are exactly right and stay exactly right. Now look.'

He switched on his flashlight to show her that they had arrived in the Temple of Luxor. Peggy gasped to find herself in a towering forest of stone pillars. On and on they stretched ahead, and again on each side, beyond the power of the torch to illuminate them. She was still trying to take in the size of the structure when Bill pointed the light at the nearest pillar and very slowly took it up and up, above their heads.

'So huge and so old and so unchanging,' he said. 'And these two little people below them, so small and so transient. Don't you sometimes get the feeling, Peg, when you're working away at whatever it is that Wrens do, that your youth is passing and that you've no way of escaping into the sort of life you really want to lead? And then you're confronted with a place like this – and you'll feel it even more strongly tomorrow, when I take you across the river to the tombs in the Valley of the Kings – and you realise that it's your whole life that's going past too fast, because it's such a terribly short time in the history of the world. It makes it tremendously important that when you find something that's right for you, you must grab it at once.'

He turned off the flashlight. Now that they could no longer be seen, the pillars were taller, heavier, pressing around Peggy so that she felt even smaller and more insignificant than before.

'The most important thing, though, is to be sure that you're right about what you think is right,' she suggested.

'Yes, of course. Well, I know. I've got just two days of leave left to persuade you.'

He switched off the flashlight and Peggy realised that he was about to kiss her. With half her mind she wanted the kiss, but the other half was still saying, 'Too fast, too fast.'

'I'm tired,' she said. 'Can we go back to the hotel now?' She hoped he would realise that the request meant that she was taking him seriously. Had she been in the market for a brief flirtation she would have needed no time to think.

42

That night, as Peggy lay in bed, she tried to look into her own future. It was not an exercise which had ever seemed worth while since she became a Wren, but the war could surely not last for ever.

Did she want to marry one day? Yes, she supposed she did. But while a man could marry and continue his life and work with very little change, it would be different for a woman. She would have to support her husband's life rather than following her own path. Was there any way in which that could be avoided? If there was one thing clear in Peggy's mind, it was that she didn't want to be like her mother.

Something else was equally clear, though. She hadn't fallen in love with Bill Brownlow when she was a schoolgirl, but it would be the easiest thing in the world to fall in love with him now.

Both in Laurie's case and in Leonardo's her feeling of physical attraction had been immediate; friendship had grown afterwards. It was part of her character, she supposed – with some sense of shame – to recognise instantly a possible lover. And Bill was not a stranger. The delight she had felt at his sudden appearance, the touch of his hand, his closeness in the darkness of the temple all convinced her that the same emotions she had felt on those two previous occasions were stirring once more. She was ready to fall in love, and her mind and her body both told her that this was the right man. Well, he had two days in which to persuade her to admit it.

'How's your kid sister?' asked Bill on the evening of the second day. He had spent much of the previous forty-eight hours escorting her round the tombs on the further side of the river. Holding her hand as the Egyptian guide explained the details of the wall paintings in a parody of English, and kissing her in dark corners. Over meals and during evening strolls and dancing after dinner they had chatted about everything under the sun: except themselves.

Soon he would be on his way back to his regiment. Peggy, already feeling desolate at the thought of his departure, was not sure what she had expected of what might be their last conversation: but certainly the subject of Jodie had not been uppermost in her mind as they sat on the terrace of the hotel, awaiting yet another sunset.

'Blossoming,' she said. 'I think she likes being the only daughter. And she's turned out to be terribly clever. I suppose I always knew she was, really. She took the Oxford entrance exam, oh, I suppose about three weeks ago. She must be at the nervous stage now, dashing for the post to see whether she's been called for interview. You know the feeling.'

'Don't I just,' said Bill, laughing. 'What will she read if she gets in?'

'The headmistress thinks she ought to be a philosopher. Jodie doesn't think there's any money to be made in philosophy, and making money is what she intends to do, so she fancies being an accountant. The headmistress points out that there's a degree called Modern Greats which would let her study both philosophy and economics – with a bit of politics thrown in – to keep her options open. Jodie argues in return that her best subject is maths and that maths is a nice all-or-nothing subject. Either you can do it well or else you can't do it at all, and she reckons she'll do it well. So she'll go to Oxford and get a First in maths and become an accountant.'

'Will she have to wait till after the war to go up?'

Peggy shook her head.

'She'd be allowed to do the first year, then she'd have to stop and join up. But she reckons that having one year under her belt would make her more certain to come back and finish the rest. She doesn't intend to make my mistake.' Upset at the memory, Peggy pulled a cigarette from her pack.

'*Was* it a mistake?' asked Bill softly, flicking his lighter and leaning forward to light the cigarette.

'Yes, it certainly was. I shan't ever go to Oxford now. I did want to, very much, when I was seventeen, but I'm not the same person any longer. It was bad enough going back to school after being a debutante. The idea of being *in statu pupillari* after so many years of being grown up and doing a responsible job – well, I just couldn't face it.'

'There'll be a lot of grown-up chaps arriving at Oxford after the war,' Bill reminded her. 'Men who've seen a lot, done a lot and aren't likely to let anyone treat them as children. The university will have to change.'

'I suppose so, but . . . If it were a training course that would qualify me for something, that might be a different matter. But learning things just for the sake of learning them . . .' She gave a sad grimace and drew heavily on her cigarette. 'What it means is that I'm not a true scholar, and never was. It's probably a good thing I found out.'

'A university education is supposed to train your mind rather than teach you particular things.'

'Well, the Wrens have done that for me. They've taught me to think logically, organise efficiently and keep the junior ranks disciplined and happy.'

'And what do you propose to do with these new talents? Organise a husband efficiently and keep your cook and house-maids disciplined and happy?'

A warning bell rang in Peggy's mind. She had been surprised that in the past forty-eight hours Bill had not returned to the subject that he had broached on the first evening in the Temple of Luxor. He had been allowing her time to think, and she had been grateful for that, but if, as it seemed, he was now anxious for her to discuss her future, she must make her feelings clear to him as well as to herself.

'One thing that seems obvious to me – and to Jodie,' she said carefully, 'is that there may not be so many women in the future who live like my mother used to before the war. Using their husband's money to buy leisure and then not having very much idea how to make use of the time. I never realised at the time how boring it must be. I suppose she took it for granted, but I want a different kind of life.'

'Doing what?'

'One thing I could do is take over my father's business. It's always bothered him that he didn't have a son to take it over one day, but he could use a daughter instead.'

'I suppose he could.'

There was an odd flatness in Bill's voice, almost as though he disapproved. Peggy glanced across at him in surprise. The light was beginning to fade and she could hardly see his face as he stared at her, fiddling with the lighter. 'You'll go up, won't you, Bill?' she said. 'To be one of the grown-ups at Oxford, once the war is over.'

'No, I shan't. Like you, I've missed my chance.'

'Oh, but Bill!'

'My mother spent thirteen years cleaning and polishing for other people to make sure that I could get a good education,' he reminded her. 'In one way it's paid off already: if I hadn't been to grammar school and got my Highers, I shouldn't be an officer now. She would have been happy to go on working while I was at university, but I promised her – and myself – that as soon as I was twenty-one I should start earning to make sure she had a bit of comfort in her life as she grew older. I've passed my twenty-first birthday, and who knows how much longer the war will last? But as soon as I can, I intend to keep my promise.'

'So what do you think you'll do?'

'Just look around.' There was a long silence before he continued. 'I'd noticed, for example, that the owner of Armitage's didn't have any sons to take over, and the young chap who was manager-in-waiting was killed at Torbruk: I knew him. I thought I might try asking for a job there, in the hope that one day I might be able to go on and marry the boss's daughter. But now I learn that the boss's daughter has plans to be the boss herself, so that won't work, will it?'

'Oh, I don't know,' said Peggy. 'Working in double harness, we might make rather a good team. A chap who's learned the art of haggling in the souks of Cairo and who can get supplies to his regiment across miles of desert and under fire would be an asset to any company. Whilst I'm a dab hand at keeping records and organising staff; and I rather fancy I'd be good at predicting what young women will want to wear once they get out of uniform. With the factories and machines already there, we could make a go of it.'

Bill slipped the lighter into his pocket and took the cigarette from her fingers so that he could stub it out. 'Would I be right in taking that as a proposal of marriage?' he asked softly.

'I thought of it more as a job offer. Assuming that I ever have the authority to confirm it.' But her heart was silently singing with happiness. Everything – the right future with the right man – was coming together at the right moment. Too fast it might be, but she was head over heels in love.

'Then that leaves me free to continue this conversation on more traditional lines. I love you so much, Peggy. Will you marry me?'

Almost unable to breathe, Peggy was unable to answer at once. Instead, she stared at the river, whose surface was already taking on a sunset tinge. A single felucca, making late for home, shattered the reflection of a row of palm trees, which then, as the sail disappeared into the distance, gradually reconstituted itself. Every night on the steamer she had seen just such a reflection of just such a row of palm trees. Then she had thought it merely picturesque: now, as the grip of Bill's hand tightened on hers, she found it romantic. This was a moment she would remember for the rest of her life.

'But it won't be like this, working from eight to six in grey, shabby old Newark,' she said, gesturing at the reddening sky. 'Perhaps we ought not to decide anything until—'

Bill was not prepared to hear her out. 'If you have one fault, Peggy Armitage, it is that you're too damn sensible. It's the way you were brought up, I suppose, with a dash of Wren discipline on top of it.' He stood up, pulling her up with him, standing so close that he only needed to whisper in her ear. 'If there are problems back in England, we can deal with them together. All I want to hear you say now is that you love me so much that nothing else matters. Because in a day or two's time I'm going to be back inside a tank, wondering whether I'm next on the menu for Rommel's Sunday roast.'

'Oh, Bill!' Appalled by the picture he painted, she flung herself into his arms.

'That's better.' He kissed her on the lips, on her eyes, on her neck, on her lips again. 'You do understand, don't you, that I have to have something to look forward to if I'm to keep going?'

'Yes, of course. And I love you so much that nothing else matters.'

317

'That's my girl!' He tugged her away from the terrace and into an unlit part of the hotel garden, tumbling her down on to the short, spiky grass that had to be so painstakingly cultivated in this inhospitable soil. Kissing and embracing and whispering nonsenses until they were both panting and breathless, they might have stayed there all night had they not been interrupted by a sinister hissing sound. Startled, Peggy wondered whether it was a snake; but a sudden drenching made it clear instead that the sun had now completely set and the hotel gardeners had embarked on the evening task of watering the lawn.

Giggling like a pair of schoolchildren, they scrambled to their feet.

'Just one thing,' said Bill before they moved away. 'If we're going to spend the rest of our lives together, do you think we might have just one night on account, so to speak?'

'Why not?' agreed Peggy. She could not remember that she had ever in her life before been so happy. Very often, when she was conversing shyly with Howard, or daydreaming about Chay, or planning how to find some privacy with Laurie, or listening dreamily to Leonardo's music, she had wondered how people recognised the real thing when it happened to them: not the instant but short-lived attraction, but the once-and-for-ever falling in love. Anne had told her the answer once, and now she had discovered it for herself: people just knew. That was all there was to it.

A second long sweep of the gardener's hose soaked them even more effectively than before. Dripping and laughing, they ran together towards the hotel.

43

'Holy cow! It's Mrs Jack!'

Ronnie looked up with interest from the newspaper she was reading. Across the breakfast table, Sandy Anderson had just unfolded a different paper, sent by post from his home town in Virginia.

'I didn't know he was married,' she said, surprised. Eight months had passed since she was first assigned to be Major Jack Donovan's driver and in that time they had had plenty of time to chat; but they rarely discussed their private lives. The American's open scorn for the British aristocracy had made her determined not to reveal her position in it, and her resulting reticence on such subjects as family and childhood home was perhaps the reason why Jack – he was Jack to her by now – refrained in turn from describing his own civilian background. Once, when she mentioned her love of riding, he had told her that his father owned a stud, but that was about all. There had been no mention of a wife.

'The ex-Mrs Jack, I should say.' Sandy was quick to correct the wrong impression he had given. 'Now Mrs Carl Greenstone.' He passed his local paper across the breakfast table, indicating a brassy blonde wearing a fox fur over her costume and a hat with three feathers tilted on one side of her head. Standing beside her, a possessive smile on his face, was a small bald man at least twenty years her senior.

'They're divorced, then, are they, she and Jack?' Ronnie tried to keep any hint of criticism out of her voice. In England divorce was still regarded as a reason for guilt, or at least shame, even when the infidelities which had preceded it were widely known.

'Since five months after the wedding. An expensive summer, my God. I warned him. This one time, he thought he knew better.'

Sandy was Jack's personal aide, summoned from the United States to take up duties with which he was clearly familiar. Ronnie still found it confusing to work out the relationship between the two men. They were the same age – had been to school together – and appeared both to have come from affluent families. Sandy, who was a Yale graduate, was if anything the socially superior of the two, but he happily accepted any kind of order and in addition was willing to act almost as a valet when Jack's disability made help necessary. Nor did the fact that Sandy held no commissioned rank appear to bother him. He was clever and cultured, but too courteous ever to make Ronnie aware of her own educational shortcomings. She liked him a lot.

Jack himself, as though to make it clear that his own rank was only a convenient formality, managed to organise his life as though he were still a civilian. Once he had realised how much of his time would be spent on the south coast of England, he had declared it to be ridiculous that he should continue to live in London. Instead, he rented a private house, Fairview, with a view of the Isle of Wight. It was run for him by a civilian cook-housekeeper, Mrs Thompson, under Sandy's supervision. Ronnie had been given the opportunity to return to the driving pool and be allocated to some other officer if she wished, but Jack, offering her accommodation in the house, had made it clear that he hoped she would continue the attachment. 'We're getting kinda used to each other,' he pointed out simply.

That was true enough. It had taken a little time for the two of them to come to terms, but by the beginning of 1944 they had developed a good working relationship. Jack no longer felt the need to test his driver's capabilities, while Ronnie was forced to admire the American's capacity for hard work.

His hard work meant long hours for her as well. As the months passed she had found herself on duty for eighteen hours of each day. There was nothing to grumble about in that: by now most people in England were so tired that they had forgotten what it was like to have a social life. If she asked for a Sunday off she was always given it, but in the spartan atmosphere of the times she did not like to ask too often. And so before very long she began to think of Fairview as her home and its other three occupants almost as her family.

Mrs Thompson, a woman of strict moral principles, had at first seemed suspicious of Ronnie's relationship with the two men, but quickly thawed after a few weeks had passed without any indications of hanky-panky – and, principles or not, did not turn up her nose at the generous, and often exotic, rations which came with an American employer.

So within a few weeks of moving into Fairview the four of them had become a tightly knit group: Jack and Ronnie and Sandy and Marge. Although Jack was nominally the boss of the other three, the fact that they were all there to look after him and enable him to do an important job without outside worries helped them to respect themselves and each other. That it *was* an important job they all took for granted. The meetings that he attended with generals and admirals and even on one occasion with the Prime Minister were proof enough of that, although he never spoke about exactly what he did on the days when he disappeared into the huge workshop he had commandeered in the dock area of Southampton.

Not all Ronnie's work was as a driver: Jack had begun, with her enthusiastic agreement, to use her as a personal assistant. There were days when, fighting seasickness, she bobbed about in a rowing boat in the English Channel, writing down the numbers he called out as he lowered a variety of instruments into the water to test temperature and the height and strength of waves.

On other days she was invited to accompany him to a shooting range; because shooting, like driving, was something he could not manage one-handed. It was the materials used for the targets that were on test, he told her, not the skill of the shooter. Nevertheless he congratulated her, with some surprise, on her accuracy. She did not like to explain that she had been killing ducal pheasants on the wing since the age of twelve. Driver Ross had become Miss Ronnie, and was now just Ronnie: Lady Ronnie was a secret self whom he could not be allowed to meet.

At Christmas Jack bought himself a present: a ten-year-old MG. He summoned her to the garage to inspect it.

'Ever seen one of these?' he asked.

'I had a Magnette myself once,' Ronnie told him. 'Before the war.' It was probably still sitting in the garage of Delacourt House, too greedy for petrol to go very far on what her coupons would buy.

'Did you so? Well, I've seen little ladies like this whizzing round Le Mans for twenty-four hours. With a bit of tinkering I reckon we could make her really shift. Would you feel up to giving me a hand?'

'Sure.' Ronnie went straight off to fetch her overalls. She was neat fingered and knew her way around an engine. Jack was adept at doing a good many things with his left hand alone, but there were some tasks that needed two or even three hands.

'You've got a talent for this,' he commented one day as he watched her carefully filing smooth a corroded surface.

'I used to watch my brother.' On this occasion she was able to speak of Chay without crying. 'I was only his mechanic – handing him spanners when he asked for them and all that sort of thing – but I did watch quite carefully, and ask questions. I enjoy fiddling about. What will you do with this when you've got it back on the road?'

'There's someone supposed to be getting a test track ready for me near the workshop. No harm in trying this out as well. Up to you, of course.'

Ronnie's grin provided a sufficient answer. 'Could you point the torch from that side and underneath?' she asked.

He had to lean over her to do as she asked, his shoulder pressing against hers and his breath warm against her neck. She was not conscious of his closeness. All her concentration was on the task in hand. There had been a time – was it as little as six years ago? – when her governess had perpetually complained about her lack of concentration. But that was because she had never been interested in French irregular verbs or the kings and queens of England or the rivers and mountains of Europe. Now she had found for herself the subject that truly interested her. It was not precisely what her mother would consider a suitable occupation for the daughter of a duke, but Ronnie was happy with it.

'It's great he has you to do his dirty work, *ma belle*,' commented Sandy that evening. He was always free with endearments when talking to her, but Ronnie knew that they need not be taken seriously. As a girl she had often heard her father burst out in disgust, 'The man's as queer as a coot!' without ever at the time understanding what it was that was so extraordinary about coots. By now she was more sophisticated. She liked Sandy and was pleased that there was no need to be cautious when he pretended to flirt with her.

'Were you afraid you'd have to do it yourself? Was that why he wanted you here?'

'No, no. I was his manager. He had mechanics for the oil and grease bit. Guess I'm here just to be a familiar face.'

'Manager?' queried Ronnie. 'What did you manage?'

'Not much since Europe went off limits. But before that, well, arranging transport, booking hotels, taking off all the worries so that all he had to do was drive. Oh, and keeping all the blondes out of his hair. I can say "Leave him alone" in seven languages.'

'But what was he doing, to be managed?'

'He's never told you?'

Ronnie shook her head.

'He was a rally driver. One of the best. Won the Monte Carlo rally twice and the Mille Miglia once in the 'thirties. With never a scratch to show for it. It was one of his father's horses that nearly did for him.'

Ronnie was impressed; not only by the achievement but by the fact that Jack had never boasted about it. 'Who were the blondes?' she asked.

'Oh, girls who hung around. You'd be too young to remember, but men who did things fast were the glamour boys of those days. Aviators were the tops, and then racing drivers. Rally drivers came third, but they still had their share of hangers-on.'

'I'd have thought he might have enjoyed that.'

'He did to start with. Until he made the mistake of marrying one of them, and learned his lesson.'

That presumably would be the ex-Mrs Jack whose photograph Sandy had shown her. It was odd what a difference a little personal information could make. Her first impression of Jack had been of a taciturn and critical middle-aged man. It had not taken her long to amend this to a picture of someone who was skilful and conscientious. Now, gradually, softer details were emerging. Jack was an enthusiast. He was a man who had loved speed and excitement and competition – and perhaps still did. He was a man who had been young once, and had made mistakes, and even now was not quite as old as she had thought at first. Little by little their working relationship was developing into friendship.

When did she first notice that Jack's feelings for her were becoming warmer than those of mere friendship? Was it on the day when he heard her bemoaning the impossibility of finding any lipstick in the shops and told her that she was a beautiful woman with a perfect complexion which needed no adornment – a comment so much out of character that they were both silenced by it.

Or was it on the day they took the souped-up MG on to the test track and put it through its paces for the first time, its tyres screaming as Ronnie, at the wheel, hurled it round and between the oil drums set up as obstacles? Jack yelled in her ear to tell her when to brake and what line to take and took pleasure in her elation as she mastered each technique. When at last the session came to an end, Ronnie staggered slightly as she climbed out of the little car. She was in no real danger of falling, but at once Jack was at her side, his good hand first of all under her elbow and then round her waist. Their shared excitement bound them together and he was slow to move away.

Those moments might have been significant, but Ronnie pushed them quickly out of her mind. It was not until a sunny day towards the end of May that she realised how much her own feelings were changing.

She had driven Jack to Dorset and was then told that she was free until four o'clock; he would be spending the day out at sea. By now, although she was careful never to speak of it, she had realised that his work was concerned with amphibious craft. Everyone in England knew that an invasion of France must come sooner or later; and everyone in the south of England guessed that it would be sooner. So much equipment and so many troops were concentrated along the coast by now that the island could reasonably have tilted under their weight. What nobody knew was the date on which the invasion would be launched.

Ronnie was not thinking about that as she drove the official Packard from Portland Bill to Bridport and then stretched herself out in the sunshine on the grassy edge of a cliff. Many feet below her the waves hurled themselves on to the pebbled sand before being sucked noisily back. The regularity of the sound acted as a lullaby. With a sigh of pleasure she closed her eyes and allowed the balmy air to envelop her.

Three hours later she awoke and stretched herself in contentment. For a moment or two she felt almost like a civilian. For a moment or two she felt almost as though she were on holiday. For a moment or two she felt almost young.

That moment could not last. What had happened to her youth? she asked herself. Between leaving the schoolroom and volunteering for war work she had enjoyed a few months of carefree gaiety; was there never to be any more? She was only twenty-four, but it was a long time since she had felt the *joie de vivre* to which a young woman was surely entitled.

Well, it was the same for everyone. Anne's dancing days had ended in tears and loss and she had become a responsible mother. Peggy had sacrificed her undergraduate years to become an equally responsible naval officer. Whatever Isabelle was doing, it was not on any social network. And some of the young men who at this very moment were awaiting the order to attack would never enjoy any youth at all. There was nothing fair about war.

Annoyed with herself for spoiling the day, Ronnie sat up, clasping her knees as she stared out towards the horizon. A sea mist had sprung up, making it impossible to see very far – she could not even make out the end of the Portland peninsula – but she could tell that the swell had increased. It was time to enjoy a walk.

At four o'clock, as arranged, she was ready to drive Jack back to Fairview. Major Donovan had not yet returned, she was told by the young sailor whom she asked to announce her presence.

It was an hour and a half before an officer came out to the Packard. 'You'd better come inside and have a cup of tea while you're waiting,' he said. 'It may be a little while yet.'

It was the officer's rank rather than his words that rang an immediate alarm bell in Ronnie's mind. A commander would normally send a message to a mere driver rather than deliver it himself. 'What's happened, sir?' she asked.

'There's been an accident out at sea,' she was told. 'A

collision. Most of the men involved have just been brought in, but there are four still missing. We'll have them back soon.'

There was a moment in which Ronnie was unable to speak because she had no breath.

'Are you telling me that Major Donovan is in the water?'

'It won't be for long, I promise you. It's tricky with all this mist, that's all. The spotter planes haven't been able to help us yet.'

'But how long has he been out there already? You do realise, don't you, that he's disabled? He may not be able to swim.' Anxiety robbed her of any respect for rank, but fortunately the officer was sympathetic.

'Come and have a cup of tea,' he repeated. 'And remember, he'll be wearing a life jacket.'

Ronnie followed him into the mess, but as she stared down at the steam rising from the hot drink she could see only the mist over the sea, and beneath it, Jack's body being tossed about by the waves. Sick with fear, she buried her head in her hands. That was the moment when she realised that what she felt for him was more than respect and friendship. She couldn't bear to lose him.

Once she had drunk her tea, she went out to sit on the dock, staring into the mist. Two hours passed before she was able to make out the outline of an RAF rescue craft as it slowly approached. There was a shout for stretchers: four stretchers. Was that a good sign, or the worst possible? Ronnie held her breath as a group of naval ratings hurried to bring the four rescued men ashore, but still she could not tell whether they were dead or alive.

She hurried along to the landing stage, but then held herself back, not wishing to hinder the operation in any way. Only when the young commander broke away from the group did she feel able to ask her question.

'Major Donovan . . . ?

'Alive and well. Very cold, of course, and probably a bit shaky on his pins, but he'll be all right.'

Ronnie let out her breath in a deep sigh. As though aware of her presence and anxiety Major Jack Donovan ordered his bearers to set the stretcher down and help him to his feet. Ronnie ran to face him, but they did not touch each other.

'All well,' he said, giving her a lopsided smile. 'Back to Fairview and to hell with speed limits.'

'Dry clothes first.'

He shook his head, although without much energy. 'That can wait.'

'Dry clothes,' repeated Ronnie. She was giving orders now, although there was no one in any service who was bound to obey her. 'And a hot drink with rum in it. And lots of blankets.'

The Navy knew what should be done, and did it. Nevertheless, by the time they arrived home, Jack was shaking uncontrollably and breathing with great difficulty.

'Hospital for you,' ordered the doctor who was hastily summoned. 'You need oxygen. And nursing.'

Jack, although on the point of collapse, shook his head.

'No hospital. Might babble.'

Ronnie understood why he was afraid of becoming delirious. No one, except perhaps General Eisenhower himself, knew exactly when the invasion force would be ordered to strike, but Jack was one of the few who could make an informed guess. 'We can nurse him here,' she said, and Sandy nodded his head in agreement.

Five years earlier, when she was making her choice amongst the different forms of war service, Ronnie had found the idea of nursing repugnant. But this was Jack's body, and she gladly learned to give bed baths and use bedpans. Nevertheless, there were many times during the next nightmare week when she wondered whether they had been right to agree to Jack's demand to stay at home as he slipped into a coma. At one moment his body would burn with fever, while an hour later he might be so cold that it was hard to be sure that he was still alive.

The moment of crisis came eight days after the accident. Given warning by the doctor, Sandy and Ronnie sat at his bedside together all night. Almost unconscious of what she was doing, Ronnie stroked his wasted right arm. 'Don't die,' she repeated over and over to herself, silently. 'Dear Jack, don't die.'

At six o'clock in the morning his eyes opened and flickered from one side of the bed to the other before coming to rest on Ronnie. 'Kiss,' he said. It was only a whisper, but it was so normal a whisper that she gave a gasp of relief. She did not in fact kiss him, but bent low to rub her cheek against his on the pillow, nuzzling him like a baby. It was going to be all right. It was going to be all right.

Two hours later, Marge Thompson prepared breakfast for the two tired watchers and went to sit with her employer while they ate it.

Sandy looked Ronnie straight in the eye. 'You'd do,' he said.

'Do for what?'

'Do for being the second Mrs Jack.'

Ronnie's mouth fell open. She dropped her fork and was glad of the need to retrieve it from the floor. Sandy did not allow himself to be interrupted, and for once he was not talking in his usual jokingly flirtatious way. 'He's crazy for you. You must have noticed.'

No, she hadn't noticed. She had even wondered, in fact, noticing the easy relationship between Sandy and his superior officer, whether there was something . . . Had that thought been only an excuse to deceive herself?

'You're twenty-four years old,' said Sandy. 'You need a man. Long overdue, I'd say. And you don't have one. If you had, I'd have noticed. You work all the hours that God gave you here and all your letters come from girlfriends. And Jack needs a woman. Someone who hasn't got her eyes just on all the money he'll have one day. Someone who'll stick with him. I told you, I've spent years pushing blondes away, but you're a brunette and I hope you're going to stay around.'

Ronnie's stomach hardened into a cold ball, but at the same time her heart beat so loudly that she could hardly hear herself speak.

'I can't,' she muttered. 'Please don't interfere, Sandy. I can't.'

'What's the problem, baby? Have you had a bad experience somewhere? I can promise you . . .'

Ronnie set down her knife and fork and stood up. She tried to leave the room with dignity but was forced to make a dash to the bathroom before she began to vomit.

It was because she was exhausted, she told herself afterwards as she lay on her bed, staring up at the ceiling; but she knew that wasn't the whole truth. Why hadn't she told him? Why hadn't she said casually right at the beginning, before it was of any importance, 'I'm actually a married woman? I haven't seen my husband for four years and I don't love him but all the same he is my husband.'

It was easy enough to answer those questions. Long before she met Jack she had put the marriage out of her mind because the thought of it frightened her. For the first year of Malcolm's imprisonment she had felt sympathy for him and had tried her hardest to persuade herself that it was love. She still wrote to him regularly, assuming that letters must be important to someone in his situation, but received in return only Red Cross postcards that did nothing to keep the memory of him alive.

Blanking out her married status had nothing to do with any wish to explore a new relationship. The memory of her wedding night, whenever she allowed it to intrude on her thoughts, was enough to keep her at a distance from any other man. Her body was her own, and that was how she wanted to keep it: untouched, unpenetrated, unpossessed. At least, that was how she had felt until an hour earlier when she rubbed her cheek softly against Jack's. In that moment everything had changed – except the fact that she was still married to Malcolm. Ronnie turned over on the bed and buried her face in the pillow, crying with frustration.

She was not, though, a woman who allowed herself to wallow in self-pity for too long. She had created a false situation and she must do something about it.

Sandy was still sitting at the breakfast table. She took a chair to face him.

'I'm afraid I won't "do for Jack", as you put it,' she said. 'I have a husband. He's a prisoner of war. I haven't seen him for a long time, but when the war ends he'll come home again.'

Sandy, who was always friendly, always light-hearted, stared at her with eyes that were suddenly cold. 'Why are you announcing this to me?'

'Because I thought – I hoped that perhaps . . .'

'You want me to tell him? To be the bearer of bad news? The messenger rewarded with the bowstring? Should I do it now, when he's still weak and ill? Or would you prefer me to wait until he's about to set off to France, when he needs to be confident and full of hope?'

'I'm sorry,' said Ronnie miserably. 'I just thought . . .' Her mood changed as she took in what he had just said. 'What do you mean, about to set off to France? He can't be meaning to go himself! He's not fit. And he's not a fighting man. He'd be a liability.'

'Correct on all counts. But he feels a responsibility for getting the Army safely on to French soil, and if he's made any mistakes he reckons he ought to suffer for them. The only person who might be able to stop him is you, but it doesn't sound as though you have any good arguments to offer.'

'Oh, bloody hell!' exclaimed Ronnie, pounding the table with her fists. 'Bloody, bloody hell!'

'Shush or he'll hear you. Go and get some sleep. It was a long night. I'll wake you at two. And Ronnie . . .'

She waited as he worked out what he wanted to say.

'It's a mess that you've dug yourself into, but it's too late now to dig Jack out without pain. Don't be in too much of a hurry to set things straight. If he dies on a French beach, let him die, well, moderately happy. I reckon you owe him that.'

She returned to her room without answering, but, tired as she was, could not at once find escape from her unhappiness in sleep. Malcolm would never let her go. He owned her, and there could be no escape. How could she even consider leaving him, when he must be having such an unhappy time now and looking forward so much to his return home? Why had she ever married him, knowing so little about what married life would be like? Unhappiness turned to anger as she struggled to answer that question. It was all Laurie's fault, for running away from her. It was all her mother's fault, for being so determined to see her married to someone, anyone, as long as he came from a good family and had enough money.

No, it was all her own fault, for not realising how young she still was at the end of her Season. She had thought that becoming a debutante was the same thing as becoming grown up, when in fact it was only a way of sheltering her from adult life for a little longer. Well, she was an adult now and she would accept Sandy's advice. It would make things worse in the long term, but in time of war the long term might never arrive.

On a blustery morning early in June Ronnie was asked to have the car ready for the first time since Jack became ill. He said nothing to indicate that there was anything special about the day, but instead simply asked her to be ready to pick him up at six in the evening – and at six o'clock there he was, paler and thinner than a month earlier, and showing signs of strain in his expression, but ready to be driven home in a normal fashion. Ronnie released the sigh of relief which she seemed to have been holding all day, and set off.

After only a little while he asked her to stop and walk with him to the edge of the cliff. It was a cloudy day with a gusty wind blowing, and the waves beneath them smacked angrily against the rocks.

'There are four things that have to come together,' he said. 'The right tide. The right phase of the moon. The right time of sunrise. The right weather.'

Ronnie looked at him in surprise. She had been in a good position to make guesses about the invasion that must surely start soon, but Jack had never before been anything but totally discreet. She could feel the strength of his need to talk to her, and was secretly pleased that he should trust her so much.

'Three of them are okay this week,' he continued. 'I wrote a message ready for you, in case I wasn't free to come back to Fairview tonight. "Bye-bye; gone hunting." But the weather forecast for the next three days is bad. I wouldn't be Ike for anything, having to make this kind of decision when there's a joker in the pack.'

'Are you telling me that you might have had to go off tomorrow?' asked Ronnie, alarmed. 'Jack, you're not fit yet. You're not well enough. You mustn't –'

He looked down on her with a smile. 'Kinda good to know that you care.'

'Of course I care.' There was no point in denying it, since he must certainly be able to see the anxiety in her eyes.

'There's a low-down trick that soldiers have been playing on kind-hearted girls since history began,' he said slowly. His good hand moved as though to unbutton her tunic. 'In every century, in every country. "Just once," they say, "because I may never come back." '

There was a split second in which Ronnie seemed to freeze. Was this to be a repetition of her wedding night? But the button remained unopened and when his fingers gently stroked the form of her breast it was only the rough khaki material that he was feeling. He was waiting for her to be ready, and that realisation was enough to warm her body and release her feelings.

'Just once!' she agreed, laughing, and flung her arms round his neck. 'Oh, Jack!'

He would be gentle. He would be kind. If she was uncertain, he would understand. Everything would happen as it ought to happen. And she loved him. This was not like the infatuation that had made her feel she had a right to Laurie; nor could it in any way resemble the alarmed repulsion with which her married life had begun.

Holding her hand, Jack led her back to the car and hesitated for a second as though considering whether to make immediate use of its back seat. But with a slight shake of the head he took his usual place in the passenger seat. 'Fast as you can,' he said.

Back at Fairview he ordered Sandy to take Marge out to the movies. Marge was delighted and Sandy, who had seen the film three days earlier, gave Ronnie a friendly wink but made no embarrassing comment. Within twenty minutes they had left the house.

The four hours that followed were the most marvellous of Ronnie's life. Giving and receiving, she learned for the first time what it meant to love. She was so happy that she could hardly breathe. She was so happy that she felt as though her life, her true life, had only just begun. She was so happy that it was impossible to believe even for a moment that this new life would not last for ever.

Sandy and Marge returned at half past eleven, closing the front door loudly behind them and clattering about the living room as they adjusted black-out curtains before turning on a light.

Pressed close beside Jack in the single bed, Ronnie did her best to remain completely quiet. But his hand was still moving over her body; stroking her, exploring her, arousing her. In a moment, she knew, she would no longer be able to restrain her shuddering gasps of desire and pleasure.

Leaning across her, Jack interrupted his explorations to switch on the powerful wireless set beside the bed. It was his habit to listen to the World Service news at midnight and the others would think nothing of it if he let the broadcasters drone on for longer than usual. Ronnie learned that Rome had fallen to the Allies and that the King of Italy had abdicated. But between the news items were statements which didn't make sense. 'Good health makes the best pickle,' said Alvar Liddell; and then, 'The fat cat catches no mice.'

It seemed, though, that they meant something to Jack. He left the bed and walked across to the window, opening the curtains and staring out to sea. As he stood without moving, Ronnie studied his body, adoring and willing herself to remember his strong neck and shoulders, slim hips and long, shapely legs.

He turned back to face her, although she could not make out his features in the darkness.

'The wind has dropped,' he said. 'It will be a fine day after all. I must get back to headquarters.'

44

Pierre's arrival in France proved to be the beginning of a happy few months for Isabelle. There were bound to be many anxious moments, but he was an efficient organiser. He knew her scheduled transmitting programme and made sure that all necessary information reached her in good time so that she could get off the air quickly. He was aware that she was never supposed to use the same site more than three times running, and not only organised a variety of safe houses but helped her to move the heavy suitcase between them.

At the same time he was busy organising new Résistance groups in the area around Chartres. There were saboteurs, who tuned in clandestinely to the BBC, listening for the 'personal messages' that would instruct them to blow up telephone exchanges or electricity pylons or railway lines. There were courier groups, collecting Allied pilots who had been shot down and helping them along the route which led eventually to neutral Spain. And, of course, there were the suppliers of information. To reduce the danger to Isabelle herself, Pierre took into his own hands the collating of everything that came in, presenting her daily with a comfortingly brief précis.

Most comforting of all, though, was the relationship that quickly developed between the two of them. It was not a romantic one, although in her secret heart Isabelle would have liked it to be – and her landlady certainly thought that the gallant gentleman who so frequently made the journey from Paris was visiting his mistress. But it was a friendship which came as near to being carefree as anything could in such difficult times.

Pierre did not gamble with money, as Isabelle's father had done, but he took different kinds of risks. He would meet her in restaurants known to be patronised by the Gestapo and the SD – because, he claimed, the true danger came not so much from them as from the *milice* – local people who opposed the Résistance because of the reprisals attracted by their activities. So he openly laughed and flirted, not caring that he drew attention to himself.

Isabelle knew that his flirtatiousness was only an act, but that did not prevent her from taking pleasure in his kisses, the touch of his hand. Perhaps one day, when the war was over . . .

That moment might be coming nearer, for on a clear night in June, 1944, a message came over the air from the BBC. 'The fat cat catches no mice.' It was the signal for her local saboteur group to set its explosives and for Isabelle herself to make contact outside her scheduled transmitting hours.

She could have had one more session in the disused signal box that she had used for her last two transmissions. But this was important. She decided to move to a new base, even though Pierre was not at hand to help her pack up and carry the equipment. At half past six in the morning she learned that the long-awaited invasion had at last taken place.

Pierre, arrived, breathless, ten minutes after she had logged off.

'Why did you move?' he asked. 'I went to the signal box and you weren't there. I've been looking for you everywhere. An urgent message. Priority. That Panzer division which was supposed to be going to the Eastern Front has been diverted towards Caen.' He pulled a crumpled cigarette paper from his pocket and held it out to her. 'Here are the details of the route. As quickly as you can.'

For a moment Isabelle hesitated. She had already spent longer on the air than usual and every extra moment brought an increased risk of detection. But this was a time of emergency. She took the paper and nodded.

'I must go,' said Pierre. 'A busy day. Tonight, six o'clock, at the café, yes?'

'Yes.' As he left the room she smoothed out the thin paper, knowing that what she was about to do would be foolish. But that could not be helped.

Two minutes after she had finished transmitting the railway details, she heard the sound that on many occasions in the past had featured in her nightmares. But this time the clattering of boots on an uncarpeted staircase was real. There was no way out. The attic which she had been allowed to use for one week in every four was on the fourth floor and had no ordinary window, only a skylight. Cold with fear, Isabelle straightened her back, took a deep breath and turned to face the door.

She tried to maintain an impression of calmness as she was arrested and led downstairs, but her thoughts were racing. Would Pierre have had time to get away before the detector van closed in? Was there anything in her lodgings that could implicate him in her activities? No, she had always been careful about that. But all those evenings together in restaurants and cafés had linked them as a couple. Would he be able to convince the Gestapo that he knew nothing of her secret activities? Worrying about Pierre's safety made it just possible for her not to think too much about her own future, but in her heart she knew that her death sentence was already passed. The only hope was that the invasion should prove not only successful but fast.

Forty-eight hours after her arrest, still refusing to show any fear, Isabelle stood in a bare room in the Avenue Foch, in Paris, facing her interrogators. Forty-eight hours. It was part of her instructions, during her training at Cleeve, that should she be arrested, she must reveal no information at all for forty-eight hours, to give everyone else in the network time to escape.

This was the period in which torture was most to be feared, because the Germans would also recognise the need to move quickly if other resistance workers were to be caught. But Isabelle had suffered no torture. Questions were being fired at her as a matter of routine, but in such minute detail that it was easy to tell that the answers were known already. She remained silent, but nobody cared.

Towards the end of the second day, the door opened to admit Pierre. She forced herself not to give any sign of recognition, but her heart swelled to breaking point with sadness at the thought that he too had been captured.

Only when she raised her head to look at him did she realise the true situation. Pierre had arrived unescorted. He was not under guard. And now he was exchanging smiles with the chief interrogator, and receiving congratulations.

She stared at him in incredulity. It was Pierre, then, who had betrayed her – and presumably many others. How could he bear to meet her gaze, knowing how much she had trusted him? His eyes, which had seemed to laugh in pleasure at her company, were laughing now in triumph; and when he spoke to her it was in the same tone of voice that he had used in a pretence of flirtation. She had always known that that was an act – or at least, had tried to make herself believe it, for fear of disappointment – but had not realised how elaborate the act would prove to be.

As though reading her thoughts, his lips – as always, pursed as though he were about to whistle – broke into a smile and he shrugged his shoulders almost as a gesture of apology.

'We have both been living a lie, you and I, Anne-Marie,' he said. 'My lie has proved stronger than yours, that's all.'

Isabelle refused to allow the heartbreak she felt to reveal itself in her expression, but her emotions were devastated. She had loved his gaiety and his willingness to take risks – but of course, for him, they had not been risks at all. Unexpectedly she remembered something that her father had said on the day he sent her off to England to become a debutante.

'Because you love me, Isabelle, you may find yourself tempted to marry a man who is like me. If that happens, your mother will forbid it, and she will be right. Before you allow yourself to become angry with her, remember that I have said the same thing.'

Isabelle had never expected to marry Pierre, but she had allowed herself to love him and it was true that in some ways he resembled her father. His apparent light-heartedness, his athleticism, the easy way in which his body moved inside his clothes – oh, stop this, she told herself. But that memory of Guy's advice drew her out of her passive silence, spurring her into a show of anger.

'I am a British officer,' she said, interrupting a question. 'And you should know that I am also a person of importance in British society. My mother is the daughter of an earl. My

337

grandfather was British ambassador to France. I am acquainted with the King of England.' Once upon a time, dressed in white and with ostrich feathers in her hair, she had located, woven into a red carpet, the golden crown which marked the place where she should sink into a deep curtsy. As she rose, King George had smiled at her. That was acquaintanceship of a kind. 'If you mistreat me in any way, the matter will not be over-looked. The British Army will be here in Paris very soon. You will have to answer for your actions.'

'Your soldiers will be turned back,' she was told by the Gestapo interrogator. 'And you will never have existed. A junior railway clerk called Anne-Marie has disappeared from her lodgings, as young women often do. No one knows where she has gone. No one cares. The King of England has other matters to think about.' He slammed together the covers of her file. 'That's enough. Take her away.'

The two soldiers standing guard stepped forward to twist her arms behind her back, but as they forced her towards the door she turned her head towards Pierre.

'And don't think that you will escape,' she shouted. 'A traitor to your country! When France is free again, there will be plenty of people to remember those who betrayed her.'

Pierre's voice was as light-heartedly casual as it had been in the days when they had flirted and exchanged information in cafés under the noses of the German occupiers; but now the words were cold. 'It's unwise to make an enemy of someone whose help you may need.'

'If you think—' But now she was outside the room and being pushed upstairs and flung into the tiny attic room which served as her temporary prison.

There was someone else in it already. A young woman sat disconsolately on the edge of the bed. She looked up in alarm as the door was flung open, but then relaxed as she realised that the new arrival was a prisoner like herself.

Isabelle remained wary for a moment or two. To have not simply company but someone she could talk to without inhibition would be a marvellous treat, but was this some kind of a trap? Was it hoped that she would be tempted into indiscretion by a stool pigeon? But then, what was there to be revealed that the Germans did not already know? The only precaution she took was to speak in French and introduce herself not as Isabelle but as Anne-Marie.

'I'm Barbara in England and Jeanne over here,' said the girl, 'and you and I have met before, on our first day at Cleeve. I remember because you spoke French so perfectly and I was having to be polished up a bit. You told me that you knew the family who owned the castle.'

'I remember.' The memory guaranteed that Barbara would prove to be who she said she was. What a relief it was to be sure that she could trust her new acquaintance! 'How did you come to land up here?'

The answer came bitterly. 'I've been in Paris for eight months, acting as a courier. Doing everything by the book. Never taking risks. And then those idiots in London send out this dimwit who can't trust herself to memorise names and addresses; so she writes every contact she's supposed to make neatly down in a notebook. And just to make it absolutely certain that she's going to get caught, on her second day here she orders a drink on a non-alcohol day. So everyone turns to stare, of course, and within five minutes she's being asked to show her papers and someone is looking through her handbag and there are the addresses. A whole circuit blown! I can tell you, if she'd been the one who was pushed through the door just now I'd have killed her with my bare hands.'

'Then I'm glad you recognised me as being someone else. Can you give me any news? I got the message which meant that the invasion had started, but I was arrested the same day. How soon do you think the Allied armies will reach Paris?'

'I don't know.' Barbara made a face. 'There's a lot of fighting. They're not just walking it. And anyway, we're not likely to be kept here if there's any chance that we might be rescued. They'll send us east.'

'Yes.' For a moment Isabelle was silent. But surely, if the Germans saw that the end was in sight, they would want to take care of what bargaining counters they had; to be able to say, 'These are some of your people and we treated them well because we never wanted this war.' So she tried to persuade herself, but in her heart she was frightened. Sitting down on the bed beside Barbara, she opened her arms to embrace her and for a long time the two women clung together in silence.

'What about you?' asked Barbara at last. 'Who let you down?'

'Probably the same idiots in England who sent out your dimwit. I only just found out.' The interrogating officers had been so pleased with themselves, so smugly satisfied with the success of Pierre's mission, that they had revealed all the details before asking her any questions; perhaps to make it clear that there would be no point in lying.

'One of the wireless operators on the Engineer circuit was caught,' Isabelle continued. 'Just in the ordinary way, by a detector van. She was ordered to transmit a message, to say that her controller had been killed and to ask for another agent to be sent out as soon as possible. Well, of course, she'd been taught, like all of us, that she must include her personal security check word in every genuine message and that if she left it out they'd know, back home, that it wasn't really her or that she was under duress.'

'So she left it out.'

'Naturally. Only to find that the people who made the rules seemed to have forgotten them. She got a message back saying, "You have forgotten to include your security check word. Please re-transmit." So of course she was forced to do it again, this time while a gun was held to the head of her landlady's four-year-old daughter.' A new agent had duly been sent out, to be arrested within two minutes of his arrival by parachute so that the way was clear for Pierre to introduce himself as the new controller.

Isabelle shivered with anger at the memory of all this; and as well as anger, there was fear. It could be that the game of disinformation by radio was still going on. The Gestapo would not have given her all the details of it so boastingly had they thought that there was the slightest chance of her ever being able to reveal them.

'Out! Out!' The guards were back, pulling the two women from the bed and forcing them down the narrow staircase with such vigour that they nearly fell. A car was waiting in the street below, and within an hour they found themselves, still under guard, locked into a compartment of a train which was moving slowly eastwards out of Paris.

The journey seemed to last for ever, for the train was continually diverted and held up in sidings to allow troop trains to rush past in the opposite direction. As a young girl Isabelle had been taught by her father that even in the darkest clouds there was a silver lining for those who were determined to find it, and she made that effort now, although no cloud could have been darker. They were being moved from Paris because Paris would soon be liberated. The troops were being rushed to the front because the German line must be collapsing. The war must be almost at an end and then she, like France, would be free.

In the meantime, she silently counted her blessings. She had not been tortured, as she had expected to be. She had not been executed, as had seemed all too likely at the moment when she was arrested. She was still alive, in short, and as long as she lived she could hope. She had survived this far; she would continue to survive.

That did not prevent her from shivering with apprehension as she wondered where they were being taken – and it certainly did nothing to relieve the discomforts of the journey. The window could not be opened and the compartment soon became like an oven. Neither of the two women had any change of clothes, nor any of their personal possessions with them, so that by the time Isabelle at last stepped out on to a small country platform she was sweating and dirty and disgusted with herself. But that did not prevent her from standing tall as she waited to discover what would happen next.

'I've heard of Natzweiler.' Barbara, close to her, seemed to be in a state of panic as she read the name of the station. 'It's a concentration camp. And only for men. Why should they bring us . . .'

'Perhaps they need nurses.' Isabelle was determined to remain optimistic.

'Nobody gets nursed here. They work in the quarries until they die. We had a deserter come to us once. He was only eighteen. German. He had to throw the bodies into the crematorium. Sometimes they weren't quite dead, he said. We had to turn him away. He was almost mad. Isabelle, what are they going to do to us?'

Isabelle had no time to answer, for already they were being led inside the area surrounded by a barbed wire and electrified fence. There were papers to be signed, acknowledging the receipt of two prisoners, so she had time to look around.

A group of about a hundred men, perhaps just returning at the end of their working shift, was trudging towards a grim concrete barracks. Their clothes were in rags, their hands in many cases were bleeding, and they were all stooped in exhaustion. Two of them, stronger than the rest, were supporting a third man whose feet trailed along the ground without going through the motions of walking. As Isabelle watched, a guard came up and knocked away the two supporters with the butt of his rifle, allowing the third man to fall to the ground.

A whistle was blown. Two very young soldiers came running. They picked up the dead or unconscious man and carried him towards a long, low windowless building with a tall chimney protruding from the roof. A moment after the three had disappeared inside the building there was a burst of flames through the top of the chimney. Then the two soldiers came out again.

Isabelle licked her dry lips with a tongue that was itself dry. But this would not happen to her: these men must have been overworked and undernourished for years, but she was strong and healthy and young, and the war would surely soon be over. It was only a question of hanging on. She would survive.

Half an hour later the two women found themselves sitting side by side on a comfortable sofa in a well-furnished living room. Isabelle's imagination began to take a lurid turn. Had they been brought here to act as prostitutes for the benefit of the commandant? The arrival of a German officer threw no light on this possibility.

'I am Dr Stiefel,' he announced. Isabelle's understanding of German was not perfect, but what he was telling them now was simple enough. 'I have to give you each an injection. Against typhus. It is very necessary here.'

The two Englishwomen looked at each other doubtfully. Perhaps, thought Isabelle, the guess that they might be used as nurses was a correct one. She made no protest.

Barbara was the first to receive the injection into her arm. She was told to return to the sofa and to press down a pad of cotton wool to prevent any bleeding. The procedure was reassuringly like that in any doctor's surgery at home.

But now Dr Stiefel, opening a second vial of the colourless liquid, was refilling the same syringe and proposing to use the same needle.

'No!' said Isabelle. Her protest was only about the re-use of the needle, but Dr Stiefel interpreted it differently. He called for an orderly to come and hold her still, and as he advanced towards her with the syringe held like a dagger in front of him her alarm grew. She turned to call Barbara to her aid and saw to her horror that her new friend was slumped unconscious over the arm of the sofa.

'No!' she shouted again and began to twist herself out of the orderly's grip. She felt a prick in her arm, but her struggle dislodged the needle, allowing half the liquid to run down her skin. Then the needle pricked again.

She was thrown back on to the sofa and there was a weird moment in which she seemed to be looking down on her own body in incredulity. That girl is Isabelle le Vaillant, who was born to be beautiful and rich and happy. An Englishwoman, who has been presented to the King and has danced with dukes. None of this can be happening to her. To me.

Now her head was spinning. She stood up, determined to keep herself alive by willpower, but there was no strength in her legs. As she fell forward she was conscious of Barbara being carried out of the room. Then she in turn was lifted up.

They took her to the crematorium. Inside the building, the oven door was opened and Barbara's body was tossed inside. The door closed. There was a moment to wait.

Isabelle began to scream. 'I'm still alive!' The words emerged in English. 'I'm still alive! I want to live!'

The door of the oven opened again. The roar of flames deafened her ears. The brightness of the flames blinded her eyes. As she was tossed inside, she screamed just once more.

45

Lady Patricia le Vaillant stared unbelievingly at the grey-haired stranger who had travelled into the country to tell her that her daughter was dead. Her ears heard the words but her mind refused to accept them.

'One day, when the war is over,' said Mr – what was his name? Mr Greenaway? – 'I hope that I shall be able to tell you something about the work she was doing. All I can say now is that she was a very brave young woman. You can be proud of her.'

What was the use of feeling proud, when Isabelle, her only child, was dead? She had been a difficult daughter, but Lady Patricia had truly loved her. She recalled bitterly how they had quarrelled during Isabelle's Season. But Lady Patricia had been right: if only Isabelle had done what she should and made a good marriage then she would have been safe. Then Lady Patricia would have felt a happy pride in her. Isabelle had been all her mother had. What was there left to look forward to, now that she was gone?

By what right had this man stolen her away? He had refused to give any details of Isabelle's work, or to say why it had been so dangerous, but if he was the man who had persuaded her to leave her safe job as a nurse, then he was no better than a murderer. Probably she had still been under twenty-one when she was recruited: a minor, whose parents should have been asked for permission. Grief and anger struggled for supremacy in Lady Patricia's mind. It was anger that won.

'You had no right!' she exclaimed. 'No right at all!' She picked up the nearest object to hand, a teacup, and hurled it at Mr

Greenaway's head. He dodged it easily enough and showed signs of proposing to mop up the tea which it had contained, so she picked up the teapot as well.

'Lady Patricia! Naturally you're upset, but—'

'Go away! Get out of here!' Her heart was filled with a rage which it pumped through her body. The fierceness of its beating increased and her eyes were blinded by a red fury, as though every blood vessel had burst. She was just able to see Mr Greenaway hurrying to ring the bell that would summon a servant before he left the room.

'My lady! My lady!' Estelle, who had once been her personal maid but was now forced to accept a wider role, had answered the summons of the bell. Lady Patricia took no notice as she moved furiously around the drawing room. 'My lady, these are not our possessions!'

That was true enough. Lady Patricia had left London as soon as the bombing started and had rented Hartwell Lodge, fully furnished, for the duration of the war. But why should she care about other people's trashy teasets? By now she was unable to control her actions. Had she known where to find the man who had killed her daughter she would have strangled him with her bare hands. If Mr Greenaway was still in the house, she would kill him too. He had no right . . . He had no right.

Mr Greenaway was nowhere to be seen, and Estelle, in the hall, was telephoning Dr Robbins to come at once, please. Lady Patricia had no intention of waiting for any doctor. Stumbling from side to side as though she were drunk, she made her way to the coach-house in which her car was garaged.

Even in her present fraught state she recognised that she ought not to drive until the red mist in front of her eyes had cleared away. As she waited, taking deep breaths, she remembered another occasion on which she had similarly been overcome by rage: on the night of Lady Ranelegh's ball. A whole lifetime ago, that seemed, but she had never forgotten the snub. Little by little her anger transferred itself from Mr Greenaway, who had put her daughter in danger, to the girls who had come between Isabelle and the position in society that she would have so splendidly graced. Peggy Armitage had turned Lord Lambourn against Isabelle, and Anne Venables, by marrying him, had dealt the final blow to Lady Patricia's ambitions.

She had no idea where Peggy Armitage was now, but the Venables girl was living with her parents at Yewley House, not too far at all from Hartwell Lodge. Still breathing deeply to bring herself under some kind of control, Lady Patricia started the car and studied the petrol gauge. Yes, there was enough there. She set out on her journey.

Mrs Venables was not at home, she was told, but Miss Anne was in the walled garden and could be told of a visitor's arrival.

Miss Anne! What sort of a duchess was that: a girl without the dignity to make the servants acknowledge her rank!

'Don't trouble yourself. I'll find her,' she said haughtily. She marched along the front of the old house and through a cobbled stableyard. A group of four boys sprang guiltily to their feet as she passed one of the old coach-houses. They were too young – aged probably between ten and fourteen – to be stable lads shirking their duties, and in fact their shamed expressions were quickly explained by the cigarette which one of them was hastily trying to stub out. Evacuees, presumably. Of no interest. She swept on.

She found Anne, as the servant had suggested, in a walled garden, bending over a row of carrots. Her long blonde hair was tied out of the way at the back of her neck and she was dressed like a farm labourer in blouse and dungarees.

Lady Patricia, her arrival not yet observed, could not contain her scorn. 'The Duchess of Wiltshire!'

Startled, Anne straightened herself and turned to face her visitor, whom she did not immediately seem to recognise. For the first time Lady Patricia realised that she had not been correctly dressed for receiving when Mr Greenaway so unexpectedly put in an appearance; and in the course of dismissing him her skirt had become stained with tea. She must appear very different from the well-groomed and formally dressed chaperone who had accompanied Isabelle to dances five years earlier.

'Lady Patricia.' Anne had made the identification at last. 'I'm afraid my mother isn't at home. I'm sorry if you've had a wasted journey. Can I offer you tea? Florrie!' She called over to the far corner of the walled garden, where a nurserymaid was watching over a small girl as she picked blackcurrants one at a time. 'Florrie, would you go back to the house and say I'd like tea in the drawing room in ten minutes.'

'So this is Lady Charlotte.' Lady Patricia hissed out the words as the three-year-old came running towards her mother, her mouth stained by the fruit she had eaten. 'A girl! Isabelle would have given the duke a son!'

Anne looked at first puzzled and then, staring more intently at her visitor, uneasy. She called the nursemaid back. 'Take Charlotte in with you, will you, and clean her up. And if you see Hans, ask him to come and join me here so that I can show him how to finish this job off.' With her instructions given, she turned back towards her visitor.

'How is Isabelle?' she enquired politely. 'She hasn't been in touch recently. Not for a couple of years, in fact.'

'Isabelle is dead. Dead two months ago, though they only told me today.'

'What! Dead! How?'

'What do you care how? It was you and your friends who killed her.'

'Lady Patricia, really!'

'If it hadn't been for you, all of you, she would never have gone to France. She should have been Duchess of Wiltshire. Living safely in England with her son. Taking her proper place in society. You would never have found *her* rooting around in the mud like a common peasant. You were jealous of her, weren't you? You froze her out because she wasn't like the rest of you. Because she was sophisticated and elegant and cultured while you were all still children. She thought she had to prove herself to you in some way that you might understand. She was a heroine, they told me. But I didn't want her to be a heroine. I loved her. I wanted her to be alive and in her proper place. And it was all your fault. All of you, but especially you, with your scheming and plotting.'

'You're upset, Lady Patricia, of course you are, but you must know, really, that there was never any plotting. Chay made his own choices. He and I were in love. Very much in love. It was as simple as that. Won't you come inside with me and rest for a little.'

'Don't patronise me, miss. Duchess! I don't want your hospitality. I don't know how you dare look me in the face. Living in the country as though nothing is happening, while other people are being tortured and killed.'

347

'If you'll excuse me for a few minutes, Lady Patricia, I need to wash and change, and then I shall be happy to give you tea in the drawing room.'

'Tea! You'll give me tea! But who will give me back my daughter?'

Anne, who had started to walk towards the house, turned back and stared at her with a firmness unexpected in a girl who had once been the shyest of debutantes. 'You're not the only one who's been forced to accept that brave men and women don't always come back to the people who love them,' she said quietly. 'I've had to learn that lesson, and so of course I sympathise with your distress. But trying to blame someone else doesn't help.'

She continued on her way towards the arched doorway of the walled garden. Even those ridiculous dungarees could not completely conceal the slimness of her tall body and the straightness of her posture. She did not look round to see whether she was being followed.

Lady Patricia's shoulders slumped in despair. She would have liked to grasp the hoe which she could see leaning against a wall and with it to scar that beautiful face so that its owner would never care to look in a glass again. She would have liked to kidnap Lady Charlotte, so that her mother would learn what it felt like to lose a child. But nothing she could do would bring Isabelle back to life. Moaning quietly to herself, she made her way back to the car and slammed the door; but she did not drive off at once.

No one in society had ever seen Lady Patricia le Vaillant weep – or, indeed, display anything but complete control over her feelings. But now, not caring who might be watching, she wept for her dead daughter as though her heart were broken; as indeed it was.

46

Before retiring to bed on the evening of Lady Patricia's visit, Anne held up her black suit and studied it critically. It was really too warm for August, but all her other black clothes were cocktail party wear rather than suitable for a funeral. Once upon a time, of course, the solution would have been to buy something new and appropriate, but in a time of clothes rationing she was not prepared to waste coupons on a garment which – she hoped – she would not need to wear again. This would have to do. She hung up the suit, ready for it to be pressed the next morning. Then the lights went out.

Anne gave a sigh, of resignation rather than surprise or alarm, and sat down on the edge of the bed to wait. There was a candle in her room, as in every other, but it was not worth the bother of lighting it. Within ten minutes Batey – the housekeeper's husband who acted as odd-job man – would have wound fiddly bits of wire round the relevant points in the mains fuse box and the house would spring to life again.

These electrical failures were happening more and more frequently nowadays, and the village electrician who might have known what to do about them was away at the war. It was rats, Batey said, and with traps and poison he had done his best to eradicate them. But there must still be a nest somewhere behind the timbers of the old house and to probe for it would cost more than Mr Venables could easily afford.

The light came on again. Anne resumed her task of setting out the clothes she would need to wear for her mother-in-law's funeral the next day. The dowager duchess had some time ago grown tired of living almost as a lodger in her own castle and, like many of her friends, had returned to London in the belief that the bombing raids were over. She had not reckoned on the new German weapon, the flying bomb, which scattered death and destruction indiscriminately across the south of England, making no pretence of being aimed at any military target. Delacourt House, in Park Lane, had received a direct hit four days earlier, killing its owner and her maid.

Anne had never developed any very close relationship with her mother-in-law, who had been hurt by the speed and secrecy of her only son's wedding and disappointed that her only grandchild was a girl. Nevertheless, this was a family occasion and Anne knew that her presence was required. On the good side, it would give her the opportunity of a chat with Ronnie. Poor Ronnie, she thought as she checked her only pair of black stockings for ladders. Within the space of only five years Ronnie had lost her beloved brother and both her parents and had been deprived of her husband's company, without a child to comfort her for any loneliness.

Her sympathy on that score led her to visit the night nursery, where Charlotte, as blonde and fair skinned as her mother, lay sleeping. Anne smiled lovingly to herself as she removed the little girl's thumb from her mouth and replaced the sheet that had been tossed aside. Then she went to bed herself, although it was still early. Lady Patricia had accused her of behaving like a peasant, and it was true at least that she had adopted the country worker's habit of both rising and retiring early.

She was awakened only an hour or so later by the feeling that something was wrong, although in her drowsy state it took her a little while to work out what it was. Eventually she recognised the smell of smoke – but even that did not ring immediate alarm bells in her mind. The lingering scent of log fires was one of the many things she loved about her old home, in which every room needed to be individually heated for eight months of the year.

But this was August! Completely awake at last, Anne scrambled out of bed. Her bedroom was at the end of a long corridor, and the smoke had only just reached her door. As she raced towards the wide wooden staircase that curved up the centre of the house the smoke became thicker and thicker and now she could hear a sinister crackle from below.

'Fire!' she yelled at the top of her voice. 'Fire!' For a split second she hesitated. The only telephone in the house – with which she could summon the fire brigade – was downstairs, but once she went down she might not be able to get back up again. People first.

Still yelling the alarm at the top of her voice, she snatched Charlotte from her bed in the night nursery and shook Florrie awake.

'Fire!' she said. 'Tell the maids and the boys upstairs to go down the back staircase. Then get out yourself as fast as you can. I've got Charlotte.' Taking a deep breath, she held it as she crossed the staircase landing and ran down the other corridor that led to her parents' room. Her father, coughing, appeared at his door to nod that he had heard her shouts. She hurried back again.

The stairwell drew the smoke upwards like an efficient chimney, and by now the crackling was becoming louder. She was unable to see to the foot of the stairs. If she plunged into the smoke, might she find herself unable to reach the ground floor? As she hesitated, she became aware that Hans had appeared from the upper floor. White faced and looking somehow incomplete without his spectacles, he was literally quivering with terror. Anne remembered that as a young boy he had watched the Nazis burning Jewish homes and shops, and could easily imagine how frightened he must feel.

'Hold on to this,' she said, pressing one end of her dressing-gown cord into his hand. 'Take the deepest breath you can and follow me down.' Using the dressing gown to shroud the head of her wailing daughter, she plunged into the smoke.

Only the bottom two treads were actually burning, though the smouldering wood higher up was hot enough to be felt through her slippers. Anne jumped them, praying that the floor would be strong enough to take her weight, and turned in time to save Hans from falling. He was crying with fear, although doing his best to control it, and Anne herself felt a moment's panic as she struggled with the heavy bolts that secured the front door at night.

Opening the door proved to be a mistake. The air rushing in intensified the blaze while doing little to disperse the smoke. Anne tugged Hans outside and put the three-year-old in his

351

arms. 'Take Charlotte over there,' she said, pointing to the edge of the terrace. 'And then you're to stay there. You mustn't let go of her, not for a minute, however much she yells and wriggles. Do you understand?'

He nodded weakly and set off with his struggling burden. Anne watched for only a few seconds before starting her search for the telephone. Once she had made the emergency call she picked up two of the heavy leather buckets that hung in the hall and threw sand that had probably not been changed for several hundred years over the bottom stairs, just in time to provide a breathing space for her parents.

Once outside, her father took control while Mrs Venables collapsed, gasping for breath, on the terrace lawn. Florrie appeared, and took Charlotte from Hans, the housekeeper was helped to climb out of her ground-floor window, and one by one the maids appeared from the back of the house.

'The boys!' said Anne. 'The Johnson boys!' Their four unwanted evacuees had returned to London at the end of 1939, when it seemed that the expected bombing raids would not materialise, but had been despatched back again as soon as the Blitz began. With their home bombed and their mother apparently disinclined to look after them, they had been at Yewley ever since.

'I should think we may take it that it's the boys who are responsible for this,' said Mr Venables grimly. As a rule he was less antagonistic to them than his wife, but the destruction of his beloved family home was the last straw to break the back of his tolerance. 'Smoking again, no doubt. They'll have made off as soon as they realised what they'd done. I doubt very much whether they'll ever dare show their faces here again.'

'No,' said Hans suddenly. 'Look!'

He pointed up to a second-floor window. All four boys were crowded there, terrified. To prevent accidents when they first arrived at Yewley, the window had been prevented from opening very wide, and its diamonds of lead made it impossible to break the glass. But Tom, the youngest of the family, was squeezing himself through the narrow gap, preparing to jump.

'Don't jump!' shouted Mr Venables. 'Stay there! There'll be a ladder here soon.'

Anne, rocking her frightened daughter on her shoulder, hoped he was right, but the fire engine had a good many miles to come. She looked anxiously across the parkland: no sign of it yet. The gardener, who lived in a separate cottage, had appeared with a garden hose, but the pressure was too feeble to make any impression on the flames which could by now be seen through the first-floor windows, leaping relentlessly upwards as they fed on the centuries-old panelling and floors. The noise was terrifying: an aggressive roaring which combined with the heat to make all of the onlookers instinctively step further back.

There was a shout from one of the maids. Anne looked back at the top-floor window. Three of the boys could no longer be seen, and Tom, who had squeezed himself halfway out, was being tugged back inside. By Hans, of all people. Hans, who was so terrified of fire and who had no reason to love the boys who persistently harassed him, must have made his way up the narrow back stairs. If he could go up, then the others could get down – and even as she watched, Tom fell backwards into the room and disappeared.

Anxious moments passed before the five boys, with Hans leading the way, appeared round the side of the house, smoke blackened and coughing and gasping for breath.

Still clutching Charlotte, Anne ran towards Hans and embraced him with her free arm. 'Well done!' she exclaimed. 'That was so brave of you. You're a hero.'

She was ashamed that the rescue had been left to the young refugee, when the family ought to have made themselves responsible for it. But Anne herself was not prepared to let go of her daughter, Mrs Venables was still lying on the ground, where she had collapsed, and Mr Venables, once he had checked that his wife had no visible injuries, was staring at his collapsing home in a despairing trance, apparently unable to speak or move.

'I must be sick,' said Hans abruptly, twisting himself away just in time before suiting the action to the words. Anne took the opportunity to comfort the other boys. Tom was crying and all four were shivering with shock.

'My books!' Mr Venables groaned in anguish as he saw that the fire, spreading sideways as well as upwards, had reached his study. Then he turned his back on the blaze and spoke more decisively.

'Anne, get the car out and well away from the house. Drive Florrie and Charlotte and Hans to the vicarage and ask Mrs Rendall if she can put them up – and you, later. Telephone from there to get an ambulance for your mother. It's the smoke, I think, as well as the shock. Then ring round and see what you can do to fix everyone else up for a night or two. The boys will have to go back to the billeting officer. And Howard: Howard must be told. When you've done everything you can, bring the car back here.'

Anne nodded her agreement. She passed the fire engine just as she emerged from the home park, but it would be too late. She would never be able to live in her home again.

At eight o'clock next morning, wearing clothes borrowed from the vicar's daughter and tired after only two hours' sleep, Anne trudged up the long drive towards the smouldering ruin. There was no petrol to spare after the journeys made necessary to find beds for all the household.

Mr Venables, equally tired and haggard, was already there, in discussion with a police sergeant.

'Your mother will be all right,' he said. 'Smoke inhalation. They're giving her oxygen. We can visit her after we've finished here. I've just been discussing what could have caused the fire. Not a flying bomb, because we'd have heard the noise. And not likely to be an incendiary bomb either; there's been no report of enemy activity last night. It must have been the Johnson boys.'

'I know they do still smoke whenever they can,' Anne agreed, 'but since I told them off about it, they've always seemed to be careful about staying in the open. If it were their fault, they wouldn't have been in the house. After all, they might have died.'

'They wouldn't have realised that wood will smoulder for hours before it flares up.'

Anne remained unconvinced. She was on the point of suggesting a much more likely possibility – that the rats had at last completely gnawed through the electric cables to set off a short circuit – but it occurred to her just in time that the cause of the fire might prove relevant to an insurance claim, so she held her peace. In any case, she was too tired and unhappy about the destruction of her home to argue. The police could reach their own conclusions. The only important thing was that the Johnson boys should not be blamed for one of the few crimes of which they must be innocent.

The day was a tiring one. With the help of the maids and the gardener Anne and her father struggled to rescue whatever had survived. All the books and almost all the pictures had gone, but a large fireproof safe had protected the most valuable silver. The kitchen quarters were also undamaged. A fire had burned down the original kitchen three hundred years earlier and its replacement had been built sensibly separate from the main house. Almost everything else had either been destroyed or was buried unreachably beneath the tiles of the collapsed roof.

By four o'clock Anne was exhausted. Only then did she remember that she had been due to attend her mother-in-law's funeral.

Unsurprisingly, there was no longer any telephone connection to Delacourt House. Anne sent a written apology instead to Ronnie, and an answer came back to the vicarage by return of post.

Of course you couldn't come. You poor, poor thing! I know how much you loved Yewley. I'm more sorry than I can say. Anne, have you got somewhere else to live? Because if not, I can offer you a choice. Delacourt House is out of the question now, of course, but until the war's over and the eleventh duke turns up to claim his inheritance, you could certainly move into Ma's quarters in Cleeve Castle. God knows what the legal position is, but who could have a better temporary right than the Duchess of Wiltshire? Or I can offer you an Orkney island. It's called Dounsay and you'll need a pretty large-scale map to find it but there's a house there which is empty. Peggy used to visit it while she was posted up there: it's where she met Leonardo, and I gather that they amused themselves by doing a bit of decorating and general maintenance around the place. Even so, it's likely to be bleak and quite incredibly isolated, so I should take Cleeve if I were you.

I'm a bit peripatetic myself at the moment, so I'll telephone your vicarage when you've had a day to think about this, and give you more details.

Lots and lots of love, and, again, I'm so terribly sorry.

The letter gave Anne a good deal to consider. No doubt her parents would soon find somewhere to rent. But it was time that she began to run an establishment of her own. She was not a daughter any longer, but a mother. Thoughtfully she tossed Ronnie's two suggestions around in her mind.

Not Cleeve Castle. She had decided a long time ago that she didn't want to lead the life of a duchess, and it would make things even worse to feel that she was taking possession only as a squatter. Dounsay, though, was a different matter.

She wouldn't mind about the isolation; and it wouldn't matter for Charlotte either, until she was ready to start school in two years' time. It would be safe: safe from bombs and safe from Lady Patricia le Vaillant. Anne was still unsettled by the violent malevolence which Lady Patricia had expressed and felt that Lady Patricia's visit had been an evil omen for the home that she loved. Whether or not Lady Patricia intended any real harm to Charlotte, Anne wanted to take her daughter out of reach of that ill will.

No one would follow them up to a remote Orkney island. The only risk would be to health, if the house proved to be uninhabitable. Peggy would know about that. Anne had almost made up her mind. There were questions to be asked, but if the answers were satisfactory, yes, she would go to Dounsay.

47

'Why didn't you tell me you were coming?' There was no hint of criticism in Anne's question as she hugged her unexpected visitor in welcome. Dounsay House belonged to Ronnie, so of course she could make herself at home whenever she felt like it. But in such a cold and wet autumn, time was needed to air and warm a bedroom. 'It doesn't matter, of course it doesn't. It's just marvellous to see you.'

'I did write,' said Ronnie. 'I expect the letter will arrive in a few days' time. But then I decided I couldn't bear to wait for an answer, and I knew . . .'

Her voice faded into a tired silence. Anne looked anxiously at her friend. She could still remember the exhausted state in which she also had first arrived at Dounsay two months earlier, after the long train journey from London and then a further eight hours in the ferry over a sea that was rarely calm; so there should have been nothing to surprise her in the sight of Ronnie's pale face and the dark rings round her eyes. But other changes were less to be expected. Ronnie had never been exactly plump, but she had been a sturdy young woman, with both her body and her voice always expressing a lively energy. Now her face was thin and strained, her voice was flat and her body listless.

'Ronnie, are you well?'

'Not absolutely.' Ronnie took a deep breath, as if to summon back her energy, and managed a smile. 'That flying bomb that killed Ma. I was two floors down, but the blast chucked me across the room. Cracked a couple of ribs, though in the general pandemonium I didn't realise that straight away. When I came out of hospital I was told to take convalescent leave and not to come back till I was fit again. Now that everyone's in France, they don't really need many people like me in London. So I said to myself, it's time that my only niece got to know her only auntie a bit better.'

'Yes, that's certainly true. Come and have breakfast. We must feed you up.' Anne opened the door and the room was filled with the aroma of frying bacon. It had taken her no time at all after her arrival here to learn that although there were a great many foods that never reached the Orkneys, there were also a good many wartime regulations that had failed to cross the water. It was nobody's business to know exactly what happened to the pigs and hens and sheep on the islands.

'Oh God, no!' Ronnie dashed for the front door and could be heard being noisily sick in the garden.

'Sorry about that,' she said, returning. 'It was bad enough on the ferry, but that rowing boat was the last straw. I don't know what I was thinking of, Anne, suggesting that you should come and live here. A crazy idea. The thing is, I've never been here before. I didn't realise.'

'I love it,' said Anne sincerely. 'Come on upstairs and rest.' She led the way up and showed Ronnie the bathroom. 'Use my bedroom to get a bit of sleep,' she said. 'I'll have a fire lit in one of the other rooms so that it's ready for you tonight.'

'But I ought to say hello to Charlotte.'

'When you've rested,' repeated Anne.

She smiled to herself as she went downstairs to give instructions for the airing of the room. Winter might alter her views, but she had been telling the truth when she claimed to be happy in the isolation of Dounsay House. She had employed two young girls to live in and help in the house, and their grandfather rowed himself over every day to join them. Until now he had been busying himself with all the repairs which had inevitably accumulated in the year since Peggy ceased to visit the house, but Anne was already drawing up plans for taming the neglected grounds and would be glad of his contribution to the heavier work there. She had appointed herself to be head nanny and governess to Charlotte, and felt sure that as a result she would enjoy a far happier relationship with her daughter in the future than she had ever had with her mother.

There had not yet been any time to feel lonely, but Anne had been quick to realise that wartime restrictions on movement and the unpredictable state of the sea would make visiting and receiving visitors the rarest of treats. So the arrival of one of her closest friends was a delight. She hoped that Ronnie would stay for a long time.

By teatime Ronnie's energy had returned and she was her old boisterous self as she watched the unpacking of a box that had accompanied her on the journey. There were toys for Charlotte, and for Anne a selection of tinned fruits and meats.

'You must have used up a whole year's points on these!' exclaimed Anne, wide eyed.

'Not a single one. I had an American friend. He bequeathed me the contents of his larder when he left for France. I didn't want to arrive and find myself robbing you of your last mouthful of food. Tell me, Anne, do you ride here?'

Anne shook her head. 'The island's too small and too rocky. And there wouldn't be enough pasture.'

'Oh.' Ronnie seemed disproportionately put out by the answer. 'I was hoping . . . So what do you do for exercise?'

'Dig. The one thing I feel I can do to repay you for letting me live here is to improve the garden. Or rather, to create a garden. There isn't really anything. I don't think any trees would survive because of the wind. But Eric and I between us are going to repair the walled garden this winter. I'm sure all sorts of things will grow here once they have shelter. Tomorrow I'll take you out and show you what we have in mind.'

'Do that, yes.' There was a pause before Ronnie asked her next question, and yet Anne had a feeling that it was not entirely a change of subject. 'How are you off for medical help? I mean, suppose Charlotte had an accident?'

'If it was a matter of a broken arm, I suppose I'd have to get her to Kirkwall. Dr Brown did call here soon after we first arrived. He gave me a list of what he called the urgencies. Things like the symptoms of appendicitis. But in general – for illnesses like chicken pox – his attitude seems to be that Nature should be left to take its course, without any meddling.'

For a second time in the conversation Ronnie seemed to find an answer unsatisfactory.

'Are your ribs still worrying you?' asked Anne.

'No. Well, not much. I just wondered . . .'

What she wondered was left unresolved, but Anne raised the same question again next morning, when she heard the sound of retching coming from the bathroom.

'Would it be a good idea to let Dr Brown check that your ribs are healing properly?' she suggested when a pale-faced Ronnie arrived in the breakfast room.

'No thanks. I'm sure they're all right. I have to put a sort of corset thing on every morning, and it's a bit uncomfortable. Nothing compared with those incredible constructions we used to wear under our ball dresses, though. Do you remember?'

'How could I forget?' Anne's own waist was so naturally slender that she had needed very little artificial help, but she could well imagine that Ronnie had been forced to submit to severe lacing. The reminiscence, however, did not distract her from the realisation that Ronnie had been deliberately changing the subject. So when on the next morning she once more heard the sound of vomiting, she decided to press her suspicions further.

'Ronnie, are you pregnant?' she asked when Grace had set the porridge on the breakfast table and left the room.

'My husband has been a prisoner of war for four years. How could I possibly be pregnant?'

'But are you?'

Little Charlotte was fortunately too young to take any interest in this conversation.

'Yes.' Leaving the porridge untasted, Ronnie put down her spoon and buried her head in her hands. 'Oh, Anne. It's all such a mess.'

Anne moved quickly round the table to hug her friend in sympathy, and for a moment neither of the two women spoke.

'So it wasn't really to see Charlotte and me that you came here,' Anne said as she returned to her seat.

'Yes, it was. I needed a friend. Someone to talk to. It's true that I wanted to get as far away as possible from everyone else. So that nobody would guess what was happening. But I've come, really, to ask for your help.'

'To do what? I mean, of course I'll help if I can, but . . .'

'To help me keep it a secret, in the first place. And then, well, I hoped I might be able to ride over rough ground here. Have a fall, perhaps. Any sort of accident. Or that perhaps your doctor would be willing . . . Oh, I don't know what I hoped. But I've got to do something.'

'You don't mean that you want to get rid of it!' In her horror, Anne spoke too loudly, causing her daughter to look up in interest. She cut a piece of toast into fingers for a distraction, and the conversation continued in a lower tone.

'Of course I want to get rid of it,' muttered Ronnie. 'I have to. You must see. I'm a married woman. If I have a boy, he'll be in line to inherit an earldom one day, because legally he'll be regarded as Malcolm's son. But everyone will know that he isn't, can't possibly be. I can't see my in-laws agreeing to let a little bastard inherit. There'd be lawsuits, publicity. What sort of a start to life would that be for a child? Even if it's a girl, it wouldn't make much difference. Malcolm would still disown her. And just think how he'd feel, after however many years it's going to be of looking forward to coming home, to find himself being welcomed by the proof of his wife's infidelity.'

'But to kill your own baby! Ronnie, you can't!'

'It doesn't feel like a baby yet. I know I've behaved badly, been an absolute fool, but now I have to start thinking about other people's feelings: Malcolm's especially. There are clinics that go in for this sort of thing, but I don't trust them to keep quiet. I might even bump into one of my dearest friends there and find the story all over London within days.'

'So you thought that if you escaped to the furthest corner of the British Isles you'd be able to find a doctor who'd risk being struck off the Register just because some stranger asked him to help her?' Anne was unable to keep a note of sternness out of her voice. 'Well, you're wrong, Ronnie. This is a God-fearing place. Puritanical, you could say. People here live very close to death. Huge battleships and tiny fishing boats set out and never come back again. So life is valued. Dounsay can certainly offer you peace and quiet, a long way from anyone else who knows you. I can promise that as long as you stay here, no one outside the islands need know about your pregnancy. But I can't help you to end it.'

'Noted.' Ronnie rose to her feet, leaving her breakfast untouched. 'I'll go out for a walk this morning, Anne, if that's all right by you. Beat the bounds. Then this afternoon I'll be happy to do some digging, or anything else that doesn't require any skill. Goodbye for the moment.'

Anne was left to feel guilty. She had been asked for help by her best friend, and had refused to give it. But how could she act against her conscience? And now she was frightened as well as ashamed. Might Ronnie try to harm herself? Perhaps not deliberately, but in some amateur attempt to induce a miscarriage she might fall further than she intended.

'Grace!' she called. 'Look after Charlotte, will you? I'm going for a walk with Lady Ronnie.'

It took her only a few moments to put on her heavy walking boots and tug the laces tight. She could easily have caught up with Ronnie, but instead she walked at the same steady pace, keeping her friend in sight but not drawing attention to herself. She needed to think.

During their breakfast-time conversation Ronnie had talked as though there were only a single choice to be made: between ending the pregnancy and greeting her husband with the living proof of her unfaithfulness. But there were other possibilities: possibilities that must be carefully considered before they were discussed.

So deep in thought was she that it came as a shock when she rounded a corner and found Ronnie sitting on a rock with her legs stretched across the path, obviously waiting for her to catch up.

'You didn't think I was going to throw myself off the cliff, did you?' Ronnie asked. The island of Dounsay was more or less flat at its eastern end, on which the house was built, but to the west it rose steeply to end in a sheer cliff, as though it had been chopped off from one of its neighbours.

'Of course not.' Anne sat down beside her. 'I like to take a walk myself every day. But you had the look of someone who didn't feel chatty, so I thought I ought to keep my distance.'

'Right. I've stopped, so I'm chatty again. If there's anything to be said.'

'A couple of questions,' said Anne. 'What about the baby's father?'

'What about him? He doesn't know I'm pregnant. He wouldn't want me to be pregnant. I have no intention of telling him.'

'Doesn't he have any rights in whatever you decide to do?'

'No. If the baby is never born, it would only distress him to know that it might have been. If it's born to Malcolm Ross's wife, so to speak, he'd have to watch it growing up either as the accepted child of another man or, more likely, as the unwanted cuckoo in the nest. Ignorance definitely bliss, I should say.'

'There's another possibility that you don't seem to have considered,' Anne said cautiously. 'You could have the baby – up here, where no one would gossip about it – and then have it adopted.'

'Oh, I've thought about adoption all right. One of the clinics I considered is run by nuns. Lovely caring ladies who think that the best way to punish a guilty mother is to take her baby away the moment it's born, without letting her see it, and hand it over to strangers whose name she'll never be allowed to know. Just think of the agony, Anne, for years and years, of never knowing whether your baby, your own flesh and blood, was being treated kindly or not. I couldn't bear it.'

'But suppose you found someone more sympathetic than the nuns. Suppose you were allowed to know who was bringing up your baby. Suppose you were even allowed to see him from time to time.'

'How are you suggesting I find this sympathetic person?'

Anne took a deep breath. Less than two hours had passed since the plan she was about to suggest had first entered her head. It was a very short time in which to consider such an important decision, but she was sure. She was absolutely sure that this would be a good thing to do.

'I don't want Charlotte to grow up as an only child,' she said quietly. 'I could adopt your baby myself.'

'Anne!' Hope and delight flashed briefly in Ronnie's eyes before she began to consider the objections. 'No,' she said sadly. 'You'll marry again one day. You'll have more children of your own. And then you won't want someone who doesn't belong.'

Anne shook her head. 'I don't want to marry anyone else,' she said. 'I want to keep the memory, although it was so short. The perfect memory.' She had been a widow for four years now, but the thought of Chay brought her near to tears and she had to steady herself with a deep breath. 'Even if I did remarry, there'd be too long a gap. It's now that Charlotte needs a brother or sister, not in ten years' time.'

'It would be marvellous,' said Ronnie simply. 'Because then I should be his aunt, shouldn't I? I wouldn't have to be just a stranger.'

'His aunt by adoption.' Anne was still struggling to find the right words to define the situation. It was important that she should get it exactly right. 'I'd have to make conditions, Ronnie, and ask you to agree to them.' Again she stopped to think. 'He'd have to know right from the start that he was adopted. Because, if the baby is a boy, he'll need to understand why he isn't a duke if the Duchess of Wiltshire is his mother. And anyway, with no father around . . . Well, that's one thing. But I should want to be his mother: his only mother. I shouldn't ever tell him who his birth mother was, and you'd have to promise that you wouldn't tell him either.'

'Go on.'

'Well, the big thing is, if you give your baby to me, you can't ever have him back. I should want to love him as my own baby right from the very first moment, and for the rest of my life. And I couldn't do that if I was afraid all the time that you might turn up one day and say, "Well, thanks very much, Anne, but my circumstances have changed and I want to look after him myself from now on." I wouldn't let you, but even thinking that might happen would spoil everything.' Anne was well aware of her friend's impulsive nature. Ronnie would find it easy to make a promise but might just as easily break it.

'There'd have to be some kind of legal document to protect me,' Anne continued. 'I think you ought not to give me an answer now; not until you've had time to think about it. Shall we climb up to the top?'

It was a steep scramble up a rocky slope that brought them to the edge of the cliff. At the bottom of its sheer face the black water swirled and broke into a cloud of white spray.

'There's a wild winter on its way,' said Anne. 'You'll find it rather dull, I'm afraid, if you stay.'

'Certainly I shall stay,' said Ronnie. 'I shall learn to knit and make tiny bootees and matinee jackets for my future niece or nephew.' She staggered a little as the wind buffeted her. 'I could say that I don't really have any choice, but the truth is that what you're offering is just perfect. Of course I accept your conditions, and I'll sign anything you like. I can't thank you enough. I've been feeling absolutely miserable for three months with the bomb and Ma's death and Jack going off to France and this hanging over me all the time. And now suddenly the sky is lifting. How lucky I am to have such a marvellous friend!'

For the first time since her arrival at Dounsay Ronnie's face was lit by the carefree smile with which Anne had always associated her.

Anne herself was not quite so carefree. The arrangement she proposed could as easily break a friendship as strengthen it. But if that were to happen, it was Ronnie who was most likely to suffer. Anne herself would have the second child that Chay had not been spared to give her; and Charlotte would have company in the nursery with whom to share and to play. And the new baby would have Delacourt blood. He might grow up to look like Chay and to have Chay's charm and intelligence and loving nature. Yes, Ronnie was right. Anne dismissed the last lingering doubt from her mind. The arrangement would be just perfect.

48

There were two good reasons – or so Peggy told herself – why she should visit Oxford in the summer of 1945. It was necessary to give St Hugh's College formal notice that she did not after all intend to take up the exhibition awarded to her in 1939. And she could take the opportunity to visit Jodie, whom she had not seen for two years.

Both these were merely excuses. A letter to the Principal would have been businesslike enough, and Jodie, who had just finished her final examinations, would be back in Newark within a week. The true incentive for the visit was more complicated. She needed to be sure that her decision was the right one and that there would be no later sentimental regrets.

She had expected this to be an easy exercise. It was, after all, almost three years since she had resolved to embark on a working career as soon as the war was over. Once upon a time she had envisaged the life of a student in terms of scholarship, but gradually it had come to present itself as not precisely frivolity but as a period of irresponsibility; of time out from the real world. Once it was seen in that light, it had to be rejected. The decision had been reinforced first of all by her engagement to Bill and later by the news that her father, overworked and overstressed, had suffered a stroke.

Oxford in December 1939 had been dark and damp, misty and medieval, silent and secret. Oxford in June 1945 was sunlit and smiling. Undergraduates in some subjects were still sitting their Finals and, as Peggy walked along The High, they were pouring out of the Examination Schools at the end of a morning session, wearing their academic gowns over the neat black and white sub fusc uniform and for the most part chattering with relief. Their friends were waiting outside to greet them with flowers or bottles of wine. It was a happy scene.

She walked a little further and leaned over Magdalen Bridge. Below her the river was crowded with punts that jostled for mooring spaces not too far from the boathouse so that the serious business of the picnic lunch could begin. Some of the picnickers, no doubt, were undergraduates who in their first or second years were free from the tyranny of examinations. A few were still wearing evening dress, perhaps after celebrating the end of their university lives at a ball on the previous night. Sleepy heads rested on companionable shoulders. There would have been proposals of marriage, thought Peggy. Lives were about to change. Oxford in wartime could not have borne much resemblance to the light-hearted Oxford of the 'twenties and 'thirties, but young people could find gaiety simply in being young.

For a moment she was tempted – touched by envy – but she was not young in that kind of way any longer. Were she to embark on a degree this October, she would be twenty-eight by the time she graduated. That would be ridiculous. Besides, she had no wish to dance or flirt or canoodle in punts with anyone except Bill, and he would not be here. So no: she must not give way. She had had her chance and had turned it down. That was that.

She had not given Jodie warning of her arrival and found her in her room at St Hilda's busily sewing – an activity she did not normally associate with her sister.

'Peg! Oh Peg, how marvellous! Are you a civilian at last?'

'Not quite,' said Peggy, returning the hug with interest. 'It won't be long, though. What are you doing?'

'Creating an evening dress.' Jodie gave a sigh of effort. 'I'm going to the Magdalen Ball tonight and I haven't got a long dress and I can't possibly spare the coupons to buy one. So I thought . . . This is only a housecoat really, but it's quite pretty, don't you think, and I've cut it low at the back and now I'm sewing black velvet ribbon round all the edges to make it really smart, and I'll wear some more of the ribbon as a choker, with Mummy's pearl brooch on it. I shall hardly be the belle of the ball, but at least I won't be a freak. I hope. But it's taking hours longer than I expected, going round the hem.'

'Let me help.' There was plenty of room for them both to work on different parts of the full skirt. Peggy couldn't help laughing as she sat down and threaded a needle. 'I think this is the first time in my life that I've ever seen you doing anything even remotely frivolous.' Jodie had never been pretty, and the horn-rimmed spectacles she was wearing made her look even more severe than usual. But there was an air of excitement about her: a lightness of spirit even more unusual than her current occupation. 'Why didn't you write home, though? You could have borrowed one of the dresses I wore for my Season.'

'Three reasons. One is that they'd have been far too grand. Most of the girls tonight will be in the same state as me: making do. The second is that I'm much skinnier than you were then. No bust at all to fill a dress out.'

'And the third?' asked Peggy, when it seemed that she was not to be told.

Jodie kept her eyes down, concentrating on her sewing. When she answered, it seemed to be with reluctance.

'The third is that my partner tonight is someone you know. Someone you used to dance with when you were a debutante. I wouldn't want to see him looking at me and recognising a dress and thinking how much prettier you'd looked in it. Secondhand and second best. No, thank you.'

'Who is it?'

'Howard Venables. One of your old flames.'

'Hardly that,' said Peggy. It was true that Howard had played an important part in her life, because he had met her at a time when she was shy and lacking in confidence in the strange new world of society. He had encouraged her to believe that she was interesting – and yes, perhaps Jodie's phrase was justified. Peggy had thought she was in love with him and certainly had believed that he loved her, but then he had just walked away. She remembered that she had been upset; but when she looked back on that time, she recognised that there had never been anything more than friendship between them. It was from Laurie and Leonardo and Bill – and, in a more unusual manner, from Chay – that she had learned to distinguish between friendship and the different ways of loving.

368

'Oh yes, he was,' protested Jodie. 'Once we got to know each other, he poured it all out. How he wanted to marry you but was too thin skinned about being called a fortune hunter. He's terribly ashamed of that. It's rather funny, really, that it's the same fortune which he may be hunting now.'

'Really? Marriage?'

'I don't know for sure, of course I don't.' Jodie's face flushed as she threaded her needle again. 'But tonight might be the night. Magdalen's such a dreamy place. There are going to be two marquees for dancing and supper and we can walk by the river or use the punts.'

'Sounds as though you're ready to be swept off your feet.'

'I've got *some* sense.' This was the old assertive Jodie speaking. 'Of course I'm going to be swept off my feet. That's why I've had to think in advance what I want to say.'

'And you'll say yes?'

Jodie's voice softened again. 'Well, I do like him very much. He's tremendously clever, you know. He's been offered a marvellous job and it won't be long before he's so rich that it won't matter at all whether or not Daddy leaves anything to me. He doesn't care that I'm not beautiful or smart or sophisticated. We talk the same language.'

'I hope you'll be very happy,' said Peggy sincerely. Reaching the end of her piece of ribbon, she snapped off the thread and gave her sister a second hug. But there was still one thing to make her curious. 'How did you come to meet?'

'By mistake. He was looking for you. He came to call at the house one day. Easter, it was, in 1940. He must have hoped, really, that he'd find you at home, because otherwise he could just have written a letter to be forwarded. Mummy and Daddy were both out, so I talked to him. His story was that he'd been invited to some kind of feast at his old college in Oxford and thought it would be nice to look you up while he was there but didn't know which college you were at. I told him that you hadn't taken up your exhibition and gave him your address in Liverpool.'

'He never wrote there.'

'No? Well, it was odd.' Flushing for a second time, Jodie stood up and held what was now her ballgown in front of her, shaking out the creases. 'He stayed for tea. I thought he was sort of sucking up to me – I mean, pretending to be interested – just because he wanted to get back with you again. I was only sixteen. Working for my School Certificate, for heaven's sake! I wasn't interested in boyfriends, and anyway, he seemed so much older that he was almost a different generation. But something kind of clicked between us. Do you know the feeling?'

'Yes,' agreed Peggy. 'I know the feeling.'

'I asked him some question that he couldn't answer, so he said he'd write, and he did write, and I wrote back, and – well, really for a long time that was all it was. We didn't actually see each other again till I came up here. You don't mind, do you, Peg?'

''Course I don't mind. I've got Bill. I shall be delighted to have Howard as a brother-in-law, if that's how things turn out.' It would provide yet another link with Anne, as well as that of being one of little Charlotte's godmothers. 'So how do you see your future?' Jodie was no more likely than Peggy herself to sink back into the kind of life their mother had enjoyed or endured.

'I'd like to start a business. I'm sure Howard will earn quite enough to support a family without my help, but I'd like to have something of my own.'

'You could always . . .'

Jodie shook her head vigorously, guessing that she was about to be offered a place in Armitage's.

'I want to start something from scratch. Just like Daddy did. It doesn't really matter what the business does or makes, as long as it's all mine. It will be fun looking around, trying to decide what sort of thing people are going to want in the next ten years or so, and how easy it would be to supply it.'

'Not easy at all, I shouldn't think.' Although shop assistants were no longer able to riposte 'Don't you know there's a war on?' to any request for unrationed goods, almost everything was still in short supply. 'Well, I'll leave you to get ready for the great occasion. Give my love to Howard. And I hope it won't be long before I see you at home.'

For a second time, as she crossed Magdalen Bridge, she paused to stare – on this occasion looking over the grounds of St Hilda's College, which she had just left. Groups of young women were relaxing happily on the lawns, savouring the last days of term – perhaps the last days of their university lives. The Cherwell flowed calmly under a white wooden bridge. And the sun was still shining.

If only, she thought, if only Jodie could find some way of packaging grass and water and roses and sunshine and selling this peaceful happiness to all the people who were tired and strained after six years of war and who would be returning, in so many cases, to cramped houses in mean streets. What a business that would be!

It was an amusing daydream, but hardly a realistic one. Peggy herself hoped that in the years to come she might be able to bring a different kind of happiness into the lives of young women by providing them with clothes that were pretty – and made the wearers feel pretty – and far removed from wartime uniforms. But her first task was to bring her own schoolgirl daydream to a final close. St Hugh's was still in temporary accommodation, as it had been at the time of her interview. She made her way there briskly to put on record the fact that she would not be taking up her Exhibition. So that was that. It was time to return to normal life.

49

All over England, now that the war was over, women were impatient with the crawling pace of demobilisation. Even prisoners of war found their return delayed by medical examinations and the requirements of military bureaucracy. But at last – and earlier than most of the men who had been actively fighting – they were free to return to their wives.

One of those wives was waiting in a state of apprehension that bordered on terror. The past few months had drained Ronnie both physically and emotionally.

All the arrangements for the adoption had gone smoothly. To guard against the possibility of bad weather, she had travelled to Kirkwall a fortnight before her baby was due, with Anne making the journey to join her only when she was admitted to hospital. For ten minutes Ronnie had cuddled baby Richard, then with a single deep sob she had handed him over and turned her face away, unable to speak. Three days later she had signed the legal papers. She had not returned to Dounsay.

Allowing her baby to be taken away from her as soon as he was born had reminded her of the indignation she felt when one of the clinics she approached earlier had made exactly the same condition. But this was different. Anne was Richard's mother now and must be allowed to bond with him from the first hour of his life.

It was a sensible arrangement. It was the best possible arrangement. That, of course, did not prevent Ronnie from shedding tears of misery and self-pity from time to time. 'All new mothers are cry-babies,' the midwife had warned her, but Ronnie felt that she had more to cry about than most.

She had returned to London even before peace was declared. Cautiously exploring the lower floors of Delacourt House she decided that they could safely continue to bear the weight of the fallen roof. In any case, she had nowhere else to stay.

It was not a good choice. For several weeks after the birth she was both physically and emotionally wobbly, and the gloom of the basement did nothing to raise her spirits. What had happened, she wondered, to the high-spirited debutante, the confident driver, the passionate lover? It was difficult, in those dark and lonely days, to believe that she would ever be happy again.

She would never see Chay again, or her mother and father. She had lost touch with most of her debutante friends. Many of them had fulfilled their mothers' hopes – as she had herself – by marrying as soon as their Season was over. They had started their families at once and for the most part had spent the war years – like Anne – living in the country as they brought up their babies and did a little voluntary work. Ronnie no longer had anything in common with them. Of those who had volunteered for war service, Isabelle le Vaillant and Julia Rutherford were dead, and she had cut herself off from most of the others when she accepted a medical discharge.

And she would never see Jack again. She had lost him even more finally than baby Richard, to whom she could at least behave as an aunt. Jack had survived the invasion unharmed, and all the nerve-racking months of advance that followed. Although it would have needed all her courage, she had felt during that period that she must make her confession to him face to face. But when he wrote to tell her that he had been put in charge of a bombed car factory in Germany, with instructions to restore it to productivity, she could wait no longer.

'I'm sorry,' she wrote – although it took her three tear-stained pages to explain it. 'I'm married. My husband will soon be coming home.' There was no answer.

And now the date of Malcolm's return was no longer 'soon'; it was 'today'.

Ronnie went to Victoria to meet the Red Cross train – looking around the crowded platform and wondering whether she was the only woman there who was longing to run away. But as the train drew in and the ex-prisoners flooded out, it

373

was only the children who drew sulkily away from the strangers who were their fathers. Everywhere else around her were kisses and embraces and tears of happiness. Ronnie reminded herself that nothing that had happened was Malcolm's fault. He deserved a welcome and she must do her best to give it to him.

And now here he came, looking fatter than she remembered him. They stood still, facing each other, for a moment in which he seemed almost as shy as herself.

'You're very thin,' he said, and then, 'Oh, Ronnie!' His grip on her arms was painfully tight as he covered her face with wet kisses. It was ridiculous that she should need to force herself not to shrink away. It was shameful that she should want to wipe her face clean.

'Come on,' he said at last. 'Let's get hold of a taxi before all this lot start moving.'

Sitting in the taxi for the short journey he took hold of her hand and stroked it along his thigh. The taxi came to a halt in front of Delacourt House and he gave a gasp of incredulity as he surveyed the ruins.

'My God! Oh, my God! I know you told me, but I didn't imagine . . . Ronnie, you surely haven't been living here! You should have gone to my people in the country.'

The possibility of living with her in-laws had never even crossed Ronnie's mind. 'I went up to the Orkneys, if you remember,' she said. 'With Anne. I came back when the war was ending. But I thought it would be best to wait . . .'

'Yes, quite right. We must find somewhere decent to live. Choose it together.' He followed her down the steps, his hands on her waist as she fumbled to set the key in the lock, and did not bother to shut the door behind him.

Ronnie had made an attempt to brighten the basement flat with flowers, but they only served to emphasise the dinginess of everything else. She could see Malcolm shaking his head in disbelief. At the time when he left England these had been the servants' quarters.

'Do you want a cup of tea?' she asked, moving towards the kitchen.

'You know what I want. Five years! Oh Ronnie, my darling. I can't tell you how much I've looked forward to this moment.

Dreamed about it.' He had caught up with her by now and turned her back into his arms, kissing her again as he began to undo the fastenings of her dress.

'Please, Malcolm. Just wait a moment. I think we ought to take this slowly. It's been such a long time. We need to get to know each other again.'

'We can do that in bed.' Impatient with the tiny buttons, he ripped open the back of her dress just as he had once torn at her wedding dress.

Ronnie began to struggle. 'No, really, please wait. Can't we just talk to each other for a bit? So much has happened to each of us. We're strangers, in a way. We need—'

'We're husband and wife.' By now her dress was lying on the floor. 'God, Ronnie, you're beautiful.'

'I'm not ready. I'm sorry, Malcolm.'

She had not intended to refuse him. As the train had drawn into the station she was still trying to persuade herself that with a little effort they could return to the light-hearted camaraderie they had shared in her debutante days. But that was when she was dealing only with the memory of a man. Faced with the solid flesh and blood of that same man, she could remember only the repugnance she had felt on her wedding night. At the time she had assumed that she was in some way to blame for the failure of their honeymoon; but a single night with Jack . . . But no, she must not think about Jack.

'What I mean,' she said desperately, 'is that we ought to step back a little. Start again with courtship instead of—'

Again she was interrupted as Malcolm picked her up and started to carry her towards the bedroom. 'This is what girls like, isn't it?' he suggested. 'A bit of sweeping off the feet. I can understand it if you're feeling a bit shy again. It's almost like a new honeymoon, isn't it?'

'No, it isn't.' Ronnie began to struggle more vigorously. 'I'm asking for courtship and you're offering – well, rape, if I don't want to do it.'

'Rape!' Malcolm let go of her so suddenly that she staggered and fell. He jerked her to her feet again with a tug that sent a stab of pain through one shoulder. 'A husband can't rape his wife. I have the right . . . I'm exercising my marital rights, that's all. I'd have expected you to want that as much as me.' His

375

expression changed as he looked at her more closely. 'Is there someone else? Are you telling me you've been unfaithful to me, Ronnie?'

For a moment she did not answer. There had been plenty of time to think about this in advance, and she had decided that it would be a kindness to Malcolm to conceal her night of infidelity from him for ever. But that was when she had still hoped that somehow or other they might find a way of being happy together.

Now that hope had died. Her marriage was a mistake. It was not Malcolm's mistake. He had genuinely loved her. It was not his fault that she had been far too young to know her own mind, far too innocent to realise what marriage involved, and far too much under her mother's influence to consider even for a moment that there could be any alternative to marriage. She was sorry that Malcolm should be the one to suffer for her own immaturity, but it must surely be best to settle the matter at once and leave him free to make a new and happier life for himself.

'There was someone,' she said carefully. 'One night, that was all. I shan't ever see him again. But it's nothing to do with that. We shouldn't ever have got married, Malcolm. I was too young. I'm desperately sorry, but I want a divorce. So that we can both start again.'

'You want a divorce, do you? That's a fine welcome home for a chap! And what grounds do you think you have? You may have found it easy enough to shag every passing Romeo, but I can tell you that my opportunities for committing adultery in the past five years have been pretty limited.'

'You could divorce me,' she said, freeing her hand and taking a step backwards. She could see the anger in his eyes and was frightened of what he might do. 'I'd give you evidence. Whatever's needed.' She knew nothing about the laws of divorce. What she did know was that a court case would turn her into a social leper – but it was not at all clear whether society, in the old sense, still existed. In any case, she didn't care about that. She wanted to be free.

'Well, perhaps I don't choose to announce to all my friends that my wife is a whore.' His anger was at boiling point now. 'I'm a married man and I've spent five years looking forward to seeing my wife again and I'm damned if I'm going to let you spoil it.' He lunged forward to grab her again, but she twisted herself away.

A blow to her face sent her staggering across the floor.

'Bloody tart! Ready to let any Tom, Dick or Harry into your bed for the night but not your lawful wedded husband. Oh no! Well, I'll show you, my girl. I have rights.'

And now they were fighting. It was a fight that Malcolm, taller and heavier, was bound to win, but Ronnie did not give in easily. Pulling just far enough away, she brought her knee up to hit him in the groin. He gave a shout of pain and responded with a blow to her nose which caused her briefly to lose consciousness, although she was just aware of hitting her cheek on the edge of a table as she fell to the ground.

'Bloody whore! Bloody whore!' With each shout he kicked her. Almost unable to move, Ronnie just managed to curl herself into a ball, pulling up her knees to protect her stomach and covering her head with her arms as she waited for the next blow to come.

'What's going on here?' It was Jack's voice. But Jack was in Germany. Was she hallucinating?

No, the voice must have been real, because Malcolm was responding to it. 'None of your bloody business!'

'You're wrong there. Leave her alone or I call the police.'

There was a tense moment of silence, followed by the slamming of a door.

'Ronnie,' said Jack. She felt something soft – it was her own dress, by the feel of it – wiping the blood from her face. 'Ronnie, look at me. Say something.' But she was unable to answer. It was enough to know that she was safe. She allowed herself to slip into unconsciousness.

When she next became aware of her surroundings she was in a hospital bed, propped up by pillows and unable to breathe through her nose. Below the waist she felt as sore as on the day after Richard's birth and every movement was painful, but she was hardly conscious of any of that, for Jack was sitting by her bedside.

'Jack. What are you doing in England?' Her voice emerged thinly, as though she had adenoids, and when Jack's smile spread over his face in the slow manner which had always delighted her, she was unable to tell whether he was laughing at the sound of it or registering pleasure at her recovery.

'Big conference going on. The industrial future of Germany. A fight to the death between those who'd like to see the country ground down and bankrupted for good and those who remember the last time and think there must be a better way. People on the ground called in to report on the situation. I skipped a lunch break to see you. You said in your letter that you ought to have talked things out with me face to face, and I thought that too. Just as well I turned up. Who was the hoodlum?'

'My husband.'

'Is that so? Then the sooner you get quit of him the better. Reckon he could have killed you, if I hadn't turned up. He'd gone berserk.'

'He had reason.' It was difficult to talk, but important to try. 'Terrible war for him. Looking forward to coming home. Expecting everything to be the same. All my fault.'

'Don't waste your energy thinking whose fault it is. Just get out.'

'He won't let me go.' By now Ronnie was coming to terms with the thickness of her bandaged nose and was able to speak more freely. 'He said he wouldn't divorce me, and I can't divorce him. Bashing your wife isn't enough. He has to commit adultery as well.'

'Then we put a private eye on him until he does. It won't take long after five years locked up. But I have a better idea.' He produced an envelope from his breast pocket and spread half a dozen photographs in front of her. 'I took these while I was waiting for the ambulance to come. And the casualty doctor will confirm the state you were in when you arrived in the hospital. How do you think this husband of yours would fancy finding himself in court on a charge of wife-beating? My guess is that there's room for negotiation. I've had Sandy talking to a lawyer here already, to see how things stand. Back home, my wife got a divorce on the grounds that I stopped paying her bills for shoes after she had fifty-three pairs in the closet already.'

'It's not as easy here.'

'So it seems. But you wouldn't have to worry about that. All I want from you is permission to do anything that's necessary to make you a single woman again – even though that may mean you standing up in court to confess that yes, my lord, you committed adultery with a worthless foreigner who ought to go back where he came from instead of taking advantage of the absence of a gallant officer and breaking up the homes of decent people.'

'Anything you say,' agreed Ronnie. 'But . . .'

'But what are you going to do afterwards? you want to know. Well, when I talked about all I want, that wasn't quite right. I want a lot more. I want you to come with me to Germany and help me plan a production line. And then, as soon as you're free, I want you to marry me and let me turn you into the best female racing driver in the whole of the United States.'

'*Are* there any female racing drivers in America?'

'Not yet, but there will be once we set up a special circuit for them. Anyway, don't start arguing about it, because who but some love-besotted one-armed cripple is ever going to take a second look at a woman with a broken nose who will probably never be able to have kids?'

'What!'

'Oh, my God!' Until that moment Jack's voice had been light and teasing, but suddenly he was overcome by horror at what he had just said. 'Haven't they told you yet? What a doggone idiot I am! I should have thought! And it's not certain yet. They won't know for sure until everything's healed up. But that husband of yours surely didn't pull any punches when it came to putting the boot in.'

Winded by the news, Ronnie felt tears beginning to run down her cheeks at the thought that she had given away the only child she might ever be able to bear. But it was done now, and could not be undone. Just as it would have been impossible to confess to Malcolm that his grandfather's earldom might one day be inherited by a bastard, so equally she could not tell Jack that she had robbed him of a son. How had she managed to get everything so wrong?

Jack was still muttering words of self-reproach when, making a determined effort to be cheerful, she interrupted with a different confession.

'It's worse than you think. You've already discovered that I'm not Miss Ronnie Ross. Well, I'm not Mrs Ronnie Ross either. I'm Lady Ronnie Ross.'

'I don't get it,' said Jack. 'Are you telling me that that son of a bitch—?'

'No. It's in my own right. I was born Lady Veronica Delacourt, daughter of the Ninth Duke of Wiltshire.'

'Wiltshire? Isn't that the family . . . '

'The family you were so scathing about the first day we met? Yes. I thought if I confessed at once, we should start off on the wrong foot, and it didn't seem important.'

'So you left me to discover for myself that even a Lady can be hard working and reliable and fun and sweet and lovely. But will a Lady agree to marry an ordinary guy? That's the big question.'

'Are you asking me?'

'What I really want to do at this point in time is cover your face in kisses before I put the question,' said Jack, 'but I've been warned in no uncertain terms that if I go anywhere near your nose it may end up even more crooked than it is now. So I have to do it cold. Yes, I'm asking you.'

'Yes,' said Ronnie. She began to cry again, but for a different reason. 'I don't deserve you, Jack, but yes.'

50

'Dear Ronnie.'

For once Anne did not need to chew her fountain pen as she began one of her regular letters to her sister-in-law. Usually she had to choose her words with a good deal of care. It was only fair that each letter should contain some news of little Richard's progress, but important at the same time that this should be balanced by references to Charlotte, to make it clear that this was merely family chat and not a report from an adoptive to a natural mother.

On this occasion, though, there was a different kind of news to tell her.

I've just had a letter from Cleeve. It's taken the lawyers long enough, but the new duke has at last managed to establish that his parents were legally married when he was born, and has arrived to take up residence. He can't believe what he's seeing! The size of the castle and the state of it, to start with. It seems to have been left in a terrible mess and no one has done any repairs for years. As well as that, all the tenants are clamouring for new roofs and better drainage and anything else you can think of, and he isn't allowed to put up their rents – and there still seems to be a legal wrangle going on about death duties.

He sounds very young and unsophisticated – younger, I mean, than twenty-three, which is what he is. He addressed me as 'Dear cousin', but when it came to the end of the letter he said, 'I'm told that I should sign myself Wiltshire, but that sounds too pretentious for words, so I hope you'll let me be simply Kingsley to you.'

Anyway, he wants me to go and visit him at the castle, and I shall. I've always been rather frightened of Cleeve, as you know, because it was so grand, but it doesn't sound as though that's true any longer, and I'm curious, and I think the children should have a chance to look around. So I'm off there tomorrow. I'll write again to report as soon as I get back.

Reading through the letter, Anne wondered whether she was being tactless. It might be hurtful to her friend to think of her old home decaying, but Ronnie had been more whole hearted than anyone else she knew in embracing a new life. In this period of chilly austerity which had followed the war, almost everyone in England – and especially the friends Anne had made during her debutante season – had been forced to realise that their comfortable pre-war lives had gone and would never return. Most of them, like Anne herself, tried to make the best of their new situation, keeping up old standards as well as they could, whilst accepting the limitations imposed by clothes rationing and food rationing and the difficulty of finding servants.

Ronnie, though, had taken more drastic action. She had divorced Malcolm and sailed off to America to marry Jack Donovan: Anne remembered the shocked gossip that had followed Ronnie's decision to turn her back on her husband, her place in society and her country. But only Anne knew the full anguish of that decision, for Ronnie had also abandoned her child. She had kept faith with Anne: Richard remained in England with his adoptive mother. Jack did not know about his son, and Ronnie could never give him another child. Instead they pursued with single-minded determination Ronnie's new career as a racing driver in the United States. It was a project that absorbed them absolutely. Jack accepted with delight the challenge of designing a new car for his wife and was planning to build at least four race tracks to be used by women. Ronnie's own challenge would have to be against the system which at present excluded females from the racing circuit. She had already gleefully described her plan to make use of her ambiguous Christian name and, with the help of goggles and a helmet and a scarf round her chin, to present herself at the last moment before the start of any race as a male. Only when she had achieved a respectable position would she reveal her gender and demand acceptance. It was clear from her letters that she was looking forward to the struggle.

How much calmer was Anne's own life! She could not have guessed, as she set out on her journey next day, that she was about to be faced with a challenge which would be just as daunting as Ronnie's.

It was just as well that the taxi driver who took her and the children from the station knew his way around Cleeve Castle and was able to show her how to reach the private quarters, for the heavy iron-studded doors of the main entrance tower had clearly not been opened for many months. After ringing the bell beside a smaller door, Anne stepped back a little to stare at the high, battlemented walls of a building that in this grey light looked more like a prison than a home. She shivered in gratitude that she was not responsible for looking after it.

The door opened. The young man who stood there was extremely tall, extremely thin and extremely black. Fifteen-month-old Richard was still so young that everything in the world was new to him and he accepted each new experience with the same look of quizzical interest, finding no single unusual confrontation of more significance than any other; but Charlotte, who had never seen a black man before, pressed close to her mother and clutched her hand apprehensively. Anne herself felt a moment of doubt, but for a different reason. Was it possible that this was the Twelfth Duke of Wiltshire? Nothing that she had been told about the reputation of the eleventh duke made a mixed-race marriage or liaison seem impossible or even unlikely. Could this be the reason why there had been a delay in recognising his son's right to succeed?

But no: there was surely no white blood at all in this young man, who now was smiling at the children and politely inviting the little group to come inside. And here in an over-furnished and slightly musty drawing room another young man, this time with a white – although tanned – skin was leaping to his feet in welcome.

'Your grace! Cousin Anne! How good of you to come!'

'Just Anne, please.' She had not bothered to work out the precise degree of cousinship, but since in her own case it was only by marriage she had no great feeling of family. 'This is Charlotte. And Richard.'

'You have a son?' Her host, obviously failing to allow himself time to calculate the gap between Chay's death and the birth of the small boy in Anne's arms, looked startled. 'Then surely . . .'

'He's adopted.' She sat down on the sofa indicated by her host and settled Richard on her lap, with Charlotte snuggling up close beside her.

'Will you have some coffee? Real coffee. I was warned about the muck that you're still having to drink over here, so I brought my own supplies.'

'That would be lovely.'

'And then, I ought to explain. I also brought with me Matthew, whom you've just met, and his mother, Leah. Just for a year, to help me settle in. Unless they decide that they'd like to stay longer, of course. Leah was my nurse when I was a baby, and Matthew and I grew up together. I helped him with school lessons and he used to take me camping and hunting. We're great pals.'

Anne couldn't help smiling. Kingsley's voice was as young in this face-to-face meeting as it had been in his letter: the voice of an enthusiastic schoolboy. His complexion was fresh and smooth and his thick hair, naturally fair, had been further bleached by the sun. It was easy to see that he was not descended from Ronnie's Italian grandmother.

Leah, when she brought in the tray, provided another surprise. Anne's mental picture of a black nurse was wholly derived from the film of Gone With The Wind, but this woman, as thin and almost as tall as her son, was silent and dignified. Only the smile with which she offered Charlotte a biscuit revealed a love of small children. She left the room quietly, leaving Anne and Kingsley to make each other's acquaintance with an exchange of unimportant questions, but returned without being summoned ten minutes later.

'I found the toys of Lady Veronica,' she said. 'Would the little girl like to play with them?'

'Auntie Ronnie's toys!' exclaimed Anne. She could sense that her daughter was still nervous. 'Let's all go and look for them, shall we? If that's all right?'

'Of course it is,' Kingsley assured her. 'I want to show you all over in any case. You'll be shocked, I'm sure, at how much everything's changed since before the war.'

'I've never been here before,' Anne told him – and now he was the one to be surprised. 'I only married Chay after the war had started. The castle had already been requisitioned by then.'

'Then you must have the grand tour.' They waited until the children, delighted by Ronnie's old rocking horse and teaset and buckets of bricks and dolls, were at ease with Leah, and then began their exploration. Standing in the middle of the Great Hall, Anne shook her head in incredulous dismay at the litter of ugly metal tables and chairs, abandoned a year earlier at the end of some final meal without any attempt even to tidy them.

'This can't be right!' she exclaimed. 'There must be some obligation on whoever commandeered it – the Army, was it? – to restore it to its basic condition or else compensate you.' Again she looked around her, this time trying to envisage it as it must have looked once, with family portraits on the walls and perhaps banners protruding from the floor of the minstrels' gallery. Of all its one-time grandeur, nothing remained but the family crest carved in stone over one of the three fireplaces.

'You can see why it's a bit daunting, the thought of living here,' said Kingsley. 'When I came over here, I really did intend to make it my home. To keep the family going, so to speak, even though I'd never expected to find myself in this position. But now . . .' He sighed. It was clear that he was tempted to return to the country of his birth and either attempt to sell the castle or else to leave it to decay. Anne could sympathise with him. But this had been Chay's home. As a small boy he had perhaps played in the Great Hall. His family had lived in the castle for hundreds of years. She was surprised by the intensity of her wish that it should continue to be cared for. By whom, though, if not the new duke?

'Isn't there some national scheme for taking over large houses and letting the public pay to come and see them?' she asked.

'Yes. But three objections to that. I'd like to be the man who saved Cleeve, not the man who gave it away. And anyway I'd have to give a money endowment with it, which I haven't got. And although I'm told that the best furniture is in store, all the walls and ceilings would have to be restored – wallpaper, panelling, plasterwork – before the rooms became grand enough to attract sightseers. Oh well. This is too depressing. Come up one of the turrets. At least nothing has spoilt the view.'

He led the way up a spiral staircase, opening the door of the one room on each floor as they passed so that she could look inside. At the top of the turret they were able to step out on to the battlements. After the musty, dusty interior of the castle, Anne was able to fill her lungs with fresh air and smile into the sunshine.

Yes, the view was marvellous. Woods and hills stretched into the distance in shades of green that gradually faded into grey. She enjoyed them for a moment and then looked straight down. The moat, which should have been lapping at the sheer stone walls of the building if it had ever been expected to serve a defensive purpose, had in fact been excavated at a little distance. The clearness of its water and lack of stagnation suggested that it must be fed by a stream. Between the moat and the castle was a flat grassy area that had once been a pleasure garden but was now, like the building itself, neglected.

There should be a parterre, she thought to herself, visualising neat triangles and sickle moons and circles of low box hedge. And the moat could be used to feed a water garden. A French water garden, and perhaps a Japanese one as well, with stone and gravel and a red lacquered bridge over a reflecting pool. And . . .

'I did intend,' began Kingsley, but Anne cut off whatever he was going to say.

'Shush just a moment,' she said as kindly as she could, needing silence for all the pictures that were painting themselves in her mind. Then she turned to him with a smile. 'Sorry. I was just thinking. What did you intend?'

'Before I left Africa, I did think it would be nice if I could persuade you to come and live here. It was such hard luck on you, your husband dying like that, and I'm sure you must have looked forward to bringing up your children in their ancestral home, and I thought you could still do that, because obviously this is such a big place that there'd be plenty of room for two households. I had hoped it might be a welcome offer, but now that I'm here, of course, I can see that really it would just be a burden. Why should you want to let yourself in for anything like this when you probably already have a home that's easy to run?'

An hour earlier, Anne would have agreed fervently with that point of view. But gradually her attitude was changing. What had frightened her in the past about the prospect of becoming mistress of Cleeve was her mental picture of ducal splendour and stuffy etiquette and an army of servants to be commanded. What was clear to her now was that life at Cleeve was never going to be like that again. Instead, it would present a challenge and a great deal of hard work. But she sympathised with Kingsley's feeling that a great house should not be allowed to die.

Since it seemed that the estate was no longer able to support it, the castle would have to support itself – and she already had an idea for that. Her plan would need money to start it off, but her brother might be able to help. Although Howard had no great capital sum at his own disposal, he mixed in the City with people who did. If she could draw up a businesslike plan, Cleeve could become an investment. And Howard's new wife might agree to become involved as well. Jodie was still studying for her accountancy qualifications, but she was an energetic young woman with a lively mind. Could she be persuaded to apply her enthusiasm to a new venture?

Anne realised that she was letting her thoughts run away with her. Kingsley himself might not have enough enthusiasm to keep him in England. She turned to face him.

'You said a moment ago that you'd intended to invite me to live here,' she said. 'Have you abandoned that idea now?'

'Only because I thought . . . But if . . . Might you really consider it? Because it would be lonely for me, struggling to do anything on my own. To have someone I could talk to if things got a bit fraught would be . . . Will you come to live in Cleeve, Anne?'

Smiling, Anne looked down again at the patch of rough grass that was going to be a beautiful parterre one of these days.

'I'd love to,' she said.

51

It took eight years. Nevertheless, as Anne awaited the arrival of the journalist who had an appointment to interview her on a July afternoon in 1954, she could honestly claim to have envisaged almost everything which had eventually been achieved at Cleeve within a single half hour of inspiration: the half hour in which she had leaned over the battlements with Kingsley by her side on her first visit to the castle.

It hadn't all happened at once. It hadn't for a long time even been possible to feel sure that the project might prove to be successful. For at least five years there had been more anxiety than achievement, and finances still were – and perhaps always would be – a worry in a building which swallowed money as a drain sucks down water. But she and Kingsley were still afloat and still introducing new ideas; and this year, at the Chelsea Flower Show, Anne had won the gold medal for Garden Design. That was why the journalist – one of several who had asked to talk to her on her home ground – would be arriving at any moment.

A bell rang. Anne went smilingly into the Great Hall to greet her visitor. 'How good of you to come all this way. I'm sure you'd like some tea before anything else, and then you'll want to walk round some of the show gardens, I expect. But before you leave I'd like to take you up to the battlements so that you can look down on the whole area.'

The timetable made it clear that she was in control of the interview. When the first journalists had appeared on her doorstep, three or four years earlier, she had been shy, reluctant to do more than answer their questions in a self-deprecating manner. It was Kingsley who had pointed out that she was in business to make money and ought to regard these conversations as a form of free advertising.

On this occasion, though, the efficiency of her programming seemed lost on her visitor. Mr Rowan Worsley was staring at her as though he could not believe his eyes. She raised her own eyebrows questioningly.

'I'm so sorry, your grace,' he said. 'Very sorry. To look so surprised, I mean. But I do an interview of this kind for *Country Life* every month, and as a rule I find my subjects to be, well, a little windswept, thick tweed skirts whatever the weather, cardigans buttoned up not quite straight, perhaps even a little dirt under the fingernails. So you . . . But I oughtn't to talk so personally.'

'I always wear gloves when I'm working,' Anne told him, 'and I shall put on sensible shoes when we go outside.' She was at that moment wearing three-inch heels which emphasised the elegance of her long legs, and although her sleeveless silk dress was in fact homemade, it would have been worthy of a place on an *haute couture* catwalk. 'If you'd called here without warning you'd certainly have found me in my working clothes. But I did know you were coming.'

She realised, all the same, that he had not been talking about clothes. At the age of eighteen she had continually been told that she was beautiful. She was thirty-four now and her face had matured into a different kind of beauty, far more striking than mere debutante prettiness. Her body was still as slender as before, but the confidence which came from organising her life independently and successfully showed itself in her posture. The admiration which she recognised in Mr Worsley's eyes was nothing new to her; but it was not important, either.

Over tea she answered his prepared questions, before leading him outside. She had spent five hard years creating the gardens that now surrounded Cleeve. The grandest, as befitted his ducal status, was in front of Kingsley's part of the castle, and for it she had drawn on memories of her childhood home. The yew features she had planted were growing well. It would be some years yet before the topiary would attain its full effect or the hedges grow high enough to secrete an avenue of statues in curved niches; but Kingsley was a young man still, and would live to see the finished effect.

In front of her own quarter of the building, the land on both sides of the moat was divided into smaller plots. The overall effect was not harmonious, nor expected to be. These were, in a way, samples from a catalogue, intended to give confidence to potential customers who might find it difficult to interpret a design on paper, even when accompanied by a painted impression of the eventual effect.

Their inspection over, they returned to the Great Hall, which acted as the entrance for all the castle's residents. Kingsley was just on his way out.

'Your grace!' Startled into forgetting his manners, the journalist turned apologetically to Anne. 'I was just wondering whether your husband could spare me a few minutes. To give his opinion of your achievements. He must be very proud of you.'

The duke, pausing politely as he was hailed, raised his eyebrows in amusement. This was not an unusual mistake for strangers to make.

'Not my husband,' explained Anne. 'I'm the widow of the tenth duke. I ought really to describe myself as dowager all the time, but I don't think that would be good for business. The word suggests either some huge battleaxe or else a little old lady with a grey bun. But I'm sure that if you want a word . . .'

'Of course.' Kingsley was prepared to be affable. His main business, since he had finally decided to settle in England, was the preservation of Cleeve. But as an escape from all the bills and account books and requests for repairs, he had developed a personal sideline, propagating plants which could be used by Anne to furnish her garden commissions, but also selling to garden nurseries and to any of the general public who found their way to this remote spot. After all, as he pointed out when the project was first discussed, if he had stayed in Kenya he would have become a farmer, although perhaps not to the extent of getting his own hands dirty. A favourable mention in *Country Life* of some of his successful hybrids could do him nothing but good.

'Bring Mr Worsley up to the battlements when you've

finished, will you?' Anne suggested, and made her own way there at once.

The battlements, like the inner courtyard and the Great Hall, could be used by all the residents of the castle. It was this element of common use that had made it so important to find congenial tenants when Kingsley decided to convert the huge building into four separate residences – not merely for the sake of bringing in regular income, but so that the whole of the building could be kept reasonably warm.

The resulting arrangements were very much to Anne's advantage – but since Kingsley had few acquaintances in England when he first arrived, he expressed himself delighted by anything which made it more likely that Anne would settle down at Cleeve. She had her own quarter of the castle, including one of the turrets and all the south-facing rooms. In another quarter lived her parents. Recognising that what was left of Yewley House after the fire could never be restored to the five-hundred-year-old home they had loved, they had taken the insurance payment, sold the ruin and its land and invested all the proceeds to give them an income on which they could live for the rest of their lives. Cleeve offered them as much atmosphere and family history as Yewley, although it was not their own; and, also, of course, the chance to be near their daughter and see their grandchildren growing up.

More surprising – but bringing equal pleasure to Anne – had been Howard's announcement that he and Jodie would like a place in the country as well. Because they used it only at weekends and for holidays, they were content to rent less than a full quarter of the property, and this had allowed Kingsley – as befitted his rank and ownership – to keep more of the state rooms for himself.

None of Anne's original plans could have come to fruition without her brother's help. From the very first moment she had realised that the idea of helping Cleeve's land to pay its way by turning herself into a professional garden designer could not be achieved overnight. The building of a reputation was bound to involve many months of expenses without any corresponding income. Howard had found the capital to set her up, while Jodie begged to be allowed to look after the business side of the enterprise. It had all proved to be very satisfactory.

Mr Worsley, panting from the steep climb, arrived to stand beside her. 'I do apologise for my stupid mistake, duchess. I try to do my homework before I come on these visits, but that's usually in terms of my hostess's special gardening interests. I didn't think to check the situation in *Debrett*.'

'That's all right.'

'Do you find your title useful?' he asked. 'I mean, do you make use of it in your work?'

'Of course.' Anne smiled mischievously. 'The customers love it. The smaller the garden, the more impressed they are. If all you own is a semi-detached patch of lawn with fences on three sides, you can really make the neighbours sigh with envy when they learn that it's about to be redesigned by a duchess.' She allowed him a little time to enjoy the bird's-eye view not only of her specimen gardens but also of the trees she had planted, before asking, 'Have you seen all you want?'

Mr Worsley was quick to take the hint. 'Please don't bother to see me out. I can find my own way. And if I may congratulate you again on your gold medal . . . I trust it will be the first of many.'

'Thank you.' She stood without moving as he disappeared.

Kingsley, who had been hovering nearby, came to join her. 'All these poor chaps falling into the same trap,' he said, laughing. 'Why don't you put them out of their misery by marrying me? You know how much I long to make you a double duchess.'

'It's surely not time for your annual proposal yet!' Anne had no compunction about teasing him. Three times, as kindly as she could, she had told him that she never wished to remarry. She was anxious not to do anything that would spoil the closeness of their friendship, but his continued pressure had to be treated either as an embarrassment or as a joke.

Sometimes she felt that every choice she made was an act of rebellion against her upbringing. Smaller things, like the decision to send Charlotte to local schools, were a direct consequence of her belief that the shyness which had affected her for so many years was the result of her secluded childhood, with only a governess for company. But far more important was her refusal to accept her mother's plan that she should become merely some kind of appendage: somebody's wife, somebody's mother. She had married Chay because her love for him was so much stronger than her spirit of rebellion, but once she had been forced to stand on her own feet it had not taken her long to realise that that was what she wanted to do for the rest of her life.

'Anyway,' she added – and this too was a comment that had been made before – 'you could solve everyone's social dilemma by marrying Jane.' Jane, the daughter of a bishop, was a bubbly, outdoor girl. She was ten years younger than Anne and had had a crush on Kingsley ever since her schooldays.

The conversation, all too predictable, was interrupted by Charlotte's return from school. It was two miles from the castle to the gate at which the school bus picked her up and deposited her every day, so she covered the distance on her pony, leaving it at the lodge all day. She was unaware of the adults who watched her from above as she passed in front of the main entrance on her way to the stables.

'What a beauty she is!' exclaimed Kingsley. Charlotte had inherited her mother's blonde hair and delicate complexion, and would be as tall as Anne one day. 'The *Country Life* chappie was burbling on about how you'd been the most beautiful debutante of your Season. He seems to have been researching in the old gossip columns, even though he failed to bring himself up to date on marriages. I reckon Charlotte is all set to take the same title when it's time for her to come out. The most beautiful deb of 1959.'

'Oh no!' Anne had moved towards the staircase, preparing to go down and greet her daughter, but now turned back in protest. 'Charlotte will have to learn to live in the real world. I can promise you, I never intend to be the mother of a debutante.'

The Reunion

'Was that really us?

They – Ronnie and Peggy and Anne – don't genuinely find it hard to believe, of course; nor do they ask the question aloud. It is a mixture of wistfulness and amusement which inspires the same thought in each of the women as they stare down at the photograph in front of them.

Ronnie and Peggy have come to Cleeve Castle for the dinner and ball which Anne has organised to celebrate the twenty-first birthday of her daughter, Lady Charlotte Delacourt. And Peggy has brought with her the album in which Mrs Armitage proudly recorded the progress of her daughter's Season.

One photograph holds pride of place. It first appeared in the *Tatler* twenty-three years ago, back in the summer of 1939. It was tiny then, just one out of half a dozen on the same page which depicted Miss So-and-So sharing a joke with Lord What's-His-Name. Or sitting out with him between dances at Lady Something-Or-Other's ball. Or enjoying any of the other endlessly repeated treats of the last London Season to be held before the war. Young men in white ties. Young women in white dresses. All looking very much the same.

This particular photograph, however, was a little different from the rest. Mr Armitage had managed to obtain a large glossy print of it from the magazine's photographer, and his wife delighted in it so much that the album automatically falls open at that place.

It shows three eighteen-year-old girls wearing full-skirted ball dresses and long white gloves. Two of them are seated, while the third – wearing a tiara which sparkles even in black and white – stands behind them so that the group form a triangle. It is a pleasing composition, very different from the pairs of heads which more usually graced the magazine's pages in those days – but artistic merit did not rate high with the society editor of the time. She would not have passed it for publication had the subjects not been worthy of her imprimatur.

Worthy they were indeed. Of all the debutantes that year, Lady Veronica Delacourt, only daughter of the Duke of Wiltshire, held the highest rank. And Miss Anne Venables was without doubt the most beautiful of all the girls who were presented at court in 1939, although far from being the most sophisticated. About Miss Peggy Armitage the editor would have felt greater doubt, had it not been for her unusual distinction in being the only non-dancing debutante at that particular ball. Her left leg, encased in plaster and supported on a low stool, is stretched out in front of her.

Isabelle is not in the photograph, and Isabelle, a casualty of the war, will not of course be attending this evening's celebration. Nor, for other reasons, will any other of the 1939 debutantes. Anne does not mix in society these days. Ronnie is here because she is Charlotte's aunt, and Peggy is one of Charlotte's godmothers.

Ronnie, as she stares down at the photograph, gives a sigh of incredulity.

'It's a different world, isn't it? A different life. When I look at the face of that girl there, that child dressed up in her mother's tiara, I can't believe that she has any connection with me at all, much less that she's the same person. It's not simply that she – I – didn't know what was going to happen to her. I suppose none of us can expect that. But I wasn't even aware that there were things I ought to be aware of, if you see what I mean.'

'We were all children,' Peggy agrees. 'I remember Isabelle saying once that girls in England seemed to move straight from the schoolroom to the ballroom, with no time to grow up in between. She was generalising madly just from a handful of debutantes, of course, but it was certainly true in my case.'

'And even in the schoolroom we weren't taught anything important.' Ronnie is still pursuing the same argument. 'I mean to say, just think. When that photograph was taken, we were only about three months away from war, and yet I didn't have any idea of what was coming. Not the foggiest. Did any of us?'

'Yes, I did.' It is Anne who admits to this. 'Because my father was so worried about it. And if you remember, the day we were presented at Court was the day Hitler marched into Prague. My mother was furious because *The Times* next morning gave so much space to the invasion of Czechoslovakia that it had to cut down on the description of the debutantes' dresses. No proper sense of what was important!'

'They had such an odd sense of values. Our mothers, I mean. It was as though the only thing that mattered in the whole wide world was the question of who was going to become the next Duchess of Wiltshire. Or, in my case, the next best thing, whoever that might be. When I think of them all sitting round the edges of one ballroom after another, plotting! Not your mother, Peggy, I know, but Anne's and mine. And Isabelle's! Do you remember Isabelle's mother?'

Ronnie pauses while yes, they all remember Isabelle's mother.

'They managed to make us believe that a wedding day was an end, a triumphal conclusion,' she continues, 'We were supposed to be making our debuts into adult life: starting to be independent. But instead of that we were being managed all the time, and led into a kind of trap.' She is talking with hindsight now, and gives an unhappy sigh.

'Well, they failed, didn't they, our mothers?' suggests Peggy cheerfully. 'They tried to imprison us in the same boring and useless lives that they'd endured themselves, but we escaped. I mean to say, look at us now! Three working women, with not a tiara between us.'

Anne looks down at the photograph once more and shakes her head in incredulity. 'How did it happen?' she asks. 'How did those three girls turn into us?'

She allows no time for an answer to that question, but instead suggests with a businesslike brightness that they had better now change for the evening, for before the dancing starts there is to be a dinner in the banqueting hall which was last used for its proper purpose on Chay's twenty-first birthday. But as she makes her way to her own quarters, she can't help wondering:

what would the three of them be doing now if their lives had gone as their mothers planned?

There is no time to answer this question either. Although Charlotte ever since the age of eighteen has been making her name – her titled name – as a party organiser, she has reasonably claimed that on this occasion someone else should take responsibility for the arrangements. So it is Anne who now embarks on all the last-minute checks: inspecting the tables and the marquee, visiting the kitchen to make sure that there will be no unexpected crises, welcoming the band and seeing that they are well looked after. And soon there will be guests to be greeted, and the night-long necessity of ensuring that everyone is happy.

Anne doesn't flinch from the task, because over the years she has become an efficient organiser; but all the same, by four in the morning she has had enough. A good many years have passed since she was able to dance the night away and still be fresh enough to greet the sunrise with bright eyes. Now that she is in her forties, by this time of the night her feet are aching and she is finding it hard to control her yawns.

As the hostess, it would be unpardonable of her to go to bed. But no one is likely to notice as she slips quietly away from the dance floor and makes her way up to that part of the battlements in which she and her friends had their earlier rendezvous.

Peggy is there already, leaning over the wall and staring down so intently that she does not hear Anne approaching, and looks up, startled, only when she is offered a penny for her thoughts.

'Oh, Anne! I was watching the dancers.' The dance floor in the nearest marquee is not as crowded now as it was earlier. Avenues of flaming torches lead from it and by their light it is possible to see young men and women strolling, sitting, kissing in the garden. Peggy's husband is one of those who have deserted the dance floor. He and Jodie, his sister-in-law, are engaged in an earnest conversation. But Peggy is not looking in their direction. 'Charlotte's almost as beautiful as you were at the same age, isn't she?'

'That's not what you were thinking when I asked. You were trying to puzzle something out.'

Peggy acknowledges the guess with a smile. 'I was remembering the evening when I met Chay for the first time,' she says. 'It was at Ronnie's ball – the night that photograph was taken; the one we were looking at earlier. I was carried into the ballroom in that ridiculous sedan chair and I looked round to see where Ronnie was. She was dancing with the most handsome young man I'd ever seen. As the music came to an end, they smiled at each other – and it was the same smile. I realised at once that he must be her brother.'

'Why should you think about that now? Just because that was a Delacourt ball and so is this?'

Peggy shakes her head. 'Because I've been watching Charlotte and Richard dancing together. A very different kind of dance, to a very different kind of music. But just like Ronnie and Chay, they smiled at each other. And just like Ronnie and Chay, it was the same smile.'

'People who live together often begin to look like each other,' suggests Anne. 'And the smile of a brother to a sister . . .' She checks herself in mid-sentence. Although they have been brought up as siblings, everyone has always known that Richard cannot possibly be Charlotte's brother. Richard himself had this made clear to him even before he was old enough to understand it completely – not just because Charlotte's father had died before she was born but because Richard would need to spend the rest of his life explaining how he had no title in spite of calling the Duchess of Wiltshire his mother.

'It made me wonder,' Peggy continues. 'Does Richard know who his natural parents are? Do *you* know, even?'

'Of course I know.' It is hard for Anne, tired as she is, to keep a slight irritation out of her voice. 'In any adoption one needs to know something about the parents, just from the health point of view. But Richard doesn't know and he never will. I'm his adoptive mother and that's all there is to it.'

'Right.' Peggy gives a brisk nod. She points down towards the Japanese garden, where Richard, no longer dancing, is chatting to Ronnie. 'It's nice that he gets on so well with his godmother, isn't it?'

She has guessed, Anne realises. 'Peggy . . .'

'It's all right. None of my business. Perhaps I feel a little hurt that neither of you ever mentioned it in your letters, but I know how to keep a secret, even one that I'm not supposed to know in the first place.' She straightens herself. Ronnie, perhaps noticing the movement, looks up and begins to stroll towards the foot of the staircase. Within a few moments she has joined her friends on the battlements.

'It's odd, you know,' she suggests without any preliminary greeting. 'Coming back to Cleeve after all these years.' She has lived in America ever since her divorce came through and allowed her to marry Jack Donovan.

'You must find it very changed,' agrees Peggy.

'In every way, yes. The most obvious is that all the rooms have lost the functions they used to have when I was a child, which is disconcerting. And in addition to that, they're warm, which is unbelievable. Chatting to Kingsley and Jane, I realised how hard they have to work, and I know you do as well, Anne. The real thing is that when I lived here it was simply a family home which the family took for granted. We knew we were privileged, but it seemed quite normal that we should be. I suppose that's what's changed: that nobody can take anything for granted. I was talking to Richard just now. When Chay went to Oxford, it was because that was the thing to do, but Richard's at Oxford because he wants to be competent to do a job. And even Charlotte . . . Did she never want to be a debutante, Anne?'

'She wasn't given the choice. It would have interfered with her "A" levels.'

'They call them debs nowadays,' Peggy tells Ronnie.

'Who does? Not the posh magazines, surely. After such a long absence, I've been startled enough by all the social changes, but for "Jennifer's Diary" to lose its dignity would suggest not so much change as revolution.'

'No.' Anne laughs in sympathy at her friend's shock. 'Certainly not the *Tatler* or *Harpers and Queen* or any of that lot. The popular press. Because the shorter the word, the larger the type it can be printed in. If your crash had happened this year it would be DEB PRANGS MG all over the front page, instead of an inside paragraph in small print headed "Duchess's debutante daughter involved in accident".'

'Don't remind me.' Ronnie looks apologetically at Peggy and the two women burst out laughing together. 'But I'll tell you the real thing that's odd. Just look at the three of us. We ought to be extinct. Debutantes and dinosaurs, equally unfit to survive in this new world. Just think how useless we were when we were eighteen, and how useless we were expected to be for the rest of our lives. And our children too, and their children. But down there we have Richard who wants to be an engineer and Charlotte who's already working as a party organiser. And here's Peggy, who has made such a huge fortune from her chain of factories that she's been able to set her designer up in his own couture house. And Anne, who has every stately-home owner in England queuing up to have his garden put right by her. And even me, with my broken nose. I may have stopped racing now, but I got the women's circuit going in the States almost single handed, and as long as I'm president of the federation it will keep going.'

'As you say,' agreed Anne, 'very successful dinosaurs.'

Peggy is unable to stifle an enormous yawn. 'Sorry,' she says. 'Will you excuse me if I retreat to bed?' She and Bill are staying in the turret that Jodie and Howard continue to rent as a weekend cottage from the twelfth duke. She kisses her two friends goodnight and makes her way down the steep stairs, followed by Ronnie, who is still in the mood for dancing.

Their hostess remains on the battlements, looking down at the young people whose lives as adults are just beginning. Once again she puts to herself the question she was unable to answer earlier in the evening: what would the three of them – Ronnie and Peggy and herself – have been doing now if their lives had gone as their mothers had planned?

But what is the point of wondering? The frivolous ambitions of the debutantes – and their mothers – were amongst the first casualties of war. The war brought times of heartbreak to each of them, but also gave them the opportunity – indeed, the need – to change direction and create new lives for themselves. That was why they grew up instead to be practical and successful women. Yes, it was the war.

Peggy has left behind the photograph album that the three of them were studying earlier in the evening. Anne picks it up to be carried inside and once again it falls open at the photograph of three young women at the Duchess of Wiltshire's ball in 1939. She smiles to herself, shaking her head in mock disbelief as she closes it again. The album is a record of a fancy-dress life in a fairytale world. All long gone now: a bubble blown away by the cold wind of war. But it was real while it lasted.